FOLKLORIC TRICKERY

BOOK FOUR OF THE FOLKLORIC SERIES

KARENZA GRANT

L'Ours

This novel is written in British English

www.karenzagrant.com

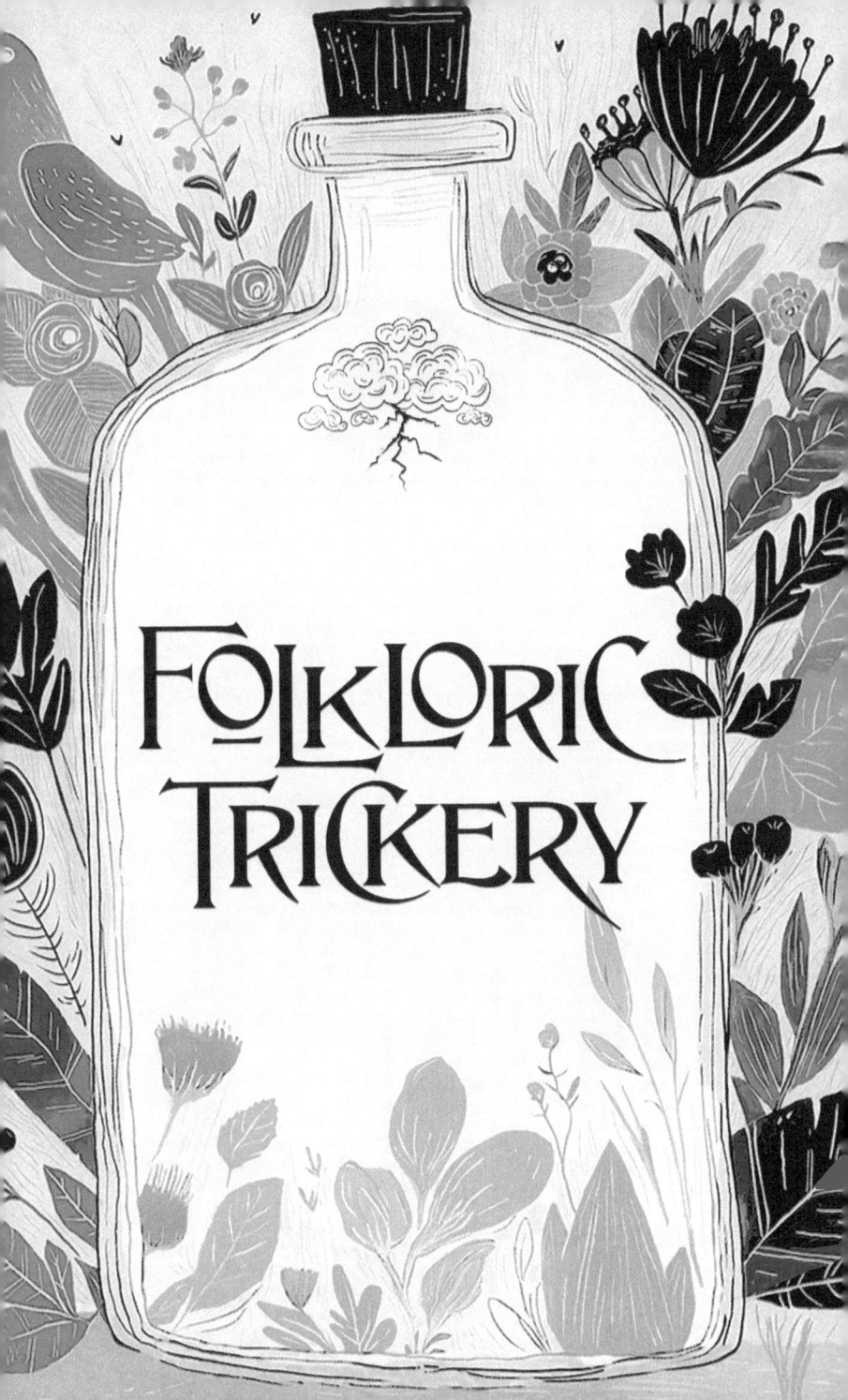

FOLKLORIC TRICKERY

*To all the readers who have
taken a chance on this series,
thank you so much*

CHAPTER 1

IT WOULD BE NICE TO HAVE THE UPPER HAND, JUST FOR once.

Fae were slippery, fickle chimeras. One moment I'd have them sussed, the next they were pulling the rug out—whether that rug was a glamour or a prank or them being totally random and impossible to understand. It was as if they couldn't be pinned to the rules that governed the human realm—rules like things go down when you drop them and one plus one equals two. In their case, the answer was whatever they felt like at any particular moment, the only influences being the phase of the moon, the flow of the seasons or whether you were holding a large cream cake.

But the fae currently meeting my blade with clash after clash, as if my retaliation was nothing more than a minor inconvenience, wasn't at all interested in cream cakes. He had a degree of self-control. A lot of them were, though, especially the more instinctual ones.

No, the fae assailing me, who actually had a T-shirt on today, thank heavens, was more concerned about kicking my butt—in the interests of training, of course. Not that he had to try. With his centuries of experience and inhuman speed and strength, my butt-kicking was inevitable, although why he had to grin while he was doing it was beyond me.

Lucas's strikes accelerated as he predicted my movements, forcing my retreat toward the trees. Urgh. I hated that he had me. His onslaught was so rapid, I barely had time to respond. Back I went until he pinned me against an oak, that grin even more pronounced. He was enjoying himself way too much.

"Raise your blade a little higher when I advance like that." He stepped away, his hair an umber mess. "Then you'll be able to put all your strength into your blows."

He withdrew to the centre of the clearing, sword lowered, gaze intense, assessing, calculating. The trees behind him sheltered us from the rumbling N2o, the sheer cliff of the foothill just down from the town looming above. The river eddied to our side, the rush slowing where its banks opened out to form a lake, whirls playing in the shallows. Beyond, another mountainous crag cradled us in the valley.

I pushed off the oak and stepped toward him, my breath ragged. Every part of my Keeper leathers stuck to me, sweat slick on my back, the slippery hilt of my blade far from ideal. On top of that, the dagger sheath strapped to my thigh was much too tight and the strands of hair that had escaped my braid stuck to my forehead and the nape of my neck.

In absolute contrast, Lucas gleamed with a sheen of perspiration that made his skin glow and emphasised the line of his clavicle where it disappeared under his T-shirt, the shape of his chest much too visible beneath the cotton. He'd been such a distraction with his shirt off during evening training, and now, on the one occasion he was fully covered, I was even more engrossed.

Damn, it was muggy. The air was still. *Everything* was still—the drone of bees, the lap of the river and the distant traffic all muted. Thankfully, a bank of billowing cloud was building from the southwest, chasing away the blue. One of the August storms sweeping in to break the heat. If only it would hurry up.

"Alright." I shook my arms, then angled my blade and body into the suggested position. "Although if I shift my weight into it, I unbalance a little." I moved my leg forward to compensate. "Though this works."

"Got it in one." His smile played as he assessed my stance.

"Right, let's do it again." But there was no chance of me gaining the advantage. I had to be satisfied knowing that with the intensive training, I was improving by the day.

He came at me, blade clasped in two hands, arcing toward my middle, his delight all too evident. I stepped forward to meet him, calculating the angle of attack. But... for heaven's sake, that grin. What was I, his entertainment?

Before he could reach me, I lowered my sword. In total control, he stilled his blade and raised an eyebrow.

"Can't you do anything without that grin?" I squared my

shoulders. "I mean, what's that lip-twitching about? Is it so amusing that I'm struggling against one of Fae's most skilled warriors?"

He lowered his blade and raised his chin, laughing. "It's not you I find amusing. Trust *you* to think it's all about *you*."

I scowled and considered driving him through with my blade. Not that I'd be fast enough without him deflecting, but he was toying with me. I was getting to know him well, this fae who was willing to do so much for others, whom since Grimmere I trusted with my life. But underneath, he was a goblin, a trickster who loved to play, and I wasn't going to react. Besides, I had to admit, I enjoyed the games almost as much as he did.

Almost.

"It's just that..." He stepped closer and studied me as though I was a puzzle, that clavicle, the lines of his neck, those sharp cheekbones, all of him too close, the scent of his sweat stoking even more heat, this time low in my middle. I ignored the hitch in my pulse and the tingling of my skin. I could pretend the crackle between us was a figment of my imagination. We both knew we were physically attracted to each other, but that was as far as it went, and we really didn't need anything messing up our Keeper partnership.

The light faded, the air even more stifling as the storm prepared to break.

"It's just that you can't help yourself," I said. The fae forces that drove him weren't logical. I could only hope that when we visited the assembly tomorrow for the night, it would give me the opportunity to untangle a little of what I found so confounding.

He drew back, a glimmer in his eyes. "I definitely can't help myself."

But perhaps I could use this to my advantage. "Then today, new rules. An additional handicap." My turn to grin. The only advantage I currently had was that my blade was sharp, whereas in training Lucas used blunted weapons. "You have to fight me without one hint of a smile, a smirk, a quirked lip. You're not allowed any of that until we're finished."

His brow lowered in a faux scowl, the glimmer in his eyes intensifying. "That might be the most unjust disadvantage yet."

I pushed past him and strode to the middle of the clearing, the musty fragrance of moss and bark heady in the oppressive air. "Starting now." I raised my blade.

He stared at me for a moment, his lips curving. He forced them down. They sprang up again, and lines of tension stole across his jaw.

I guffawed.

"This isn't fair." The corner of his mouth tugged up.

"You're doing it now. I can't believe that Lucas Rouseau, son of one of the most powerful houses in Fae, who kills with his bare teeth and fights with utter control, can't stop himself smiling." I chuckled. "That is something."

His gaze lit with mock fury, his mouth twitching ludicrously as he attempted to check himself.

"I don't think you can do it," I scoffed.

His eyes flashed. With a strangled battle cry through pressed lips, he launched himself forward.

I met his advance, our blades ringing as he twisted this way and that, the full force of his blows jarring. I was on the defensive once more, but I couldn't stop myself howling at his attempt to keep his mouth clamped tight.

"I can... do it..." he managed through clenched teeth, his face red as he escalated the barrage, forcing me to concentrate rather than laugh.

While a part of me responded to him instinctively, I assessed the likelihood of his next move. He was striking predominantly from the right. It was something he did on the rare occasion he lost focus, which meant I had him. I'd found his Achilles heel, and I was gaining ground. Even so, his speed and skill were unparalleled. He wouldn't hurt me. I knew that. Regardless, adrenaline surged in my blood.

There was no way I could beat him like this, sword on sword. But boy, was he a picture. "Lucas Rouseau, feared by many, can't keep the grin off his face."

His mouth twisted, sweat beading on *his* brow for once. This really was his vulnerability, but as much as I was enjoying it, I needed breathing space to release the laughter desperate to escape. I thrust a blow to his side. As he responded I leapt away, putting distance between us, and even though my chest was heaving, I howled and howled.

He stood there, his lips twisting as he fought to restrain himself.

"Honestly, you should see your face. It's absolutely

perfect. You look like an osencame with constipation." All I could do was crease up, losing myself completely as I bent double with mirth, tears blurring everything. But my goodness, did I need to see more of that ridiculous expression.

I raised my head, wiping my face, but he was gone.

CHAPTER 2

I GLANCED ABOUT THE CLEARING. TREES SURROUNDED me on three sides—oak, alder, hazel. The river swished at my back. The sultry air pressed in.

Where was Lucas?

In the pre-storm hush, surely I would've heard if he'd slipped into the water. He had to be in the woods, hiding, waiting. A twig snapped amidst the undergrowth. If it was him, it would've been premeditated—a distraction. He didn't make mistakes.

"Can't take the heat," I called. "Pit you against pretty much anything and it wouldn't stand a chance. Ask you not to smile and, well, you lose the plot and crumble. All you can do is hide."

My gaze darted across the forest. Nothing.

A thud came from my left—a peach had fallen from a branch. A glimmer of russet flickered ahead—a squirrel darting up a trunk. Further away in the branches, black and red flashed—a woodpecker. "*Kreey... Kreey...*" it cried.

My stomach tightened, my heart rate hitching. We'd played these games before, me attempting to defend myself from his stealth attack, and he was always too fast.

"Admit it, Lucas," I called, "I had you." I made to lower my sword but caught a movement to my right. Before I could react, he was behind me, his blunt dagger across my throat, his arm pinning both of mine to my body, drawing me against his solidity. He squeezed my sword hand. With a stab of pain, I uncurled my fingers, my blade dropping to the ground. Warmth flared through me once again at his proximity, his breath on my neck. Why did I feel like we were playing with fire?

"No way. I win." His voice was low in my ear. "I've told you before, you need to keep your wits about you in an exposed position. Fae will use all kinds of trickery. You were too vulnerable." A few raindrops dotted my skin, their rhythm irregular as if the storm was dillydallying, pretending it wasn't about to let rip.

"If I was in an exposed position in Fae," I said, "I would have a glamour. I wouldn't be lurking in the middle of a clearing like a sitting duck. The truth is, you could only run."

I tried to wriggle away. His chest pressed into me, his grip tightening around my arms, the soft edge of the blade pressing in. If he'd been foe, I would've been dead. "Well I have you now, you can't escape." There it was... that lightness of tone again. He couldn't hide it.

I cackled, my throat shifting under his dagger. "Oh my

goodness. Even now, you're smiling. I can hear it in your voice. Don't tell me you aren't." He wasn't getting out of this so easily. I could still get the upper hand.

He blew air from his nose as he fought laughter, only managing to snort, his grip loosening.

I forced myself around to face him, his arms tight, holding me, his eyes gleaming. His proximity brought back the nights we'd spent in Grimmere, and how empty I'd felt in bed since, then he threw his head back and roared with laughter. Ever so quickly, I eased back a fraction, slipped my dagger from its sheath and drew it to his gut, pressing it against him.

The difference being, my blade was sharp.

It cut through his leather trousers and into his skin, cleaving his flesh and his laughter. He snapped to attention, his eyes wide, disbelief smothering that grin. A large raindrop fell on his forehead.

"You cut me," he said with utter consternation, gazing down at the blade and his blood pooling on the glinting steel.

"First blood today." I couldn't hold the smugness from my voice. He was a drac—a flesh wound was barely a pinprick to him, and he had plenty of healing potion. Glee rose in my chest. I'd finally caught him. Yes, I'd had to use a little cunning, and he'd not been expecting it, but that was the situation he'd put *me* in over the past weeks. "What was it you said? Fae will use all kinds of trickery. You need to keep your wits about you?" A broad smirk extended across my face.

"I can't believe it." He wrapped his fingers around

mine and pulled the blade out, then tugged it from my grasp and dropped it. "You stabbed me." He just looked stunned.

He shook his head, then in one swift movement, took a step back, lowered himself and charged at me like a bull. His shoulder hit my middle, the force flipping me over it.

"What the hell are you doing?" I cried, dangling from his back, his hands gripping my thighs. "Put me down." I pummelled my fists against his butt.

"Retribution!" he yelled as he sprinted toward the river.

He wouldn't. He really wouldn't. "Don't you dare, Lucas. Or I swear, I'll wipe that smirk off your face forever."

"Never!" He twisted to the side and flung me into the air.

I was suspended for a moment, too shocked to cry out, then my back hit water. Cold pierced me as I submerged into runoff from snow still melting on the peaks. I sank down... down... fighting the urge to gasp, not only against the cold but against the fury coursing through me. I'd used my wiles to catch him out for once, and the utter bastard had chucked me in the river.

As I lowered through the glassy flow, water streaming in my ears, I made out ripples of him laughing on the bank. Well, two could play at that game. Slowing, I met weed, then sank to the rocks on the riverbed. I restrained the impulse to push back to the surface.

If I could see him, he could see me. To the side of the clearing, overhanging trees cast the water in darkness. He wouldn't be able to see me there. It was payback time. I wasn't going to pop up like a drowned rat and be subject to his taunts. He could damned well find me, though knowing a drac's affinity with water, it wouldn't take long.

Staying close to the riverbed, I swam for the shade, fighting a thread of unease and the urge to surface and breathe. As dark water surrounded my body, I made to push up from the rocks to rise for a breath, but something tapped me on the shoulder. My stomach lurching, I twisted around.

Gauzy yet fierce eyes met mine, a gaze framed with a delicate face and swirling, dark hair. A nymph, naked and almost as pale as the water, her limbs lithe, as though she was a ripple, a part of the flow. My chest tightened, needing air. I had no idea if she was amicable, and if I rose to the surface, I'd be exposed.

She smiled, a hint of mischief pursing her lips as she passed me something long and thin... a reed. "Breathe." Her lips shaped words that should have been garbled by the water but instead formed perfectly in my mind, her voice fluid. "We like a trick as much as the next fae, but when it comes to Lucas Rouseau, doubly so."

She'd gotten the drift of my plan. Wondering at the "we", I glanced about. Shimmers of other nymphs floated around her. But breathe... I needed to breathe. My chest blazing, I studied the reed. Surely it was too thin to use as a snorkel? But I could try.

I poked it out of the water, angled my head and blew the last of the air from my lungs, expecting resistance. My breath released. Hungrily, I drew in air, until my desperate sucks steadied to deep breaths, then calm inhalation.

The nymph smiled. "You're not the only one stirring our

waters, calling the storm." The others gathered around her, nodding, or was it the undulation of the current? "Though you are definitely the most noisy." At that they broke into laughter. "But we appreciate the cause is that rotter of a drac. While we surround you, you'll be hidden."

Perfect. "I could go with rotter right now." I'd said it without thinking, the words forming bubbles, the sound indistinct.

But the nymph smiled. She'd understood. "It was a couple of months ago, after that awful affair with the hantaumo, he stood up our sister."

"Viveau tells the truth," one of them said. "He left Ruisselette high and dry." The others tittered.

I took another breath through the reed, then swirled my arms to hold position in the flow. "Sounds like him," I bubbled. I remembered him saying he was going on a date with a water nymph back then. But that meant he hadn't gone, which didn't actually sound like him at all.

"Look." She swam out of the shade, beckoning.

I followed, swimming under the surface to where we had a direct view of Lucas, albeit highly distorted by the current. The nymphs gathered tightly around me and my vision grew clear, my hearing acute.

"Camille," Lucas called as he scanned the alders I'd hidden beneath. "You can't stay under that long. I know you're hiding." His frown deepened to a glower. I couldn't see him for scrub as he called my name again and again. His voice tightened each time until, "What the fuck do you think you're doing? This isn't funny."

The nymphs laughed, my chuckles joining theirs.

"Shit, Camille." There was an urgency to his tone. Served him right for throwing me in.

He returned to the clearing and made another recce of the waters. "Fuck." He kicked off his boots and dove in, his blade on his back. Thanks to the nymphs, I could see him clearly, swimming with preternatural speed as he cased the riverbed.

There was something otherworldly in the way he moved, an underwater butterfly, a fishlike shimmy that sent shivers down my spine. He wasn't swimming like the human he appeared to be, it was his drac nature coming to the fore. The aquatic creature reflected the horror folk felt for water and its power to drag them into its depths, never to return.

In moments, he'd made his way to the centre of the river. The nymphs gathered even closer, their laughter stilling, their forms lightening to translucence, becoming water itself. Presumably they were hiding me as well, because as Lucas passed a few rocks away, his T-shirt swollen and his hair billowing, he didn't notice. But the furrow scored into his brow and the tension in his jaw were all too clear.

With an undulation of his middle, he was off. He scoured the far bank, until finally he paused downstream where the river narrowed and continued its rushing course. The nymphs' smiles lit with glee, delight shining in their faces.

It was obvious what Lucas was thinking. That I'd taken in water and was unconscious, being swept off toward Foix. I was happy to pay him back with a few moments' worry, but enough was enough. I made to break surface, but Viveau pulled me back.

"Such a shame to spoil it. Just a little longer?" Devious hope shone in her eyes.

I shot her a grin and handed the reed back. "I'm tempted, but we've gone far enough. Thanks for your help."

She shrugged.

I propelled myself up into the air and trod water, gazing in Lucas's direction. He must have heard because he emerged gaping, hair plastered against his head.

I grinned. "I believe, Doctor Rouseau, that just for once, I win."

The water nymphs emerged either side, howling with laughter.

His face grew black, then he dove down. In a second, he resurfaced before me. "Of all the stupid, inconsiderate things to do."

I stared at him as I circled my arms. I just couldn't comprehend the tightness of his lips and the blaze in his eyes. "What?"

"An absolutely idiotic idea, Camille," he roared, his nose dripping as he rose and fell.

I gaped, unable to believe his reaction.

He turned to the nymphs. "What the hell possessed you to hide her?"

Viveau's chin angled. "You stood up Ruisselette."

"I didn't stand her up," Lucas yelled, "I told her I couldn't make it."

"Three hours late." Her words dripped with malice.

Incredulity creased his features. "That's not the point. The point is"—his gaze flared against mine—"Camille was out of line."

I pulled myself together. "No way. No fucking way."

"Revenge is sweet," Viveau said simply, and with it, she and the nymphs disappeared under the surface.

"I can't understand you," I shouted, threads of anger twisting my gut. "I was hiding from you just like you hid from me." Thunder rumbled in the distance. "The idiotic idea was throwing me into the river."

"After you knifed me," he growled.

My jaw dropped. "You're not going to turn *that* around. One little cut. Or is that it? I finally manage to get one up on you in training, and you don't like it. I can't believe you're being so petty."

"And I can't believe you think that of me." I wouldn't have been surprised if his glower melted the last of the Pyrenean glaciers. It bored in, going much too deep, then he shook his head and took a halting breath. "I was worried. I thought I'd hurt you."

His words held an attempt at softness, but the threads of anger cut in, indignation razor-edged. "You lost the right to *worry* when you threw me in," I roared. "What is it? One rule for me and another for you? It was totally unacceptable."

He just stared at me.

"I've had enough of this." Unable to deal with my overwhelming fury, I thrust myself into the water and swam to the shore, anger powering each stroke, my feet pounding. He was an ass. An unbelievable, conceited, complete and utter ass.

CHAPTER 3

BY THE TIME I'D SWUM TO THE RIVERBANK, LUCAS WAS standing on dry ground before me, drenched and dripping, his arms folded, his head shaking. Damn him. It was my day off, and I was due to meet Alice soon. I didn't need this.

Grappling with weeds, I managed to gain purchase on the bank. Thunder boomed as I clambered up. I usually felt relieved when a storm broke, but now I didn't. I just felt furious with Lucas, at his gaze burning into me.

Not deigning to acknowledge his presence, I headed across the clearing and picked up my blades, my limbs like lead, water trickling out of my leathers.

"Camille." Lucas's voice grated. "How could you be so irresponsible?"

"Irresponsible?" Every part of me fumed. "Me? Irresponsible? And this from the man who last week texted me that a barragognes had invaded the cinema?" I'd burst in, expecting the ghostly presence to have caused mass carnage, only to find everyone perfectly happy, if a little on edge, watching a replay of *The Lady in White*. Lucas sat at the back, a large tub of popcorn in his hands and a massive grin on his stuffed face. I'd had to explain my abrupt, unpaid entry to the manager with Lucas sniggering behind me.

Thunder crashed, louder this time... and again.

"*That* was funny." He shook his head, his jaw so stiff it looked like it might snap. "This is completely different. You were—" He glanced over my shoulder into the sky.

I frowned. It wasn't like him to give up mid-lambast.

"Uh... that wasn't thunder," he said.

Catching yells coming from the trees, I swung around.

Far in the distance, a massive round... *thing* stomped toward us. It was twice as high as the surrounding woodland, its head a part of its torso, its pit eyes as round as the rest of it. Its teeth, however, had a distinct sharpness that other body parts lacked. I couldn't say if it was more of a blob or a sort of moving rock with gnashers, but that really didn't matter right at this moment. The ground vibrated with each of its lumbering steps as it waded through the trees.

Three figures wove through the woodland toward us, their cloaks flapping. Félix, Hugo and Zach, incongruous in the open air without a Dungeons & Dragons campaign in full swing before them.

"Not again," I muttered.

"Camille," Félix cried as they approached, slowed by some bushes. "Help us!"

In the three weeks since they'd taken verity, the potion that revealed the hidden world, we'd banned them from having anything to do with fae. Despite that, we'd had to save them from an irate vestige, a guardian of high places, who'd attempted to throw them off the cliff at the Gorges de la Frou. We'd also had to placate a load of goblins at the Peppered Parsnip when they'd offended most of the clientele. And that was after they'd snuck into Stinkhorn, headed through a random door and gotten completely disoriented in a land that only appeared to exist to pull unsuspecting travellers into swamps. It was a miracle they'd made it out only having lost their shoes, Zach's mobile and half a ham and cornichon baguette to the quagmires.

It was a common reaction to verity—not being able to fully accept the reality of fae straight away, and they were treating it all as a game, unable to comprehend that if the approaching blob munched on them, it would be lights out.

They broke through the bushes and continued their approach, their faces contorted with terror.

"I'll wring their necks." Lucas dragged his hands over his face. "Men," he called. The Men of Bédeilhac were supposed to be keeping an eye on them.

Slaughter appeared from behind a tree. The foot-high warrior was dressed in carefully sewn prehistoric pelts, his blaze of hair and wild beard magnificent. He took two steps one way, then another, before spinning around, his eyes crossing. "Waaaas soooo nice of someone to leave twoooo barrels of scrapelather out for ussssss." He fell flat on his back.

Lucas rolled his eyes.

The creature thudded closer, gaining ground, though it was still a fair way off. Its general blobbiness and the fact that it was growing rapidly meant I could make a pretty reliable identification. "If I'm not mistaken, that's Pare Gégant." The giant father, well known in Pyrenean folklore for eating children.

"Spot on," Lucas said, assessing his advance.

"He's an ogre, which means he's feeding on their fear. That lot is going to have to face him and master their emotions." I was familiar with the procedure as I'd had a joyous personal experience with a croquembouche, an ogre from my childhood nightmares. I drew a breath, ignoring the panic attempting to rise. That thing didn't need my fear as well, and he was now a little too close for comfort.

Screaming, the three of them burst into the clearing and charged past. As they entered the trees again, they split up, heading for the N20.

"We need to cut them off," Lucas said, "before they reach the road."

A giant ogre eating cars on the main route into Spain would be difficult to explain.

"Get Félix," he added. "I'll get the others."

We sprinted after them.

I darted in and out of the woods. In moments, Félix was rasping ahead. He had youth on his side, but not speed. Playing D&D did precious little for muscle tone, and he was struggling. I grabbed his arm and used his momentum to fling him around, my fingers digging into his pudgy hand, which held a small sack.

"High Warrior of the Borders," he jabbered, attempting to pull his arm free. "What are you doing? That thing... that monster. He's going to eat us—"

"Shut up, Félix. Listen to me. The ogre is feeding on your fear. He will grow more powerful until you control yourself."

"You have to be joking." He tried to pull back, his sweat-slicked caramel curls shaking, his eyes wild. "We're ahead of that thing. We can escape."

"I'm deadly serious. He'll hang on in there until he finds you. If you want to get out of this, shut away your fear."

We couldn't see Pare Gégant for the trees ahead, but by the intensifying booms and the quaking ground, he would be here any second. "We need more distance so you can get control of yourself." I caught his cloak and yanked him into the undergrowth. We sprang over brambles and dodged trees, then emerged out onto a dirt car park.

Lucas burst from the woodland to the side, half carrying, half dragging Zach and Hugo by the scruffs of their necks. They were screaming as much at Lucas as the oncoming ogre.

He dropped them beside us. "I told you," he roared. "Stop. Being. Frightened."

Quivering, they glanced at each other, then made a dash for it. Before they could get to the trees, Lucas was in their path. Zach's scrawny knees bent in, wobbling.

I grabbed Félix and locked his arms, then drew my

dagger and held it to his throat. "Try to relax," I growled as Lucas seized Zach's and Hugo's cloaks.

Félix squirmed against me. "Uh, the knife wielded by someone I previously thought of as a safe and trusted adult isn't helping me feel happy and secure at this moment."

Yes, I wasn't quite sure our approach was working, but the now enormous ogre was seconds away.

"Not to mention, our doctor who turns into the beast from the abyss is about to rip us apart." Hugo's thickset chest trembled.

"We could feed them to Pare Gégant," Lucas said. "That would stop him."

Hugo fainted.

I scowled. "You aren't helping. But couldn't we knock them all out? Then the ogre wouldn't have fear to feed on."

Lucas shook his head. "Doesn't work. I've tried it before."

In the corner of my eye, I caught a movement. Two concerned faces peered out of the bushes to the side of the ogre's trajectory. Gabe and Nora.

Snapping trunks and branches, Pare Gégant broke into the far end of the car park.

"Think happy thoughts," Lucas rumbled at Zach.

I pressed the knife a little closer so Félix could feel its sting. "I am not going to die today just because you lot have been messing around in Fae again."

"High Warrior, you wouldn't hurt me," he stammered. "Not the High Warrior of the Borders, Protector and Holder of the Knowledge of Free Men and Fae?"

Lucas snorted then guffawed. Would he please concentrate on the situation at hand?

The ogre continued his march toward us, dust flying, his bulky mass shaking with fury, hunger in his eyes.

"High Warrior!" Félix yelped.

The laughter that erupted from Lucas really was quite impressive.

"Time to stop calling me that," I said into Félix's ear, glaring at Lucas.

Zach and a now conscious Hugo exchanged bemused looks, the corners of their mouths tugging upward.

"You should see your face, Félix," Zach called. "You look like you've wet your pants."

Hugo's chest shook. "Yeah, never seen you look so scared. Not even when Max stepped on your special edition rule book."

Félix stilled for a moment, then straightened in my grip. "No way. Look at you both, quaking like lily-livered flumphs. You're a sight." A slightly hysterical laugh escaped him. "It's like that time Zach thought the town had been invaded, when Ignace Gasc's crow-scarer wouldn't stop firing."

The ogre stamped closer, the cloud of dust so thick I could barely see him. But if I wasn't mistaken, he was a little smaller.

Zach laughed. "Wasn't worse than the time you drove your bike into Gabe's papa's car, denting the door. You were going to make a getaway, but he was inside. Caught you red-handed." He roared with laughter, albeit the slightly frenzied hilarity of someone who'd decided it wasn't worth spending their last moments being too serious.

"Or the time Hugo was peeing in the woods by the river," Félix added, "and a busload of tourists stopped in traffic on the road. They had full view."

They all creased up.

The dust cleared, the human-sized ogre almost upon us.

"Shit, it's working," Félix cried.

"Look at him," Hugo said. "He was a giant a moment ago and now he looks like a beachball with teeth."

Pare Gégant appeared rather disgruntled at that, especially as he shrank another foot.

I released Félix. He had the idea. Lucas did the same and the trio huddled together, howling at the approaching monster.

"That thing might be good for scaring cats," Zach cried, "but that's about it."

He shrank down to waist height and teetered around comically, which did nothing to stop the gang's roars.

"I can't believe we were running away." Félix pointed at him, his sack flying about. "It would be more terrifying running from One-Legged Lars."

"No, I don't think we should make fun of him," Hugo said. "He's too cute. I'm gonna take him home."

The hell he was.

"Men," Lucas called, still chuckling at me. "Take him back to wherever he came from."

Three rather uncoordinated Men appeared. The ogre was now smaller than they were. One poked him with the butt of his axe and he fell over, flailing. The Men tackled him rather badly, much too hammered to be effective.

Lucas snatched the sack from Félix's hand, much to his dismay, and sauntered over. "High Warrior." He didn't even try to restrain his grin.

"Unbelievable." I shook my head. "Your sense of humour actually has a use."

Chapter 4

"We crushed it," Hugo cried from the D&D nook.

I gritted my teeth as I placed a hot chocolate on the tray.

Guy swirled the cream dispenser as he made up more cups, singing something funky to himself, his words barely audible over the chatter. Pyrenee's café was full. The cosy wood beams, the displays of sunflowers with curled wheat and the aroma of fresh bread made the place a homely sanctuary against the storm that had finally broken, but it was doing little to improve my mood.

To make matters worse, Alice wasn't here and she hadn't texted. We had a date to head up to the cave for a bit of us time. I tried to release a breath to calm myself, but it didn't do much good. I was still edgy since she'd been abducted by Elivorn, the only asshole in existence worse than Lucas. What a surprise they were brothers.

I scowled at Guy as he finished squirting cream on

another cup. The hot chocolates for the gang sure as hell hadn't been my idea. Guy had taken heart, seeing them come in dishevelled and exhausted.

"That ogre was mincemeat." Félix smashed his fist against the table, now anything but tired. His large, fleshy grin was a little too broad, a little too ready, his gaze holding a slightly crazed enthusiasm.

He sat with Hugo on one side of the nook, Hugo's broad shoulders and bulk taking up most of the room. Gabe and Nora sat on the other side, absorbed in their own hushed yet heated argument. Zach was on the end, pinning them in, his elbows on the table, his hands clamped either side of his thin face, his greasy blond hair a spiky mess.

Incredulity seeped through my veins as they went on about how magnificently they'd handled everything. I hated to think what would've happened if Lucas and I hadn't been there, especially considering they'd put the Men, our early warning system, out of action.

They were also lucky that Lucas hadn't lost it in the two minutes it had taken to drive here in his SUV, all of them squashed in the back. Especially after Félix revealed how they'd stolen a couple of barrels of scrapelather from the Parsnip and left them strategically placed for the Men. They had, however, gone extremely quiet after that, seeing Lucas's skin darkening, just a hint of what lay beneath reminding them that they were in the car with a killer.

But Lucas. That utter git. He'd driven off to find sobering potion for the Men. My fury at him was worse than anything I felt for the others. He'd chucked me in the river, then been infuriated when I'd given him a taste of his own medicine. My hair was still soaked and I felt bedraggled, even though I'd dried and changed into jeans and a T-shirt. The supplies I kept in the café, in my truck and at the Keepers' post were growing by the week.

Thunder clattered and rain lashed at the windows, but the heart of the storm wasn't upon us yet. I could feel it approaching, gathering, and I wanted to be out there, not cooped up here dealing with this shit.

"Done," Guy said, before launching into another verse.

I placed the last of the hot chocolates on the tray and headed over, weaving past Ren the barman and two goblins heading out and Roux heading in.

Zach's eyes sparkled. "The whole thing was totally awesome. Best ever!"

I plonked the tray on the table, hot chocolate, cream and chocolate slithers slopping everywhere. "You don't get it, do you? Apart from ripping up the forest, you put lives in danger. Not just yours but the folk on the N20, plus mine and Lucas's. What the fuck were you thinking?"

Gabe and Nora glanced at me for a moment, before continuing their whisper quarrel, Nora's mouth puckered, her dark bob and make-up perfect as always. Gabe's glower was uncharacteristic in his usually friendly wide eyes, his silicone elf ear tips missing. I wouldn't be surprised if he'd lost them in the furore.

They all grabbed hot chocolates, catching the drips in their hands.

Félix slurped his then beamed, having developed a thick

moustache. "Chill, Camille, we sorted it. Everything turned out fine." His brow narrowed. "Though I can't believe Lucas took the bonevetch."

I glared at him.

He momentarily withered before shaking it off and grinning again. "Anyway, plenty more where that came from."

If they didn't process the verity soon and get some perspective on the dangers of the hidden world, I hated to think what would happen. "What planet do you actually live on?"

"Planet Fae," Zach said in a terrible American accent.

Félix and Hugo laughed. Gabe scowled at them all.

From a table to the side where four old men huddled, I caught, "She's a terrible waitress. Look at those hot chocolates. Spilled them everywhere." Then, "No idea why Alice keeps her on," and "Isn't she the doctor's bit of stuff?" Strong cologne wafted over from their direction.

I turned my glare on Mean Gert, Ignace, Ludger and Alf, four local farmers. At least they used to be, until their spawn had taken over their farms and they'd developed various aches and pains that stopped them helping out much. Now they hung around at the café complaining about anything they could. Alf still held a grudge against me for tripping over his gouty foot a couple of years back, even though he'd stuck it in the thoroughfare and I'd been loaded with a tray of dirties, unable to see a thing. He'd clearly been in pain, and I'd felt terrible. All until he'd started a tirade on Grampi producing a family line good for nothing but shovelling goat shit. What was wrong with goats, anyway?

Well, they could say what they liked about my waitress-ing, but Grampi was another matter, and there was no damned way I was Lucas's bit of anything. Clenching my fists, I fought the urge to mouth off. I had enough problems without starting an argument I was never going to win.

They stared daggers back at me, Mean Gert's jowls wobbling. Ignace puckered his tight lips, scrunching his scrawny face. Alf and Ludger shook their heads condescend-ingly, then Ludger transferred his gaze to the nook and shook his head some more, presumably at the gang's unkempt cloaks that were definitely not respectable attire.

I drew a deep breath and turned back to the matter at hand, leaning on the table. "This isn't a D&D campaign... or some video game. You don't get second chances. If you die, you die. That's it. Finito. And today"—I drew my finger and thumb together—"you came this close—*this close*. What were you even doing with an ogre on your asses, anyway?"

"We went into Fae for bonevetch," Félix said.

"A nice little quest, and we were the victors." Hugo slapped his chest.

Zach frowned. "Yeah, we just didn't expect the ogre to follow us back from the Bouan way marker and go berserk."

I turned to Gabe and Nora, who were still slinging heated whispers. "And what the hell were you two doing? You were supposed to be watching them."

They gaped at me, Nora looking guilty, Gabe startled. Thunder boomed again, the accompanying flash dimming the café's mellow lighting. I wanted to boom like that, to let loose and kick this lot's butts so damned hard. Actually, no, I wanted to kick Lucas's more, so much more.

"Uh, they were dead set on a quest," Gabe said. "There wasn't any stopping them. I... I... gave them the idea of retrieving the bonevetch because it was the safest thing I could think of. Before that, they were going for dragon's gold, and that really wouldn't have ended well."

"We thought they'd be able to handle Pare Gégant," Nora said sullenly, scowling at Gabe. "We didn't know that Félix's big sister used to taunt him about the ogre living under the stairs, and, well..."

I raised my hands, fingers splayed. "Why didn't you just mention it?"

They fiddled with their cups.

Exasperation tore through me. "You didn't want to tattle. Yeah, I get it, very noble. But you know what the verity is doing to them, and you know the danger." My voice rose to a crescendo. But it wasn't doing any good. Gabe and Nora were back to glaring at one another, and the rest of them were grinning inanely. Lucas had said it might be months before Félix, Zach and Hugo had processed the verity and gained a clear recognition of danger, if we were lucky. In some cases, folk remained in this state for life, which often wasn't such a long time given their behaviour.

"Take it back," Gabe said, his voice rising. He glowered down at Nora's lap.

Her hands shifted under her cloak. "No way," she hissed.

Gabe's glower deepened. Whatever it was, he'd reached boiling point. His hand shot forward under Nora's cloak and grabbed at something. They began a tug of war, Gabe almost shoving Zach off his seat. "Leave it here, then," he growled.

Nora shot me a wary side-eye.

I put my hands on my hips. "What now?"

Nora yanked back and knocked over the remains of her hot chocolate.

Having reached my limit, I held out my palm. "Right, give it to me."

They glanced at each other.

"Today, I'm pissed," I said. "Very pissed. And if you don't give me whatever you're squabbling about, I'm going to get my blade and take it by force." After earlier, it was sensible to make sure it was nothing to do with Fae.

Nora swallowed. She placed something on the table. An old digital watch.

Realisation dawned with a surge of fury. "You're still thieving." I was pretty sure this was Ren's, and he wasn't the only one. Monsieur Leclerc had lost his wallet a couple of days ago while Nora was around, and I'd caught various reports of missing jewellery. Madame Belle even lost her false teeth. I'd hoped it hadn't been Nora and that we'd seen the last of it after she'd stolen Madame Ballon's necklace and Shroom-Jean's wallet, but it didn't look like it.

I reached over and snatched up the watch. It was worthless. If she was selling stolen goods for money, this wasn't going to get her anything. I placed it back on the table. "You haven't heard the end of this." My words were deadly. "But for now, return it. I'll check you have."

With a face as dark as night, Nora seized the watch and

shoved Gabe into Zach, sliding them off the seat. She sprang up and stormed out of the café, the farmers tutting loudly at the ruckus.

CHAPTER 5

"Oh my god, you're so mad at me," Alice called as she pushed through the café doors holding a large wet box and looking almost as bedraggled as I felt.

I placed the espresso I'd been making on a saucer and transferred it to the counter for a customer. I'd channelled my frustration into helping out while I waited for her. "Never." Nope, definitely not mad with Alice. The gang were another matter. And Lucas... I couldn't shift his angry, arrogant face. Every part of me was tight. At least now Alice was here, we could get away from it all.

I grabbed a cloth and wiped the counter. Alice walked past and dotted a kiss on my cheek. Choppy hair surrounded her soft face in damp spikes, her general frazzle blending with the craziness of her rain-splattered tropical-print onesie. "Electrical outage at the cash and carry. I had to wait for everything to come online before I could pay, and I couldn't leave it, we're so short of takeout cups. Oh, and my phone ran out of charge so I couldn't text." She disappeared out back.

The kitchen clattered. Dame Blanche, Guy and José were cleaning up for the day. Across the room the farmers were still grumbling about whatever they could, several of the clientele, human and fae, glancing in their direction.

"Damn storms." Mean Gert screwed up his bullish face. "The hay won't fare well in this." The others mumbled their agreement.

Ignace scowled at Roux as he enjoyed a millefeuille by the window, dropping a splodge of cream on this cloak. "Old vagrant," he said. "I have no idea why they let him in here."

Any more of that and they would be out.

Alice returned, tying up her apron. Not a good sign for our date.

"The cave?" My voice was a little too high.

"Don't hate me, but José's aunt has taken a fall again. He has to go in a minute. We're short-staffed." Her eyebrows met in the middle, her nose scrunching. "I can't make it."

I slumped over the counter. "Crap." It had been so long. We used to go up there all the time to discuss... well, everything. After Grimmere, we had so much to talk about, and what with me busy training and there being no privacy around here, we never had the opportunity. "But it's understandable."

She bit her lip, her eyebrows still suspended. "But let's do it later in the week... when we're both off in the afternoon. I promise I won't let anything get in the way."

"Good." I pointed at her with my cloth. "But if you're short-staffed then, I'll have the Men help out."

She grimaced. "I definitely won't be."

I took another order, my voice tight, the customer eyeing me warily, then Alice began on the patisserie as I made the tea.

"Are you sure you're alright with it?" she said. "Only—"

"What?" I clattered the teapot under the hot-water faucet. "I'm fine."

"Don't give me that, Camille." She placed two plates of gâteau opéra on the counter. "You've got that expression you keep for customers who complain the crockery is dirty. And your hair is drenched. Get caught in the rain?"

I scowled. "It's just Lucas being the world's biggest asshole. Nothing new." I took the next order and Alice started the coffees.

She chuckled. "Not again. What was it this time? Another barragognes at the cinema?"

Nope. Today had been something else entirely. I transferred to steaming the milk, my fingers tightening around the jug. "This time, he threw me in the river."

Alice barked a laugh. "What?"

I glared at her. "I got one up on him in training, and he couldn't handle it. He just grabbed me and... well, threw me in. Then he was irate when I hid from him just like he hid from me."

She shook her head, chuckling.

"I don't find it funny. It's as if while we're waiting for his family to make their next move, he has nothing to do but pull pranks."

Two built men entered, their leather jackets soaked, their struts confident. The farmers, thank goodness, were heading to the door, still grumbling.

"Check them out," I said, inclining my head to the newcomers as I placed the order on the counter. The customer thanked me and headed off. "What do you reckon?"

"Definitely not local."

They swaggered in, one with razor-edged designer stubble and an equally styled ebony cowlick, the other blond and bronzed, his neck as thick as his face. As the farmers passed, the one with the cowlick knocked into Ignace's shoulder. Even though that grump deserved so much more, it was a rough move on an old-timer.

"Watch where you're going," Ignace snarled. Now the farmers had something other than me to grumble about.

The two men halted in the centre of the café, surveying the customers. They exchanged words, then strutted back into the storm. Whoever they were looking for wasn't here.

Alice took the next order. While the espressos dripped, I took my irritation out on a filter, slamming it to remove the grounds.

Alice processed the payment. "You know, you and Lucas are hilarious."

"What?" There was no one waiting, so I leant against the counter.

She tidied the shot glasses on top of the machine, her grin extending from ear to ear, her warm face alight. "You spend all your time together. He's at the café first thing. You make his noisette and sit with him. Then at lunch he's back again, you two huddled in armchairs with baguettes or whatever. And as soon as you're finished in the evening, it's training. If that's not enough, you're spending your days off going into Fae."

"And...?" I didn't get it. "I'm basically holding down two jobs, using my breaks to discuss Keeper business and training at other times. I don't have much choice." Being a Keeper didn't pay in euros. I appreciated the gifts fae left as thanks, a crocheted shawl, chantarelles, a stunning lump of quartz. Although after the whole thing with Anthras, someone had left me an assortment of charognard dung. Roux had taken it as apparently it had a use in colludes, but it didn't pay the bills. Anyway, I loved working at the café. I'd never give it up. Not to mention, I was so utterly relieved to be back on good terms with Alice. It made me appreciate my days here even more.

She opened a new bag of beans. "Apart from keeping that lot out of trouble"—she inclined her head to the nook— "how busy are you? Though I suppose Madame Bovary did sit on Monsieur Vaux's Alsatian." The tease in her voice was clear.

Yep, we'd had to pull her off with a large pair of warded oven gloves. Destroyer hadn't been breathing at that point, the sarramauca's asphyxiation having been too much even for his prowess. But a little help from Lucas, who'd cussed wildly at having to give a dog pulmonary resuscitation, and he'd sort of come round. The vet did the rest, and he was good. Well, all except for his newfound penchant for yelping at the first sign of anything vaguely feline.

"Oh..." She poured beans into the grinder. "And there was that time a load of sinagries wandered into Madame Dubois's garden. What did that take you? All of an hour to sort out?"

We'd later found out that the hell hounds had accidentally eaten a load of hallucinogenic mushrooms, which made them visible to humans. Delirious, they'd wandered out of Fae, only to give the old lady the shock of her life. She'd passed away that night, possibly confirming that sinagries truly were omens of death, but as she'd been one hundred and three and no one could figure out how she'd managed to stay alive that long, the evidence was inconclusive. It had taken a chocolate éclair to lure the hounds back into fae, with the Men guarding them until the effects of the mushrooms wore off. Both instances had been wrapped up speedily.

I fiddled with the bow of my apron. "Yes, I guess we've not been *that* busy."

"And yet you and Lucas have spent a ridiculous amount of time together."

"We have things to discuss," I snapped. "I'm still learning." And usually, I enjoyed those moments, talking folklore and fae. I liked it when he popped in all the time, and when his texts buzzed frequently in between. After everything that had happened in Grimmere, our friendship was growing. His stupid tricks aside, I had to admit he was good company—intelligent, attentive, funny. At least when he didn't go too far. But today... Damn it, he infuriated me. There was no sense to him.

Lightning flashed, accompanied by a clap of thunder. Alice flinched. The rain pummelled harder against the windows, the heart of the storm closer now, its force mingling with my irritation. But it was unlike Alice to be nervous of a little weather.

She took a breath and met my gaze. "You don't get it, do you?"

"Get what?" I cocked an eyebrow.

"Lucas is so into you."

I gaped, unable to believe her. "No... no, he's not. It's physical attraction, that's all, and we've just sort of developed this flirting thing. It's become our normal, and that's as far as it goes." She'd lost the plot.

She began sorting the cappuccino cups, a dimple forming in her cheek as she held back a smile. "Come on, Camille. It's more than that. It's so damned obvious. You two sitting in the café a bit too close. The eye contact. The mutually receptive body language." She gestured at me with a cup. "And I've seen you down by the river. Half the time you're talking or laughing or he has you in a compromising headlock, his shirt off. It's like some kind of elaborate mating ritual, you two prancing around flapping your plumage." She stuck out her elbows and waggled them.

"We're training!" I cried. "I can't believe this. And yes, we do have a laugh sometimes, like today, before it all went wrong, but it's just messing about."

The lights flickered and Alice juddered. "No way. Please don't let *us* have a power outage. That would be too much."

"You okay?" I asked. My turn for questions.

"Completely fine." She didn't look at me. "One hundred percent."

I studied her as she continued tidying. "Fine" was her default statement at the moment, but there was a lot under the surface. Considering what she'd been through with Elivorn and Raphaël, it wasn't surprising.

"And don't change the subject," she added. Those tricks Lucas pulls on you, like the barragognes. You don't see him trying them on anyone else, do you? He's completely respectful to his patients and everyone most of the time."

Would she please move on? "I... I mean, not in the human realm. He's more himself in Fae." More likely to rip someone's throat out.

She tilted her chin. "It's as though he does it to get your attention, pulling you in so that he has all of you focussed on him."

"No... I mean... double no." It really wasn't like that, and she was supposed to be siding with me that Lucas was a total jerk, not this. My irritation at him swathed out to encompass her. This was ridiculous, and from my best friend. "As I said, it's physical attraction, but that's all. There's nothing more."

Alice rolled her eyes. "Heavens help you."

Thunder broke once more, reverberating through my

chest. I was so done with this. I just wanted to be outside, feeling the wind and rain. I glanced at the deluge only to see Lucas heading in. My teeth scraped together.

"Speak of the devil," Alice said with a grin.

"Never a truer word."

He headed up to the counter, his lips pressed together as he ran his gaze over my face, assessing my annoyance level. Alice found herself suddenly fascinated by arranging cinnamon sticks.

I folded my arms and clamped my mouth, leaving no doubt about my wrath.

He lowered his chin and looked at me from under his perfect brow. "Enjoy your dip?"

I closed my eyes. He just couldn't resist. "Did you really come here to say that because—"

He raised his hands. "I have to admit... I overreacted by chucking you in the river, then losing it."

Laughter from the D&D nook rose above the chatter as the gang recounted the afternoon's escapades yet again.

"You don't say." I stared at him through narrowed eyes. He was so... out of the ordinary. I could never pin him down.

He scraped his hand through his hair. "I... uh... apologise."

I was still totally pissed, but I supposed we were learning about each other, and after Grimmere, I wasn't in any doubt that he had my back. Above all, we had to continue working together. "Apology accepted," I said stiffly.

"Good." His broad smile held more than a little mischief.

"But no more throwing me in rivers," I added.

Alice slid Lucas a noisette. "I'll sort that lot," she said, nodding to the customers heading over.

I shot her a scowl for the twinkle in her eye, then walked to the end of the counter, out of her way, Lucas following with his coffee.

"And anyway," I said, "we have another problem. Nora." I wasn't sure what I could do. I had no responsibility for her, but as her doctor, Lucas did. "She's still stealing. Took Ren's watch."

Lucas's brow furrowed. "Which makes it even more likely she's responsible for the thefts in the café lately."

I nodded. "And the watch was worthless. What's going on? Kleptomania or something?"

"I don't know, but we'll have to keep an eye—"

"Uhhhhmm." A voice came from below. Wreck, dressed in a tunic and leather trousers, teetered from one fur boot to the other, an envelope of rough, grainy paper with a black wax seal in his hand. "Bossssss," he slurred. "I think this might have been from La Vieille, but I wasss having trouble focusssssssing and it may have been from a very large spider." He hiccupped before disappearing under a table.

I glanced at Lucas. "Looks like the Men need more sobering potion. And anyway, La Vieille, the old lady? Isn't she the one who appoints Keepers?" I'd read what I could about the process since committing to the job, and an old lady had been mentioned, though the title was rather generic.

He placed his cup on the counter, took the envelope and broke the seal, the lines between his eyebrows deepening.

"La Vieille... is La Vieille," he murmured as he scanned the contents.

As clear as mud. "Care to explain in a little more detail?"

He looked up, his jaw tight. "Probably best you meet her for yourself. She would like to see us on the way to the assembly tomorrow."

"Oh?"

"And that's it. The letter doesn't go into details."

I shrugged. "Alright."

Félix's voice soared through the café. "The ogre shrank so much it was smaller than my foot. I'm telling you, we need a bigger challenge next. A mightier quest."

Lucas's face closed in as he picked up his noisette and took a sip.

"We have to do something about them," I said. "I get that they're having a reaction to the verity." The verity that had been my responsibility. "But somehow we have to make them see danger before they kill themselves." I could envision the distraught faces of their parents when we returned their lifeless bodies. "And after managing to get the Men plastered, I'm concerned about leaving them, even for one night."

"If they were fae, I would've fed them to the ogre." Lucas's jaw shifted. "But we can't postpone the trip. We have to update the assembly about my family's activities, and there's no way we can ignore an invitation from La Vieille."

I certainly didn't want to delay our trip either. More than anything, I needed to understand how Fae worked. But then, what if the gang needed that too? "Maybe it's not helping banning them from the place. They obviously want to know more, so what about taking them with us for once? If we forbid them access, they're going to sneak in anyway. Maybe with a little experience, they'll see the gravity of it all."

A rush of wind and a volley of rain drove at the windows.

He drew in a breath and rubbed his chin. "We're going to be busy. The last thing we need is them tagging along. Although... I can think of something to occupy them there. A little recompense for today." A wicked grin spread across his face.

"Sounds like a plan." I was all for recompense.

He strode to the D&D nook. "Right, you lot. Tomorrow morning, Camille and the lovely and not at all violent and never monstrous Doctor Rouseau—who holds your health and well-being as his top priority, and who would never pull your limbs from their sockets and feed them slowly to sina-gries as chew toys—are going to take you on a summer camping trip, one night only. Pack enough so your parents aren't suspicious, but there isn't anything you'll need at the assembly. Tell Nora."

They glanced at one another, eyes widening, grins pulling at their lips.

"That means..." Hugo said, bouncing in his seat.

"We're going into Fae!" Félix swung his fist through the air.

"We're going into Fae with a drac—a creature from hell," Zach said dourly.

Gabe just glared at them.

Lightning flashed, casting the room in stark white, thunder reverberating all around, wind gusting. Damn it.

After everything today, I needed to get out and clear my head.

"I'll see you in a bit," I said to Lucas, leaving him with his noisette and a raised brow. Alice was tidying the boulangerie baskets as I crossed the café. "Catch you later," I called.

She blew me a kiss, and I headed into the storm.

CHAPTER 6

I MADE MY WAY THROUGH WATERLOGGED FAE TARASCON, my shoes slipping on the cobbles, the rain cool on my skin. Even the brightly painted leaning townhouses were dull in the storm and the encroaching dusk. The foliage covering their facades whipped about in the wind, the trunks and branches of the gnarled trees that formed their joists creaking.

By the time I wove up the Coustarous steps, my jeans and T-shirt were soaked, but I barely noticed. I loved summer storms. They could be terrible for livelihoods. A single hailstorm could wipe out all the crops in the area. What with the mountainous terrain, it was one reason why livestock farming was popular. But I couldn't get enough. They held so much power, so much life, and this evening was wild.

On the summit of Coustarous, I skirted the menhir. The bounds were blessedly invisible, showing no sign of the malum, the force of oblivion that Lucas's family had used in their attempt to split the realms. Giving Fae a wide birth, I continued along the mountaintop, into the dip, before rising up toward Cap de Couronnes above the far end of Tarascon.

The squall blasted me, the amber glow of the streetlights blurred. I drew in a deep breath, the air somehow damp and static all at once. Lightning shattered over the town with a rumble that built to a deafening blast. Usually I'd be concerned about my vulnerability, exposed as I was, but today I didn't care, and damn, it felt good.

I skirted rocks and boxwood until I was above the cave where Alice and I should've been right at this moment. Relishing every blustered step, I strode to the highest point, where the ground levelled, rocks cast about. Perhaps there had been a building here at one time. Anyhow, it made the perfect spot to take in the storm... to feel its immensity.

My feet wide, I braced myself against the ravage that was freezing into hail. My shoes dug into mud as the gale whipped my drenched hair. The aluminium foundry and the hydroelectric plant lay below, the Castilla tower glowing gold across the river, the vehicles on the N20 a trail of light streaking past the café. Around the town, five mountains rose, dark in the twilight, the guardians of the valley forming the crucible that held my life.

I raised my arms, absorbing the storm. Wind streamed, caressing my skin, thunder shaking my bones. Closing my eyes, all the frustration I'd felt with the gang, with Alice, with Lucas, all the churning irritation, the confusion, the fury, it swept through me, joining with the gale, and a part of me was borne aloft. I felt as if I was soaring on the wind, sweeping above it all, rising above my agitation, and there was nothing but rushing and gusting and light and energy and power.

Yet it wasn't enough. I needed more.

I rose above Tarascon, higher and higher until the lights were mere pinpricks, static rippling through me. Exhilarated, I whirled down and flung out my arms, releasing the charge into the rocks on Cap de Couronnes, light splintering. Barrelling around, I closed in on Roc de Sédor, the sentinel mountain to the north, and let rip, dust and stone flying. I relinquished bolt after bolt after bolt, the clamour blending with deep, reverberating laughter carried on the gale, a voice thundering, "Camille..." The word drew out long and resonant as it rumbled through the valley.

And beyond it all, beyond the sweeping and surging and freedom of the storm, lurked something else. Something pallid and deathly and utterly incomprehensible.

CHAPTER 7

"HAVE FUN IN THE STORM, DID YOU?" LUCAS attempted to restrain a grin as he held open the door to Charmant, its honeyed wood radiating from a central carved sun. With the ruckus of goblins calling and bartering in Stinkhorn, I could barely hear his first effort at conversation since we'd left Tarascon. He'd spent most of the journey chewing his cheek. There was definitely something on his mind.

"Yes, actually," I replied, trying to hold the stiffness from my voice. I really had needed it. I'd been so frustrated, and getting out amidst the storm had been such a release. The fact that I couldn't remember how I'd gotten back to the farm or how I'd undressed, leaving my wet clothes on the floor, was a little unnerving, as were the images of soaring on the wind, and the feeling like absolute hell in the morning, my bones aching. But I'd been exhausted. I supposed I'd blanked the drive home, then had vivid dreams.

I followed the gang, Nora and a load of Men, Slaughter included, past the menhir that marked the way. The Men were a precautionary measure, should that lot try any more stunts.

The clamour of Stinkhorn receded, replaced by birdsong, warm sunshine and the rustle of beech forest. Lucas closed the door and it was obscured by shimmering air, then only the menhir indicated its place.

He drew level with me as we took the downhill path. "So the river was too wet, but the storm was fine?"

I narrowed my eyes. "I didn't choose to go for a swim." He was baiting me again, and I didn't need to react.

He frowned and returned to chewing his cheek.

"What is it?" I asked. "It's not like you to be so pensive."

"Oh, I have a fair few things on my mind." His eyes rested on me for a little too long, shivers rippling my skin, stirring a little of what I'd felt in the storm.

Vertes velles flitted here and there, their forms so similar to ferns that it would've been impossible to distinguish them from the fronds if it wasn't for the way they rose in small clouds, tickling my skin. One sat on Slaughter's axe.

As ever, I was beyond curious about Fae, but even more so about La Vieille, the assembly and the court of the high elf king, Belomar Rei, where the assembly was held, which apparently wasn't that far. And I wasn't the only curious one. Félix and Hugo halted a little way ahead, fascinated as a dryad merged with her tree, though Gabe was more intro-spective, staring at his hands as he walked, a glow suffusing them as he practised glamours. Nora, who wasn't talking to him, lurked a few steps away, alert and taking it all in, her cloak hanging open over her shorts and T-shirt. The two of them cast the occasional glance over their shoulders at Lucas. I had no idea what he had planned for them, but Gabe and Nora knew him too well to think that today would be a walk in the park.

Zach stared fascinated at two glowing eyes that peered from a hole in the roots of a beech. He picked up a stick and poked it in, only to have it pulled from his hands. A small golden cake flew out. He caught it and held it in his palm, examining the burnished crumb. "Everyone knows eating in Fae is dangerous."

"Stealing herbs from Pare Gégant is dangerous," Lucas called. "If you can survive that, you're good."

As we caught up with them, Félix tried his luck, poking his stick into the hole. It too was snatched, and he waited in expectation. A rock flew out, hitting him squarely on the forehead. "Jeezzz! Why does Zach get cake?"

The others laughed.

Zach tucked into his prize with ravenous bites. "Delicious—" His face turned putrid green, and he dove into the bushes, retching.

Lucas tittered. Gabe and Nora glared at him. The others snickered nervously, gazing about, wondering what this place was going to do next. I shook my head.

"What?" Lucas's brow peaked. "There's a reasonable chance he'll survive."

Stippled sunlight highlighted the angles of his face. A part of me wanted to reach out and touch what was so much of a mystery. Instead, I said, "I have to admit, you confuse me." The whole of Fae confused me. "I've seen you hold it together in the most dire circumstances, and yet you overreacted when I hid for a few minutes."

"And it didn't stop then." Slaughter turned around to face us and walked backward, adjusting the axe on his shoulder. "Got right worked up last night, he did."

"I'm sure you have somewhere else to be," Lucas said, his voice low.

Slaughter didn't appear to hear. "And then I had to help him with a potion in the early hours because he couldn't sleep. Kept going on about how he couldn't believe what he'd done, and how the hell was he supposed to wait? And then there was all that smashing his fists into walls. I think it was very sensible of you, gov, going for a cold shower, what with all you've got bottled up about—"

"Slaughter!" Lucas roared.

The others jumped, the chitters and warbles in the trees silencing.

The little guy's eyebrows rose merrily, then he marched ahead and joined Zach, who was clutching his stomach. But talk about an extreme reaction. Maybe Lucas did regret throwing me in the river, but thumping walls?

"See," I said. "Another confusing response."

Lucas drew in a breath through his nostrils. "I... uh... I find it difficult to react normally around you."

This again. "I noticed with Elivorn."

His face clouded over.

I raised my hand. "Oh, please. Forget I mentioned him.

After yesterday, the last thing I need is you getting worked up. I do appreciate your protective instinct over me as your partner-at-arms—your friend—but really, it's not necessary. You know I can handle myself."

His eyes bored into me, pressure rising in my chest. I tried to ignore him. "Partner-in-arms," he said eventually. "Friends."

"What?"

He clamped his lips together, then angled his head to Hugo, who was taking an interest in Wreck, walking in front. He poked the Man's back with his toe, then walked on as if nothing had happened. Wreck sprang onto his trainer, drove his spear deep into Hugo's foot, then pulled it out, jumped off and marched onward.

"Oooowww!" Hugo howled, hopping about on one leg.

I sighed. "As if that wasn't going to happen."

As we continued, mugwort as high as my shoulder grew in knobbly clumps, the aroma pungent. The forest grew darker, the air moist, pine replacing beech. Instinctively, the others bunched up, walking together in the centre of the path. The Men closed in around them, though they didn't appear bothered by the change.

Threads of mist swirled between the trees, glistening cobwebs hung from branches, and crows wheeled and cawed as the last of the sunlight faded. A shiver ran through me, the hairs on my arms rising. I had the strangest feeling that something was going to happen. Not terrible, exactly, just something.

"I thought the assembly was a nice place," Félix called.

I'd thought so too.

"Does this look like the court of the high elf king?" Nora snapped, gesturing to a thicket ahead. Barely distinguishable from the undergrowth was a rickety hut, its roof burgeoning with weeds, smoke rising from a heap of rocks at the back to twist between overhanging branches. Goosebumps tingled my skin.

Lucas paused, his throat bobbing. Him being nervous was an extremely rare occurrence, and one that didn't bode well.

"La Vieille lives here?" I asked.

"Yep."

"And you still don't want to tell me a little about her before we go in?"

"Nope."

When I'd read about her appointing Keepers, there hadn't been anything worrying, so I doubted she was a killer. "Best we get it over with."

"You lot, wait out here," Lucas said to the others. They drew closer, their arms folded as they gazed warily about, miniature prehistoric warriors encircling them.

"You're going to leave us in this place?" Zach cried.

"You have the Men," Lucas replied. "There's nothing to worry about. We won't be long. Keep out of mischief."

CHAPTER 8

WE PUSHED ASIDE AN OLD, WATER-STAINED HIDE AND entered La Vieille's hut. In the darkness, all I could see was a flickering fire. Woodsmoke and mustiness tickled my nose, the crackle of the flames and Lucas's soft breaths filling my ears.

Gradually, my eyesight adjusted to the gloom. High at the back of the hut, a leaded window sat between the slopes of the roof, doing little to allow in light as most of it was covered by foliage outside. Firelight danced across the rugged wooden walls, the beams above bowed with the weight of the roof, roots creeping through.

The room was cluttered. An old chair and a spinning wheel stood upon a threadbare rug before a broad hearth. Dust beaters leant against the wall. Golden combs, spindles and distaffs were piled on the sideboard. And everywhere, absolutely everywhere, hung yarn. Length upon length was strung from pegs driven into beams. Thick skeins were looped over furniture. Balls were piled upon an old dresser and a couple of stools. And in the spaces without yarn, there were cobwebs, intricate and spiralled. I shuddered, though I couldn't see the spiders that had spun them.

A large basket of fleece stood by the spinning wheel, but as I studied it, the contents swirled, dark and unfathomable. Not like the oblivion of the malum, but dark in the sense that all things might emerge from it. It was the earth sleeping in winter. It was sacrifice providing opportunity. It was life as yet unexpressed.

The shadows beside the fire shifted. Something drew logs from the stack and placed them onto the blaze, a silhouette hunched before the flames. The wood hissed.

"Come, come, my children," the silhouette croaked. "I will be but a moment. The fire must burn bright."

My heart pounded. The spinning wheel... the yarn... all of it could mean only one thing. "La Vieille du Fil," I breathed. "*That* old lady." In Pyrenean folklore, The Old Lady of the Thread spun life into existence, she measured its length, and finally, she cut it. She held the fate of men and presumably fae too. We stepped further into the room, the blaze rising, the yarn glowing gold, the cobwebs glimmering.

"Indeed." She swung around, her long slate-grey hair flying, her dress swishing. Her eyes held more than I could bear to see, her smile ever so slightly crazed. I was flabbergasted. This woman, this *goddess*, was barely comprehensible. Lucas's brow was knotted. I could understand why he hadn't wanted to explain. There weren't words.

She scurried about, checking the threads by the hearth,

then darting from one golden skein to another. She paused by a twisted loop and examined its threads, clicking her tongue, then stepped to yet another skein and muttered, "Yes, yes. This will do." Satisfied, she returned to the hearth, her arms outstretched. "Camille and Lucas. Come, come."

Firelight glimmered across Lucas's face and leathers. He met my gaze and nodded. We stepped before her, my breath shallow.

Her smile was almost maniacal. "My most recent Keepers."

I felt as if I should reply, as if there was some kind of response I should give, but "Nice to meet you" was wholly inadequate. "Andos," I managed.

"Andos. La Vieille." Lucas bowed his head, wariness in his face. "Why have you summoned us?"

"Why?" She studied us intently, her gaze piercing. "The threads that draw you together are strong, very strong indeed, and they tighten. It is time."

"It's too early," Lucas said, his voice hard.

"There is no too early or too late," she replied. "Only precisely the right moment."

I didn't get it. "The right moment for what?"

"For the Keeper bond, my daughter. We must not delay."

I stared at her wrinkled face, her eyes full of life, the life of every fae, every human. I'd read about the bond when I'd researched Keepers. It was a simple ceremony performed at a certain point in a partnership to seal commitment, and it was marked by ornamentation on the skin, the meaning of which was personal, something the pair would comprehend in time.

As far as I understood, the process was a formality, although working closely together, partners gained the instinct to sense one another whilst fighting. It was one of the reasons why Keepers were lethal and respected.

"The Keeper partnership is one of many bonds." Her bony fingers shifted as though invisible threads lay between them. "It is one of the strongest, engendering a deep understanding of the relationship between the fae and human realms. Besides, two minds are better than one. In times of great hardship, which are inevitable, you will need each other."

My thoughts had stuck on "one of many bonds", like the mates' bond we faked in Grimmere.

Lucas ground his teeth. "We've only been working together for a couple of months. Why would we—"

"It is the old lore put in place at the beginning, tied by inviolable knots." She angled her head. "If we allow the threads to pull closer still, they will cut into your flesh, your hearts, your minds. It is not something human or fae can bear. Your souls will be broken." She glanced between us, examining, assessing. "At the perfect moment, when the partnership has been drawn tight enough, the threads are knotted. They are secured in place to ensure that the relationship remains durable. Of course, that is not the only option. Before the bond is made, the threads may be cut. But once they are severed, they may never be tied as securely, and you will not be able to continue as Keepers. There is always a choice."

"There's no choice," Lucas growled.

Breath caught in my throat. I wanted to be a Keeper, but the idea that Lucas and I would be bound for life was more than a little overwhelming. But then... I glanced at him. "If we don't have the bond, what will happen to our ruse with your family?"

"If we don't continue on as Keepers"—his voice was rough, his face stony—"we won't have access to the assembly. Only the heads of states, their trusted representatives and Keepers may meet there. My father would be suspicious, and we would no longer be able to convey information to him."

And that was our only hope of preventing Lord Rouseau from splitting the bounds. "But couldn't we fake it, just like we faked everything else in Grimmere?"

La Vieille cocked an eyebrow at Lucas, then shook her head. "Assembly matters are only shared between those who have a right to attend. The wards ensure this. Lord Rouseau has his spies, just as we do. If you are not there, he will know."

I swallowed. "Then the only hope for defeating Lord Rouseau is to have the bond." The commitment was huge. I thought I'd have more time to come to terms with the idea, but I couldn't see a choice. "With the stakes so high, how could we not?"

Lucas nodded, his lips pressed tight.

La Vieille cackled and met his eye. "Indeed, my son, is there any reason why not?"

Lucas opened his mouth, then paused and shot me a glance. Hesitancy... strange. When it came to our partnership, he'd not shown a hint of reluctance before.

She chuckled. "Well then, my children, let me see that all is in place and you are ready." She extended her hands, palms open, waiting. Lucas drew close to me. His fingers curled around mine and squeezed them tight. I frowned, wondering at the gesture, but I couldn't help relishing in the security of his grip. He turned to La Vieille and placed his other hand in hers. She nodded for me to do the same. I followed suit, her palm cool, her grasp tingling. Her mouth tilted into a small smile as she closed her eyes.

And we were no longer in the hut. At least a part of us wasn't. I could still sense the threads and skeins surrounding us, still feel the warmth of Lucas's hand and the tingle of La Vieille's, but most of me was standing at the omphalos before it had exploded.

Lucas and I were together, his arms around my waist as we stared into the seething malum, the Rouseaus and the dark elves nearby. The image shifted and we were with Alice in the dungeon, then we were with Lucas's family again, this time dressed in finery at dinner. Another shift and we lay in Lucas's bed, curled close. It was something that only the two of us knew about, and yet she saw. My stomach turned. She saw it all.

"How... how can you?" I stuttered. Lucas squeezed my hand, an anchor to the present, to the hut.

"My child, I know all before it has happened, never mind afterward. At least when I want to think of it." She shrieked and cackled wildly.

The images continued, and we were back in Rancié, fighting for our lives, back in the caves near Les

Profondeurs, Lucas demonstrating an incubi's influence, his lips on mine.

"Hmmm," La Vieille murmured.

I tried to force away the images. They were *private*.

"You can't fight it," Lucas murmured. "She's too powerful."

But this was an invasion.

Back further, back... back... cutting down charognards, facing the hantaumo queen, greeting Naïs, cringing before godawful rats, back... back... Lucas fighting for Henri's life before he'd taken me into Fae for the first time.

"Yes, yes," she muttered through the replay. "The threads have drawn tight indeed." She paused for a moment, blurred images swirling before my mind's eye. "What is this?"

She cackled again, and I saw the cave above Lucas's house, Lucas in his hideous drac form as he tried to convince me that fae were real. "What a way to introduce your partner to the hidden world," she croaked. "And wait... there is more. My, my, my..." She drew in a sharp breath. "My, indeed..."

Lucas and I were back in his bedroom. It was *that* night. The night we'd both blessedly forgotten in a drunken haze. My head was thick with bourbon, and yet now I could see beyond the fog. We were laughing, saying stupid things about fae as we removed each other's clothes. Then we were naked, his firm body pressed against mine. I ran my hands through his hair. Every part of him felt so right, so damned right.

If the crushing of Lucas's fingers against mine was anything to go by, his actual fingers, not those in the memory, then he was most definitely there too. A flush rose up my neck, my breath shaking. I tried to pull my hand from La Vieille's, but she held firm and the images continued. Lucas's touch had been so alive, melting me, boiling me. But I'd forgotten, we'd both forgotten, and now La Vieille was in our heads, drawing it all back. My breath shook.

"This is unexpected." She chuckled. "Not something an old woman encounters every day."

"It's not unexpected," Lucas managed in a strangulated growl. "You know all that is."

La Vieille's cackles rose above everything.

Lucas had me up against the bedroom wall, our movements in sync, pleasure soaring through me. I couldn't get enough of him.

"Curious. Curious indeed." La Vieille's voice cleaved the image to pieces, leaving only the dark hut and the blazing fire.

My heart thumped. I didn't know what to do, where to look, how to process what I'd... we'd seen. Lucas's hand was damp with sweat, his breath ragged.

"And so, my son," La Vieille murmured, "despite your two thousand six hundred and ninety-three years on the earth, your experience commanding armies, your lordship over vast lands, your proficient bedside manner as a medic, the only way you could reveal the hidden world to Camille was to get drunk and bed her." She howled with laughter.

Age noted—the fae age. I swallowed. It was incomprehensible, but it also meant I'd slept with a two-thousand-six-hundred-and-ninety-three-year-old, which was beyond creepy.

"Mentally, I'm thirty-one," Lucas muttered.

"I would have expected better from a teenager," she hissed.

I couldn't meet her gaze. I wasn't prudish, but La Vieille had been right there. It was like my grandmother watching... Urgh. But it was worse than that. Those memories had been obscured to me, to both of us. And now, all I wanted to do was pull Lucas toward me and... and...

Shit. Shit. Shit.

I attempted to breathe away the sensations that swept through my body, risking a glance at Lucas. His eyes were wild with hunger. My chest tightened. La Vieille released our hands and my palm slid out of Lucas's.

She rubbed her chin. "Hmmm. Keepers are chosen for their suitability to work with one another. Great friendships are kindled, yes, but the work requires a degree of detachment and objectivity, and the partnership is never amorous. It is not something I usually allow to proceed—"

"We're not romantically involved," I blurted. It was the truth.

"We have to continue," Lucas rumbled. "There's too much at stake."

La Vieille's gaze bored into him. "Agreed. Everything is dependent on you taking the next step as Keepers. *Everything*. But my question to you both is"—she studied us, her chin raised—"are you ready to sacrifice yourselves for what lies ahead? For the fae and human realms?"

Lucas narrowed his eyes.

"Of course," I said. It was a no-brainer. After what I'd seen in Grimmere, I'd do anything to protect my friends and family, although the implications were so much greater than that. The splitting of the realms would mean the destruction of everything. The thought of committing myself to Lucas as his partner was massive, and it was sudden, but it hadn't been unexpected, and it paled in comparison to the consequences if I didn't.

Lucas studied La Vieille, his jaw tight. "I'm ready."

"Then, my children, the bond must take place at midday on the waxing crescent moon, in three days' time."

CHAPTER 9

"We can't determine what Elivorn is doing in the human realm." Belomar's strong, steady voice filled the chamber. Despite the length of our discourse, he practically shone, looking every bit the high elf king. He could only be described as stunningly beautiful, his eyes keen and intelligent, his robes, soft armour and long blond hair restrained by a circlet of silver, engendering stately elegance as he strode back and forth across the modest room that was part forest, part stone. He'd greeted us warmly when we'd arrived, an old friend of Lucas's.

"My spies haven't been able to penetrate his inner circle," he added, "and the loss of Branhelm weighs heavily on us all. The work he achieved in Grimmere was unprecedented."

My chest panged. The elf's death at the hands of Lord Rouseau had been horrendous, and the recollection did more to wake me up than anything had for a while. We'd been in the assembly for hours, the few fae present seated in a circle or stretching their legs about the room. A little while ago, I'd retreated to the back for that purpose, and I leant against a stone wall between two massive windows.

Lucas and I had provided an update on everything that had happened in Grimmere. Morion Auberon, the dwarf king who'd helped us with Anthras, had grilled us repeatedly. Rocbrute the troll king had helped, suspicion in his beady eyes. Hama Hêtra the dryad queen had been quieter, weighing up the situation carefully, and Wayland, Pan-European god, Lucas's old friend and the forger of my blade, had listened intently. The discussion about what to do next was circling.

I'd expected there to be more fae in attendance, but that was it. A number of leaders were occupied with their own affairs, and there were only so many races that had the aptitude or the desire to take part. Fae were wild, like the seasons or the weather, most of them ungovernable and instinctual. Sinagries, maloumbros and vertes velles came to mind, but there were plenty more. They could never work with structure, and there were lots who didn't want to try. Other circumspect species, such as the water nymphs, preferred to keep out of things. And none of this included the dark fae who had their own agendas and alliances. Of course, the goblins were by far the biggest race, with numerous subspecies such as truffandecs, minarions and osencames like Mushum, all of them under drac rule.

I'd hoped there might be other Keepers here to exchange

notes, but unless they were involved directly in assembly affairs, they were usually too busy protecting their bounds to attend. Thus far I'd only met in person one other partnership from the Alps as they'd passed through. We'd also had a video call with Keepers in the Black Forest, who'd been seeking information on maloumbro, but that was it.

Due to the low turnout, smaller quarters had been chosen. We'd passed the usual meeting place on the way, a massive amphitheatre with the potential to hold numerous fae. But I supposed with the intimacy of the group, trust could be kindled, although in the case of Rocbrute, who was picking his nose as he glared at Lucas sitting across from him, I was doubtful.

I was carefully avoiding Lucas's gaze, attempting to focus on the proceedings rather than go over that night again... and again.

We'd not had a chance to speak about it, surrounded by the others on the walk here, and when we'd arrived, we'd exchanged one lot of company for another, making formal introductions before the meeting had begun. It would've been better if we'd dived right into the subject and cleared the air, but we hadn't, and I was processing—though I had to admit, that meant trying not to remember the sense of his skin against mine, the way his touch had roused tremors. But that wasn't us. We hadn't even been able to recall that night and we'd let it go. At least I had. If the glint in Lucas's eye was anything to go by when our gazes occasionally caught, he was enjoying the recollection. How he was managing to concentrate was beyond me.

But it only highlighted how we'd gotten off on the wrong foot, and it made me question our flirting. For heaven's sake, we were going to be working together for *life*. We were never going to act on our physical attraction and risk ruining our relationship as Keepers, so what was the point? And besides, we were giving folk the wrong impression, Alice included.

"I'm having Elivorn watched," Lucas said, his words pulling me back to the discussion. "We can't get close to his property due to the wards, but we've observed him meeting with humans. Gangs, drug dealers and the like. That's all we've managed to gather." He leant back in his chair, his arm draped along the back, his ankle crossing his knee. I would've said he was relaxed if his lined brow hadn't ruined the impression.

"He's a devious one." Wayland sat next to Lucas, his dark curly locks a halo, his massive bronze arms folded before him, flattening his leather jerkin. "And if he's on the bounds in the human realm, he will be influencing people. I don't like it."

Lucas rubbed his chin. "When I returned to Grimmere briefly last week, it was clear how quickly my father is strengthening ties with the fae in his allegiance, not to mention building new partnerships and training mages. He insisted that Elivorn's presence in the human realm was simply to reinforce connections on the borders, but I'm sure there's more. He's still not telling me everything. The trust we engendered has helped significantly but—"

"It doesn't sound like trust to me." Rocbrute's voice was like an earthquake, his chair bowing precariously under his weight. He looked daggers at Lucas from a vast grey face that was almost as wide as his body, his pointy ears much too small for his head. His plated obsidian armour only bulked him out further.

"Agreed." Morion ran a hand over the centre of his three beard plaits that stood out at angles, his narrowed eyes tourmalines above a large hooked nose. His coarse walnut hair was a little wild, and boy did his armour look uncomfortable —gold, copper and platinum forged together in elaborate swirls and knots, no doubt worn as a display of his considerable mineral resources. "It wouldn't surprise me if there wasn't a soul on this earth who could gain the trust of Verin Rouseau, the monster he is, not even his sons."

"I would say that is accurate," Lucas replied.

"But if Camille and Lucas's position with Lord Rouseau is all we have," Belomar said, still striding back and forth, "we must use it."

Without thinking, I exchanged a glance with Lucas. He fixed my gaze for a little too long, his lips twitching. I knew exactly what was going on in his head, and it didn't involve clothing. My blood warmed, my skin growing clammy. We needed to talk.

I drew myself up from my wall slump and centred on Belomar's shining face. "After I saved Lord Rouseau, he said he was indebted to me. That has to stand for something, or at least it might be of use to us."

"And indebted he is, if I understand drac lore." Hama Hêtra turned away from the far window, her long limbs like rutted bark, her dress sweeping from her shoulders with the grace of a spring canopy. "He will feel that burden until it is repaid. And he *will* repay you. But we cannot for a moment take that as anything more."

"I say we attack now," Rocbrute boomed, "before Rouseau has time to fully re-establish his resources."

Belomar and Morion argued the issue yet again. Sighing, I stepped over to the window, the arched mullions formed by living alder branches.

In the distance, high forest-clad hills hid La Vieille's hut and the route we'd taken. Woodland swept downward, beeches giving way to a lush plain from which rose the huge prominence of silver limestone that bore the massive fortified city and castle of Charmant.

The place had taken my breath away when we'd arrived. The towering limestone walls were built in harmony with spurs of rock, exposed areas of masonry chiselled into intricate patterns of stars and constellations. Countless trees formed an organic structure, foliage climbing conical towers and draping over the graceful arches of innumerable windows.

We'd walked through gargantuan hallways, more forest than castle, passing massive banqueting halls and meeting chambers. Charmant was so much more than the cold stark allure of Grimmere castle. It was alive. Friends discoursed, laughter rang from chambers, knights gathered discussing tactics. It was how I'd imagined the Chateau de Foix in its heyday of chivalry and courtly life.

Our position in the central tower gave a clear view of the bustling city on the prominence below with blacksmiths, stables, cobblers, a sprawling market and home after home, all of it enveloped in greenery. Young elves ran around in jerkins edged in braid and floaty trousers, their hair flowing or plaited with leaves and flowers.

A movement caught my eye beyond the outer walls. A tiny figure pushed a massive wheelbarrow of what I presumed was dung. I was too far away to be sure, but from the figure's bearing I'd take a guess it was Félix. As soon as we'd arrived at Charmant, Lucas had ordered the gang to be given menial work. Punishment for their stupidity yesterday. Nora had been sent to the kitchens, Hugo to the dungeons, Zach to the laundry and Félix to the stables. I hoped hard labour would drive it into their heads that this wasn't a game. Félix darted toward the forest, making a run for it. In a moment, he was surrounded by an elven guard. Nice try.

"Is there a way we can take Verin Rouseau out?" Rocbrute's deep rumble filled the chamber, and I turned back to the meeting. "We must destroy him before he destroys us all." His eyes tapered to slits.

"We've considered it." Lucas glanced at me again, though this time with solemnity. "But this is so much bigger than my father. If we take him out, we lose inside access. We'll have to wait until we know who's involved and what's going on before we make that kind of move."

Wayland's biceps strained as he sat up. "One thing is for sure, the omphalos has been obliterated. Completely and utterly." His presence was both comforting that such a force was on our side and unnerving as it highlighted the shit we were in. He wouldn't be here without good reason.

"I toured the area with Belomar's knights," he added.

"Where the omphalos mountains once stood, there was only wasteland for hundreds of miles. Thankfully, there were few fae living in that area. The place did not engender life. But I can confirm that the heart of dark power is no more."

"That in itself is curious," Lucas said. "There must be a heart."

Belomar nodded as he paced. "I have men scouring the dark lands looking for sight or sign of a re-emergence, but they have found nothing so far."

"Then it seems we return to our original position." Hama Hêtra pursed her lips, emphasising the hollows of her woody cheeks. "We can do nothing until we gain insight into Lord Rouseau's plans."

Belomar paused and turned to them. "And yet if we wait, we may be too late to form a cohesive response."

"We can't delay." Lucas dug his nails into the arm of his chair. "We must approach the undecided fae races and highlight the need that they join us."

"Agreed," Belomar said. "I'll set elves upon the task immediately. And as always, my spies are at work in the dark lands. They will continue their infiltration."

"I don't like it." Morion massaged his bushy jowls with his finger and thumb. "We are on the defensive with no leads, having to wait for that monster's first move." Just like when we'd requested his help in Fae, he was showing caution.

"In the meantime," I said, "there's plenty that can be done. You must ready your defences and prepare your forces for any kind of action—an attack if necessary."

Lucas nodded. "With my father expanding the reach of his power, I don't doubt that our borders will need protection."

"Agreed," came the mutters of everyone but Rocbrute, who scowled and shook his head. Lucas returned the black look.

"I'll muster the smiths," Wayland bellowed, "and forge additional weaponry."

Lucas tapped his fingers. "As far as my father knows, Camille and I are here to sow distrust and covertly shatter our unity. He will ask more of us, I have no doubt, but for now, he won't risk our inside positions. I'll report back that we have begun the process, that there is weakness amongst us and that we are divided as to a way forward."

Belomar studied a massive map of Fae laid out on a table at the side of the room. "And it might be pertinent to feed him a little misinformation about where our strengths and weaknesses lie. We will have to do it carefully because of his spies, but it will mean that if he attacks, he will be on the back foot."

"And what of when we defeat the Rouseaus?" Rocbrute hauled himself up and stamped over to Lucas, the floor shaking. His scowl was rather deep, like rutted mud. "Everyone knows dracs can't be trusted." His voice rose, his fists clenched. "You may well be working for your father all along, passing *us* misinformation. Though more likely you'll take his seat for yourself once this is over. The rulership of half of Fae is nothing to be sneered at."

Lucas rose to meet him, his body lithe in contrast to

Rocbrute's broad dimensions, yet he stood his ground, glowering at the troll. And still I saw that night, the pleasure in his face as I kissed him... "The caveats prevent me from taking power," Lucas growled. "You have that guarantee."

"They prevent you from taking power if you kill your family," he said. "Not if you get some other fool to do your dirty work."

Hama Hêtra's brow creased in consideration, Morion's in suspicion.

Fury tightened Lucas's jaw. "Centuries of fidelity have demonstrated my worth. I have nothing to prove to you." His voice lowered. "I would never uphold what my father built. Death would be preferable."

The two of them stared at one another, the troll's muscles bulging. Every part of Lucas was taut, his glare promising a swift death.

"Enough!" Belomar cried. "I vouch for Lucas. He has fought by my side for centuries."

"I second that," Wayland roared.

"Rocbrute," Belomar said. The troll didn't move. "We value your presence here, but we must not be divided as Lord Rouseau wills. Trust is crucial to our success."

Still the troll didn't shift. If it came to a fight, I had no idea who would win, and I didn't want to find out. I strode over. "I too vouch for Lucas with my life. He is beyond trustworthy." I didn't know if my addition held any weight in Rocbrute's eyes. But, hey, it was worth a try.

"Defeater of the hantaumo queen," he said, stepping back and bowing his head before glaring at Lucas again.

"Benefit of the doubt, Rouseau. Your imminent bond with this woman means more than your drac silver tongue."

Another reason why our Keeper relationship had to work, and another very good reason why we needed some boundaries.

CHAPTER 10

"THREE ESGARRAPADONES, AND ONE OF ME..." MORION Auberon's eyes sparkled under his wiry eyebrows, his beard plaits quivering. Even here in Belomar's banqueting hall, he wore his armour. He had to be hot.

A lively melody rang through the chamber, lute, pipe and harp lifting the throng of dancers in the centre working off dinner. A host of elves conversed and laughed around the edge as they gazed upon the merriment. Above the throng, sweeping, unglazed windows revealed a wash of stars, the warm evening breeze carrying the scent of honeysuckle that mingled with spices from dinner.

"The last of them came in for the kill," Morion continued, his roar unrestrained. "I cleaved through its skull with my axe, blood and brains everywhere, but that was their final attempt on the eastern flurocite mines."

"Sounds like quite a battle," I replied, one eye on the dancing. I was interested in his exploits, and after all, he was the goddamned dwarf king, who for some unknown reason had made a beeline for yours truly, regaling me with his escapades. But I was still thinking of *that* night.

"Something about being pitted against death." Morion raised his tankard. "It burns away the pretence and leaves the shit underneath."

"I'll drink to that." I raised my goblet and swallowed a mouthful of rich wine.

As dancers twirled past, children running between them, I caught the occasional glimpse of Lucas sitting at the banqueting table at the far end of the hall, laughing heartily with Belomar and Wayland, goblets in their hands. It was curious to see him with friends. In the human realm he was the newcomer, and to the fae local to Tarascon he was a drac, one of the Rouseaus, and most definitely not to be meddled with. Here, he looked relaxed, as though he'd unwound.

And we still hadn't had a chance to talk. The assembly had continued for hours, with nothing new coming from it, then the banquet had begun, which was, as far as I could tell, how Belomar and his court ate and socialised most nights. I was now so stuffed with the magnificent array of wild meats, mouth-watering cheeses and delicious vegetables, I was glad to stand.

Nora appeared from a small doorway at the side of the hall. She passed Hama Hêtra and Rocbrute, who were deep in conversation, and headed to an abandoned banqueting table. With a glare of maleficence especially for me, she piled up the dirty plates. It was the first I'd seen of her since we'd arrived, and she was dressed in elven trousers, a floaty tunic and an embroidered apron. Not her usual look. I grinned back. But honestly, clearing tables in this place didn't look like hard graft. She had it easy. After yesterday, I hoped the others were being worked to the bone.

Morion gestured wildly, his face red as he recounted another of his exploits, something about dark elves, though my gaze was trained on Lucas. He'd risen from the table and was making his way around the hall with Belomar, greeting various officials and courtiers.

Elven children took turns to run up behind him and tug his tunic or slap his leg. "Tag the drac!" they called, then ran off laughing.

Lucas ignored them, his eyes flicking to mine, a glimmer of a smile shaping his lips. It wasn't difficult to guess that he was still fixated on that night, which only drew more images to mind, my pulse rising. They hadn't relented all day, and this was doing nothing to help. He returned his attention to the official and continued their conversation.

Lucas was tagged again and again until one of the boys cried out, "He's not ferocious. He doesn't even have teeth." Another called, "I think he's *human*," which only increased their laughter.

At the next slap on his thigh, Lucas glanced over his shoulder and extended an arm toward the children, skin morphing into desiccated hide, jagged teeth flashing, corded sinews and lethal claws grotesque. Cold ran down my spine. What hid underneath that perfection was gruesome.

The children screamed in horror and ran off crying. I shook my head. Way to terrorise sweet elven kids.

Morion had noticed my distraction and followed my gaze. "I have to say, a partnership with a drac must be quite something, never mind pretending to be mates with him in Grimmere. It must have been a challenge to pull off."

"You could say that." I sipped my wine, most of my attention still on Lucas.

"I'm amazed you managed it." Morion's armour grated a little as he repositioned himself, lantern light glinting from the precious metals. "Dracs keep themselves to themselves. Not much is known about them, though a few years back, I had dealings with one, who gave me the impression that feigning such a thing would be impossible. I'm guessing you used an advanced collude of some kind. It's something my mages would be very interested to hear about."

I glanced down at him, my brow furrowing. I didn't think Lucas had used a collude, and sneaking potion into food would've been extremely difficult, although Elivorn had managed it. But I supposed if what Morion said was true, Lucas had done something, but he probably hadn't thought it worth mentioning, what with Alice in the dungeons and everything else. "Uh, Lucas took care of that side of things."

"Then I'll have to ask him." He took a swig of ale.

Mention of Grimmere brought back the nights when Lucas's body had sheltered mine. I thought of that a lot. Too much. He'd made his way closer, and on cue, his gaze met mine once more. It was as though he knew I was thinking of him. And still that flicker of a smile.

A pair of dancers spun between us. I made to turn back to Morion but noticed the girl's rounded ears under a circlet of leaves. There was a distinct solidity about her. She was human, I was sure of it. The two were clearly besotted with one another. "How does it work," I said as the couple skipped away, "with fae and human relationships? It must be difficult with fae having such long lives?" They were immortal, unless slain or diseased.

He glanced about and caught sight of the couple. "You're asking *me*? Better you question me on minerals or smelting or warcraft." He roared with laughter, his armour shaking. On reflection, it hadn't been the best thing to ask the dwarf king.

"But, uh, well," he continued, "I believe that if their bond is strong enough, their lives equal out. The fae ages and has a shorter life, and the human has a longer one. Other than that, it tends to be rough."

"Huh." I wasn't sure if I liked the idea of outliving my friends and family, but I guessed it was better than the alternative.

"As I've got you here, Camille," Morion said, his jewel eyes gleaming fire, "let me tell you about how we removed a terrible vouivre from the caves of Bossea. It took three days and nights, not to mention a troop of five hundred dwarves and a rather large amount of lard, but—"

I felt a hand on my shoulder and the dwarf king's gaze drew up.

"Morion." Lucas inclined his head. "I hate to cut in, especially if you're telling Camille about your fascinating encounter with the vouivre, but I need her for a moment."

Morion huffed and nodded. "It is indeed one of my finest

tales. But yes, take her away. Camille, you'll have to hear it another time."

"I... uh... I look forward to it." My smile was partly genuine. I'd usually be fascinated, but I was just so distracted.

Morion strode off. "Belomar," he called. "Time we drank together once more!"

Lucas rounded on me. "We need to talk."

Finally. "The understatement of the year."

He inclined his head to where a sweep of forest-green curtains mingled with ivy. I followed him to an alcove before one of the windows. Laughter and music filled the air, but it was quieter here. Outside, beyond the lantern-lit city and high forested hills, a bank of cloud built on the horizon, erasing the stars.

Lucas sprang onto the windowsill, his hands gripping the edge, the leafy mullions framing him.

I shot him my best evil look and crossed my arms as I leant against the trunk of an alder that formed a part of the wall. "I hadn't expected La Vieille to trawl through my head."

He met my gaze. "Camille, I had no idea that she'd..."

"Rake up our shaky beginnings?" Even now, the sense of his hands running over my skin made me want to close the distance between us. My ears hummed, the rhythm of my breath much too loud. What I needed was to step out into a storm like last night.

He jumped off the windowsill and drew close. A breath

away. "Uh, I can't say I didn't enjoy the reminder. Very much... every single moment..." He drew the words out.

My throat caught, but I forced myself not to respond, and all amusement fell from his face. There was a rawness in the way he dragged his teeth over his lips. He stepped back slowly, as if it was a struggle. "Camille, how do you feel about that night?"

It wasn't difficult to answer. "It was physical, right? We've both acknowledged our mutual attraction. I had no idea there would be consequences. You..."

He rubbed the back of his neck. "I knew there would be... but I was out-of-my-mind trashed. I don't go around dosing people with verity, but I had to. The assembly insisted on it, or they were going to send someone else. It was screwing with me."

"I get it." I tightened my arms over my chest. "I'm sure there were a hundred better ways to handle the situation, but we all do stupid things." In my mind, his lips trailed under my chin. I closed my eyes against the image, only to see it more clearly. I opened them again and drew a breath. "It happened. It's in the past." What we'd gone through in Grimmere had allowed me to let go of our teething troubles.

He studied me silently, his gaze intense, his face a little too still.

"And..." I added, drumming my fingers against my arms, "we're messing with our physical attraction, allowing ourselves to get close, but..." I took a breath. "I don't think we should. I mean, what are we going to do? Act on it?" I snorted. "We can't. We're in a partnership, and it's about to be made official with the bond. We'll be working with each other for the rest of our lives. You heard La Vieille. Keepers aren't usually friends with benefits. We need to build some no-go."

Lucas's face clouded. His lips parted as though he wanted to say something, then he shook his head. "And that's what you want, is it?"

The way he drew me even now, the lines and dips of his neck, the throb of blood under his skin, it wasn't healthy. I nodded firmly. "Absolutely. It makes sense. Our partnership means too much to risk losing everything we've built."

His teeth ground. "Alright. No more flirting. Friends, yes, but professional when it comes to the job."

There was no way I could say he looked happy about it. "Isn't that what you want?"

Something flared in his eyes. "Camille, I—"

Screeching arose above the jollity of the banquet hall.

"What's going on?" I asked.

"I have no idea." We strode back in and drew up short. A figure stood before the entrance doors at the end of the hall, her arms raised, her hair streaming, a massive aureole of gold and darkness rippling from her fingers. She was at once hunched with age and at the same time colossal, eternal.

La Vieille.

Dread filled me. It was the nauseating sense of having made a decision I'd regret forever, of wishing with all my heart that I could wind back the clock and do things differently.

The elves were cowering, those nearby easing back

slowly as though she might pounce, faces ashen, bodies trembling. Rocbrute looked as though he might crumble. Only Belomar stood straight-backed and fearless.

"What troubles you, La Vieille?" he called, steeling himself against the flames and stepping closer.

"Someone has stolen my golden spindle." Her shriek cut into my head, her fire blazing brighter and darker. "And they will die!"

A murmur rippled through the hall. Folklore was clear on the matter. Death awaited the one who stole the golden spindle of fate. These fae who lived near La Vieille du Fil would've known that.

La Vieille's blaze roared as she drew her hands close to her chest, curling her fingers together then drawing them apart. Golden threads extended between them. "Who would dare do such a thing?" She thrust out her arms.

Threads extended from her fingers, streaming through the hall, seeking their quarry. They twined around a slender, dark-haired figure at the back, curling over her tunic and floaty trousers, spiralling along her arms and legs, constricting about her chest and neck.

Nora.

CHAPTER 11

OUTRAGE FLOODED THROUGH ME. NORA COULDN'T HAVE been so stupid.

"I don't believe my eyes," Lucas said under his breath, his face contorted in fury.

A slender wooden bobbin appeared in La Vieille's hands. She twisted it, drawing in the threads. Nora grasped at them, attempting to pull them from her with everything she had, to no avail. La Vieille continued winding and Nora could only step toward her.

"I have to hand it to Nora," I whispered, "she's got guts." She must have crept out of the castle and returned to the forest. I'm not sure I would've gone back there alone, never mind dared to enter La Vieille's hut without permission. "Hasn't she read any fairy tales? Stealing from the mad old woman in the woods is never a good idea."

La Vieille reeled and reeled, her eyes blazing. Nora drew

closer, shaking with terror as she was hauled into the maelstrom of black and gold.

I strode forward, dread swathing me. "There has to be some explanation." Though I doubted it.

The room drew a collective gasp at my challenge to La Vieille. But what was I supposed to do, let Nora die?

"Silence!" La Vieille raised a hand. A wall of rock-hard nothing halted me mid-stride, a blast of desolation making me want to wither and whimper.

"Camille." Lucas tried to reach me, but he couldn't move.

Nora was drawn before La Vieille. As she struggled wildly, the threads around her torso unravelled, reached under her tunic and shook it.

Clank. Clunk. Chink.

Her swag hit the flagstones. A dagger with a jewelled hilt. A silver bracelet. A glass eye.

La Vieille tutted. Belomar glanced at us, his brow raised. We'd brought a thief into his court. Nora's eyes grew wide as the threads slipped under her tunic once more. Out they came, wrapped around a golden spindle. Guilty as charged.

"Explain yourself!" La Vieille cried.

Could there be an explanation for something as illogical as Nora's behaviour of late?

"I... I..." Nora stuttered, her face ashen, almost blue, her lips trembling.

"Speak!"

"Uh... I... I..."

I got it. She had no defence. Not even a shred. Her face

flushed darker, the blue more intense. Lucas and I tried to press forward, but still our invisible bindings held firm.

"Death." La Vieille said it so quietly I could barely hear the word, and yet it bored into my skull.

"No... no... I..." Nora thrashed against her ties. The threads encircling her neck tightened. She choked and the blue intensified, but the colour wasn't right, it wasn't the pallor of asphyxiation—

"Wait!" Lucas shouted, shoving against his invisible fetters. "She's been hindered."

That was it. Back in Wayland's barrow when we'd first gone into Fae together, Lucas had held a poker to Fickle-turn's neck. The goblin had strained, unable to talk, his skin turning the same unnatural pallor. But then, how the hell had Nora gotten hindered?

La Vieille ignored him, tightening the threads. They cut into Nora's neck, blood running down her throat.

I struggled again, but it was like raging against inevitability. "She's not acting under her own volition," I yelled. "Your punishment is unjust."

The threads stilled against Nora's throat. La Vieille turned, her gaze holding death and despair. "You dare accuse La Vieille of injustice." Her shriek was agony, the burden of every bad choice I'd made descending upon me.

Blanching, I met her eye. "If someone is influencing Nora, making her steal, then they should be held accountable."

She raised her chin. Our invisible bindings dissipated. "Approach."

Lucas and I stepped either side of Nora. She gasped for breath, her chest heaving, blood spoiling her elven tunic.

"The cause of her actions is not important to me," La Vieille said. "I am consequence alone. I must have death."

"There are consequences beyond consequence," Lucas said, forcing himself to meet her eye. "There may be more underlying this, and it should be dealt with."

Belomar stepped forward. "It seems to me"—his gaze was unwavering despite La Vieille's civilisation-ending glare—"that what Camille and Lucas posit is only fair."

"Fair?" Her cackle pierced my ears as it echoed through the hall. "Only death is fair." She twisted her hands, and the threads tightened around Nora's throat once more. We tried to reach out, but we were restrained again.

Lucas's eyes flared. "You must have death... and you will have death. Give us a little time. We will find the origin of this thread of consequence and bring the guilty party to you."

"Indeed, the drac knows something of consequences. Of how they seduce and ensnare." There was hunger within La Vieille's face as she studied us both. "Very well, you may investigate, but I must have my death." She jerked her hands, and we were free, the flames of black and gold dissipating. As Nora was released, she stumbled back and grasped her throat, choking. We caught her arms and steadied her.

A single thread remained around her neck. La Vieille angled her fingers and the ends bound themselves into a noose. "You have but little time. If you do not find the cause, I will claim her life." She extended a bony finger and the noose slipped toward Nora's throat.

CHAPTER 12

"Hmmmm." Roux examined the slender golden noose that hung around Nora's neck, the knot just below her collarbone. She glared at him from her perch on the edge of the large circular table in the Keepers' post meeting room, her feet upon a chair. Despite the night in Belomar's dungeon, she was pristine, having changed into her shorts and T-shirt. Healing potion had sorted her neck wounds, and the dark lines of her slightly too thick make-up were immaculate.

What the hell had she gotten herself into?

The windows were open, sunlight casting a warm glow over the myriad of weapons hanging on the walls. Outside, fae Tarascon murmured as it awoke. Shopkeepers opening up called and whistled. Goblins who'd spent the night on the floor of the Peppered Parsnip slung insults. The new day brought welcome perspective, the fresh morning air sweeping away the warmth La Vieille had stoked in the hut, and the resolve I'd garnered last night to put some distance between Lucas and me only felt more sensible.

As prearranged, we'd slept in Charmant, the two of us in adjoining rooms that were so organic I could've been sleeping in a forest. I'd ignored the part of me that wanted to open the door between us and curl up against him as I had in Grimmere, though after what La Vieille had shown us, my thoughts weren't entirely as pure as they had been back in that cold place.

Instead, I'd listened to the storm as it cracked and crashed around the castle, wanting so much to be out in it, rather than worrying about Nora or thinking of that night. When I'd finally fallen asleep, my dreams had been filled with images of soaring on the gale that had seemed disturbingly real.

Early this morning, we'd returned to Tarascon via another way marker, so we'd not had to pass the hut, then we'd gone straight to the Keepers' post for Roux's help. We'd wanted to send the gang home. They were exhausted from their hard graft, but they were shaken and insisted on staying to see if they could help, which currently meant standing around with hands in pockets as they avoided Nora's glare. Their company was the last thing we needed, but I appreciated their concern.

I breathed deeply, trying to ease away the tension in my shoulders. Nora had gone too far this time. Lucas studied her, one arm folded, his elbow propped on it as he rubbed his chin. He'd already tried to unthread Nora's macabre necklace. That not succeeding, he'd attempted to pull it off with force. It had remained undamaged.

"Nora," Roux said, "any idea who has hindered you?" He'd been up at the bounds first thing, performing the ritual that strengthened the bonds between the fae and human realms, and he already looked tired. His cloak, if worn by another mage, might have swirled as he stepped back. However, on Roux it hung limply, a matching accessory to his beard, although at least neither was ornamented with breakfast today.

She opened her mouth to speak, but the breath stuck in her throat. And that was how it was. She couldn't confirm or deny anything connected to her hinder. Lucas and I had already questioned her repeatedly, to no avail, and we'd tried having her write and tap out answers, which also hadn't worked.

"What about you, Roux?" I said. "Do you have any idea who might have done this?" It was a question Lucas and I had asked each other many times, coming up with nothing, but Roux had another perspective.

Lucas turned to meet my eye as he usually did, but thought better of it. I had to admit, the less I looked at him, the less I was reminded of that night. He probably thought the same, what with us raising some boundaries. Even so, I could feel him, a presence in the room I involuntarily centred on.

Roux shook his head. "As the hinder was sturdy enough to withstand La Vieille, it must have been cast by a fae with a great deal of power. Other than that, I have no idea. The ingredients of the hinder collude aren't difficult to come by, and extremely adept fae can cast it by thought alone, though that is rare."

Gabe's fists balled. "But how? We've not met any unfamiliar fae, and Nora has only known about the hidden world since I..."

"Since you kidnapped her, held her at knifepoint and made her see it all." Félix raised his pudgy brow and grinned. Even now, he couldn't hold back the jest. Zach's and Hugo's tittering didn't help.

Gabe's eyes flared, his jaw tightening. "I was going to say 'For a couple of months'."

I sighed. Gabe and Félix hadn't let up griping at each other since their fall-out after the hantaumo affair.

"Way to make an impression on girls," Hugo said.

Lucas shot him a death stare, causing him to wilt on the spot.

"Uh, I mean, way to definitely not make an impression on girls. Flowers and chocolates and, uh... acts of genuine kindness are always preferable."

"And in that time," Lucas added, "we've been aware of the fae coming and going in the area. They've been harmless. It doesn't make sense." He stared at Nora. "Tell us the fae you've had interactions with."

"When I've tried a hundred times already, Lulu?" she shot out, scowling. "There's absolutely no point. I can tell you everything except—" The word turned into a strangulated gargle.

He stepped toward her, his glower a mix of fury and

concern, though the fury was winning. "You can try a hundred and one times because there might be a chance— an ever so small chance—that if you stopped that snarky crap for just one second, we might be able to find a way to help."

My feelings exactly.

Nora looked as though she would combust.

"A collude might be of use," Roux said, heading into the kitchen. "Although, in the circumstances, it would be like altering fate itself." He jostled about in one of the drawers of the apothecary cabinet and came back in with a sprinkling of dark brown herbs in his outstretched hand.

Focussing on them, he muttered, and a glow grew, extending to touch the noose at the base of Nora's thread. The knot slid a fraction toward her neck. She flinched and grasped her throat.

"Don't make it worse," Gabe snapped, his face reddening.

"By Abellion's vest," Roux said. "There's no collude that can work against La Vieille. I shouldn't have tried."

"Don't sweat it," Nora said casually, but I caught a glimmer of something in her eyes. It wasn't fear, even though I was sure that lay underneath. Relief? That didn't seem appropriate, and yet if she'd been carrying this for a while, perhaps she *was* relieved we were helping.

Gabe's eyes flashed at her. "All this time I've been pissed at you for stealing, and some creature has been messing with you." My thoughts exactly. I had no idea if we'd wrongly judged her—if whoever had cast her hinder had taken the opportunity to use her somehow because of her sleight of hand.

Roux drew a tape measure from his cloak and wrapped it around her neck alongside the thread. "I'll take note of the position of the knot. Come back tomorrow and I'll do the same to see if it has tightened. We may be able to work out a timeframe for how long... uh..."

Nora raised an eyebrow. "How long before that nutty old bat strangles me?"

Gabe swallowed.

Roux was suddenly absorbed in winding up the tape measure. "Well, yes. Sometimes it's best to call a spade a spade."

"Right, what are we going to do about it?" Automatically, I glanced at Lucas, who met my eye for a fraction of a second before focussing on the others.

"You lot," he said to the gang. "You know Nora. What do you have on her friends and family?"

Félix, Hugo and Zach shifted under his gaze. They'd only been friends with Nora for a few weeks. Gabe knew her better, but he was lost in thought, staring at the noose.

"There's the gaggle at school," Félix said. "At least that's what I call them."

Zach nodded. "Yeah, Nora used to be the ringleader of the evil spawn from hell, then she got in with Gabe and ghosted them."

Nora opened her mouth, but nothing came out. She dug her nails into her thighs. "Urgh. I fucking give up."

"Not yet you don't," Gabe growled.

Nora shook her head.

I felt for her, I really did. "Gabe. You've met Nora's family, haven't you? What are they like?"

He hauled his gaze from Nora. "Her maman is okay. Busy... works a lot as a night manager at the aluminium foundry. Gran is nice. Lives with them. Always has chocolate. Dad isn't..." He glanced at Nora.

"Whatever," she said. "Just dish the dirt. They're going to find out anyway."

He nodded. "Dad left the scene when Nora was a little kid. Six?"

"Yep." Her face tightened. "Oh look, I can answer that."

"He's a mechanic in Nîems and in another relationship. She has an older brother in Toulouse. I don't know much else."

Not much dirt, then.

"What about where you live?" Roux said. "Some fae are linked to locations."

"Rue du Bari, in the old town," Gabe replied.

"I'll look into it." Roux twirled a finger around the end of his beard. "And I'll check the Keeper records to see if the family has a connection to Fae. I also require a list of Nora's friends for the same reason, if anyone would be so kind."

"I can do that." Gabe pulled out his phone.

"I'm due at work in a minute," I said, "although I'll skip it if there's something more helpful for me to do. But the café is a great source of information. I can ask around."

Lucas looked at his watch. "I have clinic in fifteen. I'll

access Nora's family's medical records and have the Men keep an eye on the family. I'll also put out feelers."

"Uh, we'd like to help," Félix said, that crazed enthusiasm spreading over his face once again. Zach and Hugo vigorously nodded their agreement.

"You lot have gotten into enough trouble already," Lucas said.

"But you haven't even mentioned the internet." Zach practically quivered. "You and Camille are going to be at work and Roux..."

Roux was struggling to uncoil his finger from his beard. "I do have a laptop. It makes a useful plant stand."

I doubted they'd find anything on the web as this was fae related, but it would keep them busy. I glanced at Lucas, wanting his opinion before agreeing, but he was staring at Nora, though I wasn't sure he was taking her in. I cleared my throat. His eyes flickered to mine for the briefest moment before darting away. This wasn't raising boundaries, it was being completely ignored. "They can't do much harm on the internet. There are no fae involved, and it's the summer holidays, so they'll have the time."

He pressed his lips together then released them, taking in the gang. "Agreed, but don't get up to anything you shouldn't. And don't even consider messing about in Fae, or I'll send you back to Belomar's stables for the rest of the holidays."

They nodded, faces glowing.

"Right," he continued, "we'll meet here tomorrow unless

something urgent happens. See you all later." And with that, he strode to the door without a backward glance.

Weird. I'd said we needed to cool it, but I was so used to his gaze meeting mine, and his eyes tracking me constantly. Now they weren't... I don't know... it was different. That aside, we had to communicate, and a degree of civility would help us sort this whole thing out. Surely he could manage that?

CHAPTER 13

"I've not gotten anything useful on Nora or her family," I said to Alice as I tidied the bread baskets. Only a few pain complets and a fougasse remained, the rest sold out for the day. "I've asked everyone, but it seems the Ruizes keep themselves to themselves. They don't socialise much." Which didn't surprise me, considering how closed Nora was.

Shimmying my shoulders, I attempted to breathe away the tension that had set into them and my skull as the day had worn on and I'd not found anything of use. Another storm was brewing. I was sure that had something to do with it, and it wasn't the only thing bothering me. I'd been thinking of Lucas more and more, the impressions of that night not helping one bit, despite me doing everything I could not to recall them.

Alice's brow furrowed as she placed the lid on a decorative box of macarons. She piled them with the others, then set to work on the next box, glancing at the D&D nook, where the whole entourage sat, their laptops out. "She really is in it this time. Let me know if I can be of help."

I squeezed her arm. "Thanks, hon."

"Zach, I need you to look at the births and deaths records." Félix's voice rose over the bustle of the café. He was managing their internet investigation like he led their D&D campaigns—with excitement. He pointed at Hugo and Gabe. "What have we gotten from looking into the family's social media history?"

Nora's noose glinted. She sat back, staring into nothing, as they discussed one of her videos that had gone viral, and not in a good way. Gabe glanced at her from behind his laptop, worry in his eyes.

Alice shook her head. "At least they're not going into Fae—"

A crash came from the kitchen. Alice flinched.

"Shit!" Guy cried.

"Spillage in the village," Dame Blanche trilled as she hurried to help, her snowy hair a bundled crown, her long skirts swishing under her apron. "No harm done. The tray was only half laden and there's plenty of dough in the bowl." But the petit pains they were baking for a private order were ruined.

"Would they please be careful?" Alice snapped, glaring at the wreckage. Her dilated pupils and deep scowl were totally not her.

Guy attempted to pick up a petit pain. "Ouch! Hot!" He sprang back and waggled his hand.

Alice shook her head.

Max waved from a couple of tables away, his thick troll head bulging, his shirt straining. "Alice, my table is a mess. I need a little assistance over here." He had a cup and a plate before him. Hardly an emergency.

"One moment." She filled another box of macarons.

The next customer, Ignace, was stooped in conversation with Mean Gert. The other two farmers, Ludger and Alf, stood behind them. I pulled out my phone and checked my messages, waiting for them to finish, though I couldn't block out their grumbling.

"The storms the past two nights were the worst I've seen in a good many years," Ignace muttered. "The hay was absolutely ruined. All of it wrecked, just like that. Hail the size of golf balls was what did it."

I tried to ignore them. I'd not heard from Lucas for a few hours, which wasn't our norm, but given our new boundaries, it was perfect. A vision of his hands gripping my hips flashed before me, warmth creeping up my neck. Heavens, this physical attraction between us was something else. It fell away in an instant when I glanced at Max, who was leering at the woman on the next table. The perfect dampener.

Apart from that, I had a message from Grampi, the latest in a thread where I'd explained about Nora and said that I wouldn't be able to train with him until it was sorted. He'd responded with a sad emoji.

I sighed. He was at a loose end. He'd gotten a new lease of life since regaining his speech, and he'd relished helping with Anthras, but it had exhausted him, and he was taking a step back.

The farmers mumbled on about the storms, Ludger's permanent scowl deepening under his copious steel-grey hair as he complained about the damage to his grape vines. Honestly, I didn't know why anyone farmed anything other than goats around here. Hit a goat with a hailstone and it would have something to say about it.

I tucked my phone away as Ignace stepped forward. "Ah, Camille, four café serrés, please." His mouth was as puckered as usual. That and his tight face made his hooked nose much too large, and phew, his cologne could wipe out armies.

"Sure thing." I started the order.

"Did you hear about the storm damage?" he called. The other farmers had taken a table to the far side of Max.

"Yeah, I heard. Terrible." The coffees dripped, and Alice headed over to clear tables.

"Ripped up the roof of our big barn," Ignace said. It looked like he was going to give me his rendition anyway.

I processed his payment, my dreams coming back. "Huh, weird."

"That's putting it mildly. And tonight, we'll have another one, mark my word. Can't see a sign of it yet, but I can feel it." He tapped his head.

Him and me both.

I handed him the order. As he walked off, the last customer for the moment, I leant my elbows on the counter and dropped my head into my hands, scraping my fingers against my scalp as if it would relieve my tension. It didn't work.

"Hurry up, Alice," Max said.

I glanced up. She'd piled his plate onto a tray, but as she reached for his teacup, he slid it to the other side of the table. "Service is getting slow around here. Little ladies mustn't keep hard-working men waiting."

Alice chuntered under her breath. She made to take the cup again, but he slid it back. "Looks like you need to practise your waitressing." He roared with laughter.

Asshole.

Alice fumed, her mouth open. She abandoned the teacup and gripped the tray tightly, her hands and the contents shaking. If he wasn't careful, that thing was going to end up on his head. She stood there, fighting her own rule that we had to be patient with difficult customers, something she never usually struggled with.

"Don't be such a dick, Max," I called, receiving eyebrow raises from the farmers.

Managing to get hold of her fury, Alice turned away and strode around the counter with the tray. I wouldn't have been so kind. He would've been wearing it.

"I swear, if he does anything—*anything*—again," she hissed, "I'll shove his next croissant—"

I raised my hand. "Please, too much imagery."

She ground her teeth. She really wasn't herself. Although it was understandable after what she'd been through. We needed the chance to talk about it properly. "We're still on for the cave tomorrow, aren't we?"

"Of course." Her scowl broke.

"Perfect—"

"Ah, Camille."

I turned at the familiar warm voice, a smile tugging at my lips. "Grampi." With a bounce, I hoiked myself up on the counter, leant over, and dotted a kiss on his cheek.

He beamed back, his sparkling blue eyes augmented by his white hair and beard. He cradled a basket of the herd's finest cheese, his batch for the café.

Alice reached over the counter and took it from him. "Just what I wanted. We were getting low." She carried it to the kitchen.

"Find out anything about Nora?" he asked.

"Nope, not a thing." I made up his regular, a mocha.

"A very private family, the Ruizes. I could count the times I've had a conversation with Marta on one hand."

Marta, Nora's gran. "Just like Nora, then."

"She is a devout catholic, and I... well, you know me, I respect all beliefs, but the old priest from way back had an inkling about fae and used to keep his distance. The new priest hasn't a clue, though."

"Seems unlikely she'd have anything to do with fae, then." But I'd tell the others, just in case.

"I suppose so." He drew in a breath, his bushy brow lowering, worry in his eyes. "Camille, there's something I want to speak to you about. You saw La Vieille. Surely it was too early for mention of the bond?"

This wasn't about the bond per se, it was about Lucas. Grampi had done his best to let go of his misgivings, but he was struggling. A bond between his beloved granddaughter and public enemy number one would go down like a lead weight. "It wasn't too early." I continued his order, flicking him a tentative glance. But what with Nora, this was a conversation I didn't need.

"The bond is a big step." Grampi's jaw trembled almost imperceptibly.

Two figures headed into the café, all strutting muscle. The guys from the other day, though they'd abandoned their leather jackets in the heat and wore vests revealing bulging arms. They paused and glared around like last time. Nora made a double take, and I could have sworn she half cringed before laying on a cool glare.

Grampi followed my gaze. "Hmmm. Looks like trouble."

From their aggressive hunches, I had to agree. Although I had to give them credit, they were the perfect diversion.

Nora got up and approached the guy with the dark cowlick, her eyes fierce. They exchanged hushed words that built to a torrent of profanity from Nora. With a disdainful scowl and a shake of his head, the guy turned on his heels and strode out, his companion following. It had to be a lead.

"We'll talk later," I said to Grampi. "I need to find out what's going on."

I hurried over as Nora sat back down with the others.

"What was all that about?" I asked. The gang stared between us.

The annoyance hadn't left her face. "Uh, it was my..." Her breath caught. She couldn't talk about him. If that wasn't suspicious, nothing was.

Gabe glanced up. "It was her brother."

CHAPTER 14

I STRODE ALONG THE N20, THE TRAFFIC STIRRING THE stifling afternoon air, the sun blazing above Coustarous. Cloud was building in the southwest, the storm finally drawing near. The air was so muggy that my skin was moist, and on top of that, my head was thick with Lucas, thoughts of him even overshadowing my concern about Nora's brother showing up. Honestly, I'd been fine before we'd visited La Vieille. Well, sort of.

Lucas hadn't met me at the café when I'd finished my shift as he usually did, so I was heading to the surgery to meet him. After he'd blanked me, I'd wondered if I should, but that was stupid. He was my partner and we had work to do.

His consulting rooms stood ahead at the turning of Impasse Beauregard, an old building with exposed grey limestone set off nicely with white shutters. His SUV was sheltering under lime trees in the parking area with a load of other cars, so he was busy, which was unusual for the time of day. I couldn't figure out for the life of me why he hadn't texted to let me know.

I pushed open the door, catching snippets of "I had that broach stolen. The one that wasn't worth anything" and "I have no idea what happened to my cigar case. I might have dropped it." I didn't doubt that Nora was involved.

Inside was packed. Tarascon's finest over-eighties sat around the edge of the whitewashed waiting room on old wooden chairs. There was no reception desk. Sometimes I wondered how Lucas managed. In cities, multi-doctor practices had receptionists and many other bells and whistles. But doctors often worked on their own in the countryside. Although there was Madame Villy, who did Lucas's bookkeeping and some-times took calls from her laundrette. But her hearing wasn't great and folk were frequently booked in for a tumble dry.

The old folk were chatting in small groups. It had been Madame Biscotte comparing notes about lost possessions with Monsieur Sel and Madame Sanogo.

"Camille!" a few of them cried. The rest glanced up.

"Hey." I waved.

"Camille, dear." Madame Biscotte adjusted the walking poles at her side. She was still an avid hiker, though she took a more leisurely pace these days. "I'm not surprised to see you here. We were just discussing that Doctor Rouseau has a thing for you, weren't we, Kamilah?"

I stared at her, my lips parted. "What?"

Madame Sanogo nodded. "Absolutely, it's common

knowledge. The way he looks at you." She took in my expression and shook her head. "Come now, dear, everybody knows about it. You don't have to be coy."

They were worse than Alice. But, no, actually they weren't. This lot didn't know that we spent so much time together because of our Keeper partnership, whereas Alice did. But it highlighted the false impression we were giving everyone.

"We know you like him too," Madame Boulay said, sitting on the other side of the room. She tapped the side of her nose. "You don't need to hide it."

"Look at him, all dark looks and rock-hard biceps." Madame Biscotte almost sang the words. "If I was your age, I'd be jumping his bones."

My jaw dropped. I really didn't want to hear about it.

She tittered, the rest of the room joining in. Just one glimmer of what lay under that musculature would wipe the smiles off their faces.

"It's why I'm here for the fourth time this month." Madame Sanogo adjusted her floral collar. "His bedside manner is the highlight of my day. If only I had more verrucas."

"He keeps so fit," Monsieur Sel added. "Can't be much fat on that body. I'd run my hands over his—"

"Okay, okay." I raised my palms, an image of me doing just that flashing in my mind's eye. But I got it. Lucas was hot. Old folk weren't immune to his charms. No one was. "I just thought he might have finished work. We often take a, uh... walk together." It was one way of explaining the evenings we spent trying to hack each other to death.

"So sweet." Monsieur Sel sighed.

I glared at him, then the rest of them, who had far-away looks on their faces. "You lot are incorrigible."

They grinned indulgently.

The consulting room door swung open and out came Monsieur Leclerc. He hobbled across the room, a small potion bottle clutched in his hand. "Such a good doctor," he pronounced to the room at large. "He has a way of asking exactly the right questions, and this special medicine he does himself is so much better than that rubbish from the pharmacy." He paused in thought. "Devin, is what I say."

There were nods and agreements all round.

Devin. The old name for healer in these parts, the word referred to divination. I'd only heard mention of it in historic reports and folklore. It was usually bestowed on lay healers who worked with herbs and hedge magic, but never doctors, who had been viewed with suspicion in the past. It was curious that Lucas had been accepted so readily.

"Next." Lucas's voice rang out from behind the door.

"That would be me," Madame Biscotte said. "But Camille, you go in. I'm sure the doctor would be happy to see you."

The lot of them chuckled.

I ignored them. Lucas was clearly busy, but as I was here, it made sense to check what time we were meeting, or if we were meeting at all, what with his standoffishness. I strode in and closed the door.

He sat at his old wooden desk, working at his PC. A window shone to his side, covered by a gauzy blind. A couple of consulting chairs stood by the desk and an examination bed lay in the corner. The oak panelling and ancient equipment cupboards were more suited to the belle époque than modern surgeries, but they fitted his timelessness. He didn't look up. "Camille, how can I help?"

No doubt he'd overheard everything in the waiting room. I couldn't help but frown at the tone of his voice—as if I was one of his patients. He really was doing his best to maintain distance, but it was extreme, and it was so weird not to see that smile, that look of hunger as if I was his next meal.

I leant against the wall. "Uh, I thought you'd be finished and that we'd be meeting as usual." My voice was cool in response to his coolness, though his angular cheekbones and the play of his lips made me all too aware of my own body. I wasn't quite sure what to do with my hands. "Have you found out anything about Nora?"

He glanced at me for a split-second, then studied his screen intently, tugging at his collar. "Her medical records show nothing of note. I've gleaned from various patients that Nora's grandmother, Marta, is good at pétanque, when her bunions aren't playing up. Nora's mother is pretty healthy. She helps her neighbour hang out the washing but doesn't have much to do with the local community. That was it." And still the screen was the most fascinating thing in the room.

"Nora's brother came into the café," I said. "Nora wasn't happy, and she couldn't talk about him, which might be a lead. Roux and the others are making inquiries, and I've asked the Men to follow him, but I've not found out anything else."

Lucas's screen fixation was making me uncomfortable. We weren't going to get far working together like this. I rammed my hands into my pockets. "Uh, this is weird."

He narrowed his eyes, still not looking.

My clothes felt all stiff. "I appreciate that you're respecting our boundaries, but can't we talk normally? I can't believe I'm going to say this, but I might even be missing your text jokes."

His lips pursed at that. "What? Even the one about the five ore serpents and the combine harvester?"

"Nope, not that one. That one was bad."

He drew in a breath through his nose, all amusement gone. "Camille, I..." His words caught in his throat.

"What?"

He sprang up. In a flash, his hand was on the wall by the side of my head, all of him a little too close, his eyes wild, the scar beneath his ear standing out with the straining of his neck. With great effort, he pulled back a fraction. "Because," he growled, "it's taking every single ounce of strength I possess not to replay the sensation of your skin under my hands, not to recall the warmth of your body, the touch of your..." He stared at me, his breath ragged. "After La Vieille's vision, I want to rip your... Argh!" He raked his hands through his hair.

I gaped at him. "Shit," was all I could think to say, my heart racing, heat rushing through my veins.

Chuckles came from the waiting room, followed by Madame Biscotte's soprano voice. "We all know what's going on in there. Can't blame them. The doctor needs a little exercise. Sitting at his desk all day isn't healthy for a hot-blooded man."

"Do Camille good too," Monsieur Sel added. "Let off some of that steam."

Lucas balled his fists before him, ready to strike as he glared in the direction of the reception.

Yeah, I felt the same.

I met Lucas's blazing gaze. "Aren't you going a bit far? I know there's mutual attraction, but I didn't realise you had to struggle so much to control it. Usually you seem fine."

"Normally," Lucas ground out, "I am. We spend time together, we train and mess around and do whatever we do. Being with you is enough. But after the vision... Camille, you have no idea what's going through my head..."

"Uh... I'm beginning to get it."

"So forgive me if I'm not as responsive as normal." He took a breath. "I'm trying to control myself."

He raised a hand as if to brush my cheek. My eyes widened, a part of me wanting him to, then he stepped back and turned away, dropping his hand to his side.

"And this is a drac thing, right? All this intensity, this desire." It had to be. "Because yeah, I feel it too, but you... you look kind of unhinged."

He glared at me. "Dracs tend to be possessive over their..."

"Over their friends?" He was loyal. I'd seen that in Grimmere.

His glare grew even more fierce.

I sighed. "Alright, I can see you're struggling. To be honest, I am too, but it will pass. We just need to maintain our boundaries and concentrate on Nora."

He stepped away and leant on the desk, breathing deeply. "We do. I'll try to be a little more... communicative. And as we haven't come up with much, I have a home visit with Nora's grandmother this afternoon. I should be there already, but there's a bug going around, though it's nothing serious." He nodded to the waiting room. "Wait for me out there. I'll deal with everything as quickly as possible, then we'll see what we can rake up at Nora's. I'll say you're helping me out."

"It's the perfect way to get in and nose around, although me helping is highly unethical. I have zero medical training and everyone knows it."

"Ethics aren't something dracs are associated with."

I shrugged. "Alright, but give me your car keys. I'm not waiting with that lot."

CHAPTER 15

Lucas and I walked up Rue du Bari in Tarascon's old town, not far from the river. The brightly painted townhouses narrowed in on either side. There was no parking here, so we'd left the SUV at the bottom of the hill.

Usually we'd be laughing, maybe bumping shoulders. But considering Lucas's state, it seemed prudent to walk far enough apart so that we wouldn't accidentally make contact. Regardless, my sense of him was much too acute. The intensity of his desire had only added fuel to the hot mess La Vieille had created, and I was doing such a terribly bad job of not thinking of him, ripples of desire vying with goddamned common sense, and I was still so tense, my head aching. I rubbed my forehead. Gracious, I needed the storm to break. Cloud cover extended across most of the sky. It wouldn't be long.

"What do I do, then, as your assistant?" I said, attempting to make this normal. "Honestly, when Alice cut herself with the lemon knife the other day, I couldn't even get the plaster to stick."

"Here." He held out his medical bag as we continued upward. "Take this. Pass me stuff." He risked a controlled glance in my direction. He was trying to act naturally, and I appreciated it.

"I can do that." I was careful not to touch his fingers as I clasped the bag. "Anyway, why can't you just give her some healing potion?"

"She's not responsive. It happens sometimes. And I have to be cautious about what I administer. I can't go curing everyone miraculously, or people either report me to the medical council or get a little overzealous with pitchforks. There was one occasion in 1432 that I'd really rather forget."

His age boggled my mind. It was better if I didn't think about it.

He paused outside a pink townhouse that reached upward three floors, pots of geraniums either side of the doorstep. The shutters were a cheerful blue, the paint cracked a little. "This is us."

Despite the cloud cover, it was too bright to see into the window. I could only make out the sweep of curtains and the back of an armchair. "Looks pretty normal."

"Wreeeeeooooooooooouwwwwww!" I almost jumped out of my skin as a formidable ginger tom hurtled past, his fur spiked, his eyes wild.

"Jeez! What's up with him?"

Lucas gazed along the street. "That's what's up."

A little way ahead sat a massive black ball, fur puffed

ridiculously like an enormous pompom. Madame Bovary twitched her whiskers, drew a paw to her mouth and licked it in a poor attempt to look like a dear little pussykins and most certainly not a deathly sarramauca who suffocated victims by sitting on their chests. A shiver ran down my spine. "Ginger tom, you aren't the only one feeling it. I want to run the other way too." And it went to prove that cats—*and* dogs, if Monsieur Vaux's Destroyer was anything to go by—could see more than the average human eye. Madame Bovary, being fae, was invisible to most folk.

"You don't think she has anything to do with Nora's hinder?" I knew very little about sarramaucas. Something I didn't want to rectify.

Lucas shook his head. "They have a degree of premeditation, and they're more intelligent than your average mog, but they couldn't manage a hinder."

Madame Bovary paused mid-clean-up and shot him the most evil of evil glares. I doubted he would've dared say such a thing if he hadn't been more terrifying than her under that lovely exterior.

I turned back to the Ruizes' house. A large brown feather lay on the doorstep. I picked it up and rolled it between my fingers. I had no idea which bird it was from, but by the smug look on Madame Bovary's face, the winged owner had been lunch.

"It looks like a vulture tail feather," Lucas said.

"Not many vultures at this altitude." They usually hung about the peaks. I tucked it into the side pocket of Lucas's bag as he rapped on the door.

A shout came from inside. "Get the hell down here and talk to me for once. I have to go to work."

The door swung open. A tall, slender woman stood there with an expression that questioned why we dared intrude. Eva Ruiz, no doubt. Her hair was tied back and she wore minimal make-up, but other than that, with powder-blue irises and a delicate mouth, it could have been Nora wearing the grey Aluminium Sabart polo shirt and matching combats.

"Ah, Doctor Rouseau, come in. My mother will be relieved to see you." Eva stepped back to allow us into the narrow hall.

"Madame Ruiz," Lucas said. "I have my assistant with me today. Camille."

"Sure." As we waited to be directed further in, she gripped the post at the bottom of the stairs and yelled, "Nora, get here right now."

Nora stormed down the stairs. She saw us and paused like an animal in a trap. She'd changed from earlier and wore a knee-length skirt with a loose tee, her hair and make-up as immaculate as ever. "What?" she snapped, glancing from her maman to us.

"Where were you last night?" Eva demanded, her scowl deep.

Then Nora hadn't told her she'd be away. If I was Eva, I'd be pissed.

"Wouldn't you like to know." Her voice was dry. She glowered at me, her gaze laden with warning. The message was clear. Don't tell Eva about our trip. Considering the circumstances, I had to go with her request.

"Yeah, I would like to know." Eva put her hands on her hips. "Because I *care*." She turned to us and inclined her head to the door a couple of steps along the hall. "Go through."

We made our way past.

"I'm not going to put up with this stress," Nora yelled. "I'm going out."

"Don't you dare." The door slammed, and Eva cussed under her breath. Something I'd done many times myself when it came to Nora.

As we pushed inside the living room, Marta Ruiz beamed at us from her chair in the corner, her feet on a stool. The place was dark with pewter-grey walls, but kind of homely because of it, with an old wing-back three-piece, a log burner in the centre, crowded bookshelves all around and a TV to one side. A family's clutter had been cast about— books, washing piled on a chair, a basket full of knitting. A few houseplants looked as though they needed more light.

"Come in, Doctor Rouseau," Marta said, her lips a flash of carefully applied deep rouge. She wore no other make-up, her liver-spotted skin and sweep of short, perfectly coifed grey hair pale in comparison to the streak of colour. "And this is Camille, so I hear."

"Uh, yes," I said. "I get to hold his equipment."

Lucas's gaze bored into me, crimson creeping up his neck. Damn it. I shouldn't have said that. I was on autopilot. He snatched his bag back.

"I'm sure you do, dear," Marta replied with a knowing glance.

Please let the floor swallow me up. I couldn't take much more of the elderly assessing my non-existent love life.

"I'm off to work," Eva called through. "See you later."

"See you in the morning, darling," Marta replied. The front door slammed once again.

"How are you doing, Marta?" Lucas said roughly, struggling to master himself.

"It hurts like hell." She gestured to her foot. "But have a look for yourself."

Lucas knelt down and took a steadying breath before easing off her sock. A bandage lay beneath. He unwrapped it as though Marta was the most precious thing in the world. Even so, she grimaced. At the side of her foot, a huge red lump glowed, her toes bent inward at an unnatural angle.

"Looks painful," he said softly as he studied it.

The tone of his voice struck me. Despite a long day at work and having to deal with that mob in the waiting room, his concern was genuine. One thing was for sure, with his position as a fae lord, he didn't need to be kneeling at the foot of an old woman with a swollen toe. It made my chest swell, and then for some peculiar reason, it ached.

The room dimmed a little, the storm drawing closer.

"It throbs," Marta said. "Angry, it is. Doesn't give me any rest."

The poor woman, but I needed to focus on why I was here. I cast surreptitious glances about, looking for anything that might help us solve Nora's predicament.

Lucas frowned. "But you've got a date for surgery, haven't you?"

"Next week, and I can't wait to be rid of it."

He nodded. "Good."

Finding nothing in the general clutter, I studied the bookcases. Just an ordinary selection of fiction, plus some books on nature, wildlife and the likes.

"Stops me doing all sorts of things." Marta shook her head. "I even had to give up flower arranging at church. I'll be starting again as soon as I can, though. And in the meantime, I'm crocheting. It's about all I'm good for."

"And you're looking after your foot?" Lucas asked. "Putting ice on it?"

"When I can hobble in and get it. Eva is so busy. She's a manager now, at the aluminium foundry."

I frowned. Surely, whatever the hell was going on with Nora, she could take a moment to bring her grandmother an icepack. "I'll get one," I said. And despite wanting to help, it would be the perfect opportunity to look around.

"That would be lovely, dear." Marta's smile was so sweet. "There's one of those plastic bags that seals up tight in either the drawer by the cooker or the cupboard by the fridge. Probably best if you put it inside so it doesn't get dirty."

I headed out. At the end of the hall was a small but equally cluttered kitchen with dishes in the sink, piles of papers on the table, a gas cooker stacked with pots and photos of Nora pinned to the fridge freezer. There were none of her brother, which was curious. Despite most of the surfaces being covered, the place was clean. Outside lay a small courtyard garden with climbing nasturtiums and a line hung with washing. All very normal. I cracked the door at the back. A bathroom. Damn, it meant I couldn't use going to the loo as an excuse to check upstairs.

Marta's and Lucas's voices were muffled but audible as they chatted about the recent storms. Marta broke into a cheerful warble. "The wind that assails us, I shall not fear. The devil travails us, I do not hear."

I opened the freezer door and found the icepack, then went to the table and spread the papers. Bank statements, a hospital appointment letter, a wage slip and some junk mail.

"Nora seems like a handful," Lucas said as I scanned the contents.

"That girl really is," Marta replied. "She used to be so sweet. I'd sit with her on my knee and sing. But now she's a fiery one. Too much like her mother. They rub each other up the wrong way. Nora is good at heart, though. She was in with the most terrible crowd at school, but she's been a lot happier since she left them for that Thierry boy." Gabe. Yeah, recent developments aside, I'd have to agree.

I straightened the papers. There was nothing of note. As Marta told Lucas how Nora never slept as a baby, I went through the drawers and cupboards, half looking for the plastic bags Marta had mentioned, half snooping. All I found were utensils, crockery and the bags.

"As I'm here," Lucas said, "I'm going to do a brief check-up." He was silent for a moment, then, "And Nora has a brother, doesn't she?"

I dropped the icepack into the bag and found a clean tea towel.

Marta's tuts echoed down the hallway as I strode out,

wrapping up the pack. "Now that one is a different egg." She grumbled as presumably Lucas did something to her foot.

I raised my hand to push open the living room door but noticed a shape on the tiles. Another feather, this one small, though the same colour as the first. It had probably escaped from a pillow. All the same, I tucked it into my pocket and headed in.

"Romaine lived with his father for a long while," Marta continued, "then got involved with a bad crowd in Toulouse when he was fifteen. He hasn't spoken to his mother for years." Marta winced as Lucas wound a fresh bandage around her foot. I placed the icepack on the stool to the side.

"Camille, can you pass me the tape?" Lucas asked, not looking up.

I had to justify my role. "Sure." I knelt down by the bag, pulled out the tape and passed it just as his arm moved. Our fingers brushed, the sensation of his skin blazing fire through my sinews. Spats of rain drummed against the window.

Lucas stilled. A predator ready to pounce.

Marta frowned, her gaze darting between us.

I drew a deep breath, and with utmost care not to touch, passed him the tape again.

He took it, his Adam's apple bobbing hard.

CHAPTER 16

BRAKING THE TRUCK, I CHECKED FOR ONCOMING traffic at the exit of the café car park. My fingers pressed painfully into the wheel, as if clamping them tight would calm my thoughts and release the tension in my back, my shoulders, my head. It didn't. Lucas pulled out in front. He'd dropped me off after we'd finished at Nora's. We'd not found anything useful, although I supposed we'd gotten a feel for the family dynamics.

As I put my foot down and turned onto the road, rain spatted the windscreen. Cloud billowed above, trapping in the warmth of the day. It was stifling. My windows were open, but the air that streamed in was much too hot. If only the damned storm would get a shift on and break.

Lucas's lights flared ahead, bright against the overcast evening as he slowed for the queue approaching the round-about. I couldn't let go of his words at the surgery. The intensity of his desire had been crazy. It radiated off him, raw and hungry. It made me want to... to what? Follow him home? Being completely honest with myself, the answer was yes. But what the fuck was wrong with me? We didn't need to complicate things. We were going to be partners for life.

I eased off the brake and let the truck slip forward as the traffic crawled a little closer to the roundabout. The rear window of Lucas's SUV was tinted. I couldn't see in, but I could feel him, that piercing gaze focussed on me through the rear-view mirror.

"Damn you, Lucas Rouseau," I muttered. More spats dotted the windscreen. I resisted the reflex to put on my wipers, the water a shield.

My thoughts circled endlessly, though not only about that night. The way Lucas had supported Marta's foot as he'd bandaged it had kindled a whole host of other impressions—the concern in his eyes at the Keepers' post as we'd attempted to help Nora, the way he'd glanced at me back when he'd been at the mercy of the hantaumo queen, his respect for the goblins in Grimmere, and how he was doing so much for them. And that only spiralled back to the nights he'd held me in that dark place, all of it a tumult, making my pulse unsteady and my chest ache in a way that felt much too raw.

Shit, I was a mess.

I forced myself to think of Lucas's drac form. The monster was never far away, ready to kill, and it was born of such darkness. A trickle of ice ran through my veins, cooling the heat. That hideous thing made me want to wretch. Why was it I could never remember that side of him when he was close? And then there was his trickery, the bridge between the man and the beast, his goblin nature coming to the fore, which left me confounded.

Lucas turned onto the roundabout and took the first right toward the Vicdessos valley, his house a few miles down.

I indicated left, though as I passed the turning, I almost—*almost*—followed him. As I swung around toward the farm, I felt as though I was splitting myself in two. A flurry of rain dashed the windscreen, the wind turbulent like the turmoil in me.

On autopilot, I made to pull off the roundabout but stopped myself and continued on around to rejoin the N20, back the way I came. Shortly after, I turned left and headed through a residential street before pulling into the gravel parking area for Cap de Couronnes.

I jumped out of the truck, a blast of wind flinging the door wide. With a shove, I forced it closed. The rain had let up again, but the storm was nearly upon the town. My chest expanded as I drew in a lungful of air, but it wasn't enough.

I set off at a jog along the path that skirted the base of the foothill, slowing to pound over the wooden bridge that spanned the hydroelectric pipes and edge around the steep drop outside the Cave of the Lovers. A scree slope lay ahead. I scrambled upward, grabbing what little scrub clung on precariously. Rain flurried into me. That and the loose stones crunching and sliding under the soles of my trainers made the climb treacherous, but I didn't care. I clambered to the top of the cliff then rounded the curved summit, the wind at my back, goading me on.

Charcoal billowed over the mountains, my own personal tumult of impressions intensifying, begging for release. I stepped into the scattering of stones at the top, and the town stretched away before me in shrouded, endless grey. It was too early for streetlights.

The wind grew frenzied. The storm had arrived. I released a laugh, wild vitality streaming through my veins. Closing my eyes and spreading my arms, a part of me was borne aloft, the tempest embracing, caressing, welcoming. This was what I needed.

For a moment, I relished in the freedom of soaring above Tarascon, the glassy thread of the river and the dark mesh of roads growing smaller, the menhir on Coustarous a pinprick. Then I swept down upon the old town, the gate, the tower, Nora's house. I eddied and spun, sweeping past the town hall and Rene's almost rebuilt bakery. I careened and spiralled, rushing past the café and the old fae streets.

Yet as I ascended again, the tumult of impressions that bombarded me intensified until I could bear it no longer. I held out my hands.

Boom.

A serrated vein of light struck an electricity pylon on the end of Picou de Bompas, silver and blue sparking along the wires, the glare scoring my vision long after it had dissipated.

The tumult built once more, all my confused thoughts, my bewildering emotions, roiling and rolling within. The wind streamed and gushed and swirled, encouraging me. I angled my fingers and struck again, this time Cap de la Lesse to the south, and with it the torrent began, falling in swathes and cooling my skin, but not cooling it enough.

I released crash after crash, thunder blending with the deep reverberations of laughter borne on the wind, a low voice rumbling, "Camille... I need you."

My inner storm redoubled, streaking through my skull.

I needed more.

Drawn to the Surba valley to the northeast, I swept over farmland and villages, then dove down to fields burgeoning with golden wheat and verdant vines. Opening my palms, I released a volley of hail, crushing crops and shattering windows.

And on the edge of it all was something other than turmoil, other than the storm, other than the beckoning voice. It invaded the valley, seeping past my gusts.

I rushed outward, forcing it away. Screeching filled the air, horror shivering through me. And still it came—a sickness, a pestilence, an ill wind. My thoughts and my senses twisted in on themselves, colliding so I could barely think. And as it brushed me, pain cracked my bones.

Yet still the tumult stormed inside, charged and potent. I teemed with it, full to bursting.

Below me, folk were running for cover through a concrete farmyard, the modern lines of the barns jarring against the rugged landscape. And in the centre, an old man stood gazing up at me, shirt flapping, a mass of steel-grey hair flying wildly above a permanent scowl and terror-stricken eyes. And yet there was a stillness in the furrows of his face. Turned soil in the depths of winter. An acceptance of fate.

The pestilence seeped around him in a deathly embrace, and everything that roiled within me surged and erupted.

I thrust out my hands.

Searing white broke from my fingertips. It tore into the pestilence, blasting the man to the ground.

CHAPTER 17

MUTTERING COLOURFUL EXPLETIVES UNDER MY BREATH, I tossed aside the sofa cushions, trying to find my keys. I was already late for work, and boy, did I feel like hell. No, hell would be so much better than this. My head throbbed and my bones ached as though they'd been crushed to pieces in the night, only to have been stuck back together badly with noxious superglue. It wasn't helping that I'd barely had time to plaster on deodorant, tie up my hair and wash my face before pulling on cropped cotton trousers and a T-shirt. A shower would've been nice.

Frustration built as I burrowed under the old velvet seat cushions, the sofa becoming an earthquake zone, my fingers skimming crumbs. But, nothing, damn it. Where the hell had I put them?

Take a breath, Camille. Patience is a virtue.

I obeyed my inner voice, drawing in air and releasing it. I just needed a moment. Through the French windows, goats milled about in the farmyard after milking, though some of them were already tucked under bushes where the woods dropped away to the town, finding cool spots before the heat of the day descended.

I drew in another long breath and glanced around the loft. The place was a mess, and it didn't help that my head was foggy, last night's dream a jumble of blurred images. The storm. Lightning. Feeling so goddamned good out in it, and then feeling utterly awful for some reason I couldn't put my finger on. And all the tumult, the mess with Lucas, everything I'd felt, I'd released through my fingers, light blasting into some poor guy that had looked a lot like Ludger, one of the grumpy farmers.

What a creepy nightmare. I glanced down at my hands and shivered. It was more than weird that my dream self had to take out my frustration on an old farmer. It had to be some sort of Freudian crap that related to my father, which I really didn't want to think about now or ever. But I had to admit that apart from feeling steamrollered and having to hunt for my keys, inside I was so much calmer, all yesterday's turmoil gone. Outside, the day shone clear and bright, reflecting my newfound ease.

But the place really was a mess. I'd not managed to catch up on my washing before we'd gone into Fae, although I'd organised it into a heap by the bed. A massive pile of clean dishes rested on the draining board, perpetually replenishing themselves and never making it into the cupboard in one go. A load of shopping sat on the side, jars and packets I hadn't had time to put away due to working two jobs. The place being open plan meant that the whole lot stared me in the face. Now the disarray of the sofa added to the general chaos, and none of it was helping me find my keys.

It might be an idea to retrace my steps last night... Lucas had dropped me off at the café after Nora's house. I'd gotten into my truck and driven away, then I'd sat in traffic, Lucas ahead. We reached the roundabout and... Nope, there was nothing more.

When I woke, all of ten minutes ago, I'd been lying in bed naked, my soaked clothes trailed over the floor, my bag by the door, my keys missing. If I couldn't remember coming home, I must have slept heavily. I supposed we'd been through a lot in Fae. But really, blanking everything? My chest tightened. Surely I couldn't have been *that* tired.

I released a sigh. Only one option remained. Grampi kept the spare set of keys, using the truck occasionally for transporting goats and the like, not that he drove much these days. But seeing him meant more aggro about the bond, though I could plead being late for work as a getaway excuse.

I grabbed my bag and headed out. And there, on the other side of the door hanging from the lock, were my keys. Shit. I never did that. But at least I wouldn't have to speak to Grampi.

I closed up, jogged down the stairs and crossed the yard, glancing at my phone for the time. I'd only be a few minutes late. And no good-morning text from Lucas. Sensible of him. I heaved open the truck door—

"Oh, Camille," Grampi called from the farmhouse. "Glad I caught you."

I stilled, staring into the footwell. I could hightail out of here, pretend I hadn't heard him. But that was stupid. I took a deep breath and turned around.

Grampi approached, his steps stiff. "Mind giving me a lift into town?"

Great. Just great. I plastered on a smile. "Sure. But I have to get a move on. I'm running late."

We climbed in.

I cranked the ignition. It caught the second time. "Something on today?"

He rolled down the window and placed a wrinkled elbow on the frame as he frowned out onto the road, his tanned skin a contrast to his white beard. "There's a coffee morning at the town hall. I'm going to give it a try, maybe start acting my age." His words were as stiff as his steps had been. "Discussing the weather with a load of geriatrics sounds like just the thing."

I glanced at him as I took the bend. His face was void of life. He looked lost.

"And anyway," he added, "I wanted to catch you about the bond."

I clenched my jaw, tension creeping down my neck. I had nowhere to hide.

"Was La Vieille happy with your partnership?" He transferred his grip to the support handle above the window as I rounded a sharp bend.

She hadn't disapproved. If there was one word for how she'd reacted, I would've said amused, but that wasn't going to go down well. "She was aware of the consequences with

Lucas's family and the bounds if we don't proceed. So, yes, she was adamant about it."

He released a huff, his moustache quivering. "That's as may be, but the bond is for life. It's not something to step into lightly. And it's so *early* in your partnership."

"You know I'm aware of that, so let's just get to the crux of it, shall we?" I circled my shoulders so they wouldn't lock. "No matter how hard you try to get along with Lucas, you can't accept him."

He hauled his gaze from the road and fixed it on me. "Camille, he's a drac. The epitome of evil. And not only that, he's a Rouseau. When he turned up here, I thought he was some lesser family member gone rogue. But no, he's second in line to the drac rulership. You can't walk into this without thinking."

"He's the epitome of evil who I trust through and through, who cares for the town, who is beyond decent. He's all but disowned his family, and the only reason he hasn't done that is to help Fae." I'd updated Grampi on everything that had happened in Grimmere, and yet *this*.

"A decent *monster*," he snapped.

I couldn't deny it, so I chewed my cheek.

"How long has La Vieille given you?"

I dug my nails into the wheel as I tucked into the hedge, allowing a car to pass. Branches scraped along the truck. "Now... two days."

His breath caught. "And what? You weren't going to mention it until it was done?"

"Why does it matter?" My voice was razor sharp.

"We're having the bond. It's the usual process for Keepers, and our ruse with the Rouseaus depends on it. Anyway, *you* had the bond with a hantaumo, for heaven's sake. They're just as bad on the monster scale." I pulled away again.

"That was different. By the time I met Mathilde, she'd changed form, reflecting her inner orientation." He shook his head, rubbing his mouth. "There's something not right about it."

"What?" I cried. "How can you say that? It's La Vieille we're talking about. Are you telling me she makes mistakes?" Although I couldn't help wondering if it had been necessary to taunt us with images of that night. But then, fae were fae—imparting profound truths one moment and throwing curveballs the next.

"Well, La Vieille may be happy," he replied, his voice rough, "but are you... truly?"

That wasn't difficult. "The truth is, yes, I want to work with Lucas. I love being a Keeper, and there's no way I'm letting go of that." I met his eye for as long as I could, attempting to convey my earnestness before having to turn back to the road. "And I respect Lucas. He's a good person. I couldn't have a better partner. I'm more than happy to have the bond."

He slumped back and released a breath through tight lips. "I don't know how I'm going to come around to this. But I guess I'll have to find a way."

I rubbed his arm, my tension relieving a little. "Thank you."

He attempted a smile. "I have to say, there's one bonus of you having the bond with Lucas."

"Oh? What's that?"

"It means there's definitely not anything else happening."

I frowned. "Happening? What do you mean?"

"I've seen the way he looks at you." His brow knotted. "And some of the folk in town have been talking. For a moment there, I thought there might be something going on... romantically." He chuckled. "Now, *that* I would never get over."

I grated the gears. Nope. No relationship there. But what if there was? Yes, his drac form creeped me out completely, but he was one of the most honourable, strong, true people I'd met. He'd spent years being someone he wasn't, wheedling his way back in with his family even though he'd hated every moment of it, and he'd done it to help Fae, to help us all. He was witty, caring and damned good company when he wasn't being an ass, so what was the problem if we were together? Weirdly, my chest felt raw at the thought. No, more than raw. Anguished would be a better description. But all I said was, "La Vieille doesn't appoint Keepers who are romantically involved, so it's not even a consideration, is it?" I tried not to growl the last words.

He chuckled some more. "No, of course not. Thank the gods."

CHAPTER 18

THE AROMA OF COFFEE AND FRESHLY BAKED BREAD drifted from the café's open windows, meeting me as I strode to the door, the climbing geraniums that scaled the front of the sprawling chalet a welcome sight. I pushed inside. The place was heaving, mid–breakfast rush. Alice was at the till, taking orders.

"Sorry I'm late," I called as I headed behind the counter.

"No trouble," she said over her shoulder. "We have everyone in."

One of the part-time staff was clearing plates, and Inès stood by the fireplace doing the flowers. I went out back for an apron, tied it on and hurried back in. "Thanks for understanding."

But this time Alice didn't respond. Her gaze bored into one of the goblins she served, her mouth tight. They were projecting average glamours, wearing shorts, T-shirts and affable looks that hid their scrawny limbs, pot bellies and pointy ears. The tall one might've evoked Raphaël as he had the same build, but goblins were common in the café, and Alice wasn't usually bothered, or at least she never showed it.

"What will it be?" she snapped.

"Uh, ummm, I'm just making up my mind," the tall one said.

We were out of croissants. I dove into the kitchen for a fresh basket, narrowly avoiding Guy and the tray of eggs in his hands.

"Hey, Camille," he called. "Gnarly storm last night."

"Yeah, gnarly." I grabbed a full basket from the shelf, my utterly bizarre dream coming back.

"Morning, Camille," Dame Blanche called as she crossed the room, a bag of flour clutched to her chest. She beamed at me, her eyes sparkling—knowing. And all at once, I could see others in her eyes—Marta, Madame Biscotte at the surgery, and for a split-second, La Vieille.

I shook my head, attempting to fling off the befuddlement. It was always best to act naturally around Dame Blanche, as if she wasn't an aspect of the mother goddess standing in the kitchen but just an everyday old woman who definitely wouldn't set anyone's trousers on fire. I lived in hope that it had merely been a string of unfortunate events last week when Axel Tripes had stormed out after complaining his order was taking too long. His combination of acrylic trackies, rather a lot of vodka the night before and a little static—as the fire brigade later posed—had been an unfortunate combination. He'd only suffered minor burns, as Dame Blanche happened to have a large bucket of water handy, which Guy had snatched and tipped over the man's head.

"Morning," I called nonchalantly before striding over to help Alice. She was still serving the goblins and the queue was building.

"Patisserie?" I asked, ready to make up plates.

Alice's face was tight. "I've no idea."

"Umm, I'm having trouble deciding on my order." The tall one stared up at the menu board, scratching his chin.

"Hmmmm, me too," Shorty added.

Alice drummed her fingers on the countertop. "Do you think you could step aside for a moment so I can serve the other customers while you figure it out?"

"Oh, no," Shorty said. "I've got it. A cappuccino, please, and a slice of Forêt Noire."

The tall one rubbed his bristly chin. "And I'll have an espresso and a pain au chocolat." He raised a finger. "No, make it a pain aux raisins."

"Good idea," Shorty said. "Scrap my Forêt Noire, I'll have a pain aux raisins too."

"Actually"—the tall one exchanged a look with his friend, a glimmer of mischief in his eyes—"I'll have an éclair."

Alice glowered back and forth between them. Her fingers clenched around the counter edge. Boy, was she wound tight. But this pair were total knuckleheads.

"Oh, me too! Three éclairs," Shorty declared.

The tall one grinned. "No, make that a Paris-Brest—"

"And change my coffee to a latte." They broke into howls, sharp teeth prominent.

Shorty pointed at Alice. "Get a load of that face."

She hadn't moved, though a small muscle twitched under her eye.

Their idiocy would've been pushing it at the best of times, but everything was still much too raw after Raphaël. Time for an intervention. "I think you two should—"

"Get the hell out of my café!" Alice roared, her face wild, her eyes blazing hellfire.

The whole place stilled.

The goblins' mouths dropped. I stared at her, flabbergasted. When it came to the café, nothing like that had ever come out of her mouth. She was always so easy-going, taking everything in her stride.

"Go," she barked. "Go on. And don't come back." She grabbed a cake slice from the patisserie counter and brandished it before her. "I won't repeat myself. Go!"

"Alright, Alice," the small one said. "We were just having a jest."

Dame Blanche strode out of the kitchen. "Any assistance required?"

The goblins cringed and scampered away, a few of the queue following. Everyone else eyed Alice warily. She shook her head and strode out back.

"Is that a little smoke rising from their trousers?" Dame Blanche asked nonchalantly, glancing out at the goblins hurrying through the car park.

"Don't. Just don't." I shot her a glare as I followed Alice.

Drawing a breath, I pushed open the office door. Piles of boxes filled with paper cups and patisserie packaging lay all around, hiding filing cabinets, cupboards and much of the whiteboard that hung on the wall displaying the staff rota. Alice sat behind the desk, her head in her hands.

"Hey," I said softly. "You okay?"

She peered up, twisting a pencil between her fingers. "I'm fine, Camille. Just fine."

The universal answer for anything but. "You want to talk about it?"

She studied the pencil for a moment, then sat back and met my gaze. "Guess I'm just a bit riled."

"Oh?"

"Haven't you heard?" She glanced up at the ceiling and took a breath. "About Ludger..."

Well, I'd dreamt about him. "No."

She swallowed. "He died last night in the storm. Got struck down by lightning, of all things."

I squeezed my eyes closed and opened them again, my stomach dropping away. My dream had felt so real, as though I'd been soaring above Ludger's farm, my hands outstretched and... *Boom.*

"Uh, really?" I managed. "I mean, what are the chances of that?"

She shrugged. "I know."

CHAPTER 19

I SHOULD HAVE BEEN THINKING OF NORA AS ROUX studied the tape measure dangling at her throat. I *was* damned worried. But most of me was preoccupied with the storm last night, my fingers pressed tight against my mug.

We were all sitting around the meeting room table at the Keepers' post, Lucas opposite, glancing at me occasionally. He looked a wreck, his shirt creased, his stubble untamed, his hair a mess.

Roux wound up the tape measure. "The knot has slipped a little," he murmured. "If it continues at this rate, Nora will have a week or so."

"Awesome." She jutted her chin. "Just amazing."

The gang sitting on either side shuffled in their seats, casting the last of their lunch baguettes onto the table. The whole situation gave me a distinct lack of appetite too.

"Camille and I visited Marta..." Lucas began updating

everyone, but the storm replayed in my head. I'd been there, I was sure of it. I could still feel light and power blazing from my hands, accompanied by utter release.

Guilt surged through me, my legs weakening. I'd struck Ludger down. But that was utterly ludicrous. There was no way I could have flown on the wind, then somehow blasted the guy with lightning. Perhaps it had been some kind of vision.

And this morning, I'd been blissfully free of thoughts of Lucas. In control once more. But now, I could feel him, his presence filling the room. I shuddered. A front was building, cloud drawing over, vying with blue, even though today's storm was a long way off. By the looks of it, we would have rain first, the normal kind without thunder. Despite that, I already wanted to climb Cap de Couronnes to greet it. But oh my goodness, listen to me. I'd become an expert on the weather—

"Camille?"

I almost toppled off my chair. "Sorry, what?"

Lucas met my gaze, my sense of him intensifying, warmth blossoming from my middle to my fingertips. Everyone was staring. Félix was smacking his lips together like a fish. Zach, Hugo and Gabe were waiting for my response. Roux had sat down on my left and was attempting to brush down a bit of beard that stuck up, and Nora was glaring at me for good measure. No change there then.

I had no idea what Lucas had just said. His gaze lingered, his brow narrowing. The way his broad mouth straightened when he was thinking was intriguing. Why did I have the feeling that we were sitting too far apart, that I wanted his warmth to blend with mine? *Damn it*, we were Keeper partners. I had to be mindful of the distance we so desperately needed.

He drew the two feathers from his bag and placed them on the table. "I explained that we didn't find anything at Nora's, other than these. One of them is from a vulture, the other I'm not sure."

Roux leant over, peering at them. He picked the large one up. "Unusual at such a low altitude. If you don't mind, I'll study them further."

"Be my guest." Lucas centred on the gang. "Report."

Félix sat up. There was something about the creases under his eyes that augmented his eagerness. "Searches showed nothing out of the ordinary on Nora's maman, papa, gran, or the gaggle at school."

Nora folded her arms tightly.

"Her brother, Romaine, on the other hand..." Zach sat ramrod straight, his thin body quivering a little. "He's interesting."

"Oh?" Lucas said.

Hugo nodded. "From what we can gather, he left his papa at fifteen. Got in with this gang in Toulouse. The Rôdeurs, they call themselves. There are thought to be about twenty members, and they're into all kinds of stuff. Embezzlement, bribery, harassment, theft.

The Rôdeurs—the prowlers. It didn't exactly bode well.

"Been caught a few times," Hugo continued, "but they've

managed to get out of the charges, and the word on the dark web is that they're trouble. Bastien Calvi is the leader, and from photos we found, it looks like he was the guy with Romaine in the café yesterday."

"That *is* something." That lot actually had been of use. "But really, the dark web?" I glanced at Lucas.

He shrugged. "Better than Pare Gégant. But we'll need to follow that up."

I turned to Nora. "Did your brother hinder you?"

She opened her mouth, but nothing came out, which was suspicious in itself.

"What about you, Roux?" Lucas asked.

He stopped attempting to tame his beard. "I went through the Keeper records. None of the family has a connection with Fae as far as I can tell, but I'll look into the Rôdeurs."

Zach drew out his mobile. "I'll email you the names."

"Pen and paper will do nicely after the list Gabe sent yesterday, which took me forty-five minutes to open." Roux stepped over to the cupboard at the side and returned with deckled-edge paper, an inkpot and a quill.

Zach's eyes grew wide. Félix grabbed the inkpot and pulled the cork, slopping black onto the table.

Gabe glowered at him, his jaw rigid. "Be careful, you idiot. This is serious."

Félix lasered him back.

"And that's it?" I said, glancing around at them all. "That's all we have?"

They nodded. Nora sagged.

"What about the storm last night?" Considering I was feeling pretty obsessed by it, I had to raise the subject.

"Ludger was in the wrong place at the wrong time," Lucas said. "He died instantly from the lightning blast, and he was, uh, rather charred. But I can't see a connection." That was why he looked rough. He'd been up most of the night dealing with all that.

The gang gaped at one another. Even Nora was momentarily ruffled.

Félix's brow rose. "Ludger got fried?"

We nodded.

"He was a dick"—Hugo leant on the table, almost sticking his elbow in the ink—"always shouting at people, but that really was a harsh way to go."

Félix slumped back. "Totally."

Zach, who'd regained possession of the quill, looked up from the black, smeary mess he was making on the paper and shook his head.

"That's strange, though," Gabe said.

"Why?" The word flew out of my mouth, causing Lucas to frown and Nora's glare to intensify.

Gabe's brow knotted. "When I was looking through the newspaper database, I came across a listing way back, announcing that the engagement between Ignace Gasc and Marta Poirier had been called off. Marta was twenty at the time."

I sat up and stared at him, my heart thumping. "Ignace was Ludger's close friend. Could there be a connection?"

"Really, Camille," Roux said. "It's quite a stretch between a freak lightning strike and Nora's situation."

"And yet we can't dismiss the possibility." Lucas slid his jaw from side to side.

"Then could the storm be connected to Fae?" I asked. "There's a lot of folklore about the weather, but most of it has been Christianised, storms attributed to the devil, the details lost."

Lucas shrugged. "Various fae have weather magic. The hantaumo being a prime example. Many use storms."

Yeah, the hantaumo had brought godawful weather with them.

"There's Mari of the Storms in the Basque Country," Gabe said, "and the follet... uh... is related to sexual power. Whirlwinds that... uhm... fertilise women." He'd gone red.

The others sniggered, Nora chortling. Lucas glowered at them. The follet was a remnant from when fertilisation wasn't understood and was thought to be linked to the wind. Not to mention, it was a better get-out to say you'd been caught in a frisky whirlwind than admit you'd been at it in the barn with the next-door neighbour's son.

"What about the principal winds that affect the area?" Roux shifted in his chair and straightened his cloak. "The Autan from the Mediterranean is said to drive folk crazy. The devil's wind, they call it. And there are the Tramountaign, the Cers, the Eissaure, the Scirocco. They all carry a degree of elemental activity, sylphs and the like, and they're known to work people up. The Cers gives me a touch of dropsy."

Zach looked at him as though he was contagious.

I rubbed my chin. "The Autan does make me irritable." But I was pretty sure that what I'd experienced last night hadn't been any of that.

Lucas tapped his fingers on the table. "I haven't sensed or seen anything unusual in the weather of late, apart from Ludger being struck down. It's typical for the time of year, at least as far as I remember. It's been a while since I lived here."

"It's like this most summers," Félix said.

"Slaughter," Lucas called.

He appeared from under the table and saluted, grinning at everyone. "Yes, boss?"

"What have you found from tailing Nora's family?"

"Marta has been sitting at home crocheting. She had two friends pop in for tea. They chatted about the townsfolk. Nothing suspicious. Eva did a night shift at the aluminium foundry. She's back home now, sleeping soundly. Romaine and the other chap went to Toulouse. They met friends at Le Bijou, then slept in. Nora went for a walk by the river last night, skimmed some stones. After that she binge-watched *Vampire Chronicles*."

"Hey." Her eyes blazed. "You've got the Men watching me?"

"Considering everything," Lucas said, "and seeing as you can't speak for yourself, of course we do."

She scrunched up her mouth and glared some more.

Slaughter stepped back so he could see her. "Rest

assured, miss, the Men have strict orders not to go into the bathroom and to close their eyes while you're dressing."

"So reassuring," she drawled.

"Keep the Men on it," Lucas said.

Slaughter saluted again and disappeared.

"Alright." I dragged my teeth over my lip. "We need a plan of action. I'll check folklore resources for storms and anything related."

"You lot..." Lucas glanced at the gang. "I want everything you can get on the Rôdeurs. Roux, check out Marta's connection with Ignace and possibly Ludger. I'll make enquiries about fae with weather magic, and it looks like Camille and I will need to pay Marta another visit after work to ask her about her engagement."

There were nods all around, including mine.

"We'll meet back here tomorrow at the same time," he added. "Although text if you find anything."

"Perfect," I said. But it wasn't perfect. I'd spent the night flying above the town. At least I felt like I had, not to mention poor Ludger. I needed to say something. I'd had enough experience in Fae to know not to ignore oddities, and this was beyond odd.

"Right, let's get to it." Lucas rose and adjusted his cuff.

"Before you go..." I joined him. The gang disappeared out the door. Roux grabbed his staff and followed.

"What's up?" Lucas asked.

My gaze traced the shadow of his stubbled jaw to the lines at the corner of his broad mouth.

"Camille, what is it? You've been distracted throughout the meeting."

"I... uh..." He was spot on, and I had to pull it together. "The storm... Ludger..."

He frowned.

"I know this is going to sound really strange, but I dreamt of the storm, the lightning... and Ludger's death. It was so clear, as if I'd been there." Saying it out loud made it seem ridiculous. "But I'm sure it was just a vivid dream."

CHAPTER 20

"Is it possible to get any more wet?" I yelled as Alice and I ran along the path that skirted Cap de Couronnes, making for the cave. I'd clamped my waterproof coat against my head, the rest of it flailing behind, doing almost nothing to keep the pounding rain off me and my basket.

Alice squealed, holding her jacket above her as she flanked me. "Hell, no. I'd be dryer in the shower."

The rain had set in an hour ago, a little wet weather driven in by a moving front, as I'd predicted. It was a precursor to the storm, and I was glad to be out, closer to the source, though last night's dream continued to unsettle me. I'd described it in detail to Lucas, who hadn't known what to think, though he'd suggested it could've been a premonition, or that somehow I'd picked up subconsciously on the situation. He'd given me a sleep tonic that would provide hours of dreamless sleep, so thankfully, I'd be out cold tonight.

"If it would just let up for one minute," Alice cried as we thundered onto the wooden walkway, crossing the hydroelectric pipes that clung to the cliff. "I can't even see, I'm so wet."

We sprang back onto the mountainside, and with a last spurt, skirted the sheer drop outside the cave. Brushing rain-lashed hazel and honeysuckle, we made it inside, beaming at each other, our breath heaving. The rain was a little quieter here. *Everything* was quieter. Drips fell from our clothing, pitting the dusty floor.

"It's a heck of a long time since we were up here in the rain." Alice stepped deeper inside, shaking out her jacket.

I followed, my trousers sticking to me. "It's been a long time since we were here, period. A couple of years at least." We used to come here loads. With a name like the Grotte des Amoureux, the Cave of the Lovers, it left little to the imagination what people got up to here in the past, but since the hydroelectrics were built early in the last century, it hadn't been such a romantic location, and the place didn't see many visitors. Alice and I had always used it as a spot to get away from the town and talk.

Heat radiated from the rock, a remnant of the day's sunshine. "It's baking in here," I said. "We'll be dry in no time."

I placed my basket and coat down and flicked water off my fingers as I took in the walls. Prehistoric rock art decorated much of the small cave, and I couldn't resist its call. I stepped over to the dots and hatches drawn in faint charcoal, and the devils, or possibly fae, with legs and arms outstretched, painted in orange ochre, the artwork unbelievably bright considering it was eighteen thousand years old.

The cave invited me in deeper, and I paused before a complex arrangement of yellow lines and curves. The organic pattern always drew me, its meaning lost to the passage of time, though it reminded me of the foliage at the entrance. I placed my hand on the smooth limestone, making contact beside the drawing as I'd always done. I supposed it had been my personal Andos before I'd known such a thing existed. Heat warmed my palm, greeting me.

"I love this place," I said above the constant rush of rain reverberating about. "It's as if the generations echo endlessly back."

"I have to agree with you there." Alice bustled around, shaking out her hair and scraping water off her legs. She'd been sensible, wearing a short skirt. Less clothing to dry. "It's always felt like a welcoming place."

I returned to the front of the cave and leant against the wall, the soothing atmosphere easing my anxiety about Lucas, Nora and my bizarre dreams. My gaze followed the twines of honeysuckle that curved around ramrod-straight hazel trunks. The stems twisted higher until they spilled out in a tangle of dusky pink and deep orange flowers amidst broad velvet leaves. Utterly entangled, they covered the side of the entrance. I wound a strand of honeysuckle around my finger. Folklore stated that if the two should ever be parted, they would die, which was appropriate given the name of the cave. Though it was a miracle anything managed to grow here. From the look of the moss, which extended inside, there had to be a small spring feeding them.

Far below the foliage lay the grey roofs of the hydroelectric plant, the aluminium foundry and the chapel marking the place where Charlemagne had celebrated his victory over the Saracens in 778. The town extended along the confluence of valleys, the Ariège snaking through the centre, all of it veiled in rain.

It never ceased to amaze me that despite the industrial side of Tarascon, none of it, not even the pylons extending over the far side of Picou du Bompas, took away from its beauty. The sheer scale of the mountains and the overwhelming sense of nature were far more powerful than the human presence. And I'd seen it all last night from far, far above. A shiver ran down my spine.

Alice had settled on the moss and was rummaging in the basket. Grinning, she pulled out a bottle of five-year-old Mas de Daumas Gassac Rouge and two glasses. "Oh my goodness, no expense spared. Let's get this open. It's been a busy morning and—"

A boom reverberated up from the aluminium foundry. Alice jumped out of her skin.

I raised an eyebrow. "And you need a little something to take the edge off? You've been so tense lately."

She scowled. "I'm fine."

She definitely wasn't. I grabbed the bottle, found the corkscrew in the basket and pulled the cork. "And anyway, it's a celebration."

"Oh?" She held out the glasses and I poured.

"Despite everything that happened in Grimmere, I'm so relieved that we're back to...." Normal wasn't the right word, not when fae were involved. But now she knew about the hidden world, we'd returned to sharing everything.

Alice handed me a glass. "Back to being how we were."

"I'll drink to that." I lifted my glass and took a sip.

Alice joined me in the toast, then leant back on her elbows, her raglan T-shirt splaying out. Another boom came from below. She tried not to flinch, but every part of her stiffened.

"Alright, Alice, now that we finally have five minutes' privacy, tell me what's up?"

Her scowl deepened. "What do you mean? I told you, I'm fine."

I shifted my weight onto one hip and leant back against the warm rock, my trousers already feeling a little less damp. "Chucking out those goblins earlier—I can't say they didn't deserve it, but it wasn't like you. And you're so jumpy all the time... here... at the café. You've been like it for a while now."

"I'm totally fine, Camille." Another boom came. This time she couldn't hide her flinch.

I raised my eyebrows. "No, you're not."

She closed her eyes for a moment, her jaw tight, then she took a gulp of wine. "You're not going to let this drop, are you?"

"Nope." Of course I wasn't. She meant too much to me.

She sat up, drew a deep breath and released it in a tremulous gust. "It's the fae in the café. I don't mean to get at them, but they don't make it easy, playing pranks and being total asses most of the time, not to mention everything with Raphaël still hurts so much." Her words tumbled out, her lips shaking. "But what really gets me is that there's nothing I can do about any of it. *Nothing*. They have magic, and they know all the fae rules. No, scrap that. There don't appear to be any rules, which is worse, and I'm just left reeling." She shook her head, tears beading in her eyes. "And I'm scared, Camille. I'm scared all the time. There isn't a moment I don't think Elivorn will be lurking outside the café, waiting for me like before."

Shit.

"I'm so sorry, hon." I sank into the moss, wrapped my arm around her shoulder and squeezed her tight. "You took everything in your stride after Grimmere. I didn't realise what was going on, but I should have." And fucking Elivorn. My chest tightened with the deep knot of fury I'd retained especially for him.

"Why would you?" She placed her glass down on a rock ledge and dabbed her eyes with her top, smudging her mascara. "You seem fine with it all, and I was okay for a bit. Then it crept up on me."

"Ha, fine." I released a harsh laugh. "I guess I am now, but you know how Lucas introduced me to fae. All that 'dracs are real and you just slept with one'. Then I had these little Men running around my loft. I was petrified."

She snorted. "I can't imagine it was pleasant."

I shuddered, thinking of it, then attempted not to replay *that* night. "It was terrible, and I couldn't speak to anyone about it, but it was a whole lot better than being kidnapped and beaten by Elivorn, then dragged into Fae and kept in a dungeon." I gulped my wine. "It sounds to me like you're having a pretty natural reaction to what you've been through."

She sighed and leant her head on my shoulder. "I guess so."

"And remember, Roux has warded your place, and there's always a Man around somewhere. If there's any sign of trouble, he'll get help."

"I appreciate that." She pulled away and twisted her glass in her hands. "But it's just that I'm so damned helpless. There's you swinging a sword, and I don't even know how to shove someone effectively."

Annoyance wove through me. I should have thought. I would've felt so vulnerable if it hadn't been for my blade. "How about I find you a dagger, show you some moves?"

She bit her lip, her doe eyes hesitant. "I'm not sure that's for me."

I nudged into her. "If you don't try, you'll never know. Tomorrow afternoon." If I pinned her down to a date, fingers crossed, it would happen. "I'll bring some weapons and we can meet by the river where Lucas and I train. It's a good spot. Not many prying eyes."

"Well... I could give it a go." She squeezed my hand. "Thank you."

I grinned.

"And anyway," she said softly. "There's me stressing, while Nora must be going through hell. How's she doing?"

My stomach curled in on itself. "I don't know. She's a

tough one, that's for sure. I just wish we knew how to help." I scuffed my feet in the dust, chalkiness tickling my nose. "The only upside is that the gang are busy helping her so they're not currently trying to kill themselves in Fae."

"Small mercies. And you're left figuring it all out with Prince Charming."

I glared at her. "More like Doctor Evil."

"He's too good-looking for Doctor Evil." She smiled, then her lips straightened. "This bond thing you and Lucas are supposed to have... it seems weird. Quite a commitment."

I shrugged. "It is, though I'm good with it. Not that we have much choice, what with our ruse with Lucas's family. But..." My skin tingled with the recollection of his touch. "I get that La Vieille was assessing our relationship when she graced us with the flashback to end all flashbacks, but I can't see why she had to linger on our one-night stand. It's stirred everything up."

Alice nibbled her lip. "Maybe she was trying to show you how deep it goes."

I frowned. "Deep? A one-night stand?"

She studied me intently. "But what if there is more?"

"Please. Let's not start that again."

"No, Camille, I'm serious." She tipped back her wine, then met my eye. "That whole mates thing you pulled off in Grimmere. I know very little about dracs, but from what I saw of Elivorn, he was as sharp as they come, and I'm guessing the rest of Lucas's family are the same, especially as they're some of the most powerful rulers in Fae. I can't imagine they got there by being duped. And according to you, they welcomed your ruse with open arms."

I stared at her, my lips parted. Morion Auberon had questioned it too at the banquet. He'd presumed that Lucas had used a collude. But come to think of it, what collude? Lucas hadn't known I'd be there to have something prepared, and he'd declared I was his mate to Elivorn on the spot to prevent me being punished by death.

I swallowed. "What are you saying?"

"I don't know anything about mates, but it seems to me that Lucas would've had to believe in it fully for his family to be convinced."

I tugged at my damp top, the thing rubbing my skin. Mates... I got the general idea, but not the specifics. Lucas had said something about it being a deep bond possible between fae, or occasionally fae and humans. It meant his family would adopt me without question. He'd mentioned that there was power and prestige generated from the partnership, and Lady Rouseau had said it was radiating from us.

Us. Not only him.

I didn't get it, and a barrage of images were threatening to swamp me once more—the security and familiarity of those nights in Grimmere, my shudders as his lips brushed my skin. A rush of heat swept over my body, accompanied by blazing indignation. I'd had enough of it all. Those images weren't us now, and they never would be again.

"Time for a change of subject." I sprang up and grabbed the wine bottle, trying to breathe it all away. It was damned well getting to me, and I needed to forget about Lucas for a

few hours. I topped up Alice's glass and my own, then strode
to the back of the cave and examined the inscriptions just
visible in the shadows. The perfect distraction. Alice's gaze
burned into the back of my neck as she weighed up whether
to continue or let it drop. Well, she'd have to do the latter.

This part of the cave was my favourite, the prehistoric
rock art accompanied by a plethora of modern inscriptions.
Folk hadn't stopped tagging the place back in the Magdalen-
ian, they'd continued throughout history to the present day.
On top of the charcoal and ochre were scrawls of *Roger 1321*
and *Pierre 1462* and *Jean was 'ere* 2020, a continuous record
of human presence. I respected that a lot of ancient cave art
needed to be preserved for prosperity, but fencing it off
prevented the natural progression of life in places like this.
People felt the need to mark their presence in these dark
sanctuaries, an unbroken chain of life that would continue as
long as folk dwelt in the valley.

There were so many names, all jumbled on top of one
another. I traced them downward, pausing at a familiar curvy
scrawl engraved into the rock, *Lucas 1244*, and then another
in diffuse charcoal, *Lucas R. 1607*, then lower down, *Lucas
1953.*

Fuck.

Fuck. Fuck. Fuck.

My heart pounded, my body an inferno. I'd studied this
wall so many times and not noticed his name. No, that wasn't
true. I probably had, but it was before I'd known him and the
name had meant nothing, one amongst hundreds. My sense
of the storm a little way off grew, anger, desire and confusion

ripping through me, vying for dominance. What the hell had Lucas been doing up here in the Cave of the Lovers all those times, anyway? My fingers, my arms, all of me clenched. I'd told Alice to stop going on about him, and she'd brought it all up again.

I spun around to face her. "He's a monster," I shot out. "A despicable, hideous, disgusting... killer." Underneath, that was what he was.

"And?" She arched an eyebrow. "At least you know it."

I stood stock still. I hadn't been expecting that, though I got that she was comparing Lucas to Raphaël.

"Anyway," she continued, "Lucas isn't like Extreme Sports Alex or the others. I know you tried with them all and nothing truly clicked. Alex just wanted to throw himself off higher cliffs in his wing suit, with increasingly serious injuries. The two of you looked like a match because you were both so physical, but you weren't. His only goal was the next adrenaline rush. You tried damned hard, and it hurt like hell when you broke up."

I gaped at her, unable to believe she was delving into my tattered relationships. But anger mingled with a sharp pang in my chest. She was right. It had all been so difficult with Alex, a tangle of torn commitment and heartache. A big fat mess. It had hurt badly, and it wasn't something I'd consider repeating in a hurry.

"And"—she was on a damned roll—"Lucas is hardly ever a monster. He's completely and utterly gorgeous. And he's much less weird than most fae."

"Perhaps." My voice was tight.

"He's not just gorgeous," she added, a sparkle in her eye, "he's *gâteau au chocolat* gorgeous."

I groaned. "No way. Don't start on the patisserie classification of potential love interests."

"He's a complete gâteau au chocolat." She nodded smugly.

I burst out laughing, unable to believe she'd brought it up. But I appreciated the attempt to lighten the air. "Please. The patisserie scale is ludicrous. You can't measure someone against cake. It didn't work when we were in high school, and it definitely doesn't work now."

She took another sip of wine and grinned darkly. "It completely works. One hundred percent. Decadent patisserie like a croquembouche or a Mont Blanc score highest. A canele is pretty elevated too. It's totally delicious. Then take your plain madeleine. It's functional, reliable, good with a cup of tea. But Lucas is definitely chocolate. Dark chocolate."

I sat back down next to her, feeling a little lighter. "Come on. It's too subjective. Some folk love Mont Blancs and some don't. It's not a reliable scale."

"Who doesn't love a Mont Blanc? But, anyway, people have different tastes in men, like different tastes in cake. It completely works. It's just personal."

I stared into the rain. "You're right about the chocolate part," I said. "But Lucas isn't gâteau au chocolat, he's *moelleux* au chocolat." Its molten centre was dark and utterly bitter. It was hands down my favourite dessert, more so than the café's famous brioche goûter. In fact, it was so good that I rarely ate it because once I started, I was unable to stop. It would be my ruin.

"See," she said. "It totally works."

A small head popped out from the side of the cave entrance, his hair tied back, his nose prominent. It was Blather, the chef who cooked some of Grampi's meals. "Errr, ma'am. You need to meet Lucas at Place du Castella. Now. He says it's urgent."

"Of course he does," Alice said. "He can't be away from you for one moment."

CHAPTER 21

I followed Blather past the ramshackle medieval houses and the old town gate, up to the Place du Castella, rain soaking us through. Having left Alice with Wrench to accompany her home, I'd sprinted to my truck and sped here in no time without pausing to change.

We rounded the bend and found Lucas crouching on the ancient town wall, glancing surreptitiously over the railings. The Église Notre-Dame-de-la-Daurade stood on the far side, surrounded by townhouses. There wasn't a sign of life, everyone sensibly sheltering from the weather.

As I approached, I couldn't help but look at Lucas—really look—at the angle of his raised chin, at the strength in his sturdy back, at the way his rain-drenched shirt clung to him. Sometimes, it was like seeing him anew, and despite doing my darnedest not to dwell on him, I had to admit, he took my breath away.

The wind gusted the rain. The storm would be here

soon, and I would welcome it clearing the muggy heat once more. I shuddered. At least, I'd welcome it if it didn't come with another bizarre dream.

Being careful not to touch, I crouched down beside him and followed his line of sight to a narrow house across the square. "What's going on?"

"The Rôdeurs," he murmured. "Romaine, Bastien and a couple of heavies are around the corner." He inclined his head to a narrow street. "They're waiting for someone, and from what the Men overheard, it doesn't sound like they want to exchange pleasantries." He passed me a sheathed dagger. "Not glamoured. I've got a feeling it will help if our weaponry is visible."

"Best way to make a good impression." I buckled it onto my belt.

From the street opposite the Rôdeurs' hiding place came hurried footfall. Four figures hurtled across the square, their chests heaving. Félix, Zach, Hugo and Gabe. They shot past and disappeared out of sight as a dwarf came into view, his axe raised, his face contorted in fury. "I'll teach you to ask too many questions when a dwarf is having a quiet drink in the Parsnip." He stomped after them.

My fingers dug into my palms. "They're still stirring up trouble."

Lucas made to say something, but the door opened in the house opposite, and out came a hunched figure with a familiar stoop. "Isn't that Ignace?" I whispered.

"Looks like it."

Nora's brother was following the close friend of the man

I'd... who'd been struck down last night. It couldn't be a coincidence.

He scurried into the street by the church. The Rôdeurs emerged from the opposite side of the square, tailing him.

"Time to find out what they're up to," Lucas muttered.

I followed him down the steps and into the heart of the old town, the Rôdeurs disappearing around a corner at the end of the street.

"What do you want?" Ignace cried from ahead.

We slowed as we took the bend, hanging back behind a house that jutted out a little further than its neighbour. Our quarry had entered an alley with an empty parking area at the end, and Ignace was stepping backward as the Rôdeurs approached.

"You're about to find out," Bastien growled, shoving Ignace in the chest. His beret fell into a puddle, rain flattening his wispy hair as he stumbled back against the end wall.

"What did you do to them?" Romaine rumbled. He grabbed Ignace by the neck, pinning him to the stonework.

"I... I... I don't know what you mean." He was terrified, his eyes wide, his puckered lips trembling.

"Not good enough. My family. Nora. Her hinder."

Lucas and I exchanged a glance. Romaine knew about the hinder.

Ignace just shook.

"Tell me!" Romaine bawled.

Not getting a response, he drew a knife, flicked it open and held it against his neck.

And that was our cue. We strode into the alley side by side. "Good evening, gentlemen," Lucas said.

The Rôdeurs jerked their heads.

"Doctor Rouseau," Ignace cried. "Am I glad to see you!"

Bastien strutted toward us, his chest pumped under his soaked vest. "I don't think you want to be stepping into this. Best you clear off."

The two heavies were on his heels, one pockmarked, the other built like a bulldozer. All three pulled their knives.

"Call the police," Ignace spluttered. Romaine rammed him against the wall.

We drew our daggers. With their lengthy blades and decorative hilts, they were considerably more impressive than the Rôdeurs' weaponry. Lucas grinned wickedly, and I could barely restrain my smile. Time for some fun.

Ignace glanced between us. "Camille, is that you? What are you doing with a knife like that? You'll hurt yourself. Of all the stupid ideas."

"Last warning," Bastien rumbled as he headed for Lucas. He didn't think I was a threat, which gave me the perfect opportunity. No doubt these guys had experience fighting on the street, but that was nothing to being pitted against a drac every evening.

I sprang forward and drove a roundhouse into Bastien's jaw, forcing him to the side and giving Lucas easy access to the others. He hadn't quite recovered when I thrust my foot into his hand, sending his blade flying. I met Ignace's panicked gaze. "It's alright, I didn't need to use my knife."

"What the fuck?" Bastien regained himself and strutted

over, thrusting his fist at my face. As I dodged the blow and
swung my knee into his groin, I was vaguely aware of Lucas
doing nasty things with his feet to the other two. As Bastien
bent double, I drove the hilt of my dagger into the base of his
neck. Not too hard, though. I didn't want to cripple him for life,
I wanted information. He stumbled this way and that before
pitching down. "Crazy woman." It was difficult to hear him
through a mouthful of dirt. "I recognise you from the café."

Romaine glanced from us to his fallen comrades, his jaw
slack, Ignace's soaked shirt balled in his fists. Ignace just
gawped. For once, he wasn't grumbling.

"You wouldn't believe how crazy," Lucas replied
demurely. The other Rôdeurs lay groaning on the water-
logged cobbles, their blades scattered. "And you probably
don't want to find out. Only the other day she knifed me—
right in the gut." He drew a finger across his belly, his brow
raised in faux distress. "It hurt."

"You had to bring that up." I jabbed my finger at him.
"*You* threw me in the river."

Lucas's distress morphed into something carnal, his gaze
locked on to mine.

Heat rose from my depths. "Right now? Could you
please focus?" The mates thing came back, thank you very
much Alice. But the idea was ridiculous, and I needed to cool
it. I needed the storm.

Lucas just grinned.

I tore myself from that devastating smile. The Rôdeurs
staggered up, wiping their bloody mouths and eyeing us like

we were creatures from the abyss. I supposed we weren't exactly typical Tarascon citizens.

"Against the wall." Lucas shepherded them back. "And Romaine, release Ignace."

With a nod from Bastien, Romaine shoved the farmer once more for good measure, then let him go.

Ignace stared at us for a second before stooping down for his bedraggled beret, then he scampered past and disappeared around the corner.

Lucas surveyed the Rôdeurs. "What do you know about Nora's hinder?"

They glared defiantly.

I ran my finger along the flat of my blade. "We heard what you said."

Lucas glanced between them. "If you know about hinders, then you know about the hidden world. And it sounded like you were trying to help Nora."

They just glowered.

Either they really were trying to help her, or they wanted the information for another reason. In any case, it was a way in. "We want to help Nora too. So perhaps we can help each other."

Bastien spat at my feet. Every part of Lucas grew rigid, his death stare something to behold. It was a good job Bastien hadn't made contact, or this would've been his last day upon this fair earth. "You freaks," he snarled. "There's no way we'll talk to you."

I shrugged at Lucas. "He doesn't like us."

"You weirdos started this in the first place," Romaine added. "You did this to Nora."

I didn't get it. Why would they think we'd done anything to her? But whatever this was about, they weren't talking. "Leave your blades and go." The other option was to beat them to a pulp, but it was best we left them able-limbed so we could figure out what they were up to. "But find me at the café if you want to exchange information."

"Yeah, like we're going to do that," Bastien muttered as he swaggered past. They eyed us over their shoulders before turning into the street. Lucas collected their abandoned knives and dropped them into a bin.

"Ignace," I said. "The Rôdeurs have to be after him for a reason."

Lucas nodded. "Let's find him."

We headed out of the alley and paused. The Rôdeurs were out of sight. Ignace had vamoosed, and I had no idea which direction he'd taken, but at his age, he couldn't have gone far.

Lucas angled his head. "This way. He's wearing rather a lot of unpleasant cologne."

In relentless rain, we pounded up toward the Tour de Castille, our dash bringing us out at the top of Rue du Bari.

"Here again." I raised my brow. "What the hell is going on?"

A little way down, Ignace pushed into Nora's house.

"I have absolutely no idea," Lucas said as we jogged down the hill.

We slowed by the rain-streaked living room window,

unable to see in. Arguing came from inside, though I couldn't make out the words, then Ignace's voice rose. "We need your help, Marta."

"There's nothing I can do." She met his tone. "You and the others made your beds and now you must lie in them."

"You can't let it pick us off, one by one," he yelled. "You have to do something."

"Get your hands off me," she cried.

I darted to the door, but Lucas was already inside.

CHAPTER 22

WE HURRIED INTO THE LIVING ROOM. IGNACE HAD ONE leg either side of Marta's chair and was shaking the life out of her. Lucas yanked him off, Marta yelping as the old man caught her bunion. He stumbled back and knocked over a potted plant, then regained his footing.

"Dick move, Ignace," I said, "beating up old ladies."

Marta stared between us as she clutched her foot, her nightdress rucked up, her face pale without lipstick. "Doctor Rouseau, Camille. Uh, I wasn't expecting you."

"What are you doing here?" Ignace puffed out his non-existent chest, eyeing our sheathed weapons. We ignored him.

"Are you alright, Marta?" Lucas asked.

"I'm a little shaken"—she adjusted her nightdress and glared at Ignace—"but I'll do."

"We have to ask her about the hinder," I whispered.

He nodded.

Ignace headed for the door, making a run for it. I stepped in front of him and drew my dagger.

He paused, gawking at it. "Utterly idiotic, running around with knives. What are you, some kind of vigilantes?"

"Something like that."

"But Camille, you can't even cut a gâteau straight." He scoffed nervously.

He was such a git. "True. But I can cut off arms pretty well."

Marta's eyes widened, and Lucas scowled at me. Okay, I got it. I was scaring the old lady.

"Marta." He studied her. "It appears there's something going on between Ignace, Romaine and you. As Nora is having trouble speaking to me about certain things, do you by any chance have an idea what's going on?" He was treading carefully.

She opened her mouth to speak. "I... I... uh..." Her skin turned grey, then blue. *She* was hindered too.

"It's okay," he said. "I can see you're having trouble."

I turned to Ignace, ignoring my phone vibrating against my leg. "What do you know about Nora's and Marta's hinders?"

"As I said to that good-for-nothing in the alley, I have no idea what you're talking about. And unless you're going to use those weapons on me, I'm going to make my way home. If you follow, I'll report you to the police." He glanced at window, his jaw quivering.

He was nervous. I'd take a bet that he wanted the police involved as much as we did. And no, I wasn't going to use my blade on him, although I'd like to very much. "Go." There was no point holding him if he wouldn't help.

He scuttled out, and the door slammed.

"Oh, you two." Marta placed her hand on her chest and released a long breath. "I'm so glad you came when you did. What fortunate timing with Eva and Nora out. Were you passing?"

"Kind of." I sheathed my dagger. "We heard shouting."

Lucas picked up the plant and tidied the books. Marta goggled at my scabbard, then as if deciding to set the matter of me carrying a lethal weapon aside in favour of the rescue, she gathered herself. "That awful man. I can't believe the audacity, him barging in like that." She winced again and repositioned her foot.

Lucas fussed around her, pulling a shawl off the back of the chair and wrapping it over her shoulders. His phone buzzed in his pocket, which he ignored, though it reminded me that mine had done the same a moment ago. I pulled it out as he headed to the kitchen for an icepack, leaving Marta to rearrange her messed-up crochet. It was a message from Félix. *We found something. Marta is a tempestaire.*

I stared at the screen.

Tempestaires were folk with a connection to the church who used prayer to control and chase away storms. They were usually priests, sacristans or old women. When the region had converted to Christianity, many of the old beliefs had remained, one of them being that evil forces drove bad weather, and the population demanded protection. Whether the church actually believed in the tradition was another matter, though perhaps a face-off with a town full of peasants furious that their harvest had been wiped out by hail was a lousy alternative to saying a few additional prayers. But this was another possible link between Nora's family and Ludger's death.

I texted back, *Are you sure?*

Félix's reply came almost immediately. *Hundred percent. Dug up a newspaper article from years ago, around the time Marta dated Ignace. There's nothing more recent about it tho.*

Lucas returned, placing a glass of water on the table at Marta's side and an icepack against her foot.

"Marta," I said. "Do you mind if I ask you something?"

"Of course, dear." She smiled amicably.

"You were a tempestaire, weren't you?"

Her eyes widened, her skin flushing blue once again. "I... well... I..."

Lucas raised his brow.

I stepped over and squeezed her hand. "It's okay. Don't try to speak."

"I'm good, dear. Just a little something in my throat." She took a sip of water. "I'm perfectly alright."

Lucas adjusted her icepack. "Marta, I hate to leave you so suddenly, but Camille and I have to be going." Yep. We had to discuss this.

"Of course. Don't let an old lady hold you up. You be on your way, and I'll get back to watching *Les Enfants du Paradis.*"

He nodded. "Alright. But call if you need me." And the Men would keep an eye on her.

"Take care of yourself, Marta," I said as we left the room. "And lock up after us."

"Will do, dear. As soon as my foot eases a bit."

We headed out, the rain soaking us in an instant. The moment I pulled the door closed, Lucas turned to me. "If she's a tempestaire, that means she has weather magic."

"But they were linked with the church, right? So did they know about the hidden world?"

He frowned. "It's highly unlikely. They used incantations in the form of prayer or hymns, but that was as far as it went."

"One thing is for certain, Nora and Ludger's death have to be connected."

"It seems likely. I'll get the others to focus their investigations on storms and tempestaires." Lucas chewed his cheek, the play of his skin intriguing, glinting with moisture. "And it was curious that Romaine said we were to blame for the hinder. I'm not sure what he meant by that."

My gaze fell to his solid chin, his firm, straight lips. Frustration tore through me. With the distraction over, I was back to thinking about him again. Talk about a one-track mind. All I could do was dig my fingers into my thighs, trying not to show it, but I'd had absolutely enough. I took a deep breath. "If only we could make Ignace talk. And the hinders have to be a family thing as both Nora and Marta are affected. I wonder if Eva is involved?"

"We'd better pay her a visit at work." Lucas reached out and brushed a raindrop from my nose.

I froze.

The gesture had been nonchalant, yet it had been so familiar, so intimate, my chest excruciatingly raw. I wanted him to do it again. I wanted to take his soaking wet face into my hands, cup the solidity of his jaw and draw him toward me, and...

No, no, no, no, no.

I wasn't supposed to be thinking like that, for heaven's sake.

Thunder rumbled softly, the storm breaking. What with this, my dream and the jumble of emotions from Ludger and Alice, I was exhausted. "I'm going to give Eva a miss. I'm tired after last night. But you go." It wouldn't take both of us. All I wanted to do was return home, take the sleeping draft and sink into oblivion until morning.

CHAPTER 23

I STEPPED OUT OF THE SHOWER, WRAPPED MYSELF UP IN towels and headed into the living area of the loft. I'd had to fight myself not to drive back to town and climb Cap de Couronnes to immerse myself in the storm once more. It was as though it called me, its vitality stirring my blood and stoking the rawness in the centre of my chest, which had only worsened since earlier.

Despite the wind blustering about the loft and the squall driving against the windows, it was hot again. I was hot. All I could think of was how Lucas had brushed the raindrop away. I'd wanted to respond. I really had. But it didn't make sense. Nothing made sense. He was so confusing. We were partners, and I had to hold on to that. Being a Keeper was damned important to me, and I wasn't going to ruin that or the firm friendship we'd built.

I pulled on knickers and an oversized T-shirt, then grabbed Lucas's tonic from the bedside table and knocked it back. It tasted of rosemary and something earthy. Of him, or at least how I expected he would taste if I...

Heavens, would I give it a rest?

I opened the French windows in the sitting area and the small casement near my bed. The wind gusted through, but did little to cool me as I sank into the mattress, shoving the covers aside. My eyelids were heavy, my limbs deliciously relaxed thanks to the tonic, yet still so much roiled and whirled through me. Desire... frustration... resolve to preserve what Lucas and I had...

But as sleep swept me away, I could still feel the rawness, the piercing anguish that hid behind everything else. And all of it stormed at the edge of my dreams, gusting and twisting, until once more, I was borne on the wind.

For a moment, I resisted, hovering over the farm, Delphine casting a wary eye up at me from her bed amidst the bushes on the slopes below the yard. I was supposed to be resting, but how could I with the tumult inside me. No, better I release it so I could sleep properly.

With that resolution, I rose above the farm and soared high over Picou de Bompas, thoughts of Lucas vying with my determination to protect our Keeper partnership, all of it swelling, rolling, gathering charge, building momentum, drawing me across the valley to Cap de Couronnes. I swirled around the stones on the summit, the conduit between land and sky lending me vigour, then I rose once more and scarred the sky with a myriad of blazing ribbons, thunder cracking, rain lashing in torrents.

And yet I needed more. I always needed more.

"Camille..." That voice again, rumbling my name, the air reverberating with it. And deep, sonorous laughter echoing about.

Curiosity unfurled amidst the tumult. "What do you want?" I called as I circled the town.

"I want you," the storm boomed. "I need you, Camille. A life, a focus. I need you, as you need me."

I did need it. If it wasn't for the storm, there would be no release, no respite from the turmoil that was surging again.

I soared higher, then swept along the Vicdessos valley, wheeling over Lucas's house, the tempest within a dizzying spiral at the thought of him beneath. It spurred me onward, and in moments, I was careening above Sem, the dolmen below, and then Rancié, the dark openings of the mine where Anthras had done his worst leading into the underworld.

All about lay small fields, clinging to the mountainside as if they might be reclaimed by nature at any moment. In their midst stood a grey limestone farm, an ancient tractor parked in the lane.

A figure shifted in the farmyard, a man attempting to pin a tarp down over open silage bales. Rain blasted into him, his waterproofs streaming, his hood blown off. And still the tumult inside of me swelled and crackled.

But in the back of my mind, beyond the storm, something tugged at me. A memory, recent and raw. Another farmer struck down.

I couldn't do it again... I couldn't.

But I wanted release. I *needed* it.

I rushed over the farm in a fierce ravage, fighting what I

so desperately wanted, my gusts unfocussed, tearing the tarpaulin from the figure's hands so it flailed about. But something scraped along my flurries, something pale and slick and horrendous. Pestilence slunk into the farmyard. I gusted against it, but still it came, its touch nauseating, crippling. My thoughts twisting, I contorted and spasmed, pain splintering my bones.

With an ear-splitting screech, it furled about the rain-drenched figure, small eyes bulging amidst a bullish face. My tumult surged. But I couldn't do it again. "I don't want to," I cried.

"Let go, Camille," the storm resounded. "I need you to let go."

"No," I screamed, desperately trying to hold back everything that brimmed. "I won't do it."

The pestilence wove its way around the man, shrieking a single drawn-out word. "Death."

I could resist no longer. I extended my arms and let rip into the farmer's chest. He slammed down onto the drenched concrete, a smoking, blackened husk. Whipping about the farm, I stared at him, dumbstruck.

Yet still I needed more.

"Rrraaaaaaaaaagh!" The storm roared and cracked. "You resist me, Camille. You who cannot even confront yourself. Why do you persist in holding everything within?"

"You," I bellowed, hurtling over the mountains to sweep along the Ax valley toward Tarascon, needing to get away. "You made me do that."

I rose above the town, fury impelling me to a frenzy. And

there, standing on the summit of Picou de Bompas, high above the farm, was another figure. He was lithe yet robust, anchored to the land, his hair a mess in the wind. My tumult raged, close to flashpoint at the sight of him.

"There," the storm rumbled. "That is the reason you restrain yourself..."

I swept over the peak, swaying bushes and bending trees. And right at the top, I stilled, coming back to myself, planting my feet firmly on solid earth.

Lucas stood stock still a little way off, gaping.

I was vaguely aware of my sodden T-shirt and drenched hair thrashing about, of my bare feet digging into mud and stones, but I was more aware of the energy shuddering within.

"Camille," Lucas called. He took a tentative step forward, his hands raised, water running down his face, his shirt and trousers saturated. "I don't know what's going on, but let's just get you back to the farm, and we can sort everything out." More tentative steps, his gaze wary, assessing.

I could feel his fervency, his fealty stirring me to my core, tugging at feelings he had no right to disturb. The storm spoke the truth. Everything swelling within me, absolutely *everything*, was down to this one man, this passionate, committed, brave, stalwart fae—*he* was the root of my desire, *he* stirred the rawness in my chest, the agony I would do anything to avoid, *he* made me storm and fly and release because he scraped at my heart and cut into my soul. "Damn you," I cried. "What are you doing to me?"

Lucas's eyes grew wider. "Camille, let me come to you." More steps.

"No, it's you. You're my problem. You're the reason I'm losing it." I propelled the gale into him, shoving him back. But pushing him away wasn't enough. I had to be rid of him, to protect myself, to shield all that was defenceless and exposed. My tumult within gathered force, one with the storm, static swathing me. I thrust out my hands. A luminous bolt rent the air, streaking into Lucas's chest.

He stood there, stunned. I sent another bolt, then another. Convulsing, he fell to the ground, but I could still feel life flowing in his veins.

He raised his head, then struggled up. Damn him, he was indestructible.

Unfurling my fingers, I released everything I had into him. This time, he dropped down, lifeless.

CHAPTER 24

STRUGGLING OUT OF RAGGED DREAMS, I TURNED OVER IN bed, my covers tangled around my limbs. Unease seeped through me, woven with a multitude of impressions— swirling above the town, writhing in terrible pain, releasing bolts of light into an old man and... Lucas. My heart beat heavily, as though it would bury me. I'd done that to him. I'd hurt him. But while the images seemed so real, they were fuzzy, distorted, distant. A nightmare.

Of course it had been a nightmare.

I turned over again, my blood cold, and shit, I ached, although ache was much too mild a word. I felt as if my bones had been put in a coffee grinder, and for some reason my chest throbbed terribly. And still I could see Lucas lying upon the ground. I'd dreamt of Ludger, and he'd died—what if the same had happened to Lucas? The chill in my blood seeped to my skin.

Tearing myself from the images, I sat up and forced my

eyes open, clasping the sheet before me, an anchor to reality. The blurry room eased into clarity, the dresser opposite the bed, the seating area by the French windows, the heaps of washing. It was all so normal, so why was dread a dead weight in my chest? And there was a clinking sound... as if someone was cooking.

I struggled to focus on the kitchen. Lucas stood behind the unit, a frying pan in his hand. Everything slowed, relief washing over me. I couldn't believe it, he was fine. It really had been a nightmare. I rose and tucked the sheet around me, wobbling a little. I wanted to rush over, to wrap my arms around him and bury myself in his solidity. Instead, I took a few stumbling steps, then paused, my breath erratic, my limbs stiff.

Those intense eyes narrowed as he met my gaze. His white linen shirt was rolled up to the elbows, the sinews along his arms flexing as he shook the frying pan. The aroma of coffee and something delicious wafted through the loft.

"Morning, Camille," he said softly with a ghost of a smile.

For a moment, I didn't know how to reply. The shadowy impressions of my nightmare blended with the memory of him close to death in Grimmere, and a wave of desperation crashed over me. The idea of him dying was terrible, awful, too much. I shook myself and tried to swallow everything away. "These dreams are really screwing me up. I thought you were... I thought I'd..."

He went to the sink, ran a glass of water and passed it to me, then stepped back to the pan and gave it a shake. He was cooking an omelette, and it was totally incongruous. I had no idea why he was here.

I drew the sheet tighter, cotton brushing against my skin. Other than wearing half my bed, I was naked, and Lucas was in my loft. I groaned. "We didn't, did we?"

"Didn't what, Camille?" His gaze lingered, the corner of his mouth flickering up.

"Didn't get plastered and... I mean, of course we didn't. But I have the hangover from hell, and what other explanation is there for you being in my loft?"

"You don't remember last night, do you?" His expression levelled.

"No, I... uh... well, I took your tonic and went to bed." He had to be here for another reason. If only I could clear my head and think straight. I gulped down the water, tracking his movements as he handled the pan. The last person, other than me, who'd cooked anything here had been Extreme Sports Alex. He'd managed to burn pasta, and weirdly, it fed into the aching in my chest.

Urgh, *Extreme Sports Alex*. I'd tried, I really had, and finishing it had been beyond painful. I hated that someone had made me feel so damned awful—that he'd cut so deep by mere negligence.

And now, the place appeared tidy, the sofa straightened, the kitchen surfaces clear and the pile of perpetually replenishing clean dishes gone, as though Lucas had broken a dark enchantment.

Shooting me a side-eye, he slid the pan from the heat and clicked off the gas. "It was a rather electrifying night."

My stomach lurched. "What the hell does that mean?" It had been a little too close to my nightmare for my liking.

He undid a button at his chest, then another. I narrowed my brow. He pulled his shirt up over his head and tugged his arms out of the sleeves.

"Uh, why are you undressing?" He looked better than anyone had a right to, all ridges and V-cut and solid bronzed pecs scattered with hair. I couldn't pull my gaze from the strong lines of his neck and the light that glinted along the sturdy curves of his shoulder muscles. And yet strange, fractal-like patterns mottled his skin, tattoos forking smaller and smaller. Intrigued, I stepped forward and ran my fingers over the darkest of them scored across his chest. He inched back, his throat rising and falling.

"There's a small problem we need to talk about. The matter of three hundred million volts shooting from your hands."

"What?" Blood drained from my face, from every part of my body. "It wasn't real. It couldn't have been." And yet I knew the truth in my aching bones. Dismay coursed through me.

"What do you recall?"

I could only stare at him, unable to comprehend that somehow I'd been one with the storm, and that I might possibly have hurt him. "I... I was riding on the wind again, but it's all hazy, a muddle." My fingers tightened around the sheet. "But I couldn't have been." I let out a brusque laugh. "I can't fly like Superman."

Lucas's face grew dark.

I drew into myself, trying to remember. "I couldn't think straight, and there was so much pain, and it was speaking to me—"

"What was?"

"The storm, it wasn't happy. I... I think it was using my emotions, as if they were fuelling it, but they weren't enough." It had wanted me to let go, which was strange because, as far as I could remember, it had used me just fine.

"And it was angry with you—no, *I* was angry with you." I'd been furious with Lucas because *he* provoked the pain in my chest. I could feel it now, an agonising wound open and exposed. It was *him*. *He* was stirring everything up.

My heartbeat grew heavier still, all of me weak because... shit... it *did* go deeper than physical attraction. Far, far deeper, and it was so excruciatingly painful that I had absolutely no idea what to make of it. All I could do was stare at him, my pulse thudding in my ears.

"What then?" he asked.

I was at a loss for words, my tongue thick, but I had to pull myself together. There was so much more at stake than whatever was going on between me and Lucas. "Uh, then I... uh... let rip." I winced. It was all too ridiculous, flying on the wind, blasting Lucas, but considering Ludger the other night, I had to go with it. What's more, the evidence was branded into Lucas's skin. He should have been dead. "How did you...?"

"Survive?" He pulled his shirt back on. "One of a drac's strengths is resistance to lightning. Although apart from a rather unpleasant encounter with a giant electric eel in a flooded copper mine, I've never had to try it out. I think I passed out back there... at least twice." He shuddered.

"I'm... I..." How could I ever apologise for *that*?

"Hey," he breathed. "I do know that in your right mind you wouldn't have hurt me."

But I had. Nausea swirled my stomach. "What the hell is happening?"

He opened his mouth, but I raised a hand. "Wait, there's going to be an utterly bizarre explanation for this, and I need the basics first, like how I got back here and"—my voice grew shrill—"why the hell I'm not wearing any clothes."

Lucas walked past and grabbed the heap of dirty underwear by my bed. I wanted to protest that my partner shouldn't be tidying my things, that my laundry wasn't the most pressing matter at the moment, but it was so inconsequential after what I'd done that I couldn't bring myself to say anything, and by the look of his face, he was attempting to piece together his thoughts.

All I could do was watch as the bundle made its way into the kitchen in his hands. He opened the washing machine door, then turned to me. "After what you told me about the night before, I had the Men watch you. They alerted me when you left the farm wearing nothing but a T-shirt for a midnight walk in the storm."

He put the washing in the machine, added liquid and switched it on. Such an everyday act, so incongruous against the bizarre images in my head. "They followed you up to Picou de Bompas," he continued, "where they lost you. I came as quickly as I could, and well, when I got there, you greeted me warmly." He pressed his lips together. "When I came to, you were slumped on the ground unconscious. I carried you back to the loft. The Men brought over a few supplies, and I've taken healing potion, so I'm good." He palmed his chest. "At least, I'm getting there."

I shifted the sheet. "And, uh, my clothes...?"

"You were soaking wet and unconscious, not to mention the *crack, crack, boom.*" He did an impression of me blasting him, then leant against the machine. "I had no idea if you were hurt, so I cut off your T-shirt and examined you."

He'd had his hands on my naked body, *again.* Despite everything, despite the horror and guilt, heat rose in me.

"What's the matter?" He smirked. "It's not like you to be bashful."

Embarrassment hadn't caused my flush, but I wasn't going to say that.

His gaze drew steady. "I'm a doctor, Camille. It's my job."

"I can go with that," I murmured.

"How are you feeling now? No residual sensation?" He peered at my fingers with morbid fascination.

I stretched out a hand and he flinched.

"I'm fine." More images flashed before me. The mountains, Rancié... a terrified face. My nausea redoubled. "Please tell me no one else died."

Lucas froze. "I can't do that."

A bullish expression and beady eyes. "Mean Gert," I scraped out, a fresh swathe of dismay closing my throat. I could see him, a burnt shell on the ground.

Lucas drew a breath. "We have a serious problem on our hands."

My throat tightened a little more. "And I'm it."

"I think you're linked in some way."

"Alright, tell me what's happening. I need to know."

His lips grew thin. "I can't be sure, but we have to entertain the possibility that a demonic presence is involved."

"What?" I gaped.

"There's a chance you're being possessed."

I shook my head. I wanted to laugh it away, but I couldn't. Something had me under its control.

Lucas massaged his jaw. "Actually, considering what happened, I don't have any other explanation."

I met his gaze, dread seeping through me. "Tonight, it's going to happen again. Why wouldn't it? I can feel the storm building already."

"Ludger and Gert were part of a close-knit group of farmers, weren't they?"

"There were four of them, with Ignace and Alf. And Ignace was terrified when he called in on Marta. I think he knew something was going to happen." I could still see Gert's face, the terror, then the stillness. "We have to find a way to stop me. I can't take another innocent life."

"I'll have the Men watch the other farmers, although there's not much they can do against lightning. And I'm going to keep an eye on you, stick by your side." He fixed me in the eye, sussing my reaction.

I appreciated it, but it didn't make sense. "You were my target. It's too dangerous."

"Given that I'm the only one with resistance to lightning, we don't have a choice. Anyway, I was the storm's target, not yours."

I wasn't so sure about that. But I'd done my worst to him, and I hadn't managed to kill him—that was something. "Alright. But I want you to use any means necessary to stop me striking again."

"I'll do whatever it takes." His jaw stiffened. "You said the storm was using your emotions somehow."

Using my utter turmoil about him. "I'm certain of it." And it wanted more. It wanted everything I was holding back. But I would never leave myself so exposed.

"Then there may be something I can do."

Chapter 25

"Where the hell are Nora and the rest of them?" Lucas paced back and forth along the length of the Keepers' post library.

"It's most unlike Gabe to be late," Roux muttered from his seat at the head of the reading table with a large ornate volume, *The Frippery of Storms*, propped open before him.

And it really was late. When I'd woken it had already been midday. I'd showered quickly and Lucas had insisted I have some lunch. Despite my churning stomach, I'd eaten a little omelette because he'd made it for me, and because I was utterly drained. And even though I'd forced it down, I had to admit, it was the best I'd tasted.

Lucas paced faster, which was doing little to calm my nerves, his restlessness a visual of my dire predicament. The thought that an unknown quantity could take hold of my mind and use me to kill was incomprehensible. I wasn't in control of myself, and if we didn't figure out what was going on, I would strike again, tonight. On top of that, Nora was in danger, and somehow, through the farmers and Marta, it was all connected. I fought to breathe steadily and maintain focus, but it was a struggle.

What I wouldn't do for a normal day at the café. At some point while I'd been out cold, Lucas had called Alice to say I wouldn't be in, and he'd arranged a locum for his practice. All we needed now was the gang. So far, their research had been invaluable.

I shifted on my stool, my elbows digging into the reading table as I flicked through a chapter on storms in *Demons and Demonic Fae*. The heavy velvet curtains were open, sunlight illuminating the books sprawled over the table, and the scents of sage and peppery chasteberry wafted in from the potion Lucas was brewing in the kitchen. He was convinced it would help with the storm, though he'd sent a message to La Vieille to check it wouldn't interfere with the bond tomorrow. My fingers were firmly crossed that she'd give the go-ahead. I'd do whatever it took to prevent a repeat of last night.

"What I don't get," I said, putting my book down, "is that the word 'demon' has been used to describe so many creatures. Practically anything with a negative connotation, from the various manifestations of Aherbelste to dracs and maloumbro, so what are we actually looking for?" I picked up my mug of hazel leaf tea and took a sip, the heat warming me through. Roux had made it, the hazel a protection against lightning. I doubted it would do me much good, but I could do with all the help I could get, and it had been sweet of him.

Lucas swung around and paused. "In theory, a demon is a powerful entity of any kind with harmful intent. Sometimes the more incorporeal types use a human focus to channel power." He continued wearing out the flagstones.

"I was pretty sure the storm had said that was why it needed me."

Roux nodded, his bony fingers and ragged nails gripped tight around his tome. "A demon with a human focus is extremely potent, although it's very dangerous for the subject. And it goes without saying that we're looking for a being with forceful storm magic. More so than your average fae with influence over the weather."

Their words stirred a memory, one I couldn't quite put my finger on. I picked up my book and continued leafing through.

Lucas's phone pinged. He glanced at the screen. "It's Félix. They're following a lead and can't make it, though they're emailing some information." His jaw grated. "They better not be in trouble again."

"You're telling me," I said. "I'm going to give them hell about that dwarf last night."

Lucas slid onto the stool opposite and opened his laptop. "Nothing yet." He cast the briefest of looks at me. Not one of his carnal scorchers of late, but one filled with rock-hard tenacity. I was getting used to his mannerisms, and it was his default cover-up for serious worry in dire circumstances.

And I'd almost killed him.

My throat grew unbearably dry as mortification swathed me—mortification and everything I'd felt for him last night...

that I still felt for him. That pain, that rawness... it was *horrible.*

"Camille, are you alright?" He'd noticed. He always noticed. And I was so utterly far from alright. "I'm good." I attempted to draw a deep breath into my tight chest.

"We will sort this." There was a surety in his voice that I didn't possess.

Roux placed his tome down. "I do think it would be best to get on with the update if we are to help Camille."

I tried to straighten my thoughts. Best I channel my nerves into this. I drew a shaky breath. "So Marta is a tempestaire who can control the weather. Ignace went to her for help, which means he and possibly Alf are wise to her abilities, and there's a chance they know what's going on— and maybe Marta does too." I drummed my fingers on the table. "But she and Nora are hindered. Something that Romaine and the Rôdeurs are aware of. If we can figure out who cast the hinders and why Nora has been stealing, we may be able to get her off the hook, and that might give us information about the storm."

Lucas fixed me in the eye. "Although right now, our priority has to be you. I'm hoping the potion will help, but"— he glanced at Roux—"if Camille takes off up the mountain again, is there anything I can do to restrain her? Obviously, I have physical means, and I have the Men."

I had a vision of a hundred pint-sized prehistoric warriors sitting on me. "Wonderful."

Roux massaged his chin. "Well, there's the bonevetch the boys stole from Pare Gégant. It's one of the few herbs that offer significant protection against malevolent entities, and it's the only one we have here. That's all I can think of."

"Good. I'll grab some on my way out." Lucas went back to scrolling on his laptop.

"Any leads on our research?" I had zero to contribute, although demonic possession was a legit excuse, and there was still that something at the back of my mind I couldn't quite grasp.

"I had a chat with Mushum," Lucas replied. "He said that whatever was going on, it didn't involve his friend, the wind. And I've asked around about unusual fae activity in the area, but there's been none."

I rubbed my face. "Roux, please tell me you have something."

"Well, the Rôdeurs aren't fae." He squirmed a little, his stool creaking. "And both feathers from Nora's house were indeed from a vulture, which is anomalous, although there is nothing peculiar about them. However, the Men did find a couple more at Gert's farm. As for Marta and Ignace, I've not found anything. We only have the newspaper report mentioning their engagement."

He'd been busier than I had, that was for sure.

"Oh," he continued, "and I went to Notre-Dame-de-la-Daurade and asked Father Sédir about tempestaires. He informed me that Marta was the last in the area and that she didn't indulge in the practice. He was quite a friendly chap, I have to say. Although he kept glancing at my socks, which was somewhat unsettling. But that could have been because I was wearing my lucky Aherbelste pair that Jean gave me."

I glanced down at his sandals perched on the rung of his stool. His luminous orange socks sported a large black effigy of the horned goat god surrounded by various occult sigils. Yep, that probably did it. Aherbelste had been adopted by Christians as the devil, even though I could attest from experience that he was really quite amiable.

I drew myself from the neon stinging my eyes. "But with Marta being a tempestaire, what if she's doing something to the storm—to me? She can't go out with her foot hurting, but could she be influencing things from home?"

"If she was," Roux said, "she'd be recounting prayers or possibly singing. The old enchantments were adapted by the church. Oh, and interestingly, I've read in here"—he tapped *The Frippery of Storms*—"that tempestaires were thought to run in families on the female side."

"Now, that *is* curious," I said. "It extends the whole tempestaire thing to Eva and Nora."

"Slaughter," Lucas called. "What has the Ruiz family been up to?"

The leader of the Men of Bédeilhac popped out from under the table, his eyes shining, his beard smartly puffed. "Marta has been crocheting mainly. She's managed a whole basket of kitty-warm jackets for the cat's shelter. The lads are bringing her icepacks when she's asleep. She thinks Nora has turned over a new leaf."

"Any sign of praying or unusual activity?"

He shrugged. "She did say, 'Jesus Christ in Heaven, Mary Mother of God and all the saints, my foot hurts.'"

"I think we can let that slide," I said.

"Eva's been sleeping and doing chores," Slaughter added. "And Nora has spent most of the time with the gang doing research. Right now they've gone for a walk by the river."

I scowled. "*A walk by the river?* And they're too busy to make it?"

Lucas ground his teeth. "And what about the Rôdeurs?"

"They went their separate ways. Been texting one another, though, and we're not able to see what they're writing, as we're not good with electrical equipment."

"Thank you," Lucas said.

Slaughter disappeared behind his leg.

Lucas's laptop pinged. "The email." He scrolled through, his gaze darting across the screen. "This is interesting. The gang appears to have gathered information from news reports and forums. They've flagged up a number of crimes by suspected gang members as having possible connections to fae. In two counts of bribery, five charges of harassment and numerous thefts, the police noted that the victims were involved in 'unusual herb usage', 'pagan rituals', or that there had been some sort of correspondence mentioning fae."

"Telling, indeed," Roux muttered.

"When we rescued Ignace, I mentioned the hidden world, and the Rôdeurs called us freaks..." I grasped my tea and took a mouthful.

Lucas nodded. "Could we be dealing with some kind of vigilante fae prejudice?"

"It's not unheard of," Roux said.

"And that would denote a degree of knowledge of the

hidden world," I added, "even if the Rôdeurs couldn't actually see it."

Lucas met my gaze, those dark irises holding so much, seeing way too far into me. "Camille, is there anything else at all that you can remember about the storm?"

I closed my eyes and forced a replay whilst desperately trying to blank out Gert and Ludger. I could see myself gusting over Tarascon, releasing light, swirling, spinning above the town and... Cap de Couronnes. That was odd. I'd been compelled to walk there each evening, although I'd resisted last night and ended up on the summit with the storm anyway.

"Up there." I pointed roughly in its direction. "There are stones. I'm sure the place is connected as I was drawn to it each time."

Lucas rubbed his forehead. "I do remember seeing a building on Cap de Couronnes, but it was years ago, and I only noted it from the town."

With his fae age, I hated to think what that meant.

"There are ruined huts and barns all over the place," Roux said, getting up stiffly. "Although Cap de Couronnes is a rather exposed position." He headed to the stack of scrolled maps, pulled out a couple and rolled them out on the end of the table. "Here it is." He ran his finger over one, then glanced between us. "It was an exconjuradora, a storm oratory."

My lips parted. "Tempestaires used them for conjuring."

Roux returned to the head of the table and picked up his

tome. "I'll see if there's any mention of the place." He flicked through, mumbling to himself.

"If only we could persuade Romaine to talk," I said to Lucas. "But fat chance. Though it might be sensible to pay Alf a visit."

"Agreed," he said. "And Roux, can you put up wards around the farmers' properties, and strengthen those around Camille's, ideally without worrying Izak."

He looked up from his book. "I can certainly do Camille's, but as for Ignace and Alf..." he cleared his throat. "Well, it would mean access to their properties, and as I'm... uh, not regarded well in that circle, I doubt they'd be receptive."

He had a point. The eccentric town drunk doing a ritual on their land wouldn't go down well.

"I may be able to sneak in, though," he added.

Lucas nodded. "Do it. And the only other person that might have an inkling of what's going on is Eva. I didn't have a chance to visit last night, what with everything. We should talk to her before..." He glanced out of the window.

I tilted my chin. "Before your partner goes all demonic again?"

"Got it in one." He began rifling through the mess of books on the table.

I drew a deep breath as I skimmed *Demons and Demonic Fae* once more, and still the niggle remained that there was something I was missing. But maybe I was looking in the wrong place. I pulled out my phone and scrolled through one of Margo Joly's folklore papers that I'd downloaded from JSTOR.

"As for Romaine, perhaps I can persuade him to be more friendly." An evil glint lit Lucas's eye.

If it took persuasion to help Nora, I wasn't totally against it. I continued scrolling, and "demon" caught my attention. My heart thumped. There it was—the niggle. A brief entry in a paper I'd read years ago about a Mesopotamian entity with a connection to the area.

I placed my phone down and ran my hands through my hair, glancing from Roux to Lucas. "Uh... I think I may have found our culprit."

Their heads shot up.

"Pajuzu," I said.

Lucas's lips parted. "That sounds a lot like Pazuzu, the Assyro-Babylonian god."

"The personification of the southwest wind," Roux murmured, "and the sovereign over the wind demons of Mesopotamia."

The back of my neck prickled. The storms had come from the southwest.

Lucas's lip twitched. "Wasn't Pazuzu in *The Exorcist*? Is your head going to start spinning?"

I glared at him. "If it does, you're the one who will have to deal with it. And anyway, that wasn't an accurate portrayal."

Lucas frowned. "But that's Mesopotamia, Camille. Pazuzu is not a Pyrenean deity. Fae tend to stick to their regions, having power in their locales. Why would he be here, using you?"

I had an answer for that. "Over the centuries, the old storm lore was thoroughly replaced by a Christianised version. Storms were attributed to the devil or witches under his command, and in this area we lost all knowledge of specific storm demons. Except for one. Pajuzu... most likely a corruption of Pazuzu. Prayers were recited in the exconjuradoras mentioning his name. The Priest of Saravillo is recorded to have evoked him to cast hail on the village of Plan, and the priest of Abiego did the same on Bierge. It's probable the demon was introduced to the area along with the oriental saints at the beginning of Christianity."

"Plan and Saravillo aren't far as the crow flies." Roux twisted his fingers together. "On the other side of the massif to the southwest."

"This might be it," Lucas said. "We need to look into him. Myths, legends, lore."

Roux's finger-twisting grew more frantic. "Though what good is it going to do us? Pazuzu—Pajuzu—is a god. He will have masses of power."

I bit my lip. No matter how potent he was, I wasn't going to let him use me to kill again.

Lucas's face hardened, his cheekbones appearing more severe than ever. "At least we have an idea of what we may be dealing with. And if I remember rightly, Pazuzu is an apotropaic entity. Yes, he's dangerous, but he's also known to repel evil."

I nodded. "He protects mothers and children. In

Mesopotamia, amulets depicting his image were worn and carvings were placed around homes to prevent the lesser wind demons causing havoc."

"Well, in this case," Lucas muttered, "he's up to no good."

"And what about the priests?" Roux asked.

I frowned. "What priests?"

"The ones who evoked Pajuzu to cast hail on rival towns. Could we be looking at a similar situation? Someone having evoked him. And could he have hindered Nora and Marta?"

Lucas nodded slowly. "I think we have to entertain both as strong possibilities. Pajuzu would certainly be able to cast a hinder." He met my eye. "But no matter how powerful he is, if he's using your emotions, the potion should help."

At this point, it was my only hope. "When will it be ready?"

"This afternoon."

"Alright." The sky still shone iridescent blue. We had time.

"Uh... boss?" A voice came from beneath the table. Slaughter had returned. "The Rôdeurs are following Nora, and I don't reckon they're up to much good."

CHAPTER 26

WE STOLE THROUGH WOODLAND ON THE EAST BANK OF the river, skirting willowherb and elder. Led by Slaughter, we headed for the Rôdeurs, who had left their pickup on a track a little further along.

I repeated to myself that we would sort everything out. That I wouldn't be used again tonight. Even so, my chest was still much too tight, although the physical activity was helping. And despite it all, I was painfully aware of Lucas—how his trousers shifted over his thighs as he walked, how his shirt bunched tight under his dagger hilt. It was as though I could sense him. If I closed my eyes, I'd know where he was, and it only went to stoke that rawness. Frankly, after my tumult of feelings last night, it was way too much, and I needed some headspace to process it all.

A shout came from beyond a clump of hazel ahead. "Get your hands off me, you asshole." Nora.

"Charge!" And that had sounded suspiciously like Félix.

"They've gotten themselves into trouble again, the idiots." It was the last thing we needed.

"We'll take it from here," Lucas said to Slaughter. "Go keep an eye on Marta and Eva."

"Yes, boss." He disappeared behind a tree.

Lucas and I slid between the hazels. We were much too close, his body pressed against mine, my blood humming in response. Given, this was the only way we could fit in the bush together, but it wasn't doing much to calm my nerves. At least there was no sign of the storm yet.

We peered out.

Romaine was dragging Nora down a wide track toward their truck a little way off, his arm locked around her neck, her cusses wild enough to shame the wicked. So now Romaine was abducting his own sister. What did he know that we didn't?

Bastien and the other two Rôdeurs were all vests and bulging, oiled brawn. They brandished knives, amusement flickering across their faces as the gang hurtled toward them. Félix and Zach were roaring and waving swords. Hugo almost knocked out Zach's eye with his quarterstaff. They'd taken weapons from the Keepers' post, damn it. And there was Gabe, standing at the back, muttering at something in his hand.

"Retreat, you foul, dungeon-dwelling scum!" Félix cried, his eyes burning with frantic fervour. Frustration swelled in my chest. Was he reciting a D&D script? Zach thrust his sword at nothing, his maniacal grin only making his thin face appear fragile.

"You shall feel the sting of our weapons," Hugo yelled, tripping over his quarterstaff.

They weren't going to help Nora, they were going to maim themselves. Mind you, Nora was doing a good job of helping herself. As Romaine attempted to pick her up, she twisted and writhed and drove her heels into his shins. "Get the fuck off!"

I made to spring forward but Lucas placed his hand on my arm, his touch rippling through me. "Perhaps they need some consequences," he murmured, his breath tickling my ear. "Something has to stop them interfering where they're not wanted, and the Rôdeurs won't do more than rough them up. They're thugs, not hit men."

"Watching teens being pulverised isn't exactly my thing," I whispered. But he had a point.

Zach lunged at the pockmarked Rôdeur, who side-stepped. As Zach nosedived, the brawn thrust his knee into his jaw.

I winced.

"Cleric down," Hugo cried, swinging ineffectually at the bulldozer.

Félix wasn't doing much better with Bastien. The leader of the Rôdeurs shifted his weight, avoiding his slow and predictable swipes. Félix's face contorted in rage. "Don't mess with us. Your information is in our hands, NightDestroyer. Who'd use MyMemberIsLarge as a password?"

The pockmarked Rôdeur snickered.

Bastien glared at him as he circled Félix. "How did you find that out?" he growled.

"He's the little faker who got into our group chat," Romaine yelled, his struggle with Nora unceasing.

For heaven's sake, they were in over their heads again. And why the hell did Félix think it was a good idea to divulge their cyber infiltration? If only the verity would get a move on and work its way out of their systems.

"Looks like I'll have to deal with you." Bastien slammed his fist into Félix's cheek.

My stomach lurched as he fell to his knees, blood gushing from his nose.

Lucas just grinned.

"Are you really taking pleasure in this?" I hissed.

He shrugged. "Yes."

The bulldozer caught Hugo's quarterstaff with one hand. With the other, he smashed into his gut. Hugo collapsed, gasping.

"Nope," I whispered. "I can't watch any more of this. You're so sadistic. And anyway, you're going to have to clean up their injuries."

"Not a chance," he rumbled. "I'll leave them to suffer."

As the other Rôdeurs secured the gang's wrists with cable ties, Bastien prowled toward Gabe, who was muttering wildly at his hand. "Gabe is most likely the innocent party in this."

Lucas ignored me.

"Freaky boy in a cloak," Bastien said. "What the hell do you think you're doing. Casting spells?"

Gabe dropped the contents of his palm and threw a punch into his face. I had to give him points for effort.

Bastien caught his fist and twisted his arm. Gabe screamed. The pockmarked Rôdeur tied his wrists and shoved him into the dirt.

I elbowed Lucas.

He grunted. "Alright. Do you want Bastien or Romaine?"

"Bastien and his lackeys. I feel like working off a little angst."

I stepped out of the bushes and strode over, not bothering to draw my dagger. I wanted to help Nora and get information, not take more lives. "Bastien, Rôdeurs, how lovely to see you. And yet, once again, you are messing with the townsfolk of Tarascon."

They turned toward me, eyes wary.

The gang groaned from the floor.

Bastien swaggered over, spinning his knife and mustering more confidence than he had a right to after yesterday. "If it isn't the waitress with a fancy for blades. My kind of kink. My kind of woman." His gaze trailed down my T-shirt to the dagger sheathed in the belt of my shorts. He licked his lips.

"Gross. Didn't anyone ever tell you, Bastien, that lip-licking is the ultimate turnoff?"

"High Warrior of the Borderlands," Hugo muttered from the ground, delirious.

Romaine and head-locked Nora were closer now, Lucas ushering them with his dagger from behind, his gaze blacker than black, no doubt from Bastien's comment. "Unless you want a repeat of last night," he growled, "don't move."

"Let them all go." I gestured from Nora to the boys sprawled about in various states of consciousness. I was pretty sure the Rôdeurs weren't interested in the gang, but they wanted Nora for a reason, and I doubted they'd give her up without a fight. She tried to shrug away from Romaine again, but he held firm.

"I don't think so." Bastien smirked.

"Do we really want to repeat yesterday?" I shook my head as condescendingly as possible.

Bastien nodded to the bulldozer. He came at me with his knife.

I swerved and struck my palms into either side of his wrist, a nice move Grampi had demonstrated. His blade fell from his grip.

Before he could respond, I booted his kneecap at just the right angle. A little well-applied technique was far more dangerous than pounds of muscle. He dropped like a stone. "Please don't make it too easy."

The pockmarked Rôdeur thrust his knife at my gut. I swivelled, grabbed his hand and used my momentum to bend his arm behind him. He crumpled forward and I drove my heel between his shoulder blades rather nastily. The dust cloud that rose when he slammed down was impressive.

In the corner of my eye, I caught Lucas laying into Romaine, Nora sitting a few steps away.

I turned to face Bastien, but he was already close, his blade plunging toward my shoulder, though an easy recovery would leave him vulnerable to a facial attack. As I slipped to the side, a roar filled the air. "Noooooooo!" Nora cried.

A blast of cold hurtled into me, and I hit the ground.

Something repugnant and deathly gusted over my skin, nausea rising in my throat.

I drew my head up. Wind whipped about, but not the typical gusts that tunnelled through the valleys, and not the whirr and rush of the storms I rode upon, but a pallid and sickening and utterly horrendous presence. It tore along the track in pale streaks, whipping around the Rôdeurs, its screeches joining with their panicked cries and the gang's moans, though it gave Romaine a wide berth. And... it was familiar, the way it shredded my thoughts and made my skin creep. Everything was hazy, but I was sure I'd felt it with the storm.

"What is this stuff?" Bastien yelled as the presence twined about him.

Lucas gritted his teeth against it.

Nora just stood there, unaffected, her hands on her hips, those cool eyes blazing. "I told you to get the fuck off me. And you can get the fuck off my friends too."

I gaped, my breath shallow.

Grimacing against the wind, Bastien turned on her. "She's one of them."

Romaine rose to face his sister. "You're as bad as the others," he shouted above the screeching. "We were trying to help."

"No way. We don't help freaks." Bastien made to knife me again, but the presence gathered around his chest and squeezed. His eyes bulged, his breath leaving him in a strangulated wail.

I tried to move, but embraced by the lifeless miasma, I

couldn't shift a muscle. I had no idea how to help him, and by the look on Lucas's face, neither did he.

"Enough!" Nora roared.

With an ear-splitting shriek, the wind twisted about her, then dissipated to nothing, leaving brown feathers eddying in the air.

Bastien and the stooges exchanged glances. As one, they hurtled off through the trees.

"You're sick," Romaine spat at Nora. "An abomination like the rest of them." With a withering glare, he sprinted off in the Rôdeurs' wake.

CHAPTER 27

Nora stumbled forward. Before I could move, Lucas was there, steadying her. When she raised her head, tears streaked her dusty cheeks. Whether they were for what happened with the wind or from Romaine's words, I couldn't tell. But I'd not seen her cry before. Lucas helped her to the ground, where she hung her head between her knees. "Crap, I feel sick." She wiped her face with her T-shirt.

"Take a moment," he said.

I knelt down by her side. "I'd like to ask you what the hell just happened. But I'm pretty sure you can't tell me."

She glanced up, her skin unnaturally blue. We weren't getting anything out of her.

Lucas strode over to the gang, who were groaning on the floor. He dug his boot into Félix's stomach, provoking a yelp and more groaning. "What do you lot not understand about keeping out of trouble?" he roared. "Why the fuck didn't you call us?"

"We only wanted to help," Félix muttered, the manic edge to his voice much too evident.

I rose and brushed the dust off my shorts as Lucas cut Félix's cable tie, then stepped over to Gabe and set him free, in no way being gentle with his injured arm.

"The others are having a reaction to verity," Lucas rumbled, the fury on his face a sight to behold, "but you..."

"We caught the Rôdeurs following Nora." Gabe was on the verge of tears, his voice high. "We knew the Men would warn you."

I shook my head. "And then you went in with weapons raised like you knew how to use them." My tone met Lucas's. "Weapons you stole from the Keepers' post."

"I... I... was trying to raise a protective ward," Gabe stammered. He managed to push himself up, his gaze fixed on Nora.

Lucas's eyes blazed as they locked on mine. "We could feed them to a maloumbro now and save us months of hassle."

"I'm all for the idea, but right at this moment, let's get a move on. I doubt the Rôdeurs will come back, but I don't want to risk them making another grab for Nora and that, uh... wind returning."

"Get up, you lot." Lucas cut Zach's and Hugo's ties, then gestured across the track. "Take the footpath. My car is by the road."

They stumbled to their feet, groaning and swaying.

"Men," he said. "Circle them. If they do anything, cut off their feet."

Zach turned green.

Gabe came over and offered Nora a hand.

She glared at him, her tears gone. "I'm fine."

He waited until she rose, then stuck by her side. They headed along the footpath with the others, ringed by Men. Lucas and I took up the rear.

"What just happened?" he whispered as we entered the woods, a deep score between his brows, his white linen shirt marred with dust. "I take it that presence wasn't your storm. It was nothing like last night."

Ahead, Félix's bloody T-shirt caught on a bramble. As he yanked himself free, he stumbled backward and fell into the thicket. Zach and a host of Men tried to haul him out.

"Jackass," Gabe muttered.

I pulled myself from the spectacle. "It definitely wasn't my storm. But I think I may have encountered the presence when I was with it." I tried to make sense of it all as I stepped over a fallen branch. "And it looked like Nora was in control back there. It must have been some sort of tempestaire display. It happened right when Bastien attacked me, and it shoved us apart." My brow furrowed. "I think she was trying to help."

"If she was, it was unlike any tempestaire activity recorded. They're known for controlling weather fronts, and that's it. And it means she may have a direct connection with the farmers' deaths, though I have no idea how."

I winced. As much as I didn't want to consider that she might be involved, we couldn't rule it out.

"And Romaine wasn't affected," he added. The road lay

ahead, Lucas's SUV tucked into the bushes at the side. "You lot," he called, "get in the back."

"One thing is for sure." I scraped the escaped strands of my ponytail behind my ears. "We need to talk to Eva... and Alf, if he's receptive. And we should probably do something with the Rôdeurs."

"I'd be tempted to report them to the police, if it wasn't for us needing them accessible and out of custody should we have to get heavy with Romaine."

"Agreed. And that's looking more and more likely."

"But for now I'll assign additional Men to Nora—"

A clamour rose from ahead. The gang was clambering into the SUV with fifty wild prehistoric warriors, who were cussing and hollering as they jostled for space. I hated to think what they were doing to the upholstery.

Lucas gritted his teeth. "Everyone in the back *but* the Men."

———

We strode up Rue du Bari, Lucas and me on either side of Nora, my sense of him acute. The street bathed in the afternoon sun, the scent of geraniums making my nose twitch. After we'd updated the gang about Pajuzu, we'd deposited them unceremoniously in the café car park, Lucas refusing them healing potion. He had, however, given them a large guard of Men, not just to prevent more stupidity but for protection in case the Rôdeurs retaliated against their cyber exploits.

Lucas studied Nora as we walked. "Roux was supposed to measure your thread at the meeting earlier. Has the knot moved?"

The noose hung low around her collarbone, sunlight catching gold where it emerged from under her bob, which was for once a little dishevelled. She rolled her eyes. "Of course I measured it. It's slipped about an eighth of an inch."

"The same amount as yesterday." At least it wasn't tightening more quickly.

"You really don't have to escort me home," she snapped for the third time since we'd gotten out of the car.

With Marta hindered, I had to wonder if home was the safest place for her. But after today's display, perhaps I should be more concerned for her family.

"The Men said the Rôdeurs are heading back to Toulouse," she continued, "so what's the trouble? What are you, anyway? The gendarmerie?"

"Nope, not the gendarmerie," I said. "Only a murderous drac and a woman possessed by the demon Pajuzu."

"Call it as you see it, Camille," Lucas muttered.

I glanced at Nora. "We just want to see you home safely, and we need to find out if Eva is hindered."

She didn't deign to give me an answer. Instead, she attempted to torch the street with her glare.

Madame Biscotte was striding down the hill, walking poles in hands.

"Afternoon," I called, waiting for a smirk or a comment about me being with Lucas again. But as we paused at Nora's house, she scurried past without a word, her face sallow.

I raised my brow. "What's up with her?"

"I have no idea." Lucas frowned. "That wasn't her usual cheery disposition."

Nora stepped up to the door and pushed the handle. It opened without a key. Clearly, Marta hadn't levelled up her security. As Nora entered, she swung the door back in our faces.

Lucas stuck out his foot and eased it open again. "Nothing like a warm welcome."

"Oh, Nora." Eva hurried into the corridor, dressed in her grey uniform, a pile of washing in her arms. "Doctor Rouseau? Camille?" She scoured her daughter's face, her brow creased in concern. "Is everything alright?"

Nora took a breath. "Completely. I was feeling a little sick and they gave me a lift home, that's all. They were just leaving."

"Doctor Rouseau," Marta called from the other room. "Fancy you being here again."

Lucas stuck his head around the door. "Marta. We're dropping off Nora. Foot alright?"

I turned to Eva as they continued their small talk. "Actually, Madame Ruiz, now I'm here, I wonder if I could ask you something?"

Nora blasted me with laser eyes.

"Of course," Eva said. "If it's quick. I've tons to do before work."

For a moment I wondered what she would say if I brought up Romaine. Did she know he was in the neighbourhood? But I had no idea what was going on, and I needed to focus on why I was here. "I was reading up about tempestaires, and the Ruiz name was mentioned. Do you know anything about the subject?"

Eva stared at me, her eyes widening. "Uh, uh—" Her breath caught, her skin flushing with a hint of ashen blue. She was hindered too. She tried to speak again, but only managed to croak, her hand reaching for her throat, her washing falling. Nora grabbed it and Eva released a volley of coughs.

"Can I help?" Lucas said. "A glass of water?"

Eva waggled her hand, indicating that she was fine. She looked anything but.

"I think you need to go." Nora caught some socks falling from her pile.

Eva managed to clear her throat. "I'm sorry, Camille, Doctor Rouseau." She coughed again. "But, uh, I'm not feeling a hundred percent. Perhaps we could talk another time?"

"Of course," I said. "Sorry to intrude."

As we made our way to the door, Marta called a cheery goodbye. We headed out, and Nora slammed the door behind us.

"So they're all involved," Lucas said.

Shouts came from inside. I couldn't catch the words, though some of them bore the gunshot force of Nora swearing her heart out.

Lucas tilted his head. "Eva wants to know where Nora

has been, why we had to bring her home, and why she hasn't done her chores. Nothing about tempestaires." The argument died away. "We'd better get to Alf and see what he knows."

I pulled out my phone for the time as we set off down the hill. "You go. I'm due to meet Alice for a self-defence lesson. I'd give it a miss, but she's struggling, and it won't take two of us to question Alf."

Lucas glowered at me. "You have to be joking. I'm not letting you out of my sight."

I glanced at the sky. "There's no way I'm going to risk zapping any more farmers." And that was the truth. The thought made my breath catch and an icy chill run down my spine. "But the storm is a long way off. I can feel it. It will come in tonight, as usual. But for now, I'll be fine."

"No," he said flatly.

We reached the SUV and climbed in.

I got that he was concerned, and the guilt about what I'd done to him last night was never going to release me, but the fervency in his set jaw and the fury he was giving off were damned unnerving. I had the notion it was directed at the storm, and frankly, it only made me more freaked out. But if the storm wasn't here, nothing would happen, and the distress in Alice's face when she'd explained how helpless she felt had been harrowing. "I'm meeting Alice, and I'm not going to argue about it. Send a load of Men with me if you like, but drop me off at the café. We'll meet later and I'll take the potion as soon as it's ready."

Lucas switched on the engine, the air conditioning

cooling my skin, his gaze boring into the road. "Camille..." His hands were ridged as he gripped the wheel. He was struggling with this, but there was something more, I was sure of it. Without thinking, I reached out to touch his arm, wanting to reassure him that I'd be fine, but I paused, thinking of those boundaries.

He turned and caught my fingers. I flinched as a surge of fury and frustration ripped through me. *His* fury and frustration. He gazed at me from under his brow, his eyes dark. "What is it, Camille?"

"I... I..." I didn't know how to shape the words, breath leaving me. "You..." I said. "Sometimes it's like I can feel you. What is it? I... don't understand." My throat stuck, his fingers burning into mine. "I guess I'm projecting... but, shit, this is so screwed up."

His lips parted as if he was searching for the right words.

But it struck me. "It's the Keeper bond, isn't it?" Keepers gained an instinctual awareness of each other for combat. It had to be a sort of foreshadowing.

His gaze lowered to my lips. "Yes, it's the Keeper bond. Maybe we're starting to feel it. But there's also the possibility of—"

"But that means you must be able to feel me too..." I hadn't even considered it.

His grip tightened around my fingers. He studied them for a moment, then hauled his eyes upward to mine. "Yes, a little. It's like you're the other half of me, and when you're out of sight, I'm on edge, irrational, completely out of it until I have you close."

"Half of you?" His words gouged at my chest, making the pain there so much worse. "I expected something to happen with the bond, but... this is all so intense." And I really wasn't sure I could handle it. I pulled my hand away and gazed out the window. "I need to meet Alice."

CHAPTER 28

"I just don't understand why my sense of Lucas is so strong." The rock I was sitting on by the riverbank dug into me, the sun blazing down as Alice, dagger in hand, repeated the move I'd shown her—an upward thrust that would slide under the ribs of an attacker to do serious damage. "The Keeper bond is supposed to heighten my awareness of him during combat. I can see that it might extend to other areas, but... I don't know. It's so *overwhelming*."

Alice tried the move again, then jumped up and down and shook out her arms. "I'm probably not the best person to ask as I know so little about fae."

I'd explained everything that was going on. Well, not quite everything. With her worries, I'd conveniently left out the part about me being possessed by a demon and slaughtering farmers. To put it another way, I'd updated her about Lucas and the gang's latest escapade.

Wrens scolded from the woodland at the edge of the clearing, their calls mingling with the lap of water at the riverbank and the soft grunts of the ridiculous amount of Men that Lucas had insisted accompany me. Most of them were dozing under the trees, their backs against trunks. A few stood alert, though. Slaughter gripped his axe tightly, his eyes narrowed on the sky as if it might put up a fight, which considering everything, wasn't beyond the realm of possibility.

Every part of me was tight, although I was attempting normality for Alice, my forearms resting on my knees, my dagger gripped loosely. But the storm would come. We hadn't gotten much closer to figuring out what was happening, and now my only hope was Lucas's potion and the bonevetch. But so help me Abellion and all the Pyrenean gods, I wouldn't kill another farmer.

Alice shimmied her shoulders and stepped back into an attack position. Her loose crochet top above floral shorts combined with abundant tinkling bangles weren't exactly the perfect combat gear, but she was trying, and that was what mattered. "Honestly, I think you need to look at your feelings. Like I said, maybe there's more there beneath the surface. At least you should explore the idea."

Yes, there was something under the surface. There was so much there that I couldn't come up for air. Her lips bunched as she thrust out at an invisible foe, managing to muster as much aggression as a wet lettuce, but she'd gotten the technique.

"You're doing great. Keep trying. If you repeat it enough, it will become second nature."

She stepped back. "But, Camille, I know you have feelings for that hot slice of moelleux au chocolat. I mean, even if they're friends-level feelings, you have them, and they might give you an insight into what's going on."

I shrugged, twisting the dagger in my fingers. "Yes, we have friends-level feelings. And"—I couldn't deny it after last night—"there may be something deeper under the surface, but the Keeper bond has nothing to do with that. It's a professional relationship."

"I knew there was more." She smirked, as satisfied as a cat licking cream from its paws. "But that's quite a turn-around. Yesterday you were adamant that there was nothing."

"Yeah, well. A lot has happened." I dug my shoes into the dust, my fingers tightening around the dagger. "And anyway, what Lucas and I have as friends—as partners—means so much. I'd never risk losing that."

She sighed and tried the move again, driving the dagger upward before sagging. "Honestly, what am I going to do? Kill someone? Wielding a dagger is just not me."

"It's for self-defence. A flesh wound will make an attacker think twice, but if you're in danger, go all out. You have nothing to lose." All she needed was some confidence.

I got up and tried a few lunges. She shook her head, watching me intently.

"What?"

"Look, Camille." She pressed her lips together, then released them, her cheeks flushed. "I get that you want to preserve the friendship you've built with Lucas, but I also know that you don't find it easy to open up. You never have. But maybe you should at least consider that these feelings might be important."

Yes, they were very important. They were crippling me. Oh, and they linked me to a murderous storm demon.

"And anyway," she continued, "it would do you good to have a proper relationship."

I stopped mid-lunge and faced her. "What the hell do you mean by that? I have relationships."

She snorted. "Screwing around doesn't count."

"I can't believe that came out of your mouth." Irritation raised my voice, consternation a wedge in my gut, though I had to admit, it wasn't entirely untrue. Even so, I'd had enough. "Alice, change the track. It's old, so old. I can't discuss anything without you taking apart my emotional state."

Her eyes flashed, her brow furrowing so deeply that lines puckered around her nose. "What the fuck, Camille. The whole town knows there's something between you and Lucas. Would you just take a look?"

I stared at her open-mouthed, my pulse hammering. "I can't believe you're pushing me on this. You're going off on one, like you always do." Anger swept through me. I couldn't wrap my head around her stubbornness, not after all we'd been through in Grimmere. I'd almost lost her. "You're not listening. It doesn't matter what's between me and Lucas, because I'm not going to risk what we have."

She strutted forward and poked her dagger at my chest, then thought better of it and threw it to the ground, replacing it with her finger. "No, you're not going to get out of this so easily. I'm going off on one because my best friend is ruining her life. Things with Extreme Sports Alex hurt like hell, not to mention that business with Madame Truffle. Add to that a lot of shit with Raoul and Gilles." She came right up to my face, her skin red, her jaw jutting. "What are you going to do?" she cried. "Live some half-life, denying yourself because you're too scared to face the consequences?"

My pulse hammered harder, my breath shallow. I was being sensible, keeping what was important safe. And she was totally out of line. "No, it's you. You've changed. You're struggling to cope with the hidden world and you're taking it out on me." I seethed the words. And damn it, I didn't need this now. Not with worrying about Nora, not with having almost killed Lucas, and most definitely not with the prospect of tonight.

"I've had enough of this," I growled, and stormed off along the riverbank, a host of miniature prehistoric warriors trailing in my wake.

CHAPTER 29

My blood boiling, I strode along the bank toward town, unable to comprehend how pig-headed Alice actually was. She was so out of line. It was like that time when we were eight and she locked me in a closet with scrawny little Mael. She wouldn't let me out until I'd invited him to see my comic collection. And maybe it hadn't been the worst move ever—I supposed I wouldn't have gotten the nerve otherwise —but she hadn't predicted that he'd be claustrophobic, because she didn't think. She *never* thought. After Mael's panic attack, the commotion with the ambulance crew and the wrath of his parents, he'd never made eye contact with me again. It was so typical of her, pulling her weight around because she knew me well. But it didn't mean she could make off-the-wall assumptions that she had no right to—

"Trust you to be disturbing the peace again," came a voice from the riverbank.

I spun around, a wave of Men drawing up short. The

river was narrower here, boulders lining the bank. On one sat a stunningly beautiful woman with sweeping ebony hair and light blue robes that tumbled from her shoulders. There was something familiar about her.

"Viveau?"

"Why, of course." She shot me a mischievous smile.

"I didn't recognise you." Underwater, she'd been barely distinguishable from the flow, not to mention naked, and now she looked so human.

"If it's not you being thrown into the river, it's you arguing on the bank." She rolled her eyes. "As if it hasn't been enough with our waters stirred each day, with stones cast in. But now, we're having to put up with *that*..." She gestured downstream, where a large branch had wedged between rocks a little way from the bank. Something black and rather bedraggled clung to it. She jutted her slender chin, her eyes glinting. "*That* is the last straw."

I didn't need anyone else's angst at the moment. But curiosity got the better of me. "What is it?"

Something thin stuck up in the air. A tail. "A cat?" A horrendous yowling issued from its mouth. I'd recognise that sound anywhere. "Madame Bovary?" But it couldn't be—the creature was too thin.

"Precisely." Viveau ran her hand down her robe, smoothing the edge. "And she's harming my waters. I have nymphs barely able to breathe under the surface."

Madame Bovary hissed and spat, the current gushing against her. She wouldn't hold on for much longer. "Shit." It looked like I'd have to do something, and it definitely didn't make me feel any better.

I spun around and scoured the Men. They were so crammed together, they formed a multitude of beards and skins and weapons. "Slaughter," I called.

He stepped out from amidst the throng. "Yes, ma'am."

"Get me the oven gloves from the Keepers' post."

"The ones woven in the Mount of Purity and blessed with the waters of protection, then triple-warded on a full blood moon against the most ferocious creatures of the night?"

"Yep, those." Roux had taken a lot of effort to create the perfect gauntlets. He had to remove the occasional sarramauca from a tree because unsuspecting folk developing severe asthma at the top of a ladder never ended well.

He disappeared behind a bush. Once I'd kicked off my trainers and socks, he was back, the gloves in his hands.

I pulled them on and took a deep breath. Chuntering to myself, I clambered down the bank and waded out, the water rising to my knees, then my waist. Honestly, I couldn't believe I was taking another dip because of a creature that was likely to suffocate me in my sleep.

"A little to the left," Viveau cried. "There's a trench ahead."

I glared back at her. "So helpful."

The water rose to my chest, the icy current rushing hard. I reached Madame Bovary, and the glare she cast me was beyond evil. Other than that, she really didn't look herself, her fur plastered to her body. It was surprising how thin she was under all that fluff. Only her gnarled whiskers remained proud. I shuddered and gripped her middle, but her claws were wedged into the branch. With another tug, she relented. She had to be exhausted. I held her in front of me, flailing, hissing and spitting, a blur of legs and teeth and tail, the water taking some of her weight.

"There, there, girl," I tried half-heartedly.

She only spat louder.

Okay, time for another tactic. "Why don't you calm the hell down," I growled, "and let me get you out of the water before you drown your little kitty ass."

She stilled, peered at me as though she was a spectre of death and it was my turn to feel the scythe, then continued her hissy fit. I shook my head and waded on. As the water grew shallow, I held her out before me, and damn, she was heavy, but there was no way she was going anywhere near my chest.

As I passed Viveau, she shrank back. "Don't bring that thing near me."

I clambered up the rocks, stepped onto the bank and placed Madame Bovary down.

"Wreeeaooooooowwww." She shook herself once, twice, three times, and her fur popped out, a resurrected pompom of doom. The fluff barely allowed her to see, only four feet and a tail escaping its bounds. She shot me a death stare for luck and sauntered off toward the bushes, the Men parting in a frenzy to allow her through.

I turned back to Viveau. "How the hell did she get into the river?"

She glanced up from examining her nails. "She was thrown in."

"What?" The thought that someone had actually chucked a cat in the river did nothing to improve my mood, and I didn't know anyone stupid enough to touch her voluntarily. "Who?"

"We didn't see. The first I heard of it was a splash as she hit the water over there." She nodded to the far bank downstream. "The reverberations of her yowling spread to every part of the river. By the time we investigated, she'd caught onto the branch. She's been there maybe ten minutes."

Viveau dangled her legs in the sarramauca-free flow and sighed, her skin a mere shimmer. "It was probably the miscreant who's been stirring our waters every day."

"Stirring the waters. Yeah, you said." It seemed like something a child would do, dangling over the bank, stick in hand. But throwing in a cat—a *sarramauca*—was another matter entirely. But then... both stirring the waters and throwing a cat in a river were traditional ways of evoking the weather, well documented in folklore.

I gaped at Viveau, my stomach knotting. "Someone has been calling the storms."

But more than that, now I wasn't so consumed with fury and didn't have a hellcat in my grasp, I could feel the cloud, building, rushing, billowing.

The sun darkened, and dread flooded through me.

Here it came.

Chapter 30

I sprinted through the woods, pulling my phone from my pocket, fear spiralling up. Fumbling to unlock the screen, I sprang over a bush, but before I could call Lucas, he rang.

I slammed the phone to my ear. "I'm almost at the parking area by our training spot."

"I'll be there in a second." He disconnected.

As I burst out of the woodland into the car park where we'd had the face-off with Pare Gégant, Lucas's SUV hurtled in, spun a handbrake turn and screeched to a halt. I jumped inside and we sped off, wheels spinning.

"I want to go home," I said through breaths. Roux had warded the farm, and I felt safe there. My only concern was Grampi, though there was no indication that the storm was malevolent to anyone other than the farmers... and Lucas.

"Alright." He pulled out onto the N20.

"Tell me the potion is ready and La Vieille approves."

"It's in my bag, and she's given her consent. She wrote that we had bigger things to worry about than a little potion. I take it she meant the storm." His lips tightened. "I also have the bonevetch with me and some, uh... rope."

I raised an eyebrow.

"In case I have to restrain you."

"This is going to be a bundle of laughs."

Flooring the accelerator, he overtook a lorry and slipped in before an oncoming camper, provoking a volley of horn blasts. A few dots of rain spotted the windscreen. I glanced up at the sky. Cloud covered half of it, building in angry billows from Rancié way. I ached to join it as much as I had every evening.

"I shouldn't have left you." His voice was a deep tremor. "It's coming in early."

"Someone evoked the storm. They threw Madame Bovary in the river. "

"The 'ol cat-in-a-river trick. Beats the shake-my-shoe-at-the-sky ploy anytime, in my opinion." He swung a right at the roundabout and we hurtled through the edge of town. "I'm taking it that's why your clothes are soaked... again?" Despite everything, the corner of his mouth tugged up.

"Yep." I was a sight, my socks and trainers squelching from having to put them on wet, my shorts and T-shirt sticking to me. "And whoever threw Bovary in has been stirring the waters all along. At least, that's Viveau's theory."

He dropped a gear and took the corner. "The Men said Nora was skimming stones yesterday."

I turned to him. "Shit, of course. That's it. And they

thought nothing of it to report back. Although if she'd thrown Madame Bovary in, surely they would have noticed. It just doesn't make sense—neither does her little show earlier, the Ruizes' hinders or the farmers."

We crossed the river. On the pavement at the side of the bridge, Ren was firing off at passing cars, his fist balled and shaking.

"That's unusual for him." He was as mellow as they came.

Lucas frowned. "I spoke to the locum earlier. He mentioned that Madame Sanogo, Monsieur Sel and some of the other patients are feeling very unsettled." He nodded to the edge of the road, where Axel Tripes was screaming, his hands clasped against his face. Not good. Definitely not good. Though at least his trousers weren't on fire this time.

I clenched my fingers around the armrest as we wove toward the farm, taking the bends at speed. In moments, we pulled into the farmyard and drew up by the loft. A faint rumble echoed through the valley as we sprang out. Lucas grabbed his bag, and we headed to the door.

"Oh, Camille!" Grampi emerged from the barn.

We paused mid-stride, my stomach twisting. "I don't want him involved," I murmured. I wasn't going to put him in danger.

"Agreed," Lucas said softly. "But we need to get a move on."

He didn't have to tell me.

Grampi hobbled over, looking me up and down. "You're all wet... and Lucas is here." A scowl dug into his bronze skin before he forced it away and smiled. "I wondered if you fancied some of the cassoulet I've made. It turned out very nicely, if I do say so myself. And I wanted to catch you before the bond tomorrow, to say, uh... I hope it goes well."

I attempted to return the smile. "I'd love a bowlful, but we have something to deal with right away. I'll grab a helping in the morning, if it's okay with you?"

His face fell. He just looked empty. "Of course, tomorrow. I'll see you then." With a nod to Lucas, he headed back to the barn.

I led the way to the loft entrance, my throat dry. I'd sounded so cold, but with the prospect of being Pajuzu's plaything, I wasn't myself. I would have to make it up to him.

"He'll be alright," Lucas said as we took the stairs. "He's made of tough stuff."

"Tough stuff that has always had something to do. He's not used to being out on a limb."

We headed into the kitchen, and I turned to Lucas. "It's just that—"

He reached out and cupped my cheek.

My breath caught, the light dimming, the cloud darkening. His touch was something else, his eyes tender, and yet my chest gouged unbearably.

"It's just that you're scared," he said softly, "and right at this moment, you have more to contend with than his problems, even though they're important to you."

He drew his hand away, leaving emptiness. I swallowed and leant back against the counter. I needed to insist on some distance, but I couldn't bring myself to speak.

Lucas placed his bag on the floor and rummaged inside.

My argument with Alice returned, red hot—her insistence that I should dig deeper, her assertion that I was denying myself. She had no right to tell me what to do or make assumptions about how I was feeling. What I needed was to release everything that churned for her and Lucas out in the storm. I *craved* release. But it was the one thing I couldn't have.

Lucas rose with a duck-egg-blue vial in his grasp.

I dug my nails into the edge of the worktop, doing my best to hold it together. "So what is this potion?"

"It's a mixture of sage, wild oats, chasteberry, seeds harvested by a valerian verte velle, and the nasal discharge of—"

I raised a hand. "Nope. Don't tell me. But what will it do?"

His jaw tightened. "It will subdue you, leaving you flat, not able to experience joy or sadness, excitement or fear."

I let out a breath. "Sounds like a riot." Although with everything storming through me, perhaps it was just what I needed.

"It means Pajuzu won't be able to use your emotions." He swirled the liquid. "There are a number of fae that feed off feelings, so it's used frequently for defensive situations, and it has a reliable track record. Having said that, messing with emotions isn't something I do lightly." There was a flicker of agitation in his gaze.

He took a glass from the cupboard, placed it on the worktop and poured a measure. "You may experience nausea on ingestion. The potion will last approximately three days, and then, if necessary, you can take another dose. If there are problems, or if it makes you too uncomfortable in any way, there's a simple antidote."

I nodded. "Sounds good to me."

He passed me the cup, and I tipped the contents back. Sharpness filled my mouth, lingering after I swallowed. I stared into nothing, waiting for a reaction.

"How are you feeling?" He studied me.

"I... think I'm fine—"

My stomach tightened and lurched, my body flushing cold, nausea rushing through me. I ran to the sink and retched. In an instant, Lucas's hand was on my back, warm and soothing, his fingers brushing my hair aside as I heaved and heaved. Nothing came out but mucous.

"It will pass," he said softly. "Just give it a moment."

Another wave of cold and nausea swept over me, then dissipated. I retched again and felt a little better. He passed me a tea towel. I wiped my mouth before rising and releasing a few breaths, the last of the nausea easing. "I'm good."

Attempting to gain a sense of myself, I stilled and searched inside. It was peculiar. There was no anger for Alice, no attraction for Lucas, no confusion, no gouging chest, no pain at all. I had the notion that it lurked deep within, caged and inaccessible, but that was fine by me. I really *was* good.

"Alright now?" he asked.

We stood there, a step apart, and instinctively, I reached out for the connection between us, but there was an utterly empty void, and it was such a relief. I let out a long breath, my shoulders sinking. "That's better. So much better."

Something flickered in Lucas's eyes. I could have sworn it was dismay. My imagination, no doubt, because in an instant it was gone, replaced by battle-ready hardness.

CHAPTER 31

As I paced from my bed to the kitchen and back again, sonorous thunder rumbled in the distance, barely audible, accompanied by the occasional half-hearted flash of sheet lightning and a little rain. It had been hours now, the storm hugging the far side of town, the bank of cloud shrouded in night. Perhaps the potion was holding it back, its advance hindered by my lack of emotion. But instinctively, I knew it would come.

Wind flurried through the farmyard. Grampi's bedroom light had gone out a while ago, and the goats, who usually spent the night on the mountainside in the summer, had taken shelter in the barn.

I was restless. I'd had a shower, changed into yoga trousers and a fresh tee, and attempted to sleep earlier, which hadn't been successful, so I'd scrolled on my phone, paced, and read up on Pazuzu, not finding anything of use.

Lucas sat on the sofa, his ankle crossed over his leg, his

chest rising and falling in a steady rhythm. His gaze tracked me constantly as I paced. I indulged in not feeling him, in being deliciously calm. Willpower and logic had replaced emotion, and that made the resolution that I wouldn't kill again unshakeable. I had the potion, Lucas's help and the Men if needed, not to mention we had the bonevetch and the farm wards had been strengthened. But logic also reasoned that Lucas was being odd. "Do you have to do that?"

"What?"

"All that staring."

His jaw shifted this way and that, then he glanced out of the French windows and watched the volley of rain for a split-second before returning his gaze to me.

I sighed out of habit, unable to muster the exasperation I should have been feeling.

Thunder broke, louder this time, the storm closer.

Slaughter appeared from behind the sofa. "Uh, boss."

Lucas didn't take his eyes off me. "What is it?"

"The Rôdeurs are back on the bounds. They've stopped at a brasserie in Foix for a bite to eat. They haven't been talking much as they're paranoid about being overheard. But we caught that they're returning to Tarascon."

"Let me know what they do when they get here."

"Righto, sir." Slaughter shot me a reassuring grin before disappearing behind the sofa.

I paced some more, this time from the comfy old armchair piled with cushions to the bookshelf—the shelf Lucas had arranged so carefully the night he'd commanded the Men to destroy my loft. I could barely believe that arrogant asshole was the person sitting on the sofa, boring his eyes into me. Still arrogant, yes. Still an asshole, most definitely. But so much more. Fervent, honourable, strong, brutal. Thank heavens my emotions were blissfully absent.

Lightning flashed, followed immediately by thunder. Gold sparked around the farm. The wards. I glanced at Lucas, who only grated his teeth.

Minutes passed, the wind whipping about the place. Bolts of light tore the sky, cracking and clattering again and again, gold sparking on and on. An almighty crash shook the loft... then stillness. Lucas's muscles tightened, his fists clenching.

I went to the window. It was a little too still outside, the farm dark and quiet, the gold gone. "What happened? Are the wards holding?"

Lucas just stared at me, his fists clenched tighter.

"You're full of conversation tonight." I continued pacing. Back and forth I went, the floorboards creaking.

A flurry of hail battered the windows, breaking the silence. Blazing white cut the sky, the crack of thunder synchronous, calling to the storm within me that was locked away tight. I headed back to the bookcase, then turned to walk across the room for the hundredth time, but I just didn't feel right. I needed to go outside.

I strode to the door. Before I could reach the handle, Lucas slipped in front of me, his back against the wood. "Where do you think you're going?" His voice was a deadly rumble.

"Out. I need some fresh air." I tried to push past, but he was unmovable.

"The wards have failed. You're not going anywhere."

"Oh for heaven's sake." I tried again.

He gripped my shoulders and pushed. I could only step backward as he guided me to the living area.

This was ridiculous.

Wind rose, shaking the loft. It sent shudders through me, stirring something I couldn't quite reach. Even so, I could feel the storm in my blood, surging, streaming, filling me with vitality. I grabbed Lucas's hands and pulled them off as though he was nothing and made for the door.

Before I got there, his arm wrapped around my neck. As he pulled me back against him, the vitality ebbed. "Camille, listen to me," he growled in my ear. "It's the storm. Try to detach yourself."

"Don't be absurd. I'm going out." I struggled "Get off me!"

He pinned me against the door, grabbed my hands and jerked them behind my back. Coarse rope encircled my wrists. "What the hell are you doing?" I roared.

He shoved me back into the room, the wind rising again, and it rose in me too. I tried to wrench free, to no avail, but by the strain on Lucas's face and the sweat on his brow, he was working for it. Tugging and twisting, I almost pulled free, but he rammed me into the corner between the bookcase and window, pressing his body hard against mine.

I writhed under him. "Get the fuck off me!"

"You're not going to Pajuzu," he rumbled. "You're mine."

He rammed a forearm across my chest, trapping me, then raised his other hand. There was something in his palm. The bonevetch. He muttered under his breath, a glow encircling the herb. I couldn't catch his words, but his eyes... They bored into me, his gaze an inferno, the scent of his sweat and the pressure of his body overwhelming. The glow swelled, reaching toward me.

"Aaaaargh!" I arched into him, a thousand unseen needles piercing my flesh as the glow suffused my body. "What are you doing?" I thrashed, pain driving into my muscles and bones, until every ounce of strength abandoned me. I didn't have the fight. Releasing myself, I hung limp in his arms, groaning, agony coursing through me.

He stroked my hair. "I'm so sorry, Camille, but I won't let you go through the pain of killing again."

I moaned into his chest. There was nothing left but excruciating torment. But the storm rose once more, its clamorous gusts building to a deafening roar, light discharging repeatedly, hail pummelling the roof. As I rested against Lucas, my senses were filled with it. The soft draft that coiled over the floor soothed my skin, easing the pain a little, and the vitality of the storm trickled through my blood once more. It built to a gush, and then it consumed me.

I drew up my head and met Lucas's gaze. "Let. Me. Go." It was my own voice, and that of a thousand ruthless tempests. I pushed against him.

He gritted his teeth, the veins in his temples throbbing. "Never."

Unable to tell myself from the storm, I pulled my wrists

apart, the rope tearing. Before Lucas could act, I thrust him away. He flew back and crashed into the far wall, plaster cracking. I was vaguely aware of innumerable Men grabbing my arms, my legs, my clothing. I angled my palms and released a gust. It swept the warriors back, holding them off.

Lucas came at me once more, fast. But he was nothing compared to the storm. I struck out with a hook kick. He didn't have time to angle himself into a defensive manoeuvre, and my heel struck his jaw with a crack, hurtling him down. Groaning, he struggled to get up, but I was on him with a stomp to his gut. He collapsed, then tried to rise again. He really was tough. I thrust my foot into the side of his head. This time when he crumpled, he was out cold. The mass of Men still restrained cussed and hollered, their grimaces fierce.

I strode out of the loft and into the storm.

The track up to Picou de Bompas was shadowy and indistinct. Hail turned to icy rain, which drove down in sheets, soaking my hair and clothing. The wind enticed me in spiralling caresses, and on I climbed until I reached the scrubby summit. Boulders and trees loomed black below, and beyond, the deluged town glimmered.

The gale whirled about my body and surged through my blood. It spun faster, and I drew up my arms, waiting to rise, to fly as I always had. My own tumult lay within, imprisoned somewhere beneath the surface. I couldn't reach it, but all the same, its pressure burgeoned. The storm rose to an utter frenzy, until an almighty fork rent the sky, splitting into innumerable spears.

"Raaaaaagh!" Pajuzu boomed. "What have you done?" A barrage of wind blasted me to my knees. "You restrain yourself. You keep everything tightly wrapped, and now...." His voice merged with an onslaught of thunder. "Now you hide away everything I need!" His roar was so loud I thought my skull would shatter. "I need you, Camille, I need your focus. Without it, she will gain power. She will take lives. She will destroy us all."

Screeching arose from all around, a sick, gleeful keen, and with it, nausea filled me, my skin abraded by fetid pestilence. The world spun, and with it, my bones shattered. I was barely aware of Pajuzu storming against the presence. Yet still it came, driving him back.

"There is nothing you can do now," an agonisingly shrill voice cried. "I will take revenge on those who opposed and bound me. I will destroy the sons and daughters of Tarascon. It is time..."

Hideous wings swept across the sky, and oblivion descended.

CHAPTER 32

"CAMILLE... CAMILLE..."

The voice was distant. Nothing like the uproarious decibels of the storm. For a moment, I thought it was Lucas, but it couldn't have been. I couldn't feel him. Someone shook my shoulders. I was too exhausted to respond. My eyes wouldn't open and pain coursed through me like every one of my bones had been cracked.

More shaking. "Come on, Camille." The tone *was* familiar. Strong and resolute, with just a hint of murder. Something touched my lips and ran under my tongue. Cardamom and nutmeg, sweet and potent. It drew warmth into my limbs, then fire, a blaze of life flowing through me.

I hauled my eyes open.

Slaughter stood at my side, holding a small lantern. And next to him, Lucas leant over me, his face a little bruised, his shirt splattered with blood. A flicker of a memory came back —me driving my foot into his head. "Shit. What did I do to you...?" He must have had healing potion, because I was pretty sure I'd caused him more than a few bruises.

"It's not important," he murmured softly. "Lie still and let the potion do its work."

I groaned and closed my eyes again. But... I'd not ridden on the storm. It had called me, it had given me the strength to escape Lucas, but it hadn't taken me. I dug my elbows into gritty mud and pushed myself up. The sky was clear though hazy, the stars dim as the morning encroached. A faint breeze flitted about, though it lacked freshness. No, that was being generous. It was utterly lifeless. But what mattered was that we'd made it through. "We did it... I think. At least, I didn't kill anyone." I scoured my memory, all of it thick and elusive, but there was no tormented face in the throes of death. "It was the potion. Pajuzu couldn't take me." Although I felt as though there was something I was missing.

Lucas studied me, his fingers playing with the vial. "For tonight, at any rate."

A shudder ripped through me, my body responding to something far deeper than emotion. Survival instinct, perhaps. "There's no way we can repeat that." I couldn't hurt Lucas again, and the pain from the bonevetch had been a whole other dimension. I glanced at Slaughter. "Are the Men alright?"

He grinned. "You don't need to worry yourself about us, ma'am. We enjoy a bit of a challenge, and you were certainly that."

"I tried to hold you." Lucas's voice was edged with fury, his face clouding. "He took you."

"Pajuzu is a god," I said. "You did everything you could."

He shook his head. He wasn't going to let himself off that easily.

I swept my gaze over his bruised face. What I'd done was so wrong. He'd helped me, and I'd pulverised him. "I'm so sorry."

"I've had worse." His lip quirked. "At least it wasn't lightning."

"Small mercies," I muttered.

"No, actually." He raised his brow. "Rather large mercies, believe me."

I huffed. "I think the potion affected my electrical abilities too. I didn't even get as far as lightning. But the main thing is, no dead farmers."

"Exactly." He smiled softly.

Blather appeared and whispered something in Slaughter's ear, then vanished behind a rock.

"Uh, gov." Slaughter fiddled with his axe handle. "That was a report from the Men watching the farmers." He looked anywhere but at us. "Alf passed away from unknown causes a few minutes ago."

"What?" Lucas cried.

"No way!" I sat upright. "That's not possible. I didn't hurt him. At least, I don't think I did."

"He wasn't struck down by lightning, ma'am. The Men reported a presence, a pestilent wind. Alf was in his tractor shed doing jobs because he couldn't sleep. He kept looking up at the sky. But then this stuff swept in, not at all like Camille's storm. It seeped through the farmyard and encircled Alf, and he snuffed it, just like that. His wife found him a minute later. They've called an ambulance."

Lucas's grip tightened around the potion vial. "It sounds like the noxious wind Nora evoked."

I should've been seriously worried, but due to the potion, I only felt flat. Despite that, the gravity of it all hadn't left me. "It doesn't make sense. The farmers were killed by lightning." I could see it. "Each time, I felt power building and extended my hands..." I'd been about to say that then I'd struck them down, but that wasn't what happened next. My gaze flicked from Slaughter to Lucas. "The presence was there when the farmers died, I'm sure of it. It's hazy, but I think it bound itself around the farmers' chests *before* I did anything." My thoughts had been so tangled, but, "What if, guided by Pajuzu, I wasn't aiming for the farmers, I was attempting to take out the presence."

Lucas rubbed the back of his neck. "But why would Pajuzu wait until it was encircling someone before attacking? It doesn't fit. Another possibility is that he's controlling it."

I frowned. "I don't think so." Though I couldn't substantiate my answer in any way.

"Gov." Slaughter tugged at his arm. "The farm..."

Lucas examined my face again. "You're looking a little better. If you can manage it, we should get back. As if we didn't have enough to deal with, the Rôdeurs have returned. Seems they found out where you live and want payback for earlier. Last report from the Men, they were creeping through the woodland toward the farmyard."

"Grampi—"

"There are more than enough Men to protect Izak. The Rôdeurs will be lucky if they don't get their toes hacked off."

I struggled to my feet, wobbling a little.

Lucas extended a hand. "Can you make it, or shall I carry you?" Knowing my independent streak all too well, he couldn't resist a smirk.

I accepted his hand to steady myself, the lack of connection disconcerting. "I'm good." And really, I was, thanks to the healing potion.

The three of us set off down the path in the early-dawn grey. I drew in a lungful of faintly nauseating stale air, which stuck in my throat, bringing back images of the sickening presence. "The pestilence... I think it spoke. It said something about the sons and daughters of Tarascon, and that it would take revenge—"

Wrench appeared from behind a bush. "Uh, boss. You better come quick. The Rôdeurs are being attacked by that horrible stuff near the farm."

Slaughter sped ahead with the lantern as we ran down the hill. Damn, he could shift. And other than being a bit achy, I managed. Rounding the last bend, the farm came into view, and cries of utter torment rent the air.

We hurtled into the farmyard and paused. The place was empty, the commotion coming from the woods below.

Then silence...

Lucas and I exchanged a glance as we followed Slaughter into the trees. There was no sign of the presence, but amidst the dim boughs of oak and hawthorn lay three Rôdeurs. Romaine's broad shoulders hunched over one of them. As we closed in, he didn't react. He just stared at a bulky figure. Bastien. Even in the shadowy light, his deathly pallor was all too clear, as were the deep purple lesions seeping blood and pus. They were like the sores that had covered Henri's body when he passed away a couple of months ago. An indication of an affliction by a fae cause.

Lucas dropped down and checked his pulse.

Romaine turned to him, desperation warping his face. "You're the doctor, right? You have to help him. For fuck's sake, help them all!" He resorted to muttering under his breath, and I caught "demon" and "evil".

"Bastien is still alive," Lucas murmured. "Just. And by the look of his skin, not for long. Slaughter, get my bag."

The little guy placed the lantern down, disappeared behind a tree and returned with it in an instant. Romaine was too absorbed in Bastien to notice anything out of the ordinary.

Lucas drew out a potion case and handed me a vial. "Quickly."

I took it and knelt at the side of the pockmarked Rôdeur. Grabbing the back of his head, I poured it in with considerably less skill than Lucas administering to Bastien. I could only hope I wasn't going to choke the guy. Lucas headed to the other Rôdeur. Romaine continued muttering as he gripped Bastien's vest.

My Rôdeur took a breath. That had to be a good sign, though his eyes remained closed.

Lucas rose. "They need shelter."

"The barn." The goats had emerged at some point while

we'd been distracted. They'd assembled at the edge of the yard and were eyeing us with curiosity.

A group of Men surrounded each Rôdeur. They jostled their shoulders underneath, lifted the prostrate forms into the air and floated them toward the barn in much the same way they had for Lucas a few weeks ago when he'd been trashed in Foix.

Romaine stepped back, his jaw slack as he watched Bastien soar along, accompanied by Delphine and Rose, who were assessing his clothing as potential fodder. Lucas grabbed his bag, and we took up the rear.

"Are you going to deal with Romaine or am I?" I asked.

The Men carried Bastien through the open door, catching the side of his head on the frame with a crack. "To the right, Men," Slaughter ordered. The other two Rôdeurs followed Bastien in.

"You go," Lucas said. "I need to examine this lot more thoroughly."

I strode over to Romaine, who had frozen, staring at the spectacle from amidst the trees. "They... uh... they appear to be floating. I think I'm seeing things." He fell to his knees and threw up in a bush. Nope, he definitely couldn't see the hidden world, which made his knowledge of it even more curious, although he *had* sensed the presence.

"Tell me something," I said. "Why did you try to take Nora?"

He shook his head, trembling. "I wanted to protect her... from that stuff."

For some reason, the pestilence hadn't attacked him

again. "Then you know what's going on. Don't you think it's about time you gave us a little help?"

He clambered to his feet, swatting a branch out of the way. Doing his best to square his shoulders, he glared down at me, but what with his flattened cowlick and his struggle to focus, he really didn't cut it. "Why the hell would I want to do that?"

"Because"—I mirrored his tough-guy stance and added a rather mean glare that I didn't feel—"we want to help Nora too, which was why we turned up in the woods earlier. We don't know what's happening, only that she's in deep trouble. We also don't know what floored your buddies, and *you* may be the only one who can help." My voice rose, and I jabbed my finger at him. "So it might be an idea if you leant us a hand. Or are you going to let that thing strike again?"

"No, I'm not." He glowered. "I'll help."

CHAPTER 33

ROMAINE FOLLOWED ME ACROSS THE YARD, DAWN casting the limestone walls in soft grey. A few goats milled around the door, waiting for milking and the feed they would guzzle whilst on the stand.

He took them in warily. I couldn't blame him. They really were quite daunting, with shaggy brown hair and size-able horns that curved backward, though it was probably the look in their eyes that made him nervous. It spoke of wild gods, death, rebirth and relentless butting. The herd had been through a lot with the hantaumo, and they weren't going to let anyone forget it.

With that attitude, a few of them pushed inside. I closed the door after us. The three Rôdeurs were lined up in the straw on the opposite side to the milking stand, a group of men surrounding them, weapons ready should they wake. Delphine chewed on one of Bastien's rather expensive-looking trainers as Lucas listened to his chest with his stethoscope.

After a moment, he tugged out the earpieces. "They're not showing signs of coming round. And with lesions this advanced, there's only a chance they will pull through."

Romaine's breath hitched.

"Romaine is willing to help," I said. "But ideally, he'll need to come with us to the Keepers' post. It's going to make everything a whole lot easier if he can see the hidden world."

Lucas rose and scoured his face.

There was defiance in Romaine's eyes, but also something more. Fear, uncertainty. He tried not to shrink from Lucas's dark gaze. "What do you mean, hidden world? I don't want to be involved in any of your creepy shit."

"Tell me, Romaine," Lucas said. "Are you aware of the existence of fae, creatures of the night, monsters, that sort of thing?"

He shrugged. "I feel stuff sometimes, like today. And there are rumours... idiots messing with things they shouldn't." He shook his head and smacked his fist into his palm.

I tipped my chin. "And the Rôdeurs put those idiots in their places."

"If they're causing trouble, yeah, we do. What of it?"

"Targeting folk on hearsay doesn't sound like a solid strategy to me." I arched a brow.

Lucas folded his stethoscope into his bag and pulled out a blue vial and a small plastic dispensing cup. "Looks like it's time for some creepy shit." He poured a few drops and held out the cup. "If you want to help your sister and friends, you'll have to take this. It will allow you to see everything that's going on. The dose is considerable to ensure immediate effect, and it can't be undone. None of this is going to be easy."

I drew a long breath. Verity would change Romaine's life irrevocably, and a large dose was dangerous, not to mention he had no way of understanding the consequences, but Nora's and the Rôdeurs' lives were on the line, and possibly others too.

"None of it has been easy, not ever." Romaine's jaw strained as he eyed the cup. Verity had a way of drawing folk, and Romaine was fighting the urge. "But there's no way I can trust you lot."

"I know that," I said. "But can you trust that Nora trusts us? You saw how she helped me yesterday."

His eyes bored into mine. "Fuck, I'm that desperate for Nora, for all of them." He grated a hand over his designer stubble, then swiped the cup from Lucas's hand and downed the contents.

There was a creak from behind. The door swung open. Grampi stood there, brandishing a medieval knightly sword.

Romaine goggled. "Another wacko with a blade, and this one is geriatric. What is it with this place?" Something caught his attention by Bastien. Slaughter shot his best black-toothed grin from amidst the circle of men. Romaine leant forward, blinking hard.

"I thought I heard a noise," Grampi said. "Looks like you

might be needing some help." His eyes gleamed. He hadn't appeared so keen since we'd dealt with Anthras.

"That would be perfect." I stepped over and squeezed his arm. The Rôdeurs wouldn't be able to see a guard of Men, and there would be problems if they woke to invisible captors.

Grampi sniffed the air. "There's something unpleasant about. I take it you're following it up, and that giving me a full update right now isn't going to be helpful."

I nodded. "Got it. I'll fill you in later."

Romaine's eyes had grown even wider, his body trembling. "Is it me or are there about thirty miniature wild men standing around the edge of the barn?"

Slaughter's grin widened. He really was trying to look friendly.

"Uh... uh... and some of them appear to be massaging goats." Indeed, Lavender and Daisy had lowered their heads. Blather and Trounce were rubbing behind their horns and ears.

Lucas ignored him and turned to Grampi. "That lot will need healing potion every hour. We don't know exactly what happened, and I don't rate their chances, but if they regain consciousness, they'll be dangerous."

"I'll restrain them just in case." He grabbed a coil of rope from a rusty hook on the wall, a hint of a smile pulling at his lips. "Beats pétanque with One-Legged Lars."

———

The aroma of baking bread met me as I headed into the café, my stomach rumbling. The place wasn't due to open for an hour, and it was empty and peaceful. One good thing about being here this early was that Alice rarely made it in at this time. I hurried to the kitchen anyway. I didn't want to risk bumping into her.

As I entered, Dame Blanche strode across the flagstones, her floury hands raised as she homed in on the mound of dough on the worktop. "Camille, how lovely to see you, and so early."

"Morning." I fought the urge to curl up in a ball at her feet and forget everything. I was here for a reason. Breakfast. Lucas had called everyone, and we were due to meet at the Keepers' post in ten. I scanned the kitchen for goodies.

"Today is the big day." Dame Blanche eased the heel of her palm into the dough, her long skirts swaying under her apron.

I frowned. She couldn't mean the bond—she knew nothing about it. Although that was rather naïve of me, as she knew about most things. "Uh, yeah."

"Don't be late." Her keen eyes sparkled. "The whole of Fae is relying on it."

I stared at her. "No pressure then."

Something caught her attention over my shoulder. "Tut, tut, tut. Look at that."

I followed her gaze through the door and across the café to the car park, where Max was slumped on the ground, weeping into his hands. On the way here, the few people up at this hour had appeared lost or distraught. It was the air, I was sure of it.

Dame Blanche turned the dough and continued kneading. "It looks like you're going to have quite a day."

I studied her, wondering if I should ask for an explanation about that and the Fae comment, but she would only say something even more enigmatic, and my brain would fry. "Uh, I need breakfast for nine. I'll settle the tab later."

Guy entered from one of the back kitchens, holding a basket covered in a cloth. The top of the logo on his favourite *Carve the Chaos* T-shirt was just visible above his apron. "Camille! We've got plenty. The Unnatural Gardener's Association had Breakfast and Blooms this morning, but they cancelled due to the lot of them feeling out of sorts. No idea what's got into them, but it's a major wipeout."

There really was something in the air, but in terms of breakfast, it sounded promising. "What was their order?"

"Croissants including almond ones, brioche buns, pain au chocolates and chausson aux pommes. Go for it." He shoved the basket at me.

As I grasped it, the aroma rose, buttery and sweet, the fresh viennoiserie warming my hands through the wicker. "Perfect, thank you. I'll see you guys later." Time to make a speedy exit before there was any chance of Alice appearing.

I turned and bumped straight into her.

We faced each other, her glower fierce, mine habitual. My lack of feeling didn't change the way she'd forced her opinions on me yesterday. She never would let up, and by her blazing eyes and the fierce, rock-hard set of her jaw, she still wasn't ready to see the light. With my mess of emotions safely hidden and all of me blissfully calm, it was even clearer that she'd been wrong about absolutely everything.

I turned away and headed out.

"Oh, Camille, dear," Dame Blanche called from behind. "Just remember, a few emotions never did anyone harm."

She was as bad as Alice. They could both go to hell.

CHAPTER 34

WE SPRAWLED AROUND THE TABLE IN THE KEEPERS'
post on various rickety chairs that Roux and Lucas had found
upstairs. Lucas had just finished updating everyone, the gang
wolfing down patisserie as if it was their last day on earth.

Nora hadn't eaten anything. She sat next to Romaine, her
noose dangling over her boat-neck T-shirt, the knot in the
same position as yesterday. Romaine, face pale, was alter-
nating staring at the glinting gold and gazing out of the
window. Elves and goblins strolled past as Tarascon awoke,
most of them in various states of torment, crying or cussing.

Romaine really had been dropped in it. Lucas had
explained as much as he could about fae and Nora's situation, and he was taking it pretty well. There had been more
vomiting, a little raving, some weaponry tossed off the walls,
Roux hiding in the pantry with a colander on his head, a
violent threat from Lucas to calm the fuck down, and a

couple of dead faints, but Romaine had settled nicely once Nora had gotten here, although they'd only bickered since. Considering Romaine's motives with the Rôdeurs, I supposed he already believed in much of the hidden world, and that was helping his transition.

Gabe hauled up the coffee pot from amidst bags of patisserie, mugs and bottles of fortifying potion, and poured a top-up. "So let me get this straight. The thing that took down the Rôdeurs at Camille's was the same thing that was in the woods yesterday?"

"You got it." Lucas sat at my side, a half-eaten almond croissant in his hand. His chair was a little too close, no doubt so he could spring on me should I take on demonic tendencies once more. His proximity should've stoked at least some warmth, but there was still nothing, and although I was enjoying the respite, weirdly, it left me without an appetite.

"And," he continued, icing sugar dusting his leathers, "it was the same presence that attacked Alf, according to the Men, plus it was there when the other farmers died." He glanced at me for the hundredth time since we'd sat down, scouring my face as if he'd lost something there.

"Curious, indeed." Roux juggled his mug and a chausson aux pommes. "Gabe and I were certainly feeling out of sorts before taking the fortifying potion. It seems the presence has encompassed the town."

The potion had helped me too after the exhausting night, but I hadn't experienced the atmosphere like them. Perhaps I was more accustomed to the presence than they were, or perhaps it was my general insensitivity at the moment. Everyone else was fine. Lucas because it took a lot to affect him. Nora and Romaine because they seemed to be immune, and Félix, Zach and Hugo because their crazed verity enthusiasm appeared to be shielding them. However, they were still in various bruised states. Zach sported a particularly impressive shiner around his left eye.

"What remains to be seen," I said to Nora and Romaine as I sat back and cradled my warm mug, "is your involvement. Romaine, the presence didn't attack you earlier. I hate to say it, and I know Nora probably can't answer, but is either of you controlling it?"

Fury swathed Romaine's face. "Did you see what it did to my friends?"

I'd take that as a no.

"You're right that I can't answer," Nora snapped, folding her arms and shooting me the dirtiest look in the history of teenage condescension.

"Personally, I don't think you killed the farmers or hurt the Rôdeurs." She was a lot of things, but I doubted she was a murderer. "But then, *I'm* being possessed, and *I* almost killed my partner." Twice.

"It's not out of the realm of possibility," Lucas said. "Nora, you appeared to be controlling the presence when Romaine tried to carry you off."

She shrugged and lasered Romaine instead, though he didn't notice. He was staring at Gabe's ear. The silicon elf tip had shifted a little, revealing the real elf ear underneath. By

Romaine's contorted frown, I'd say it was adding to his general fae overwhelm.

"Romaine," I said. "As you're not hindered like the rest of your family, perhaps you'd like to tell us your side of things?"

He shook himself and dragged his hands over his face. "All I know is that it was bad at home, very bad."

Nora narrowed her eyes. "The next instalment of the Nora show."

He placed his hand on hers, but she snatched it away.

"I only want to help," he said, fixing his jaw. "We're going to sort this, once and for all."

She turned to the window, Gabe watching her intently.

Romaine took a long breath through his teeth. "The atmosphere at home was shit. A bit like how it is outside right now. I don't know if there was something in the house, but it was as if I had to fight it off. It affected Maman worst of all. She used to get so mad, shouting and crying." He grabbed his cup from the table, his oversized biceps straining as he gulped his coffee. Félix goggled at them. I wouldn't be surprised if the gang's next pursuit was the gym. "It didn't affect Gran much, though, but Nora... she did weird shit. When Maman got bad, Nora would leave stuff out in the back yard, like a ribbon or a shoe. Stuff she stole from folk. It was so random, but it seemed to make Maman better. The real kicker was that no one would talk about it, and it freaked me out completely, but now I'm thinking maybe they couldn't speak because of their hinders."

My lips parted. Romaine had left a while ago. They'd been going through this for *years*.

He placed his mug down. "Anyway, I hung out with friends all the time, then made an exit as soon as I could. I hated leaving Nora, but I was a total wreck. I couldn't think straight and felt like hell. A while after moving in with Papa, I met up with Bastien and some others in Toulouse. He was the first person not to write off my experiences. I joined the Rôdeurs to target spooky shit like at home." He glanced at Nora. "I tried to get you out so many times, but you wouldn't come."

Her gaze didn't shift from the window.

"That's why you took her yesterday?" Lucas asked.

He nodded.

Roux leant back in his chair. "Certainly sounds demonic."

"I appreciate your openness, Romaine," I said. "But we still don't know what we're dealing with, and from my rather fragmented memories of last night, I'm pretty sure the presence is furious and wants revenge, not to mention there are people out on the street weeping." I took a sip of coffee, absorbing the bitterness.

"The wind is coming from the east," Roux said. "It's the Autan, reputed to cause illness and madness."

"It's certainly not my storm, which is more... uh, stormy and most definitely from the southwest." Look at me getting possessive over my own personal demon.

"Nora was stirring the waters, right?" Gabe twisted a brown paper patisserie bag between his fingers. "Though I can't imagine her dunking a cat in the river—"

"Madame Bovary is not a cat," she snapped.

He shrugged. "Anyway, that's what they used to do in the old days to raise a storm. So is it possible Nora was calling Pajuzu for help?"

I studied his dark eyes and intense face, a face that had grown a little stronger since Grimmere, his determination less naïve and more forceful. He had a point. "It fits with my hunch that Pajuzu was attempting to take out the presence."

"Despite Pajuzu's reputation, he's also a protector of women and children." Lucas picked a flaked almond off his croissant and nibbled on it.

I trawled back over my interactions with the storm. "I never felt in danger from him. Not once. I thought I had, but that had been the presence." It was the opposite, in fact. I'd felt amazing, letting rip and releasing my turmoil.

"Well," Félix piped up mid-chew of a brioche bun, "if he's the good guy, who is the boss?"

"What?" Lucas's eyebrow lowered on one side.

"The big bad, the archenemy, the nemesis, the one Pajuzu opposes. There's always the opposition."

He was right. And after an evening reading up on the subject, I had the answer. "Traditionally, in ancient Mesopotamian lore, it's Lamashtu, daughter of the sky god Anu."

Everyone exchanged looks.

I pulled out my phone and scrolled through another of Margo Joly's papers until I found the relevant part. "Lamastu, as she was called in the Pyrenees, was invoked by the witches of Upper Aragon to sicken young brides and kill newborns. She's generally known for harming mothers and children, killing foliage, infecting watercourses and bringing nightmares, sickness, disease and death." I scraped my teeth over my lip. "It also says she was introduced into the area with Pajuzu in the tenth or eleventh century."

Lucas's fingers tightened around the remains of his croissant, crushing it. "It looks like we may have found our problem."

A few crumbs fell from Roux's lips to his beard. "My, my. A goddess with as much power as Pajuzu."

"More," I said. "If Pajuzu was trying to stop her, he didn't manage it."

"Uh, we have something." Zach's thin lips quivered, his greasy blond hair trembling. "We were working on it all at Félix's late last night, and we found another article."

Félix nodded, his cheek stuffed full. Hugo grabbed the last croissant.

"Oh?" I asked.

Zach tucked his hands under his legs. "Twenty years ago, four farmers from Saint-Girons were killed in a violent storm one night. They were inside a barn when it struck, the roof collapsing. It was a major tragedy at the time."

"I vaguely remember hearing about it," I said.

"And get this..." Hugo waved his croissant around, his eyes sparkling. "Ten years earlier there was an article about the same Saint-Girons farmers. They'd been in a nasty fistfight with a group from Tarascon—Ignace, Mean Gert, Ludger and Alf. Apparently, it was a long-standing feud, though the article didn't say what it was about."

I clenched my mug. "In the past, rival towns evoked

storms to take revenge on one another, and Roux raised the question yesterday of whether we were facing a similar situation. Back when Ignace was engaged to Marta, could he have enlisted her to evoke a storm in retaliation?"

"Indeed," Roux murmured.

Romaine shook his head, looking rather dazed. "If I hadn't felt that thing last night, I would be telling you where to go."

"What?" Nora bit out. "The goblins walking past outside aren't enough to convince you of anything out of the ordinary?"

He drew his hands to his chest and slumped back as if shot through the heart. "You got me there."

Nora almost managed a smile, though she restrained it on principle.

"Well, whatever they were doing back then"—Lucas glanced at his mangled croissant as if he'd just remembered he was holding it—"after last night there's only Ignace left."

Félix shook his head. "Ignace is toast."

"He's a goner," Hugo muttered through a mouthful.

Zach's lips quivered some more. "He's checking out of the building."

"And after the other deaths," I said, "I'm sure he knows it."

Lucas looked pointedly at me. "Which might mean he's willing to talk. We'd better pay him a visit ASAP." He shoved the croissant into his mouth.

"Definitely." But I still couldn't piece it all together. "What I don't understand is why Lamastu didn't kill the farmers straight away, or years ago? I also don't get why she's picking them off one by one?"

"She may be building power," Lucas said. "Though as she's a goddess, I have no idea why she'd need to."

Her screeching filled my head, my ears ringing with the recollection. "I'm sure she mentioned something about 'those who bound her'."

"If she was bound, then she could be in the process of unbinding herself, and maybe she's doing it through Nora, Eva and Marta." Lucas grabbed his mug. "Slaughter reported earlier that Eva had returned home from her nightshift and was going to bed, and Marta was up and crocheting. There's nothing unusual going on at the Ruiz house at the moment."

But then, Nora had been stealing way back, leaving unusual things out in the yard to help Eva, and she was still doing it now... I pulled myself upright. "Yesterday, Ren and Madame Biscotte were acting strangely, and the locum said that Madame Sanogo and Monsieur Sel weren't feeling well. There may be a connection. Nora stole Ren's watch, and I'm almost certain that she stole Madame Biscotte's bracelet, Madame Sanogo's broach and Monsieur Sel's cigar case. She was supposed to return Ren's watch, but I'd bet anything she didn't."

She met my gaze, her brow raised as she chewed her tongue.

"You're *still* thieving?" Romaine's lip curled.

"And you're still a member of a violent street gang?" She returned to staring out the window. Touché.

I placed my cup on the table. "All those folk she stole

from were feeling rotten before Lamastu spread her influence over the town this morning, when everyone else was affected. What if Nora has been attempting a sort of appeasement, stopping Eva being victimised by leaving offerings for Lamastu? And through those personal items, Lamastu managed to link with the owners and draw power from them, regaining strength gradually over time, until today, when she became powerful enough to draw from folk directly."

Nora remained fixed on the window. This had to be ridiculously difficult for her.

Lucas rubbed his chin. "And as Lamastu could only regain power little by little because of her binding, those Nora stole from may not have noticed the drain. A headache here, a nasty cold there. And Nora's been stealing more lately, if the number of reports are anything to go by. Perhaps she's had to work harder to stop Eva being used as Lamastu recovered."

Gabe's eyes widened, the paper bag woven tightly around his fingers. "And maybe stealing La Vieille's spindle was the ultimate offering."

"Or the ultimate cry for help." Nora didn't do anything without calculation. She turned to me, her face expressionless, the lack of a glare highly unusual. We may well have hit the nail on the head. "Only, Nora didn't understand that taking the spindle would have such dire consequences."

"But then why is this all about Nora's maman?" Hugo rubbed his flabby cheeks. "Marta is the tempestaire who was involved with the farmers."

I hadn't a clue. And by the looks of everyone's blank faces, no one else did either.

"And Romaine," Lucas said. "Do you have any idea why Lamastu didn't hurt you back at the farm?"

He thought for a moment. "Nope. No idea at all."

"Well, if the atmosphere in town is a reliable indicator," Roux muttered, "it looks like Lamastu is making her move."

"The question remains, what are we going to do about it?" I dug the toe of my boot into the floor.

"Uh..." Gabe had untwisted the paper bag and was pulling it to shreds. "When the hantaumo thing happened, didn't everyone get some kind of potion to slow the effects? We could do that now."

"The potion takes days to prepare," Lucas said. "Presuming Lamastu will strike Ignace tonight, never mind what else she might do given her strength, we don't have the time to make it, although we can begin the process in case this stretches out." He glanced at his watch. "At this point, it will have to be when we get back from the bond as we need to see Ignace first."

"I can prepare the initial ingredients to speed things up," Roux said.

Lucas nodded. "That will help."

I got up and paced back and forth along the length of the room. I should have been feeling urgency or concern for Nora and perhaps some empathy for the townsfolk, but I only felt unsettled. That aside, we really needed to be ready for tonight. Outside, the wind had developed an eerie, sickening keen as it blustered about, and cloud had drawn over the sky, a pale, lifeless pall. "What do we have that we can use against Lamastu?"

"The bonevetch," Roux replied.

Félix folded his arms and scowled, still riled that his prize had been confiscated.

Lucas swigged his coffee. "It didn't work on Camille, though it might have a stronger effect on a demon directly."

"It didn't work," Gabe said, dropping the shreds of the bag onto the table and pulling a book from his cloak, "because it wasn't wielded by the person who gathered it." He opened the volume, slapped it on the table and jabbed his finger at a paragraph, a little dust rising from the pages. "Says it right here in *Demons, Darkness, Desolation and Ducks*."

I really wanted to ask about the ducks, but now wasn't the time.

Roux took the book. "Now, now. Well, yes." He glanced around at all of us before examining the text. "The boy is widely read indeed. It's been many years since I picked this one up. It's very good, especially the chapter on duck husbandry and beak care."

Nope, I wasn't going there.

"Félix will have to wield the bonevetch with help from Zach and Hugo, in the same way they stole the herb in the first place." Gabe fiddled with the edge of his cloak, looking more than a little worried at the prospect.

"If we divide the bonevetch between the three boys," Roux said. "we only have enough for one potent collude."

Félix grinned—the slightly inane grin that we'd seen all

too much of lately. By the looks on Zach's and Hugo's faces, they were teetering on the edge of ecstasy.

I didn't like the sound of it. "That would be serious trouble. They've had no preparation."

Lucas's gaze drove into Félix, his foot drumming against the flagstones. Félix squirmed, his grin drooping. Finally, Lucas met my eye. "We don't have any choice. Even so, does anyone know how effective the herb will be?"

"According to *Demons, Darkness, Desolation and Ducks*," Gabe said, "it has the power to paralyse a demon temporarily."

Damn it, I couldn't get the ducks out of my head.

"Doesn't sound too effective to me." Zach fidgeted. "I mean, it's not like the ultimate demon-destroying weapon or anything."

"Totally not," Félix agreed.

"Nora," Lucas said. "You appeared to have control of Lamastu yesterday. Is there anything you can do?"

She stared blankly at him.

Roux closed the book. "Lamastu is a goddess. There's very little we can do at all. The only one who may be able to help is Pajuzu."

"And he was pretty ineffective," I said, then paused, a rush of images coming back, my unease gaining strength. "I think we might have made a big mistake."

Lucas frowned. "Oh?"

"Pajuzu chose me as his focus, heaven knows why. But to attack Lamastu, he has to use my emotions. He was ineffective because I was holding back. I didn't want to give him more."

Lucas's face hardened. "And when you took the potion, we stopped him in his tracks, allowing Lamastu free rein."

"That's it. And if I give him full access to me, he may have what he needs to defeat her." I shuddered, thinking of everything locked up tight. "I need the antidote to the potion. I need to feel."

CHAPTER 35

"No." LUCAS SAID IT SO ABRUPTLY THAT EVERYONE flinched. "You're not having the antidote."

I raised my brow. "What?"

He rose, his jaw rigid as he leant toward me. "There is no way in hell I'm going to allow my partner to be used by a demon again."

Scouring his face, I bit back a retort. "Roux, make up the antidote."

Lucas's eyes blazed.

The others were staring at us. I inclined my head to the kitchen.

"Gabe, instruct Félix in the bonevetch collude," Lucas called as we headed in.

We positioned ourselves either side of the central unit. I leant over it and glowered at him. "I get where you're coming from. Last night was awful, but there's too much at stake not to risk me having the antidote." Roux shuffled in and busied himself, gathering supplies and most definitely not looking our way.

Lucas shook his head. "This is a *god* we're talking about, not a load of wraiths or dracs. It's next level, Camille. The power Pajuzu and Lamastu have at their fingertips is staggering."

"I get that, but what am I supposed to do? Let everyone die?" I would be so pissed with him right now if I hadn't had the potion.

He gripped the edge of the worktop, his eyes wild. "It's too dangerous."

"What would *you* do in my place?" I poked my finger at him. "Would *you* allow Lamastu to terrorise the town?"

His nostrils flared, his chest rising and falling.

"I know you'd help. And as much as I'm enjoying not feeling, I need to, because Nora's and Ignace's lives are at stake, not to mention the rest of the folk out there aren't looking too hot, and neither is the weather." The keening had grown louder, gusts rattling the windows.

He took a deep breath. "Believe me, I'm not against you feeling." His words were surprisingly soft, considering the state he was in.

Roux lit a spirit lamp on the worktop and held a small vial over the flame with tongs, the contents dark brown. From the other room, Gabe's voice fought with the wind as he explained the collude to the others. My phone buzzed. I pulled it out.

A text from Grampi. *The men are still out cold, but One-Legged Lars and some of the over-eighties are in a state. There's a nasty storm brewing and I'm feeling a bit rough. Hoping you have everything in hand?*

As always, we were right on top of things. I sent back a smiley emoji. *All good. Take fortifying potion.*

He replied with, *Will do. I hope the bond goes well. x*

Which proffered the question of what could go wrong with it, but that was the least of my concerns.

"I do believe," Roux said as he studied the antidote, which had developed a pink blush, "considering Pajuzu hasn't harmed Camille, and taking into account the state of the townsfolk, she may be our only hope."

Lucas's hands tightened around the worktop, a low growl emanating from his throat.

"What the hell is up with you?" I really couldn't figure him out. "More drac possessiveness?"

Still no answer. Just a lot of heavy breathing.

Roux raised an eyebrow as he swirled the vial.

"Roux," I said. "Is there anything else I can do to help Pajuzu defeat Lamastu?"

Lucas's arms became taut, the sinews much too pronounced. For some reason, he was having a hard time restraining his inner drac. I ignored him.

Roux glanced warily at him as he blew out the flame. "I couldn't say, other than make yourself fully available. He will guide you."

"Alright." I'd try.

He poured a dose into a measuring vial, then tipped the

contents into a cup and slid it over. "It should be cool enough, but be careful just in case."

Time to be swamped with my shit once again. I grabbed the cup.

Lucas's gaze bored into me. "Camille, don't."

"The matter isn't up for discussion." I raised the antidote to my lips and took a sip, Lucas shaking his head. It was warm but not scalding. I drew a breath and tipped it back. Ginger and something I couldn't identify warmed my throat. Placing the cup down, I waited for the onslaught. "How long will it take to work?"

"It has immediate effect," Roux said. "Your emotions will return straight away."

I peered into the meeting room, waiting. Gabe had developed a scowl and was tapping his fingers nervously as Félix acted out blasting Lamastu with fireballs, Hugo and Zach whooping. It didn't look like the collude training was sinking in. Romaine and Nora had pulled their chairs to the side and were arguing with one another. And still, I couldn't feel a thing.

Perhaps I could help the antidote along. Under normal circumstances, I'd be worried about Lamastu. I tried to centre in on that and how Nora's life was at stake. But nothing.

Best go for my strongest trigger. Lucas. I wasn't going to meet his gaze with him in his current state. Instead, I studied his hands. They were a little too striated, the wood under his fingertips splintering, but the breadth and strength always drew me. That and the elegance of his fingers. They bore a dexterity that healed and cared, and the way they'd run over my... I shook myself. I didn't need to go that far, and that should have been more than enough to kindle something. But inside, I was flat... dead.

"It's not working." I shifted, my Keeper gear much too restrictive. I just needed more of Roux's mixture, that was all.

Lucas released the worktop, leaving crushed indents. "Impossible. The antidote has a proven track record."

Roux nodded. "Indeed, it does."

Were they listening? "Well, it's not working now."

Lucas's brow lowered. "Give her another dose." It was almost a shout. Panic wasn't a word I associated with him, but his eyes had broadened to saucers.

"You didn't want me to take the potion a moment ago, and now you look even more unhinged." I should've been the one panicking.

"Of course I'm concerned if a reliable antidote isn't working," he said stiffly.

It was more than that, I was sure of it.

Roux poured another measure into my cup. "Yes, a second dose will do the trick." He passed it over.

I downed it and stood there waiting, my arms folded, my fingers drumming. "Nothing yet."

Lucas turned away and raked his hands through his hair, before snapping back and fixing on me again, as if the moment I'd been out of his sight had been way too long.

"Still nothing." This really wasn't good. "What's going on?"

Roux kneaded his beard. "The potion and antidote are

used frequently in fae. It's extremely rare for problems to occur. In fact, I've only heard of one such case."

"What happened?" I wasn't sure I wanted to know.

"The elf in question had been through a lot, and he didn't want to feel. His emotions never returned."

"It has to work," Lucas growled. He picked up the vial and sniffed it.

Roux drew himself up. "I can assure you, it is the correct antidote, prepared with the utmost care."

I closed my eyes. Even though I didn't want to face everything inside, living life without feeling was incomprehensible. But talk about jumping the gun. Roux had heard of one case in thousands. There was nothing to say I was in that league, and despite my concerns, we had other matters to deal with.

I glanced at Lucas. "It's getting late. We'll have to go now to catch Ignace before the bond—"

A scream came from the other room.

"We have a problem," Gabe cried.

I strode in, Lucas and Roux following. Nora was clutching her neck, her chest heaving.

"Show them," Romaine said.

She drew her hands away. Her noose had slipped right up to her throat.

I stared at the hellish necklace. It was so utterly *fae* for that damned thing to tighten suddenly, rather than be measurable or in any way predictable. Nora had put up with so much over the years, and we were *that* close to unravelling what was going on. I wasn't going to lose her.

Brushing her hair to the side, Lucas eased his fingers around the thread. "It's taut, but it's not cutting into your skin. How does it feel?"

She shrugged. "It just took me by surprise, that's all. I'm totally fine." Tears beaded in the corners of her eyes.

She was anything but.

CHAPTER 36

WE SPED DOWN THE ROAD TOWARD IGNACE'S FARM AT Miglos, the sheer face of a foothill on one side, the Vicdessos river on the other. The wind contorted trees and scattered debris. Outside a cluster of houses on the far bank, two women screamed at each other and a man writhed on the ground, attempting to pull out his hair. It was more of the same. The town had been in shambles, folk crying, arguing and fighting.

I was beginning to feel it too, despite the fortifying potion. No emotions, only nausea stirring the pit of my stomach. Lucas changed gear much too hard. His face hadn't lost its severity.

"Are you sensing Lamastu?" I asked.

His lips tightened. "A little. It's... not pleasant."

I tipped my head back against the rest, images of never being able to feel again strobing before me. Given the circumstances, it was the least of my problems, so why couldn't I stop thinking about it? I'd told Roux to call if Nora's noose slipped further, but at least we had an inkling of why she'd stolen La Vieille's spindle. I had no idea what we could do about it, though. La Vieille had insisted on a life for a life, and we couldn't take down Lamastu if I couldn't help Pajuzu.

I'd taken a third lot of antidote before we'd left, and still nothing. We could only hope that Ignace would provide something of use, and we really had to get a move on or we were going to be late for the bond. Despite Lamastu's threat to the town, the risk of the bounds splitting because we couldn't infiltrate Lucas's family was ultimately so much worse.

We overtook an ancient Citroën 2CV.

"Uh, boss?" Slaughter's head appeared between the two front seats, his gnarly hands gripping the headrests on either side.

"Report."

"Ignace has driven off with a packed bag. He's in a right state."

"He's making a run for it," I said.

"What's he driving?" Lucas put his foot down, and we hurtled past a truck.

"A Range Rover the colour of cat sick."

"He'll be coming this way." It was highly unlikely he'd take another route as they all led further into the mountains. "We can cut him off."

"My thoughts exactly," Lucas said. "And it shouldn't be long until we see him."

We rounded the corner, and ahead was a tan four by four.

"That's him." Slaughter joggled about.

Lucas lowered the gear. "Hold tight."

I grabbed the overhead handle, and Lucas thrust the wheel around. My stomach lurched as we twisted into a screeching side skid and slid to a halt, the SUV spanning the road. Penned in by rock and river, Ignace couldn't pass. His Range Rover drew to a stop.

We sprang out, adjusting our dagger scabbards over the Keeper gear we'd donned for Fae. Burnt rubber filled the air, mingling with the noxious wind, which turned my stomach and abraded my skin. Despite the heat, I wished I'd covered up, but we'd worn summer tunics that revealed much of our arms, and goose bumps skittered over mine. The truck and the car we'd overtaken pulled up behind Lucas's SUV, the drivers peering our way.

Ignace climbed out stiffly. "What the hell do you think you're doing?" His scrawny face tightened, his lips puckering. His wispy hair thrashed about along with his shirt, which was roughly buttoned and open at the bottom. "Get out of the road."

"What we're doing," I called as we strode over, "is stopping you from running away and leaving us all in it."

"You two again." He stepped backward and made a dash for his car.

Lucas got there first. He slammed the door and leant on it. "It's lovely weather, Ignace. Such a pleasant breeze." He glanced around. "How about you tell us what's going on."

"What are you talking about?" Ignace blustered. "What with the other day at Marta's and now this, you two are so far out of line. I'll be reporting you to the National Council of the Order of Physicians."

The drivers of the car and the truck began fighting.

I joined Lucas. "I think you know full well what's happening. You're the last of four, Ignace. Are you looking forward to tonight?"

His jaw slackened.

"And it's not just you," I added. "The whole town is taking it rather badly. What about your wife, how is she?"

"We may be able to help you and her," Lucas said.

Ignace sneered. "What can a doctor and a waitress do?"

"We know about Marta being a tempestaire for starters. Fill in the gaps."

"Ridiculous. A lot of old mumbo jumbo."

In one swift move, Lucas stepped behind Ignace, drew the dagger from his thigh and positioned it against his neck.

A little blood trickled onto his shirt. "What are you doing?" he stammered.

"Talk," Lucas growled.

Ignace raised his hands, his throat bobbing on the blade. "Alright... *alright*. Where do I start?"

"The beginning would be nice." I smiled, though I was sure it didn't reflect in my eyes.

"It was the farmers from Saint-Girons," he said, trembling. "It's all their fault. They started it. Gert lent one of them his good spade, but the wretch denied it. We got in a fight, but those wastrels were all talk. We pummelled them, and they didn't like it, so they set storms on us. Everything was ruined—the hay, the vines, the sunflower crop, the little wheat we managed in the mountains—it was all destroyed."

"So you got Marta to help you out," Lucas said.

"She wouldn't. She broke off our engagement. Said that our behaviour was reprehensible and that calling storms was an ungodly practice." His jaw shook. "They kept sending weather at us, and all the time their women were overly competitive with ours in the regional baking competitions. Spiteful, they were."

"Baking competitions," I said. "That'll do it."

"You weren't there." He glared at me. "There was nothing we could do. Eva wasn't interested in helping, either. She didn't believe she or Marta had control over the weather. But when her husband left her for some woman from Bagert, she was in a state. She had young children and her house was about to be repossessed." He shifted and winced as he stung himself on the blade. "We offered her a lot of money to perform an incantation on Cap de Couronnes, where my great-grandfather remembered his great-grandfather saying there had been an oratory. She insisted she didn't have a clue what to do, and that all she could manage was to recite the verses her mother had sung to her as a child. We didn't care at that point. Anything was better than nothing. She didn't think it would work, but she was willing to do it for the money."

"But it did work." Spats of rain struck my skin and marked the dusty road.

He made to nod, then glanced at the blade and thought better of it. "Eva evoked something terrible." His eyes shifted from side to side as if he was trying to see the horrendous presence. "It finished off the Saint-Girons farmers. They deserved every little bit of what they got, and so did their families."

Lucas met my gaze and shook his head, rain spotting his face. Yep, this guy really was a jerk.

"Marta told me that Eva was pretty vexed about the deaths," Ignace continued. "She went back to the oratory. I don't know what happened up there, but afterward she was never the same. Apart from that, I have no idea what's going on. I swear, it was all Eva's doing. She's to blame." His voice grew shrill. Talk about passing the buck. But perhaps when Eva had returned to Cap de Couronnes, she'd bound Lamastu, and somehow they'd become linked.

"He may have explained a few things," Lucas said, "but he knows nothing of use. We're wasting our time."

"Agreed." We were cutting it much too fine for the bond. If only Eva could talk. But right now, we needed to get to Fae.

He pushed Ignace forward, releasing him. The old guy stumbled to his Range Rover, cussing under his breath and dabbing at his neck.

Before he could climb in and start the engine, I drew my dagger. "I'd like it if you hung around." There was a chance we might need him, and it was only right that he stayed to face his own mess. I'd have the Men ensure he didn't take off again, but for now... "It's not such a long walk home." I stepped over to his Range Rover and drove my blade into the nearest tyre. Circling the car, I repeated the process. Hissing air mingled with Ignace's rather heated response.

CHAPTER 37

WE SPRINTED DOWN THE HILL THROUGH THE FOREST near Charmant, vertes velles scattering, wrens diving for cover. We'd run all the way here, and my chest heaved, though the air was blessedly clear. I didn't know how far Lamastu's range extended, but it appeared to be limited to the human realm. And after the rain had built to a torrent back there, I was almost dry from the warmth of Stinkhorn and the woodland.

The sun was as high as it could be. It was time. Through the boughs, the pale glimmer of the waxing crescent moon shone in the pristine blue.

As we continued on, the forest grew dense, mugwort skirting the mist-wreathed path. Cobwebs draped the branches, spirals ornamented with dew, and musty mulch tickled my nose, the scent pungent and otherworldly. The hut came into view, smoke rising from the ramshackle chimney. We slowed to a halt. I bent over, leaning on my knees as I fought for breath. Lucas was fine, as usual.

He glanced at his watch. "We have a minute."

"A *minute*," I said through gasps. "Let's not cut it this fine next time."

With a wry look, he shook his head. "There won't be a next time."

The gravity of the moment descended. There had been so much else to think about, but we were going to be bonded for life. I was going to be bound to this brave, stalwart, courageous drac. I drew a deep breath, fixing him in the eye. "So this is it."

He scoured my face. "You still can't feel anything." It wasn't a question.

I shook my head, my jaw tight. "Nope."

"Well, there's not much we can do about it now." He inclined his head to the hut. "Ready?"

"You asked me that last time we were here, and in no way was I ready for La Vieille." I released a snort. "I don't think I'm ever prepared for Fae. But yes, let's do it."

We strode to the door. Lucas held the hide and I ducked under.

Once again, I was blind in the darkness but for the glow of the blazing fire. He placed his hand on my shoulder, his touch warm. My vision adjusted slowly, revealing the curves of the spinning wheel and the skeins of golden yarn hung all about, mingling with cobwebs. At the end of the hut, the sky shimmered from the window in the eaves.

"Come, come." La Vieille stood before the blazing

hearth. She dusted her hands on her dark dress, her long grey hair falling either side of her wrinkled face. "You have cut it fine."

"Andos," Lucas murmured.

"Andos, my children." She met my gaze. I fought not to look away. Her eyes held so much... too much. "Well now, my daughter, it seems you're not feeling yourself at the moment." She cackled.

"Andos," I replied. She was spot on, and there really was nothing else I could say.

She clasped her hands in front of her. "But you are both here, and that is what matters."

It wasn't the time, but there was something I had to ask. "Nora's noose has drawn tight. We believe she stole your spindle to appease Lamastu, who has sway over her family. Is there anything at all you can do?"

"Child, I must have death for the stealing of my spindle. The threads demand it—there is no alternative. Now, the fire is blazing, and we are ready to begin." Her voice was as firm as the earth. There was no argument to be had, and I wouldn't risk delaying us further.

She beckoned us closer until we stood with her on the threadbare rug before the hearth. Lucas's hand brushed mine. I should have shivered at his touch, I should have felt something, but I didn't. We entwined our fingers, gripping each other tightly.

La Vieille held out her palms. We placed our hands in hers, just as we'd done when she'd trawled through our heads. "Good, good," she muttered.

I glanced at Lucas. He was already looking at me, his eyes questioning. I didn't need to feel him to know he was seeking confirmation that I wished to proceed, not that we had much choice where the bounds were concerned. But from the depths of my being, it was what I wanted. I nodded and asked the same question with my gaze. His eyes hardened with absolute certainty, and he dipped his chin in return.

"Yes, indeed." La Vieille cackled softly. I had no doubt that she was aware of our exchange.

"Camille Amiel, my daughter." La Vieille studied me, then turned to Lucas. "Lucas Rouseau, my son. The threads that draw you together tighten. They must be bound this noon, otherwise they will be rent asunder lest they break you. You have declared your fealty to each other, but you must affirm your decision to me. My children, I ask you once more, are you ready to sacrifice yourselves for what lies ahead?"

Lucas stared at her a little too hard. "Yes," he pronounced.

I wanted this. I wanted to continue on as a Keeper and work with Lucas. The answer fell from my lips. "Yes."

"Then by the old lore, by the earth and the sun, by fae and humankind, by the balance that must hold with all things, so be it."

Her hands tightened around ours as steadfast as night follows day, and the hut darkened, or was it that the yarn glowed brighter. But the threads weren't only draped about the room, they wove about our waists, our chests, our limbs, our clasped hands. The fibres were firm and strong, bearing the weight of our souls. My lips parted. Awe had to be instinctual rather than emotional, because I brimmed with it. I met Lucas's gaze, his pupils wide.

The threads gleamed, but something even more luminous suffused the hut. The small window at the end shone, its radiance overwhelming, its warmth indescribable.

"I wondered when you'd get here, you old fool," La Vieille cackled. "Always one to make an entrance, Abellion. As if we couldn't do anything without you. Tut, tut, tut."

The room grew brighter still. The threads, the air, *everything* was so radiant, I could hardly bear it. All I could do was stare flabbergasted at Lucas, as he stared back, open-mouthed. The yarn tightened, weaving into knots that fastened me to him. I could feel every one of them, though the yarn joining our hands and twining up our arms burned.

When I thought I could bear the radiance no more, the light dimmed to nothing. As I adjusted to the gloom, La Vieille squeezed our hands and released us. But still, Lucas and I held each other. For some reason, I didn't want to let go.

"There we are, my children. It is done." She turned to the fire. It had burned to ashes, only a few embers remaining. She piled wood on once more and flames kindled, light glinting on our skin. My hand still in Lucas's, I angled my arm toward me. Where the yarn had burned were golden patterns, thick lines that twisted about both our hands and curved along our arms to fade at the shoulder. Our bond markings. I had no idea what they signified, though I was sure I'd seen something similar before.

Yet despite the awe I'd experienced, unease made me rigid. Lucas and I were bound, but as I met his eyes, I couldn't feel the slightest hint of him. He may as well have been dead to me. And deep in my bones, I was certain of one thing. It wasn't right. The potion had taken away more than I could comprehend. His gaze flickered over my face, searching for that link I couldn't make, its absence so utterly wrong.

CHAPTER 38

We stepped through the old verdigris door in Stinkhorn and emerged out by the menhir on Coustarous, rain blasting into us, driven by the screeching, repugnant wind. We were soaked in an instant, icy water oozing into my leathers.

I forced myself not to wretch, nausea coursing through me, not only from the rank atmosphere but from the large dose of antidote Lucas had given me on our return. Once again, it hadn't done a thing.

We'd sprinted back after Slaughter had sent word that things were deteriorating in the human realm. Despite all that awaited us, I couldn't stop thinking of how much I'd lost. My mess of emotions had been unwieldy, so damned unmanageable, but they'd been more than mere overwhelm. They were everything I used to connect with others. They were me.

Through sheets of blustered rain cast from pallid cloud,

something glimmered amidst Tarascon. The Ariège was swelling fast. Beside it, the N20 was snarled and water-logged, downed electricity lines blocking the route, and at the far end of town, part of the roof of the aluminium foundry had been blown off.

I glanced at Lucas. "Shit."

"That's putting it mildly." Rain ran over his bond markings, which were now little more than water-streaked golden ochre.

"Lamastu is gaining strength fast." If the farmers' deaths were anything to go by, when she reached full power, we'd be goners. My phone vibrated repeatedly against my thigh as a host of messages came in. I pulled it out as Lucas's rang. We had no choice but to huddle together, shielding our phones from the deluge.

"Roux, what's happening?" Lucas yelled above the wind. He tapped the call onto speakerphone.

"Oh, thank heavens you're back." He was only just audible. "It went well, I take it?"

We glanced at each other. I wasn't sure how to answer that. We were bound, and yet we were so terribly far from well.

"All good," I said, cringing at my words.

Lucas lasered me. "You call this good?" He didn't mean Lamastu.

"We have Eva in the Keepers' post," Roux continued. "She drove to the base of Cap de Couronnes and took the path to the oratory in a daze. The Men overpowered her and brought her here. She got violent and they had to tie her up.

Nora and Romaine have been trying to calm her without success. The Men are continuing to guard Marta at home."

Lucas dripped onto his phone. "It sounds as if Lamastu wants Eva as her focus, and that she needs her at the oratory. If she succeeds, her power will spiral. Keep Eva there at all costs." As he shot out instructions for the readying of weapons and herbs, I scanned my texts. Most of them were updates from Roux, but there was one from Grampi, who was just about coping, the Rôdeurs still unconscious, and another from Alice. *What the hell is going on?*

Damn it. She'd broken our silence to text, which meant she was freaking out. Hoping with every fibre of my being that she was alright, I tapped out, *Difficult to explain. Stay inside and keep a weapon on you. Defend yourself if necessary.* Though I had no idea how she could protect herself from the wind.

Lucas finished his instructions and we set off toward the steps, but thunder rumbled, low and threatening. I paused, the rain stinging my skin. Dark cloud had built behind us. It swirled against Lamastu's pale maelstrom, two mighty weather fronts clashing, vitality stirring in my blood. Pajuzu.

"Wait," I said. "I have to try again."

Lucas's glower should have been enough to chase both storms away. "Pajuzu couldn't use you last night. He won't be able to now."

I brushed water off my face. "I'm the only real chance we have, and I have to give it a shot before Lamastu grows stronger."

He studied me from under his brow. "I don't want you to, Camille. I've said it already."

"Our alternative is the bonevetch, but Lamastu is too scattered right now. If she uses Eva as her focus, we'll have our target, but if things get that far, I hate to think what will happen to her and the town. I have to give it a go."

"No," he growled, his fingers clenching.

I couldn't figure out his protectiveness. Heaven help us working together if this was going to be his norm. I took his rigid hand in mine and drew him to me. His breath hitched. He was feeling it more than I was, that was for sure. "You're not going to stop me," I said as softly as I could in the commotion, "because I have the right to choose, and if you don't respect that, our partnership, our bond, is nothing. I'm going to the oratory."

His hand tightened around mine, his gaze darker than night. For a moment I thought he'd crush my fingers, then he released me. "I'm coming with you."

I hadn't expected anything less.

With the wind and rain pummelling us, we jogged along the length of Coustarous, then descended a little before rising again toward Cap de Couronnes. As we approached, the screeching grew louder, the wind wilder. The nausea seeping through my veins vied for dominance over Pajuzu's vitality as the fronts clashed above, lifeless grey meeting enraged black.

We reached a protective clump of box trees just below the summit. "Stay here."

Lucas nodded, though he looked far from pleased.

I strode on, skirting the edge of the peak. Pajuzu's rumbling and Lamastu's keening were a physical thing, reverberating through my body. On the southwest flank, I paused and closed my eyes, trying to open myself... to feel something... anything... Some of the most fraught moments of my life strobed before me. My dismay when, years ago, Grampi had returned home only able to speak about goats. Everything I'd felt in Les Profondeurs. Alice being hurt by Raphaël. That absolute asshole, Elivorn. Lucas almost dying in Grimmere. My thoughts stuck on that one, but they were thoughts, nothing more.

Pajuzu twisted about me, probing for my tumult. "No, Camille," he roared. "Still, I cannot use you. What have you done?"

If I could feel panic, it would've been building. Instead, my thoughts raced through the possibilities if I was to fail. None of them were pretty. "I'm trying," I cried.

Thunder broke, light streaking the sky. "I need more," he bellowed. "I need all of you."

Washed-out cloud met Pajuzu's immense billows, condensing and forcing him back. The lifeless air thickened, and tendrils of pestilence coiled around my body, seeping into my skin. I sank to my knees, agony swathing me, my thoughts tangled. Damn it, I couldn't feel emotion, but I could sure as hell feel pain. Lamastu bored into my bones, my vision darkening as every one of them shattered. I caught Lucas charging from the far side of the summit, then the world fell away.

Chapter 39

My soaked body shook, my face pressed against solid leather. Arms cradled me, a familiar scent soothing my aching bones. I tucked myself into Lucas's neck, inhaling wild rosemary and earthy sweat. By the undulating, which wasn't helping my sickness, he was running. I forced my eyes open to a blur of colours. "Where are we?" I managed.

"Fae Tarascon. Almost at the Keepers' post." After a moment, he slowed to a walk and paused before a riveted oak door. We were back.

"Put me down," I murmured. "I'm fine." Though it was far from the truth. I felt as though I'd been crushed, my nausea was indescribable, I was dead inside and I hadn't been able to help Pajuzu.

He released me gently and held my elbow with a steadying hand, the beamed overhang of the Keepers' post sheltering us from the worst of the wind and rain. The boughs and trunks from which fae Tarascon was built creaked, and the leaves that covered much of the street thrashed about. Water streamed down the slope toward the café. Three goblins lay in the flood, groaning and heaving.

"You sure you're alright?" He scoured my face.

"Completely." So completely not.

"Let's get you some healing potion, anyway."

"I can't argue with that." I took a step toward the door and wobbled, then steadied myself against the wood, my failure swamping me anew. I hadn't wanted to feel for so long, and now I couldn't. I was so completely and utterly screwed.

"Camille?" His brow rose.

I met his gaze as shouting came from inside. "Really, I'm fine." Taking a breath, I headed in.

An uproar met us. At the back of the room, Eva thrashed and bellowed upon cushions. She'd been tied to rivets in the wall by her chest, waist and wrists, and her ankles were bound.

"Nora, Romaine, release me," she snarled an octave higher than usual, her voice blending with the screeching wind that shook the timbers of the Keepers' post.

Nora leant on the table, her fingers raking through her hair. Her noose didn't appear to have tightened further, thank goodness. Romaine sat beside her, wringing his hands. Poor kids, seeing their mother like this, though considering their history, perhaps it wasn't the first time.

The gang huddled on the other side of the table, Félix's, Hugo's and Zach's faces much too jolly as always.

"I can see it now," Félix cried. "I'm casting the collude,

and Hugo and Zach, you're backing me up, and the demon swells and swells, her tentacle appendages bulging until she explodes." He thrust his hands over his head and splayed his fingers.

Hugo punched the air. "Yesssss!"

"Slime splattering over everything!" Zach hollered.

Gabe slumped back in his chair. Dark rings circled his eyes.

"You lot holding up?" Lucas called.

"Hundred percent," Félix said, along with hoots from the others.

"I feel like shit, though I'm not quite ready to weep in the street," Gabe replied. "The fortifying potion is helping."

Roux hurried from the kitchen to meet us, his face pale, his cheeks sunken. "I'm glad you're here. I have to say, I was expecting you sooner. I was worried something had happened."

His worry was justified—something had happened. I'd fucked up so badly that we were about to be at Lamastu's mercy. I trembled. Even though I couldn't connect to my emotions, my body sensed the hopelessness of it all.

Roux inclined his head to Eva. "That's the third lot of restraints. She's getting stronger. Tell me we have a plan."

"Right now, the plan is healing potion." Lucas strode into the kitchen, Roux and me following. He rummaged in one of the apothecary cabinets and passed me a vial. "Drink."

"Happy to oblige." I pulled the cork and tipped it back. My trembling eased a little, my bones felt whole once more and my nausea lightened. If only the potion could help me feel.

"Tell me we have a plan other than that," Roux muttered.

I shook my head. "I still can't access my emotions. I'm useless to Pajuzu."

Roux ran quivering fingers down his beard. "Well, we can't use the bonevetch with Lamastu dispersed, so we're empty-handed."

But there had to be something I could do. I couldn't contemplate the alternative.

The gale thundered into the building, the whole place shaking. Eva shrieked, pulling a hand free.

"I'll sort it." Lucas strode out and grabbed a coil of rope that hung over a chair.

Roux made to busy himself with the herbs laid out on the worktop, but I caught his cloak. "Wait, I need your help."

"Alright, alright, Camille. No need to manhandle a mage, especially one who's had as many run-ins with lesser-spotted scritchouts as I have. I'm not as steady on my feet as I once was, and what with this terrible atmosphere, I'm most definitely not myself."

I released him. "My emotions. I have to do something about them. Is there anything you can think of?"

His brow peaked as he shook his head. "The only thing that comes to mind is the elf I mentioned. Like him, could there be something painful you would rather not feel? He certainly had a few matters to deal with, and he chose not to confront them. Perhaps, in the same way, there is something troubling you."

Lucas was struggling with Eva, Nora gazing on fiercely, Romaine's face broken.

"Something troubling...?" I stared at Lucas.

"Indeed." Roux nodded, his brow raised and wrinkled. "Something so troubling that you dare not even consider facing it."

My trouble was there, in the other room, wrestling Eva. That wasn't difficult. Lucas had been trouble from the moment we'd met. But I'd attempted to reconnect to the flames he stoked and it hadn't worked.

I leant back against the apothecary cabinet and dragged my hands over my face. There had to be something more, something I was missing... So much had happened to us lately. There had been our flirting, and La Vieille's interference. There was the way Lucas fought to control himself over me, and the bolts of light I'd released into his chest. I'd never forgive myself for that, but he'd provoked pain that I couldn't even consider facing, and my reaction in that possessed and definitely-not-me state had been to protect myself.

My breath grew shallow, my fingers pressing into the solid wood of the cabinet. *Something I dare not consider facing...*

Oh, fuck.

There was *that*.

There was the gouging in my chest, the agony that hurt so badly because Lucas tore at my soul with his warmth, his company, his teasing, his trickery. He pierced my heart with all he'd done in Grimmere, with everything that made up him. He cut so deeply that he was already tearing me apart.

It hurt so much that I'd struck him down in a demon-induced overreaction. I'd shied away from it because I didn't want to risk our friendship and our partnership. They meant too much... *He* meant too much.

I began to tremble again, my fingers, my hands, all of me.

The truth was, I couldn't put myself in a position for him to hurt me. He could do that in an instant—no, he was doing it already. He hacked at the wound of every broken relationship and every stupid mistake that littered my past. He left it all smarting so terribly that I would do anything to seal it shut.

That was my trouble.

Lucas rose from Eva and cocked his head as if he'd sensed something, as if his presence filled every inch of me.

As his gaze met mine, I couldn't ignore the desire to step over to him, to reach out and feel his warmth, his fervour. But my chest panged, the pain worse than anything Lamastu could inflict. All I could do was brace myself against the cabinet and gasp as every single tormenting emotion I felt for him battered into me.

Shit, I wanted to lock it all away with every fibre of my being. I couldn't, though. Alice was right, it was holding me back. No, more than that, it was destroying me. The thing was, I had no idea how to handle being so utterly exposed.

The room narrowed, my heart thrashing against my ribs. There was only one thing I could think to do. I strode through the meeting room to the door without meeting Lucas's eye. "I need to see someone. I'll be back soon."

"Camille..." he called.

I pushed out into the street, the door slamming shut. Wind and rain thrust me about in the ghastly air, horrendous keening piercing my ears. Every part of my body pounded with my heart as I waded through the torrent that gushed past the shops. Doors stood open, the ironmongers, the cobblers and the florists all flooded. Some of the goblins that lay about groaning or crying had developed faint lesions similar to the Rôdeurs'. The din of a godawful brawl came from the Parsnip as I passed.

Out on the N20, drivers were shouting, several in fights, one slamming the head of another against a car. I wanted to help them, really I did, but I was so utterly raw. I stumbled through the car park to the café and pushed open the door.

Calmness hit me, the room warm and peaceful. Folk of all ages huddled together, talking in hushed voices. Some sat on chairs, some nestled in sleeping bags on the floor. None of them were cussing or fighting or pulling out their hair. It didn't make sense.

The events room door opened, and I glimpsed folk sheltering there too. Dame Blanche emerged and wove in and out of the tables, collecting empties, warmth emanating from her. She was doing this. She was protecting the place. She paused on the other side of the room and inclined her head.

I made to nod back, but the rawness in my chest was too much to bear. "Alice!" I cried, hurtling behind the counter. I dove down the corridor to the office, but it was empty. My stomach lurching, I headed to the kitchens and paused at the entrance.

She was standing at the worktop by the window, making up plates of food. Thank heavens she was safe. She turned and flinched as she registered me, her eyes widening then narrowing. Our argument hung in the air, and my chest hurt so terribly, I couldn't speak.

"Camille, what's wrong?" She made to rush over, but I raised my hand, then clung to the doorframe. Biting her lip, she searched my face.

"Uh... you're right," I managed, my voice shaking. "About me and Lucas."

She glanced out the window. "This... now?"

I nodded, hoping she could see the insistence in my eyes. "The thing is, Alice... I have no idea how to handle it. No idea at all."

She snorted. "That much is clear."

My eyes pricked, my chest smarting. Everything that had happened with past breakups, I'd brushed off. I'd picked myself up as if they'd been nothing. A self-defence mechanism that stood me in good stead for combat. But they hurt so much that it took my breath away. "I'm scared, Alice, I... I'm so damned scared. I have all these feelings and they're so painful. This is worse than the hantaumo, worse than Grimmere, worse than anything else." Tears ran down my face.

She rushed over and drew me close, wrapping me in her arms. "Oh, hon... Oh, Camille."

I shook against her, sobs wracking through me. "I can't do it, Alice, I can't."

"Hey," she said softly, squeezing me tight. "Being a little vulnerable isn't such a bad thing. Not with people you trust, right?" She drew in a breath. "Not with me... and not with him."

"Oh, shit. Oh, shit. Oh, shit," I murmured into her shoulder. She smelled of bread and childhood sleepovers and laughter. "I don't know if I can do this."

Pulling back, she tucked a strand of hair behind my ear, just as she'd always done. "Camille, you're the strongest person I know. You've got this."

I swallowed and nodded slowly, everything whirling and spinning through me. I could hardly comprehend what I felt for Lucas, all of it spiraling with deathly fear and excruciating pain, but there was something I had to do.

"I love you." I dotted her cheek with a kiss. "But I have to go."

Grinning, she squeezed my arms. "Love you too."

CHAPTER 40

OUTSIDE THE CAFÉ, WIND AND RAIN DROVE HARDER, THE air so sickening I had to force myself not to double over. But more than that, my chest was raw, my fear a physical thing gouging at a wound so great that I had no idea how I was still standing. But I had to do this.

My phone buzzed. I pulled it from my pocket, the screen instantly spatted. Lucas. My stomach leapt, so many emotions whirring through me. I was going to be just the person Pajuzu wanted to see.

I read the text. *Nora flipped. She and Eva are making for the oratory. They were too strong to hold. Ignace and Marta are heading up there too. The Men say he found a car and forced her, desperate for help. We can't intervene as Lamastu is protecting them all. We're following but the wind is holding us back.*

I tapped out, *I'll be there soon. I'm ready.*

I made to head for fae Tarascon to take the steps up

Coustarous, but that was human thinking. Time to think like a storm. With Lamastu whipping about, I strode to the centre of the car park. Pajuzu's vitality stirred in my blood, stoking my tumult. He seethed and grumbled in the mountains beyond Rancié, waiting for a chance to challenge Lamastu.

I raised my hands in the air. "Pajuzu," I yelled.

The sky blazed with light, and thunder shook my bones as Pajuzu ripped in and spiralled around me.

"Yes!" he roared, the reverberations filling the sky as he swept me up. "That's more like it."

Reason insisted that I really shouldn't be soaring above the town, and that as I was, panic might be the preferred option, but that part of me sank back, and I was fully present, though immaterial. There was no Superman impersonation, and I wasn't standing in the car park in a trance. I *was* the storm, within and without. I spun and gusted, the rawness in my chest unrestrained. I was the tempest that cleared the air, that brought turmoil and release, and it was time to blast some serious demon butt.

We rose high above Tarascon, Pajuzu's immensity reaching far to the southwest. Beneath us, Lamastu's pallid tendrils wove about the town and streamed along the valleys, a blight on the land. Nora, Eva and Marta stood at the oratory, their arms raised in supplication, Lamastu gathering amidst their forms. Ignace was staggering between the women, and a little way off in the dip before Cap de Couronnes were Lucas, Roux, Romaine, the gang and a load of Men, heading to the summit.

I swept toward Lucas, rawness churning amidst heat and bewilderment.

"This is what I need," Pajuzu roared. "This is why I chose you... for your colossal disarray!"

That was one way of putting it, though I wasn't going to deign to reply. All the same, I could feel Pajuzu using my turmoil as a focus that honed his power into a mighty force.

As I wheeled over the summit, Ignace grabbed Marta by the shoulders and shook her, ranting in the poor woman's face, her floral granny dress flapping about. I tried to surge forward to help, but Lamastu wouldn't allow me close. Marta took an unsteady step back, bunched her fist and clobbered Ignace on the side of his head. He dropped into the mud. Possessed or not, way to go, Marta.

She retook her place in the oratory, and ashen streams flowed from the three women to Lamastu, feeding her presence. Roux had said that a demon with one focus was potent, but a demon with three? It didn't bear thinking about.

"We must stop Lamastu using them," Pajuzu bellowed.

We hurtled toward them, pristine air striking lifeless miasma, the sky crackling. Lamastu's hideous presence wracked through my bones. With a mighty screech, she drove out against us. Nora, Eva and Marta fell to the ground, and the mirk that sprawled along the valleys multiplied. Countless dark fragments broke off and swept into the sky. Birds... vultures, all of them with massive wingspans and mean, beady eyes.

I wasn't sure if I had a heart rate right now, but it definitely hitched.

"Lamastu is in her full power," Pajuzu boomed. "It is time."

Lucas and the rest took cover in the boxwood thicket under the summit.

We tore at Lamastu's rank gusts with volleys of hail that scattered the vultures asunder, the two weather fronts twining, struggling for dominance. The vultures swooped at us in retaliation, beaks and claws shredding our blasts. Pajuzu's anger roused my whirring emotions, and tension built until I could do nothing but throw out my hands, releasing a searing blaze into Lamastu and her flock. She shrieked, blackened carcasses dropping, then she rammed against us harder, expanding, thickening, extending, as if all we'd managed was to incite her.

"I need more," Pajuzu growled.

"More?" I cried. "What else is there?"

Vultures flew in from all sides, diving at us and everyone sheltered in the boxwood. Lucas and a load of Men cut down as many as they could, but they were bombarded. I flurried over the trees, chasing them off and brushing Lucas's moist cheek. My bond markings warmed, despite me not possessing an arm. Old habits died hard.

The lull allowed Lucas to pause. He stood up straight and stared about. "Camille?"

Fire blazed through me, the rawness in my chest searing unbearably. I desperately wanted to shy away from it, but I held firm, the smarting tearing me up.

"That's it," Pajuzu boomed.

In the town below, vultures swooped on folk. They broke

windows and barged into buildings. We rushed downward, buffeting them away and driving them into the cliff below Cap de Couronnes.

The café doors were open, the glass broken, the wood battered and scratched. Inside, vultures fluttered about.

A chill shuddered over me. Alice.

I swirled through the building, the wooden walls shaking as I chased the awful atmosphere away. Dame Blanche was defending the place with a frying pan. Even she hadn't been able to hold Lamastu at bay. And Alice... She was in one piece and driving a dagger into a vulture that had taken an interest in the croissant basket. She was good.

And we were off, soaring upward.

The two fronts crashed above the town in a frenzy of thunder and lightning and hammering rain, but as we fought against Lamastu, she condensed once more, each of her toxic gusts stronger than the last, her shrieking everywhere, my thoughts splintering.

"Give me more, Camille," Pajuzu roared.

He had to be joking. He had everything, and my mind was being torn asunder.

"Vengeance is mine," Lamastu screeched. "Death embraces the mountains, and it embraces you, Pajuzu, once and for all."

We withdrew, then blasted into her again, but she expanded further, her sickening tendrils reaching out to Ax, Foix and beyond. Beneath us, folk writhed in the torment of her excruciating grip, vultures barrelling into them, my heart breaking at the sight.

"She's too big," I cried.

CHAPTER 41

"We must force Lamastu back into herself," Pajuzu roared as we circled the summit, his deluge ceasing. "She's too dispersed to target."

"How the hell can we do that?" It was the question I'd discussed with Lucas and Roux, and we hadn't come up with an answer.

I gazed down at Nora's, Eva's and Marta's prostrate forms. There had to be a way to help them. They'd been innocent victims in all of this. But... perhaps there was something we could do. What if we finished this the way it had started? "Put me down on Cap de Couronnes," I cried. "And cover me."

With a deafening crack, Pajuzu cut a channel through Lamastu and scudded toward the summit. And just like that, I was standing in the mud a little way from Lamastu's seething centre at the oratory. Pajuzu was holding off her gusts, his own squall pelting down. The vultures were another matter. They flew at me. Without thinking, I reached over my shoulder for my blade, but it wasn't there. Dodging this way and that, I avoided them as best I could, striking out as they closed in.

"Camille!" Lucas charged from the boxwood.

For a moment, I could say nothing as this wonderful, frightening, brave drac fought for me. The Keeper bond throbbed between us, augmenting my sense of him. It left me speechless.

"He is causing trouble again," Pajuzu boomed in my head. "Shall we strike him once more?"

"No," I yelled.

Lucas spun around mid-hack, thinking the reply was for him.

"Don't," I murmured so only Pajuzu could hear. "Don't touch him." I couldn't comprehend everything I felt for him, and now wasn't the time. "We need to draw Lamastu back here."

Without waiting for a response, I sprinted to the boxwood. Men stood on rocks and clung to soaked boughs, their razor-sharp flint weapons doing a great job of defeathering vultures. Amidst eddying plumage, I ducked in under the branches to where the others crouched, equipped with daggers and blades.

They stared at me, open-mouthed. Gabe was as white as a sheet, Roux's beard was bedraggled, the gang still appeared way too enthusiastic and Romaine's eyes bulged. I fell to my knees, Lucas joining me, my awareness of him at my side overwhelming.

"Romaine," I yelled above the commotion. "We need a tempestaire."

He scraped his wet and most definitely not styled hair back. "What are you asking me for?"

"Because we have to draw Lamastu in. She's too spread out for Pajuzu to have an impact. Once she's focussed, Pajuzu and I will keep her here. Then you lot cast the bonevetch collude, and we'll do the rest."

Lucas nodded. "It could work."

"I don't get where I come in," Romaine said. The others stared between us.

"You have to call Lamastu here."

A hustle of vultures breached our cover, borne on a repulsive squall. Lucas sprang up to meet them, joining the Men.

Romaine released a humourless laugh. "I can't do that. Anyway, tempestaires run in the female side of the family."

"Really?" I raised my brow. "There has to be a reason you've not been affected by everything. It's possible you possess the ability like some of the priests in the past, but maybe because you kept out of Lamastu's way, or because you fought off her influence when you were at home, she wasn't able to hinder you."

He opened his mouth, then closed it again. "Even if I could, I don't know what to do."

"What did Marta sing to you when you were little?"

His breath caught. "Well, yeah, I guess there were those songs. She always used to sing the same stuff. It stuck in my head. Maman and Nora used to hum them too."

"Then you're good." I clapped him on the back.

"No." He shook his head. "It's enough seeing all this shit. It's completely freaking me out. I'm not going to take part in it. Hard no." He glared defiantly at everyone.

My eyes blazed. We didn't have time for this. "Have you noticed that your maman, sister and grandmother are demon fuel over there? How much longer do you think they're going to last?"

Romaine swallowed.

"If they die," I added, "will you be able to live with not having tried?"

"Fuck." His shoulders dropped. "I can give it a go... not that there's any point."

"Do it. Now. Get as close to the oratory as possible. We'll provide cover. The rest of you, be ready with the bonevetch."

There were nods all around.

Romaine drew his dagger, his fingers trembling against the hilt. "Nothing for it." He sprinted out of the trees toward his family, Lucas at his side.

I followed them out. "Pajuzu!"

In an instant, I was borne aloft, leaving startled faces below. I could only guess that I'd vanished before their eyes.

Romaine paused at the side of the oratory near Lamastu's fetid concentration, Lucas defending them from the vultures. It was difficult to tell from this height, but Romaine appeared to be singing. We streamed toward him. Lamastu wouldn't allow us close, but I caught shreds of "The wind that assails us, I shall not fear. The devil travails us, I do not hear." But it wasn't anything like Marta's warble. It was the forceful blast of rap.

Lamastu's shrieking rose to a crescendo. She fought to reach him with her deathly flurries, but her closest gusts could only wither toward the oratory, gathering in the centre between the Ruizes.

"I like this boy," Pajuzu roared.

The vultures, however, weren't restricted. They swooped at Romaine. He swung his dagger as he continued the chant. Lucas took the brunt, cutting down the throng faster than humanly possible. They hurtled into us too, and I felt each one as though they pierced my ribs, yet we blasted against them and surged forward, Pajuzu's raging billows speeding Lamastu's retreat.

Seeing her fall back, Romaine gained confidence, his voice rising, the incantation a rhythmic rant accompanied by his foot stomping in the mud. He skilfully dropped a new beat, the chant mesmerising. Not exactly in keeping with the old tempestaires, but it worked for me.

The D&D gang and Roux had noticed too. They ran out of the thicket, heading for the oratory, swinging blades at their winged assailants. I could only hope the boys would do better than the last time they'd held weapons. The Men shielded them as well as they could with their height disadvantage, maiming anything that came near.

Pajuzu and I whipped about Lamastu, encircling her in the valleys, light streaming from my fingers, weakening her further, though I was seriously flagging. Pajuzu had taken so much.

Unable to resist Romaine's call and our onslaught, Lamastu shrank back to town. We persisted, and she withdrew to Cap de Couronnes, vultures swarming the summit. As if they were Lamastu's last desperate defence, they tore into Romaine and Lucas. The Men did their best to help, but one sliced open Romaine's arm, his dagger falling from his grip, the chant leaving his lips. We swept in to force them off, but Lamastu shielded them with her last sickly tendrils.

The rest of her, restricted to the oratory, whirled about, spinning faster until she elongated into a tornado. Her swirling top drew out to form colossal wings. In their midst, a head emerged with a streak of black that led to a red-ringed eye and a sharply hooked beak. And below, a body extended with a tremendous fanned tail. Her wingspan shadowed the land, her end feathers spreading. Utterly terrifying, she rose above us, talons at the ready.

"What's happening?" I cried.

"She's building power again," Pajuzu rumbled.

Damn it, we needed Romaine, but he and Lucas were so overwhelmed with vultures, I could barely see them. Fairing only slightly better, Félix, Hugo and Zach had taken positions around the oratory, brandishing bonevetch, with Roux and Gabe beside them. The Men, who'd resorted to climbing on their shoulders, continued their defence.

Lamastu tilted her head, taking my measure with a single beady eye. Bitter cold ran through me. She could sense that I was Pajuzu's focus. She flapped her wings in a forceful beat, then drew them in tight and dove.

As one, Pajuzu and I careened to the side. He wanted to

protect me, but Lamastu was too quick. Her claws tore through our gusts. I cried out as excruciating pain ripped into every part of me. With Romaine out of action, she was gaining too much strength. She attacked again, driving her beak through my middle, then she swept around to slash me once more. The world dimmed and spun as I fought to hold on to consciousness. My weakness meant Pajuzu's impotence. He released me, and I hurtled down. As I hit the ground, I was in my body, tumbling over and over. I came to a stop where stones delineated the oratory. Agony wracked my drenched limbs, my nerves searing.

Lamastu circled, making ready for another attack.

I drew in all the air I could muster. "Now!" I cried.

Félix stared at me, then gazed at the enormous vulture. All his frantic zeal of past weeks had gone, leaving absolute horror in his eyes, his lips parted and trembling. Hugo's and Zach's faces were aghast.

"Come on now, lad," Roux stammered. "Give it a shot." He swayed precariously as the two Men on his shoulders hacked about, using his hair for support.

Gabe, with a Man anchored in his drawn-back hood, looked as though he might pass out. "Do it!" he bellowed.

Félix flinched and held out his hand. Slaughter, on his shoulder, took down several vultures with his axe. "O mighty... demon of the air," Félix stuttered. "O bringer of pestilence and disease." Zach and Hugo joined in, their voices halting. "O destroyer of women, children and families. O destructive force of oblivion."

"The alder leaf," Roux cried, wobbling as he drew a

bundle from his cloak. The others did the same. They threw the leaves toward the oratory, though they blustered about in the wind.

"O darkness of the depths," Félix continued, his voice barely audible above Lamastu's screeching as she held Pajuzu back. "O blackness of obscurity—"

"We don't have time," Gabe yelled. "Just do the important bit."

Félix focussed on the bonevetch, and a glow encompassed his hand. He jumped back, almost dropping the herb, his fleshy mouth gaping.

Lamastu drew in her wings and plummeted toward me again. One thing was for sure—grounded in my body, I wouldn't survive another attack.

"Do it!" Lucas roared from amidst a feathery throng.

Félix hauled in a massive breath. "I bind you!" he yelled.

Brilliant gold surged from his hand to Hugo's and Zach's. It met with the alder leaves flying about, then blasted upward to encircle Lamastu. Her enormous body thrashed against it, but she was unable to break free of the glow. She shrank a little, the stream of miasma from the Ruizes severing. The vultures fell back, fluttering into one another.

Despite being torn and exhausted, Pajuzu stirred in my blood once more, his booming filling the air. "Lamastu, I will destroy you!"

His vitality permeated me. I extended my hands and lightning streaked from my fingers into Lamastu's chest, the force blasting me down. There was nothing left in me, nothing at all.

She plummeted, stunned. I was too tired to tell whether the others were gawking in horror at the massive creature as she fell or at me because of my light show. But just before the ground, she regained her senses and swept upward again, though restrained by gold. She was smaller and weaker, but by the glint in her eye, her resolve was unshakeable. She writhed in the air, attempting to cast off the glow.

"Not enough," Pajuzu bellowed. "I need more."

"Uh..." I was too exhausted to speak. He always needed more, but what more could I give? He'd had everything. Through blurred vision, I caught a movement in the oratory. Eva raised her head, Marta groaned and Nora turned onto her side. Thank heavens they were alright. But the gold around Lamastu was dimmer. The collude wasn't going to hold much longer, and still she thrashed against it.

"Come on, Camille," Pajuzu rumbled.

Yeah, I was trying, but even a glance at Lucas shaking Romaine's slumped form, no doubt willing him to chant again, only stirred a faint mixture of concern for Romaine, who was beginning to stir, and relief that Lucas was alright.

The glow encircling Lamastu dimmed further. Then, with a brutal thrash of her wings, it faded to nothing. My breath grew shallow, despair seeping through me. She swept around the summit, impervious to Pajuzu, then hovered above us once again, a beady eye flicking about, then fixing on me.

"You!" she screeched. There was no way she would stop until her arch-nemesis's focus was down.

She dove toward me. Pajuzu attempted to meet her, but

without my help, he was powerless. I closed my eyes, ready for impact, but all I felt was a rush of wings and a gush of nauseating air. She rose once more, building speed, then she plunged toward Lucas, screeching a malevolent laugh.

Panic seared my veins. She could sense our Keeper bond, and she knew what he meant to me. This was vengeance. He leapt out of the way, but she was too fast. She tore through his leathers, piercing his gut.

He cried out, the momentum rolling him to his front.

Something stirred in me then, burning in my chest, white hot and violent. That was my partner she'd hurt. No, not only my partner... That man—that fae—was *everything*. Fury coursed through my blood, and it possessed me entirely, goading my sinews to life. I rose to my feet and raised my arms, drawing Pajuzu until all the storms of the earth writhed and churned and raged within, until he and I were a single entity formed of nothing but unadulterated power.

That hell demon had to die.

"Raaaaaaagh!" Pajuzu and I roared together as I released everything in an almighty bolt of white. It ripped into Lamastu, who shook, then stilled. As she tumbled down, she shrank until she was little more than a large vulture, her noxious gusts falling away. She struck the ground at my feet, mud splattering.

"Yes, Camille!" Pajuzu cried. "She's almost dead. One small blast will finish her off."

She lay there, her feathers twitching as she cawed softly. The others came over and encircled her in morbid wonder. I glanced at Lucas, who was groaning in agony, Romaine kneeling at his side. I wanted to go to him, but this had to end, and my fury knew no bounds. I raised my hands, everyone stepping back in alarm. But before I could do anything, a figure pushed into our midst, her jaw firm, her eyes blazing, Romaine's dagger in her hand.

Nora.

She knelt by Lamastu and regarded her for a moment, then drew back her arm. With a guttural cry, she thrust the blade into the demon's heart. Lamastu released a faint screech, then stiffened, the light fading from her cold gaze, the world growing still.

Nora stared at the lifeless creature, her chest heaving. The gang gazed at her in awe as Lucas's groans filled the silence. I made to head over to him, but Nora gasped and clutched her throat, her eyes bulging.

The noose.

With a strangulated gurgle, she slumped to the ground.

CHAPTER 42

I FOUGHT TO FOCUS AS I KNELT AT NORA'S SIDE. SHE didn't appear to be breathing, but everything was a whir, my mind consumed with Pajuzu, who was drifting away, and I could barely grasp my thoughts.

Marta yelped behind me, clutching her foot. Ignace lay next to her, unmoving. Roux and the gang gazed on in various states of panic.

"Nora?" Eva clambered up and stumbled over. "That creature... I... I tried to get rid of it... to trap it years ago... but I couldn't. It wouldn't leave..." She dropped down by Nora. "Her neck."

It was swollen and crimson around the noose, which dug in viciously.

Romaine pushed through the others and joined his mother, his skin a bloody mess.

Eva's breath caught. They'd not seen each other for

years. But in a heartbeat, she returned to Nora and gripped her hand, tears beading in her eyes. "My darling. My sweet girl."

"You have to help her." Romaine blazed at me as he fumbled in his pocket, at a guess for his phone. It wasn't there. "Someone call an ambulance," he yelled.

That focussed my thoughts. "No. We have to get her to La Vieille." But Lucas was still groaning, though that was so much better than silence. "Roux, give Lucas healing potion and sort everything out here."

"With much rapidity." He darted over, rummaging in his bedraggled cloak.

I turned to Romaine. "Can you carry Nora?"

"Yeah, of course." He raked his fingers through his grimy hair.

"I'm coming." Eva tried to rise but fell back. A shell-shocked Félix caught her arm.

"No, Maman." Romaine met Eva's gaze. "We'll get help faster without you, but I promise I'll look after Nora." He hoisted her over his shoulder.

Pain streaked through me as I hauled up Lamastu's lifeless vulture form, her feathers slick in my hands. Damn, she was heavy.

Romaine shifted, and I caught sight of Lucas. Roux was at his side, still rummaging under his cloak. "I know the potion is in here somewhere."

Lucas turned his head and met my gaze, and a cascade of connection rushed between us. He would be alright. He had to be alright. Drawing a deep breath, I pulled myself away. "Romaine, let's go."

We dashed for the Coustarous menhir. A surge of adrenaline spurred me on and dulled my pain, although I still hurt like hell. But I wasn't going to lose Nora. Down we went, past the boxwood and into the shallow pass. We rose once more and tore along to Coustarous, the menhir ahead.

Romaine made for the steps to town, Nora gripped tightly in his hands.

"This way," I yelled, heading to the stone.

He paused, heaving, his face red. "What? We have to get an ambulance."

"No, we don't. There's no way they can remove the noose. There's only one chance. You have to follow me."

Nora swung lifeless from his shoulder, her hair dangling. There was a possibility we'd lost her already. But no, I couldn't think like that. Romaine's eyes flickered back and forth as he considered my bizarre request. "Alright," he managed.

We rushed to the menhir, the air glimmering as we crossed the bounds.

"Andos," I cried, then turned to Romaine. "Say what I just said to the stone. No time to explain."

He paused, wide-eyed. "Uh... Andos?"

The boy was doing better than I had the first time I'd entered Fae.

We stepped past the menhir, the old verdigris door appearing. I pushed it open.

Romaine's eyes widened some more. "What the fuck?"

Before us lay the chaotic market square in Stinkhorn, the place bustling with goblins, elves, dwarves, trolls and creatures of all shapes and sizes. They chatted, laughed and expressed themselves in the worst language possible.

"This is Fae," I said as we made our way into the overwhelming hustle. A myriad of doors set into the stone buildings beyond the market stalls opened and closed as fae came and went. Spices, cooking meat, and sweat assaulted my senses. "We don't have far to go."

Romaine's face paled, his mouth slack, his knuckles white against Nora's thighs.

"You can do this," I said.

He shook his head. "After this, I'll believe anything."

We shouldered past a dense crowd, provoking hearty cusses. Lamastu's neck lolled to one side. It felt like she was growing heavier, which wasn't helped by every part of me hurting so much. A group of trolls stood in our way. As we skirted around them, one eyed Nora and nudged a sack out to trip us up, a sneer on his bloated face. We stepped over gingerly and headed through an archway into a broad street.

It was clearer here, fae walking with purpose. We hurtled past, dodging this way and that, then turned into a side street. At the end stood the honeyed door with the carved sun. I pulled it open and shoved Romaine into the forest, beech leaves stirring either side of the path.

Romaine swayed precariously at the change. He was tiring now, sweat trickling down his face and neck. "I don't know what just happened, but I need to throw up again." Attempting not to retch, he clutched Nora tighter.

"Stay with it." My voice may have been strong, but my limbs were jelly. I didn't know if I could muster the energy to carry on, but I had to try. I hoiked Lamastu under my arm, and we ran down the path.

Passing the mugwort, the deciduous forest morphed to cobwebbed pine. A little further on stood the hut, the hide door undulating in the breeze, smoke billowing from the excuse of a chimney.

It took everything I had to force myself to the entrance, my legs shaking, my chest heaving. I pulled back the hide and entered, then held it for Romaine, who ducked inside.

"La Vieille," I cried, only able to see the glow of the hearth in the darkness. "Here is your death. We have the culprit. Release Nora."

My eyes adjusted to take in the faintly glimmering threads all about, and the barest outline of La Vieille sitting at her spinning wheel, her foot rising and falling on the treadle, her hands teasing fleece as the flyer snatched it hungrily onto the bobbin. Romaine's face was fixed in bewilderment.

"Ah, Camille, my daughter. How are you finding the bond?" Her cackles shook her thin body, her long hair swaying. Firelight glinted in her crazed, fathomless eyes as she gazed upon Romaine. "My son, welcome."

He shifted nervously.

This really wasn't the time for small talk. "Put Nora there." I pointed to the threadbare rug before the hearth.

Cradling her head, he laid her down, then knelt beside her and stroked her hair. "Come on, Nora. I know how tough you are. You can make it through this."

Nora's eyes were softly closed, her face alabaster. I hated to think it, but she looked like a corpse. My heart rate hitched. It had taken us too long to get here. The golden noose glowed from her swollen neck, one thread amidst countless others within this place, all tangles of consequence.

"Tut, tut, tut." La Vieille shook her head. "The young thief. The life due to me."

"Here is the culprit." I held up Lamastu's floppy form. The damned thing was beginning to smell.

La Vieille leant forward. "Oh dear, Lamastu, what have you been up to this time?"

Romaine glanced between us, confusion peaking his brow.

"A life for a life." I eyed La Vieille warily. "Lamastu hindered Nora for years, tormenting her family. She was stealing to ease her mother's burden." I dropped the vulture at her feet, stirring up dust.

"Hmmmm." La Vieille placed her fleece in the basket and studied the bird, shaking her head. "But Camille, Lamastu is a goddess. She is immortal and cannot be killed."

I gaped, my heart thundering. "What...?" I tried to say that it couldn't be, that it wasn't fair, that fucking fae were so damned tricky, but the words stuck in my throat. Yet I wouldn't give up that easily. Not after Nora's relentless struggle. "No way. Absolutely no way." My voice was steel.

"My daughter, are you telling the bearer of the fates of fae and humankind what is and what is not?" Her eyes flared.

I shuddered, sensing her utter presence, cold trickling

through me. She was the way things must be, she was the passage of night and day, she was birth and death and every moment between. But Nora had suffered for years. She'd done everything she could to help her family, even evoking Pajuzu. I met her gaze. "Yes, that's what I'm telling you."

La Vieille studied me, then tipped her head back and broke into uproarious laughter. "Indeed, my child. Indeed." She reached down, her sinewy hands curling about Lamastu, long nails meeting dirty brown feathers. With a cackle, she threw Lamastu into the fire.

An eerie draught drove through the hut, my spine tingling as it converged on the hearth. A tornado of flames soared up the chimney, an inferno driven by malice. The blaze roared, and Nora's noose glowed, the light so intense that Romaine and I had to shield our eyes. Then the flames subsided, and Lamastu was gone.

The golden knot at Nora's throat unravelled, and the cord slipped away. She flung up and clutched her neck, gasping in desperate breaths.

La Vieille's dark eyes fixed on me. "My daughter, you are right. This incarnation of Lamastu is no more. She will manifest again, though not here, not now."

But even the depths of her gaze couldn't hold me. All I could see was Nora as she coughed and spluttered, and Romaine as he rubbed her back, repeating her name over and over. As her breath steadied, he drew her into his chest and held her tight.

Relief flooded through me. Utter, welcome, wonderful relief.

"But Camille," La Vieille said, "don't think your work is done. There is something you need to finish... or perhaps start."

Fear and desire and pain tumbled within, my exhausted body trembling. She was right. There was someone I needed to face.

CHAPTER 43

TAPPING MY FINGERS AGAINST MY THIGHS, I GAZED OUT onto the road. Nora would be here at any moment. At the entrance to the farmyard, the old five-bar gate was propped permanently open, sheltered by an ancient gnarled oak. After everything, the familiarity of home was such a comfort.

"Yeah, you aced the bonevetch collude." Gabe's voice rose from the yard as he scratched Lavender behind the ears. "I couldn't have done it better."

Félix grinned. "I was awesome. I totally slayed it."

Those two talking amicably was a welcome turn up for the books.

Near the trees, Hugo teased Daisy with a dandelion leaf, and Zach loitered about, scuffling stones as he gazed at his phone. The mellow limestone buildings baked in delicious warmth. I drew in a breath, absorbing the sun. It was already late afternoon, but over the town to the southwest, the sky shone blue. There wasn't even a wisp of cloud. I could still feel Pajuzu a little, and because of it, I knew in my bones there would be no storm tonight. We were done.

"Come on, Camille." Félix wandered over, Lavender following and chewing at the back pocket of his shorts. "Tell us why we're here."

"You'll find out soon enough." If only Nora would hurry up. Grampi would be out any minute. I was due to give him a ride to over-eighties samba, something he was most definitely not looking forward to. He was going purely to appease Madame Biscotte, who had threatened to cut off his cheese sales to her daughter's deli if he didn't try it out.

After Lamastu's near cataclysm only the day before yesterday, and the town still being cleared of debris and rubble, I was impressed that samba was going ahead, but the over-eighties were a robust bunch.

The whole incident had been put down to freak storms and an unprecedented surge in the vulture population, the creatures forced from the peaks by the weather. I honestly didn't know how anyone could justify the presence of so many vultures, but I supposed that to most folk, it was a more likely explanation than a storm demon set on tearing the town apart.

Only a few buildings had suffered major damage, and the townsfolk had found themselves remarkably chipper after the storm had abated. And actually, we were all appreciating life a little more. Being released from a hellish pit of demon-induced desolation did that.

Unfortunately, there had been plenty of injuries, mainly from flying masonry and vulture gorging, though the single fatality had been Ignace, who'd died of suspected heart failure in addition to head trauma. What the farmers had started so many years ago had well and truly ended.

Lucas, the locum and a number of volunteer healthcare professionals had been raced off their feet, dealing with everything at a makeshift treatment centre in the town hall.

Lucas.

My chest grew tight and buoyant all at the same time, my heart squeezing.

We hadn't had time to talk since Romaine and I had returned from Fae. No, scratch that. We probably would've had time if I'd had the nerve.

What the hell was I doing? I had to face him, of course I did. Pajuzu might be satisfied, but the storm within hadn't settled. Besides, I ached to see him, though I was still swamped with the rawness in my chest and more fear than I knew how to handle.

I placed my hand on my arm, feeling my bond markings beneath my fingers, the lines etched in my mind. I was certain I'd seen the pattern somewhere, and this morning, as I'd awoken to a tumult of images that La Vieille had stoked, I'd remembered where. But I needed to see it for myself. I took a sharp breath. It would have to wait a little longer. First, I had Grampi to deal with.

Delphine emerged from the barn, which was now free of the Rôdeurs. They'd woken around the time Nora had killed Lamastu. Considering they had been trying to help her, we'd let them go, and Romaine had decided to have some space from Bastien and the rest of them, knowing that his newfound knowledge of the hidden world wouldn't go down well. He had a few loose ends to tie up in Toulouse, then he was returning to Tarascon to spend time with his family.

Delphine glanced at Félix, who sidled away. A typical reaction. Folk often took a mere carrot-seeking glance as the casting of eternal damnation.

"They're really quite harmless," I called. "Though they're kind of indestructible now, since the whole hantaumo thing. They're favourites of Aherbelste. He strengthened them somehow." I scanned the woodland below the farm. "Actually, sometimes you can get a glimpse of him. He likes to hang around here."

"Uh, what? Aherbelste, the goat god that folk call the devil?" Félix's brow creased.

"That's the one."

He glanced nervously into the trees.

"What's up?" Hugo called, pinned against the barn wall by Daisy, the rest of the herd peering on.

Zach drew his gaze from his phone. "Camille says the devil lurks around here."

"I completely didn't mean that, I—"

Félix's eyes hardened. "I don't care what you meant, Camille. Give it a rest."

I frowned. "What? No battling dragons, teasing ogres or anything else that would get you killed if Lucas and I weren't about?"

He shivered. "I don't know. After everything Nora went through, and seeing Lamastu... I'm good for now." He glanced at the others. "We all are."

I shook my head, unable to believe it. And truly, his crazed expression had been replaced by something steadier. There was still enthusiasm in his air—that would never leave him—but it was more restrained. "Well, thank the heavens."

A Renault estate pulled up by the gate, the windows rolled down. Eva was driving with Marta alongside. Nora sat in the back.

Finally.

I strode over as Eva and Nora climbed out. Eva tugged her daughter into a tight hug. "Look after yourself."

"Sure will." An unaccustomed smile spread across Nora's face as she pulled back, though it quickly morphed into controlled indifference. And although her hair and make-up were as perfect as usual, they were a little softer, the lines of kohl not quite so harsh.

"Bonjour, Camille," Marta called.

"Hey, Marta. How's the foot?"

"Just heading to the hospital to have it sorted." Her face was alight, her lipstick a bright flash. "I'll be as good as new in a few weeks."

"Wonderful." That family deserved some let-up.

"Camille." Eva climbed into the car. "Thank you once again for everything."

After Romaine and I had delivered Nora safely home, I'd gone over recent events with the family. Eva had wept for the years of torment, Nora's and Marta's arms around her. When she'd been reassured that Lamastu was gone for good, she'd cried again. Best guess, there wouldn't be any more tempestaire dabbling for her, and hopefully not for the rest of them either. She drove away with a wave.

"Why did you ask me here?" Nora's eyes narrowed.

"Wait and see." I made to walk over to the others, then paused. "I owe you an apology. I gave you a hard time about stealing. There was no way I could have sussed your motives, but even so, I wanted to say that."

She raised an eyebrow. "With Maman in such a mess, I guess it might have been quite nice to know that someone cared enough to have a go at me. And anyway"—her eyes glinted—"I can't say I haven't taken the odd lipstick for myself... and maybe a couple of—"

I raised my hand. "Nope. I don't want to know."

She shrugged and glanced at Gabe. He was sitting on the grass next to Lavender, trying a collude as she munched on one of his fake elf ears. "Get off." He swatted her away, but the end had already received a good munching, and it lolled sideways.

"You know," she said, "it was so much better after Gabe made me see the hidden world. Life was hell before—and it was hell after, but I could make out Lamastu possessing Maman and feeding off her."

"That must have been bad." Understatement of the year. It must have been utterly terrible.

"Yeah, it was. But I knew what I was dealing with, and at least I could attempt to do something. I found out about storm deities in an old book in the Keepers' post. With Lamastu gaining strength, calling Pajuzu was my last hope."

I breathed out slowly. "I'm so glad you did." For her and

her family's sake... and the town's. Though there were a couple of things I didn't get... "You appeared to be controlling Lamastu when Romaine kidnapped you."

"Nah. My stress levels spiked when the Rôdeurs attacked. She saw them as a danger and went for them. She was protecting me because she wanted to use me. Same for Romaine. She didn't harm him in case she needed him, that was all. When that load of thugs returned later, she went for them again, but by that time, she was stronger and did more damage."

"That makes sense, but... you threw Madame Bovary in the river to call the storm." I couldn't hold the sharpness from my voice. "And I have no idea how you escaped the Men to do it."

"The Men were easy. I just got them into *Vampire Chronicles*, gave them a large bowl of corn snacks and said I was going to the bathroom."

I sighed.

"Madame Bovary, on the other hand..." Nora shuddered. "Uh, I didn't exactly throw her in the river. I grabbed her with a thick pair of sheepskin gloves, which wasn't a pleasant experience, and I placed her in the shallows where she could wade back out. I hid in a bush to check she was alright, but she had a monumental hissy fit, threw herself into the flow and got carried off downstream. I was going to raise the alarm, but I caught sight of some nymphs heading her way and figured they were her best bet."

"The nymphs left the delightful honour of fishing her out to me." But at least that was sorted.

Grampi stepped out of the farmhouse backward, muttering to himself as he pulled the door closed. He turned around and paused. "What's all this?"

"That's what we want to know." Gabe extinguished his collude and got up as Grampi walked over with the others.

"Camille won't tell us anything," Hugo added.

I grinned at Grampi. "We're waiting for you. I've cancelled samba. Madame Biscotte won't stop the cheese as I've assured her that I have the perfect activity for you this afternoon... and, well, every afternoon, if you're happy with it."

"Oh?" His bushy brows narrowed.

"I have five people who urgently need weaponry training and instruction in the ways of Fae."

They all studied me with various looks of incomprehension.

"Currently," I continued, "this lot are a danger to themselves and others. I need your help." Félix, Zach and Hugo *had* calmed down a bit, but did I think that any of them, Gabe and Nora included, would keep out of Fae? Nope. Not a hope in hell.

Grampi studied me, then his lips parted and his eyes widened. A wry smile crossed Gabe's face, and Nora actually grinned.

Félix slapped his hand over his mouth, then let it drop to his side. "Oh. My. God. Weapons training with the grandfather of the High Warrior of the Borders, Protector and Holder of the Knowledge of Free Men and Fae. He's the freaking Keeper who trained her in swordsmanship—"

"The Keeper who originally fettered the hantaumo queen." Zach's lip trembled.

Hugo shook himself. "The Keeper who defended the swamplands from the invasion of the horned wobbling shammy newt."

I glanced at Grampi, my brow raised. "I haven't heard that one."

"Uh, it wasn't my finest moment. Best forgotten." He shook his head. "So what you're saying, Camille, is that you want me to train this lot?"

I nodded. "That's it."

A broad smile drew across his face, his eyes sparkling. "I think I'd like that very much."

"Yes!" Félix fist-bumped the air. The others beamed ridiculously.

"Looks like I've got my hands full, though," Grampi muttered.

He certainly did.

A car turned into the farmyard and parked alongside my truck. Alice's Citroën. I wasn't expecting her. After we'd taken Nora home, I'd checked in on the café, and despite the damage, Alice had been fine. Since then we'd texted as usual, and she hadn't mentioned dropping by.

She jumped out and walked over, a small smile tugging at her soft lips, her choppy hair swinging at her shoulders. "Camille, Monsieur Amiel. I, uh... got quite a feel for the dagger when we were raided by vultures and, well..." She met my eye. "I liked being able to defend myself. I don't suppose you'd have space for one more in your training sessions?"

"Of course we do, Alice," Grampi cried. "This is getting better and better."

I wrapped my arms around her, absorbing that familiar scent. "I'm so pleased."

"Me too," she murmured into my neck. "Thanks for the encouragement. It woke something, and I don't feel quite so vulnerable anymore." She drew back and grinned. "The next fae who messes with me..."

I laughed. I'd watched her skewer a vulture. "I don't rate their chances."

"And"—I lowered my voice, though the others were too busy making enthusiastic plans with Grampi to hear—"thank you for being straight with me."

"It doesn't take much to see through your crap. Anyway, have you seen him yet?"

"Uh..." I avoided her gaze. "I was planning to after this... or maybe later."

She rolled her eyes. "Oh Camille, what are you like?"

My stomach twisted. "I know. *I know.*"

CHAPTER 44

MY STOMACH HAD TIED ITSELF INTO A THOUSAND aching knots by the time I strode along the path toward the Grotte des Amoureux. Heat radiated from the mountain even though the sun had sunk behind the far side of Cap de Couronnes a while ago, and the light breeze was a welcome relief. The town rested below, imbued in an evening glow.

I'd finally made it here.

After finishing up at the farm and finding, oh, so many other jobs to do, I'd not been able to ignore the insistence in every part of my being that I had to see Lucas. I'd texted him to meet me at the cave. I had questions that needed answering, and it had to be there.

As I crossed the wooden walkway over the hydroelectric pipes, a gust swept around me, tugging at my shorts and T-shirt and casting my loose hair across my face.

"Camille..." a voice rumbled.

"Pajuzu." I stopped and searched for an oncoming storm. There wasn't a cloud in the sky, though he swished about.

"You finally let go." He sounded content. Pleased, even.

"It only took the town almost being destroyed."

He chuckled softly. "Lamastu is no more, and I am satisfied. Though I believe you have a little of your own storm left to... hmmm, how to put it? Discharge?" He laughed again, and this time it bordered on raucous. I was getting used to his comments on my emotional state. But he was right, I was still a mess inside.

"Fair thee well, Camille," he rumbled. The gust whirled about, then drifted away, and something released in me. He was gone. I was no longer possessed by a demon. The day was looking up.

I jumped off the walkway, climbed the scree slope and skirted the sheer drop. Clambering into the cave, velvet hazel leaves brushed my skin. The honeysuckle that twined about the branches was a defiant splash of dusky pink and deep orange amidst a harbour of vigorous green. The cave was warm, retaining the day's heat. I stepped past the expanse of moss to the wall of prehistoric drawings.

There it was. The painting that always drew me.

I traced my forefinger over the lines, the smooth rock undulating beneath, then with a twist of my arm, I studied my bond markings, which were now barely visible. I'd read that for each Keeper partnership, the pattern was unique and the meaning personal. If the lines on the wall represented an arm, it was the same design with curves rising upward. On the rock it was jumbled in with dots and pectiforms, which

I'd thought were part of the composition, but they could have been added at another time. I had no idea why our bond markings were inscribed on the cave wall, but if I looked at the drawing without the other shapes, I knew what it meant. I glanced out to the hazel and honeysuckle, the lines so alike I couldn't be mistaken. I followed the pattern with my finger once more, then paused.

Lucas was here. I could feel him.

His soft footfall scuffed rock as he approached. Unable to move, my stomach knotted tighter, my heart pounding, my breath much too shallow.

"Camille..." He paused behind me. My heightened sense of him was almost unbearable. But even now, I couldn't face him. He was close, so close. We weren't touching, but I could feel his heat, or was it the bond? I couldn't tell, but the space between us thrummed. And still, he tore at my chest, leaving me open and exposed. I stared at the curved artwork. It was all I could do. I needed to figure this out.

"Hazel," I managed, my voice trembling as I drew my fingers along the vertical lines, recalling the tree lore I'd gathered over the years. The leaves stirred a little at the cave entrance. "It has protective qualities with an affinity for air, and it's mutable, like you. It also has an affinity for water, like your drac form, and it's mercurial, difficult to pin down, a trickster spirit. The tree is associated with the caduceus, the symbol of a healer, a devin, a doctor."

Lucas stepped closer, his body against mine. His lips brushed my neck, placing a soft kiss on my skin. My breath hitched as desire rippled through me. But I couldn't respond.

Not yet. Not before I knew. Setting my finger on the wall once more, I ran it over a curve that wound about the hazel.

"Honeysuckle—couteteo," he murmured.

He *knew*. "Representing tenacity, strength, affection and fidelity."

His arms encircled my waist, drawing me close, his warmth surrounding me entirely, his scent stoking fire. "Also symbolising undying passion and enduring beauty."

I swallowed. "Its medieval name was chevrefoil... goatleaf." Despite everything, I released a snort. "So you get to be a protector and a healer, and I get to be goat girl."

He chuckled into my hair. "But goats have so much going for them. Their resilience..." He kissed me where his lips had rested. "Intelligence... bloody-mindedness." He grunted a little. I refrained from responding to that. Yeah, I could be bloody-minded.

"The honeysuckle twines about the hazel," I whispered.

His arms tightened. "The two grow into one another. If they should be separated once they have been bound, they will die."

I shuddered. I knew it so deeply that it hurt.

But there was more I needed to know, and I had to face him. My stomach spiralling, I turned around in his arms and met his dark gaze. He drank me in, his eyes astute and ephemeral, his lips playing, his broad mouth begging to be kissed, and those cheekbones... they were otherworldly, divine. His jaw flexed, casting momentary ridges along his neck, which followed the scar that ran down from under his ear to disappear under his white cotton shirt. His collar was open a few buttons down and his sleeves were rolled up to his elbows, revealing bronzed skin.

I couldn't get enough of him.

But I needed to find out where I stood. "I don't understand why I can feel you. I presumed it was the Keeper bond, but that's supposed to be subtle and linked to combat. This is much more."

His throat bobbed, his gaze fixed on mine. "Camille—"

"Our mates act in Grimmere..." When we'd met his parents for dinner, there had been something intense between us, and I'd put it down to physical attraction—I'd attributed so much to that—but, "It wasn't a ruse, was it?"

He shook his head. "Not in the slightest. My family would've never been fooled."

I narrowed my brow, my body stiffening. "So what does mates mean? That you're going to throw me over your shoulder, take me home and..."

"And what...? Would you care to explain?" His eyes glimmered.

I gritted my teeth. "You know what I'm getting at. Where is my choice in the matter?"

His face became solemn, his grip tightening. "You have a choice. I know that I am your mate, and I will hold true to that. But it's not always reciprocated. If you choose not to be mine, I will respect your decision, and yet I will be yours until the end of days."

My lips parted at the weight of his words. But it only raised another question. "You knew this the night we slept together?"

He winced. "I knew deep inside, but I wouldn't allow myself to believe it. I thought if I had you, I would get you out of my system."

"Such a charmer." I shook my head, thinking of his name inscribed multiple times on the cave wall. "Is that how you dealt with the women you brought here? You *had* them?"

"We used to come here back when I served Charlemagne, and then when I was in the service of Raymond Roger in the eleventh century. It was a tradition amongst the chevaliers. We marked our names and declared for another year that we were awaiting our one true amour. That is why the cave is called the Grotte des Amoureux. It's a sanctuary to the highest ideals of love."

"Huh." I studied his face. "But there's no way you've been celibate all this time."

He chuckled. "Celibate, no. We weren't abstaining, we were waiting."

Once again, I had to adjust my preconceived notions of him. "But... why me, why us? A fae and a human. I... don't get it."

A smile flickered on his lips, his gaze tearing into me. "You mean apart from you being beyond brave, tenacious, driven, mouthy, maverick, headstrong and utterly beautiful?"

I gasped, his sincerity a physical thing weaving about me.

He tilted his chin. "Apart from that, perhaps some people are made for each other. I also appreciate that you're not afraid of me. That goes a long way when you're a lethal predator from one of the darkest families Fae has seen."

I barked a laugh. "Afraid of you? You can't even eat a

baguette without spreading mayonnaise all over your face, or make it home drunk without the Men's help, or tackle an ogre without cracking up."

He grinned. "There's that."

But my laughter caught in my throat. I wasn't afraid of him in his human form, but the drac was another matter, not to mention his goblin heritage. The problem was, I spent so much time with the man, I could barely equate him with the monster. And try as I might to use it as a defence against my vulnerability, I couldn't.

And all of that was nothing compared to the rawness in my chest. Truth be told, what had begun to unravel throughout the hantaumo affair had torn open in Grimmere during those nights we'd spent together. I hadn't wanted to acknowledge it, but all the while he'd enfolded me in warmth and protection, his claws had pierced my heart.

My chest tightened, the pain of everything that had prevented me opening to Pajuzu ripping through me, my thoughts more chaotic than when I'd soared on the storm. I bit my lip hard, Lucas's gaze following the movement, his pupils flaring.

"This is awful..." I muttered. "Terrible. I'm totally defenceless." I'd never felt this way. Not with Extreme Sports Alex, and I'd fallen hard for him, and certainly not for the others. My broken relationships hurt so much, but this time... hazel and honeysuckle. If something happened, I wouldn't survive. But it was more than that. "We're supposed to be Keeper partners... We can't mess it up. It's too important. *You're* too important."

"Camille, I'm yours. Every part of me. I always have been and I always will be." The light on the side of his face delineated his elegant nose and those beguiling laughter lines. He was so unearthly, so difficult to grasp. "So many years passed as I watched empires rise and ruin..." He brushed his fingers across my cheek, his touch a firestorm. "As I hid in the shadows while countries formed and reformed... as I fought at the side of kings who blazed through Europe and burned to nothing, and throughout it all, I hoped for you." He drew out the last words, said them tenderly, as though each one ached with as much vulnerability as I felt. "I will do whatever it takes to make this work."

I couldn't hold back any longer. I couldn't restrain what I'd denied myself, denied us. Wanting him so damn much devastated me, but sensing that he felt the same way was my absolute ruin. I cupped his cheek and drew him to me. Our lips grazed, releasing more blazing light through my sinews than any storm could. I tasted him, earthy and recondite, his kiss shuddering me to my core as he savoured me in return, his solidity vast and unshakeable.

We pulled apart, our foreheads touching as we shared breath.

"It's just like you," I murmured, "always having the upper hand, keeping me one step behind and leaving me totally confounded." I drew my fingers along his jaw, his stubble prickling. He leant into my hand and kissed my palm. "Except by the river, of course," I said, unable to withhold my smile. "I had the upper hand then."

"You really don't get it, do you?" His nails dug into my back, which only heightened everything I was feeling.

"Get what?" Nope, I didn't get him. I barely comprehended anything about him.

"You..." he rumbled. "It wasn't me who had the upper hand. It was you. From the moment we met, I was destroyed, undone. All my reactions, *everything* has been in self-defence. A desperate, untenable attempt to protect myself."

My brow knitted, my gaze flickering across his face. I couldn't believe it, yet the truth shone in his eyes and reverberated between us, and it only made me want him more. "So what? Now you won't play tricks on me?" I ran my hands through his hair and knotted his messy locks between my fingers.

"Oh, I wouldn't say that." He grinned. "I rather like keeping you on your toes."

And for some reason, I liked it too. Coming up against him was irresistible. The challenge stoked me. My heels rose as I reached up and kissed him again, tugging at his lip just as I'd done in the caves near Les Profondeurs. "I'm on my toes now."

He growled, his reciprocating mouth unruly, his hardness digging into my middle. "See what you do to me?"

"Perhaps I can do more." I undid a button of his shirt, then another, my gaze flitting from the fabric to his eyes. His head lowered, his breath ragged, his hands tightening around my tee. I worked down to the bottom button and hauled his shirt from his shoulders. He shrugged out of it before gripping my top and drawing the cotton tight. He made to pull it up, but I laid my hands on his chest, feeling his strength. "Wait."

My lips pursed as I ran my fingers over the rise of his abs and the furrows at his ribs, his gasps mesmerising. Wanting more, I kissed the hollow at the centre of his chest and the dip where his pecs met his collar bone. I liked it there, and if his moans were anything to go by, he liked me there too.

As I worshipped his skin with my lips, his moans morphed to growls and his gaze deepened to a glower. He was struggling to restrain himself. But really, I'd tried not to look at this body so many times during training, how could I resist? I loved that he was at my mercy, though in truth, I was completely at his.

And there, glowing faint gold along his arm, were his bond markings. *Our* bond markings. I brushed my fingers over the curves, our connection deepening, the threads that bound us never to be undone. Relishing the intimacy, I kissed him slowly, tenderly. Then, unable to restrain myself, I deepened the pressure. His untamed response made me ravenous. His grip tightened around my tee and he tore it apart.

"That was one of my better tops," I muttered as he undid my bra and tugged it off.

"I don't care." He devoured me with his gaze, his chest rising and falling. "You're awe-inspiring," he breathed.

I pulled him close, and his kiss was so forceful that I couldn't think. His hands met mine. Our fingers entwined, and we stilled, our tattered breath synchronising as we bathed in each other.

After a moment, he grasped my butt, scooped me up and laid me down upon the moss, the mantle deliciously soft. Lowering, he took his time to scatter kisses over my breasts, my ribs, my belly, his touch sublime. "Retribution for your treatment of my chest."

I could only moan, the ripples he aroused all-consuming. His kisses morphed to mind-blowing, barely restrained bites that rose to my neck. He found the hollow behind my ear and nuzzled into it. "Are you sure?"

Clasping his head and drawing his gaze to mine, I drew in a slow, shaky breath. "Surer than anything in my life." I needed him with every fibre of my being. "I'm sorted for contraception."

"Me too." His eyes shone.

"Taking responsibility. I like it." No doubt he'd concocted some potion.

"I'm sure I can find more for you to like than that." He grabbed the waist of my shorts and ripped them open.

I couldn't help my grin as I wriggled out of my knickers. "I can see I'm going to get through plenty of clothes."

"Tons of them." With a scorching gaze, he descended, caressing my thighs and pausing delectably at the place between to swirl elation through my body.

But I needed more.

I pulled him up and tugged at his belt, undoing the buckle as if it was the most cumbersome thing in the world. "I prefer the slow method of undressing."

The desire in his eyes was contained by a thread as I

worked at his button and zip, and yet he was allowing me to take my time, even though it wasn't his preferred tempo of clothing removal.

Together, we hauled off his trousers and trunks, my skin flushing as I took him in. I'd seen him naked on countless occasions, and of course, our one-night stand had been rekindled by La Vieille, but it wasn't the same. This time, I was fully present and brimming with admiration for his magnificent form and ample rigidity. He looked different. Primal yet ethereal. Utterly irresistible. He sat back, his eyes wide with reverence, and we were caught in time, unable to believe this was happening.

"Camille..." he said. "I don't have the words... I—"

I rose to my knees and clasped his face in my hands, my kiss lingering. But I wanted him closer still. I straddled him, and as we sat together, my legs wrapped around his body. He filled me entirely, his heart thudding against mine. Kissing him fiercely, I rocked into him. He thrust in response, and we found an incandescent rhythm as ancient as the mountains where the fae and human realms were bound.

Sweat beaded on our skin as we snatched desperate breaths between urgent kisses. He consumed me—his taste, the scent of his pheromone-drenched body, the exquisite friction between us. I was so exposed, so defenceless, and yet I wanted this. My senses expanded, and there was nothing but movement and pleasure and connection.

There was nothing but Lucas.

I surrendered to everything I'd held within for such a

long time, everything that had stormed and raged, tempted and taunted. I surrendered to *him*, and he cast me to the edge of oblivion, where he held me in sublimity until I shattered with his release, his roar claiming me.

CHAPTER 45

NIGHT FLOWED AROUND US, THE STARS, BRIGHT ABOVE the guardian mountains, swirling with the inky darkness of the cave. The enduring rock under our bodies anchored us to the land as we consummated everything we felt for each other again and again.

I tasted every inch of Lucas, unable to get enough. He reciprocated, desperate to provoke the utmost pleasure and whirl me into senselessness, our declarations of fidelity in this ancient place knotting us tighter.

At some point during the early hours as I nestled into him, my head in the crook of his neck, our bodies so entwined that I wasn't sure which arms and legs belonged to me, I began to shiver.

He stroked my hair, his gaze scouring my face as though he couldn't get enough. "You're cold."

"A little." There had been so many ways to keep warm,

and heat radiated off him, but I was exhausted. All I wanted was to lie in his arms and rest.

"Slaughter," he called.

I glanced around, conscious of my nakedness and the state of us.

The miniature warrior appeared from the entrance. I needn't have worried about the intrusion. His hands shielded his eyes. "Yes, boss." He walked into the cave wall.

"Get blankets from my house. Plenty of them."

Slaughter swayed a little from the impact, his fingers twitching over one eye as he fought the urge to salute. In the end he resorted to flapping his elbow. "Yes, gov."

He disappeared. A second later, he returned, walking backward and carrying a couple of blankets that were much too large for him. He dropped them by Lucas, disappeared, then came back with more, still facing the other way. I had to love his discretion.

"Is that all, boss?" He turned around, his hands over his eyes again.

"That's it." Lucas tugged exquisite cashmere about us.

"I'll be going then." For some inexplicable reason, Slaughter was still in reverse, backing away. I couldn't help but smile as he disappeared into darkness, but then frantic scuffling echoed through the cave. "Aaaaargh," he cried, his voice growing distant.

I sprang up. "Shit, is he alright? He must have fallen down the cliff."

"I'm fine," a faint cry came from below.

Lucas shook his head, pulling a blanket up to my shoulder as I lay back down. Slaughter was pretty indestructible. I curled into Lucas, my fingers entangled in his chest hair, my knee hooked over his hip, the blankets deliciously warm.

He kissed my forehead and drew in my scent, then held my hand in his, gripping me tight. "Mates," he rumbled, and the utter surety of that one word had me pulling off the blankets, to begin all over again.

We did get some sleep, waking as the sun skirted Picou de Bompas across the valley to shine directly into the cave, hazel and honeysuckle dappling light over the walls. Well, I awoke. Lucas was watching me. I winced, aware of my dishevelment, though he'd seen me in worse situations. I scraped my fingers through my hair, finding only knots. My cheeks burned with the lingering sensation of his stubble, and most of me ached. Especially my arm, for some reason. My chest tightened. In the clear light of day, it was all very real.

"Good morning," he said with a soft smile, one I couldn't resist mirroring.

"That's one way of putting it." My partner, whom I'd committed to serve with as Keeper of the Bounds, the man who had fought by my side and saved me innumerable times, the fae who had given me verity and chucked me in the river and gone all out for the goblins in Grimmere, was naked and pressed close.

As I attempted to detangle my hair, he caught my fingers, drew them to his lips and kissed the tips. "Everything I said last night, I meant. I'm yours. Every part of me, body and soul, is in your service." His words were strong, almost ferocious, as though his pledge was carved into the mountain.

I swallowed hard. "This connection between us, it's so much. I've never felt anything close." Despite it, or perhaps because of it, lightness filled my chest. "But does that mean you'll milk the goats and clean the loft at my command?"

He grinned. "Without a doubt. I'll also continue doing your washing."

"And then throw me in the river?"

He shrugged. "After you blasted me with lightning, I might think twice. Although you were pretty hot as a demon-possessed storm." His eyes glinted.

I wiggled my fingers. "Nothing. Damn, it would've been useful to keep you in check."

He only winced a little.

I reached up and dotted a kiss on his lips, bringing my thoughts back to practicalities. "As much as I want this to last forever, I should go to work, and we'd better move before we make a nice surprise for the next hiker passing this way."

His gaze flicked across mine. "Camille, this *will* last forever." He said it with such surety that I shuddered.

Desire stirred once more. I could do nothing but pull him to me and kiss him with abandon. He responded in equal measure, an inferno building. An inferno and... excruciating pain in my arm. "Owwww!" I cried, clutching it.

Lucas shot up. "Did I hurt you?" He looked as though he'd rather traverse the dark realms blindfolded.

"No... no." I sat up, holding my arm, the blankets tucked

around me. "I have no idea what I've done. Too much exertion, most likely. I'm sure a little healing potion will sort it out." But still, pain lacerated through my arm. I glanced at it, my throat tightening. The lines of my bond markings, where they extended out from under my fingers, were *black*, the pattern brightening to faint gold just beyond.

Lucas gaped. "Let me see that."

I didn't want to release my arm for fear of it hurting more, but that wasn't going to help. I peeled off my hand. Beneath, near my shoulder, my skin was deeply scored with gouges so dark that it was as if oblivion filled them. I gasped, my heart racing. "What the hell?"

"I've never seen anything like it. Keep still." He sprang over to a pile of clean clothes that Slaughter must have left out while we slept. He grabbed a shirt and ripped it into a long strip, then knelt beside me and wound it tightly around my arm, finishing it with a knot.

"What is it?" I wanted to claw the darkness from me.

"Are you ready to sacrifice yourselves for what lies ahead, for the fae and human realms?" he murmured, his body tightening. "It was the question La Vieille asked. A sacrifice for the bounds..."

I frowned, not understanding.

As he shifted, the sinews along his arms tensing, I caught sight of his shoulder. My breath hitched. He followed my gaze and turned his arm. The lines of his bond markings, where they faded to nothing, were utterly black, mirroring mine.

"It's like the bounds cracks," I whispered, "the malum." It was the substance Lucas's family had used in their attempt to separate the realms. "Tell me what's happening."

Fury blazed in his eyes. "I don't know. But I'll damned as hell find out."

Find out about Camille's first encounter with an ogre...

Get Folkloric Fae,
the Folkloric prequel novella, FREE at
www.karenzagrant.com

Perfect for reading at any point
during the series

A MESSAGE FROM SLAUGHTER...

The Men of Bédeilhac would be exceedingly grateful if you
would leave a star rating for the book on Amazon to signal
your appreciation for their little-known fae race of fearless,
violent and only occasionally inebriated warriors.

Thank you very much!

FOLKLORIC GUILE

THE FOLKLORIC SERIES
BOOK FIVE

KARENZA GRANT

AFTERWORD

It's been wonderful to immerse myself in the Folkloric series once more and expand it further. It gives me so much joy to write these novels (and many sleepless nights, a little tearing my hair out and then utter relief when the plot comes together, but hey, it's all part of the ride, and I wouldn't be without it).

Folkloric Trickery is the most folklore-rich novel of the series to date, so for those of you who like to indulge, here's the essence of what was introduced in this story and also a few notes on the locations.

All the folklore is based on actual Pyrenean mythology. Occasionally, I do have to make up elements because real-life doesn't always fit perfectly with fiction, though when I do, I aim to respect the old traditions. It goes without saying that storms are at the heart of *Folkloric Trickery*, and their impact on survival in the Pyrenees was so great that a lot of folklore developed around them, so this time, there was ample material to draw from.

Looking back, the initial inspiration for the story came from hiking in the area a few years ago during one of the typical summer storms that descend in the afternoon or evening after a hot day and let rip.

Back then, I was standing in an exposed position near the top of a foothill not far from the Dolmen of Sem. The furious tempest swept over the mountain on the other side of the valley, barraging it with lightning that cast sparks along the electricity pylons. Then it surged toward me. Needless to say, I made an impressive dash for shelter. Being English, and living in such a temperate climate, it made a deep impression.

When I began my research into storms and the weather, I was intrigued to find that the prevailing winds of the area are named (for example, the Autan, the Tramountaign, the Cers, the Eissaure and the Scirocco), with various effects attributed to them such as illness and insanity. In addition, there is a local wind spirit called the Follet that was believed to fertilise women. Fearing its whirls, they threw wheat or sand behind them as it was compelled to stop and count the grains before approaching.

There is also a considerable amount of storm lore in the Basque Country at the western end of the Pyrenees, which has its own distinct traditions. Despite all that, I couldn't find any ancient lore specific to the fierce southwest storms I'd experienced, which seemed odd as these were the storms that would wipe out an entire harvest in one violent burst of hale, meaning starvation for the population. These storms meant life or death.

But it was precisely because storms were so important that there is little lore. The ancient storm deities were thoroughly replaced during the advance of Christianity, and storms were attributed to the devil and his witches, despite the fact that in other areas of folklore, even those that were Christianised, echos of the old deities may still be recognised.

However, some of the bygone traditions remained. For example, methods of evoking a storm included throwing a cat in a river (sorry Madame Bovary!), shaking a shoe at the sky, stirring the waters or casting stones into a river.

But where storms were concerned, the church took over as protector of the people and the land, with priests or tempestaires (often old women or sacristans) recounting prayers and performing rituals to chase away bad weather. The last tempestaire in the Pyrenees was Marie-Louise Endart of Bascassan in the Basque Country. She passed away in 1990.

So important were storms that storm oratories played a role in the protection of the population. These were chapels, hermitages and sanctuaries that specialised in storm warding. Ancient practices at such places may have been simply for protection, although they may have been a gesture of hostility toward the storms and the devil. Another idea is that sacrificial offerings were made to storm deities with the intention of controlling them. It is also possible that these practices related to the ancient worship of sky gods such as Zeus, Jupiter and Thor.

Although storm oratories were common in the region, there is no record of one upon Cap de Couronnes above the town. I took the liberty of placing one there because keeping the story within the crucible of Tarascon and the surrounding area helped create a compelling narrative.

Pajuzu, or Pazuzu as he was known in Mesopotamia, is a wild wind demon associated with the west wind. He was often evoked to chase away the even more demonic baby-snatching, women-terrorising bringer of disease and destruction, Lamastu (Lamashtu). Both were recorded in the Pyrenees, and Pajuzu was indeed invoked in storm battles between rival villages—the accounts mentioned in the novel are recorded folklore. I love to imagine the population battling in this way, and it doesn't take much to guess that this was the inspiration behind Ignace and the exploits of the grumpy farmers.

Pazuzu's most famous recent appearance is in *The Exorcist*, where he is portrayed as the epitome of evil. He does indeed have a dark side, but he is also a protector of women, children and the home. Furthermore, he's useful for warding against unwanted guests!

It's often necessary to flesh out folklore for a story, and in this case it meant personifying Pajuzu and Lamastu. In particular, I needed Lamastu to be embodied for the finale, and I wanted to use a creature that has an affinity with the air. Although the bearded vulture isn't normally associated with her, I thought it was the most suited of all the Pyrenean birds, being quite fearsome. It really is a curious creature, feeding almost exclusively on bones, which it drops from great heights to shatter against rocks.

Nora did her best to subdue Lamastu with offerings. This is known as appeasement magic, where gifts are made to a malevolent demon or spirit in the hopes of avoiding harm. It's a form of ancient defensive magic that has its origins in Mesopotamia, so it tied in nicely.

Of course, I couldn't complete this overview without mentioning La Vieille. She stole the show in many ways, and she was a joy to write. Her origins lie in the Fata (the Fates or the Norns), who are widely known in Europe for spinning the thread of life, then measuring it and finally, cutting it. In La Vieille, meaning The Old Lady, I wanted to portray the three Fata combined in one powerful being, whilst also bringing in some of the local Pyrenean lore. In the area, the Fata appeared as fairies, and there are many myths about them spinning, washing and beating garments. They possessed golden spindles and were the guardians of *la fil du vie*, the thread of life. It was said that death awaited anyone who stole from them.

Before moving on, *Folkloric Trickery* briefly mentions a few other snippets of folklore. Devins were lay healers of the area, so it seemed only right that Lucas should be crowned with the title.

The region is also home to a whole host of child-snatching, people-eating and generally pretty terrifying creatures known as *peurs* or fears. These include ogres, demons and apparitions of various kinds, and most of the mythology that follows falls into this category.

Pare Gégant, the Giant Father, is an ogre with enormous teeth who eats disobedient children, so it seemed appropriate for him to hound the D&D gang. There are many other ogres, and Camile battled a croquembouche in the prequel novella, *Folkloric Fae*, which can be downloaded for free on my website.

Vestiges, another of the fae provoked by the unruly gang, are guardians of high places. They are thought to fascinate travellers with songs, then drag them to the bottom of abysses. The barragognes reported by Lucas to be lurking in the cinema is a type of ghostly presence. The esgarra-padones, which Morion mentioned fighting, attack mountain dwellers who look for wood at night.

Moving on from the *peurs*, Morion spoke of his conquest of the voivre. This is a monstrous snake from medieval French mythology. And the caves of Bossea, where the creature hid, are in Italy, not far from the French border. And finally, I couldn't move on without mentioning the water nymphs. As in most regions throughout the world, they are a common feature of the area's folklore.

As for the locations featured in *Folkloric Trickery*, the Grotte des Amoureux (the Cave of the Lovers), sits as described, just beyond the hydroelectric pipes on the side of the majestic Cap des Couronnes (Peak of Crowns), which looms over Tarascon.

There are many massive cave systems in the valleys around the town, which reach miles into the belly of the earth. Prime examples are Lombrives (the biggest cave in Western Europe), Niaux and Sabart. There was a period early in the last century when these were thoroughly explored by spelaeologists, but for some reason, the cave system of Sakany, to which Grotte des Amoureux belongs, was missed and only investigated more recently. I have no idea why this was the case, though I wonder if it was because of the hydroelectric system that runs through the mountain a stone's throw away.

The hydroelectrics themselves are a feat of early 1900s engineering, and they still transport water collected high in the mountains to the pipes running down the side of Cap des Couronnes, where electricity is generated in the plant at the base. This is right by the site of Charlemagne's legendary victory over the Saracens in 778. I love how industry, history and myth combine.

The actual interior of the Grotte des Amoureux is unlike the cave in the novel. It is smaller with a drop leading into the cave system. It does have a little cave art, but not as much as described (my inspiration for the prehistoric drawings in the story came from Niaux, and the inscriptions from Sabart). My aim was to evoke the spirit of the area's caves, which are decorated from ancient prehistory to present day. There are caves where eighteen-thousand-year-old drawings are accompanied by names carved a few hundred years ago and those made very recently.

At a certain point during the ice age, the Earth's population dwindled to mere thousands. People dwelt in this area and the narrow band of terrain that stretched eastward across Europe and Russia. It was the only hospitable land at the time, and it is why the region is known as "the cradle of civilisation". These caves are truly places of *our* ancestors.

It is curious that with all my research, I couldn't discover how the Grotte des Amoureux came by its evocative title. Did lovers from the town actually use it as a retreat? My interpretation that the chevaliers would inscribe their names inside is fictional, but based upon the strong tradition of chivalry and courtly love that abounded in the region in the Middle Ages. I detailed a little of this in *Folkloric Ruse* with mentions of the Trencavel family and the Chateau de Foix. If anyone knows the real reason for the cave's name, please let me know.

And finally, hazel and honeysuckle. I thought the plants fitted Camille and Lucas perfectly. The inspiration came from a 12th century poem by Marie de France known as *Chevrefoil*, which once again links the novel with chivalry and the progressive values of the region in medieval times.

If you'd like to find out more about the folklore of the Pyrenees, there's not much published in English, but as always, I recommend Martin Locker's *The Tears of Pyrene*. If you read French, try one of Olivier de Marliave's books, such as *Trésor de la Mythology Pyrénéenne*, which is excellent.

Finally, I'd like to thank everyone who has taken a chance on this series and made it this far through. I appreciate your support from the bottom of my heart.

Unending thanks goes to my amazing ARC team, who has been unbelievably helpful in so many ways. As always, my gratitude goes out to Octavia Denning and Dorine Maine. A huge shout-out to my writing group: Viktoria

Dahill, Katie Mouallek, Rachel Cooper and Abhivyakti Singh. Special thanks to Jack Barrow and P.M. Gilbert. Many thanks to Toby Selwyn, my super editor. Thank you to Minerva Grant for keeping me on my toes in the best of ways and brightening my days more than I can say. And Finally, Rillian Grant, thank you for your indispensable input and so much more.

About the Author

Karenza Grant writes folklore-inspired fantasy of all kinds with delectable slow-burn romance.

Her early years in Cornwall were largely the source of her fascination with all things mysterious. She lived below a hill reputed to be the Cornish residence of the Unseelie Court, and the local myths got their claws in. Now she's inspired by a broad range of creators, from Jim Henson and Arthur Rackham to a whole host of amazing contemporary authors.

She has three black cats known as The Three Guardians, and a crazy lab x spaniel who is just about the only thing that can extract Karenza from her writing desk—if the pooch isn't walked, the legions of hell will be released.

Find Karenza at www.karenzagrant.com. Subscribe to her mailing list for the latest news.

Connect

There's nothing better than hearing from readers. Drop me a line, find me on social media, or if you'd like to keep in contact, sign up for my newsletter.

You can find all the links on my website:
www.karenzagrant.com